The Canterbury Tales

HANDBOOK

The Canterbury Tales

HANDBOOK

ELIZABETH SCALA

*Ellen Clayton Garwood Centennial
Professor of English*

University of Texas–Austin

W. W. NORTON & COMPANY
Independent Publishers Since 1923

W. W. Norton & Company has been independent since its founding in 1923, when William Warder Norton and Mary D. Herter Norton first published lectures delivered at the People's Institute, the adult education division of New York City's Cooper Union. The firm soon expanded its program beyond the Institute, publishing books by celebrated academics from America and abroad. By midcentury, the two major pillars of Norton's publishing program—trade books and college texts—were firmly established. In the 1950s, the Norton family transferred control of the company to its employees, and today—with a staff of five hundred and hundreds of trade, college, and professional titles published each year—W. W. Norton & Company stands as the largest and oldest publishing house owned wholly by its employees.

Manufacturing by LSC Harrisonburg
Book design by Pamela Schnitter
Production Manager: Sean Mintus

Library of Congress Cataloging-in-Publication Data
Names: Scala, Elizabeth, 1966– author.
Title: The Canterbury tales handbook / Elizabeth Scala.
Description: New York : W.W. Norton & Company, [2020] | Includes
    bibliographical references and index.
Identifiers: LCCN 2019031007 | **ISBN 9780393624441** (paperback)
Subjects: LCSH: Chaucer, Geoffrey, -1400. Canterbury tales.
Classification: LCC PR1874 .S34 2020 | DDC 821/.1—dc23
LC record available at https://lccn.loc.gov/2019031007c

W. W. Norton & Company, Inc., 500 Fifth Avenue, New York, NY 10110
    wwnorton.com

W. W. Norton & Company Ltd., 15 Carlisle Street, London W1D 3BS

1 2 3 4 5 6 7 8 9 0

FOR CLAIRE

CONTENTS

PREFACE AND ACKNOWLEDGMENTS

This book was an absolute pleasure to write—most of the time. It is largely based in my teaching of *The Canterbury Tales* at the University of Texas at Austin. The lively questions of my students (nearly every fall semester since 1995) have prompted many of the ideas, exercises, and creative explanations in this book. I am grateful to Norton for its support for the project from its inception. Julia Reidhead (then editor), my editor Marian Johnson, and my copyeditor Alice Falk were pleasures to work with. Alice made this book tighter and more accessible with her sharp eye and lively turns of phrase. Its writing was made possible by the support of my husband, Douglas Bruster, whose copyediting not only clarifies but often gives my ideas their punch. He is the one who first suggested I write the kind of introductory book for which I had long been searching for my students.

I began this book in the late afternoons at the Folger Shakespeare Library, where I spent a lovely month doing primary research for another book to which I will shortly turn in earnest. Late in the day, when I could no longer pore over the Chaucer editions at the Folger, I would sit and type out my basic ideas on each of the Canterbury tales and try to explain why we were going to spend a semester reading them. The individual chapters were read by a number of friends and colleagues: Patricia Clare Ingham, Frank Grady, and Tom Goodmann were each enthusiastic and exacting in just the right measure. I also appreciate more than I can say how a really short turnaround seemed to mean nothing to them!

Three undergraduate students in particular were extraordinarily helpful with this book. Katelyn Connolly and Emma Holt, both of whom toiled in the UT English Honors Program, volunteered to help me with these materials. Emma, especially, was tireless in helping to check my quotations and track down sources. Claire Bruster (and some of her friends at Barnard) were invaluable in reading various chapters while they were studying literature of the Mediterranean their freshman year and giving me feedback from the trenches. It was a very happy coincidence that I had these new undergraduate readers for chapters when I needed to road-test them. But Claire also double-checked all the corrections to the primary text citations and helped me get the final manuscript to Norton in something like a confident form. And that is why this book is dedicated to her.

ELIZABETH SCALA

The Canterbury Tales

HANDBOOK

WHAT IS
THE CANTERBURY TALES?

Given the remoteness of Chaucer's culture and language, the question in the above title is worth asking: what, exactly, is *The Canterbury Tales?* Chaucer is one of the earliest English poets, *The Canterbury Tales* his best-known work. It is a collection of stories supposedly told on a pilgrimage to Canterbury, the most important shrine in medieval England and the site of the "murder in the cathedral" of Thomas Becket.[1] One or another of the tales is typically included in most British literature surveys. While famous, it's also funny, especially the parts that tend to get anthologized: tales of trickery and illicit love (the Miller's Tale) or hypocritical self-exposure (the Pardoner's Tale). There's also a wild and over-the-top animal fable illustrating human foibles (the Nun's Priest's Tale). But *The Canterbury Tales* also gets translated in some editions, thereby losing its character and signature wordplay. Because he writes in an earlier linguistic form, Middle English, which is somewhat more distant from us than Shakespeare's language, Chaucer is often encountered in an oversimplified form, translated or rewritten in prose. Turned into a minor literary figure, he becomes a curiosity of the distant past. This book helps you enjoy Chaucer by showing you how to read him more fluidly in the

---

[1] The allusion here is to T. S. Eliot's famous verse drama about this event, *Murder in the Cathedral* (1935). Becket was archbishop of Canterbury, the most powerful prelate of the Roman Catholic Church in England. He was assassinated in 1170 by men loyal to King Henry II, who found him "troublesome" for resisting the king's authority.

language in which he wrote. Some careful work at the beginning of the semester pays dividends later. We must learn *to see into* Chaucer's language, not merely to look up what his words mean and memorize them. *How* his words mean what the glosses say they mean is a large part of the fun. Figuring that out makes reading Chaucer easier.

Why does Chaucer have a course devoted to him in most English department curricula? Chaucer is the first important English poet for whom we have a name. There are a lot of moving parts to that claim: "first," "important," "name." We can begin with the last of these: "name." The vast majority of medieval literature is anonymous. The word *medieval* (from the Latin *medium aevum*) here means "period in the middle"—the age between the classical period of ancient Greek and Roman culture on the one hand, and, on the other, the modern period after around 1500. Chaucer wrote before the advent of printing, a technology that eventually developed features of books that we take for granted, such as title pages (making authorship clear) and the idea of "copyright" (making ownership of one's work possible). When we think of books we tend to take these matters for granted: authors write books and their intellectual ownership of that material can be read on the page. But books have a long history, as do the ideas of authorship, ownership, and originality. Chaucer worked during a much earlier stage of textual and literary production, before the genre of the novel or literary realism had been "invented." So we have to reset our expectations to an age before such conventions had been developed.

In the Middle Ages, books were individual handwritten objects produced by professional copyists called *scribes*. Composed by one person, they were written down by another. Many if not most books were produced in monasteries for clerical and academic use by students. Only in the late Middle Ages, at the time Chaucer is writing, do we have anything we might call a relatively commercial form of book production. As a result, books and the texts contained in them were more separable from their authors than we are conditioned to think, often circulating out of their control. Not surprisingly, then, English poetry before Chaucer is largely anonymous. In the late fourteenth century, when Chaucer is writing, only one other poet signs his name to his works: John Gower, Chaucer's contemporary and his friend. Gower's name is attached to his writing both in English and in Latin.[2] But the creator of two of the most remarkable poems of the era, *Sir Gawain and the Green Knight* and *Pearl*, did not sign his poems, and no one thought to write down his name when they were copied. Around this same time, William Langland, the presumed author of *The Vision of Piers Plowman*, left his name in a punning acrostic: "'I have lyved in *londe*,' quod I, 'and my name is *Longe* Wille'" (my emphasis).[3] But this is hardly the kind of authorial self-identification we are used to. There were no poet laureates in this era and not much royal privilege to be given for such activity, at least not in any official capacity that might have been recorded. We are lucky that Chaucer's name survives attached to his writing through inventive forms of inscription discussed in the chapters that follow.

While Chaucer has a significant relation to "name," our next three terms are harder: "first," "important," and "English." Chaucer was not the first writer in English: centuries of writing preceded him. But English is far from the only language under consideration, for Britain was a nation of many languages and cultures in the Middle Ages. It had native Celtic and Briton languages, such as Irish, Welsh, and Cornish. It had been conquered by the Romans, which brought Latin to its shores. It was then invaded by Germanic tribes and the Danes, who arrived with Scandinavian as well as Germanic speakers: Angles and Saxons, among others, whose various dialects form the basis of what we now recognize as English. The ascension of Christianity guaranteed that Latin would retain a hold. Finally, England was conquered by the Normans, French speakers, in 1066, which brought

---

[2] Gower inscribes his name into the closing framework of his English poem *Confessio Amantis*. It also appears in the Dedicatory Epistle of the All Soul's College (Oxford University) manuscript of his Latin *Vox Clamantis*. For discussion, see the edition by G. C. Macaulay, *The Complete Works of John Gower*, 4 vols. (Oxford: Clarendon P, 1899–1902).

[3] See William Langland, *Piers Plowman*, ed. Elizabeth Robertson and Stephen H. A. Shepherd, Norton Critical Edition (New York: W. W. Norton, 2006), 15.152 (the B-text).

yet another dominant vernacular to this realm. By the time Chaucer is writing in the last quarter of the fourteenth century, England is a trilingual region: Latin for the church and universities; an insular form of French, Anglo-Norman, for the aristocracy and the law courts; and English—the Middle English we must learn—for those "not sitting on a cushion."[4]

Chaucer is preceded by writers in Old English (also called Anglo-Saxon) and early Middle English, and many anonymous romances, pious treatises, debates, and songs predate Chaucer's writing, even providing the foundation that enables him to compose in English and adapt French and Italian materials to his own native use. So there is *writing* in English before Chaucer, to be sure. But most of us would be hard-pressed to agree on the text or to name the author that might centrally represent medieval English writing before Chaucer came along, whereas few would argue about his claim to that status after he appears on the scene. Here lies Chaucer's importance as the "first." It's not that he writes in English so much as what he does to English writing. While he could have written his poetry in the more elegant French of the court that he served as a bureaucrat (and we do have a manuscript of some lyrics, written in French and signed "Ch," that may be his), he instead used his native English and wrote poetry on elevated topics and in Continental forms (philosophic dream visions and epic romances) that attempted to raise English to the dignity held by French and Latin at that time. First. Important. English. Poet.

Chaucer's importance continues to be marked after his death in ways we still notice today: with the prestige and value accorded by money. His *Canterbury Tales* may have been the first work ever to be printed in England; it was certainly one of the first four books produced by the nation's inaugural printer, William Caxton, on his Westminster press. His works were never out of print for long, with a near continuous history of

---

[4] The reference is to Chaucer's address to the tournament audience in *A Knight's Tale*, a film written and directed by Brian Helgeland (Miramax, 2001).

print, translation, and "recovery" stretching from 1477 to the present.[5] Lest that sound like a mere historical curiosity, we might remember that Caxton's first edition of *The Canterbury Tales* is still the most expensive literary work ever publicly auctioned. (The only books that have gone for a higher price were an original edition of Audubon's *Birds of America* and da Vinci's notebooks.) Since its first public appearance, *The Canterbury Tales* has never ceased being the most important of English books. Yet its print history is not nearly as interesting as its manuscript history, which tells an intriguing story of an unfinished tale collection.

It may come as something of a surprise that Chaucer's most famous work is in a state of disarray, left in an uncertain arrangement and not fully pieced together at the time of his death. In its General Prologue, Chaucer describes a group of pilgrims. These are the prospective narrators for his stories, and the fiction is that he is merely reporting what he heard on his travels. But while he counts "nine and twenty in [this] compaignye" (I.24) at this beginning, there are fewer than twenty-nine tales (and more than twenty-nine pilgrims). The numbers throw us off balance from the start. Chaucer never wrote a story for the Plowman or the Yeoman. Some pilgrims are described in groups, like the five guildsmen or the Nun's three priests, and we are unsure how their collective status works. To make matters even more confusing, he invents a new pilgrim tale-teller who joins the group on their way to Canterbury, the Canon's Yeoman. Breaking the opening frame of the General Prologue in this way makes it seem that almost anything is possible.

The poem's state of incompletion is also telegraphed by the uncertainty of its tale order. The tales survive in clusters, typically called "fragments," in which some kind of conversation links one tale to another. In those links, the Host, Harry Bailly (I.4358), a London innkeeper who has joined the pilgrims at the outset and undertaken to guide their journey, often comments on the story and helps shift from one teller to the

---

[5] The longest stretch without any new edition of Chaucer is between 1602 and the reprint of that edition in 1687.

next. Some fragments link a number of tales together. The famous first fragment links the General Prologue to the tales of the Knight, Miller, Reeve, and Cook, the last of which breaks off after 58 lines. But there is no link from the Cook's Tale to anything. We don't know if Chaucer meant to cancel the Cook's Tale or finish it later.[6] He may have been looking for a story to replace the one he started but never got past his preliminary work. He may have planned to have the Cook interrupted at the point he stops speaking and begin a different, more decorous tale in its place. Or maybe he had not yet made up his mind about what to do. The only thing certain about the fragments, and there are by convention ten of them, is that their final order was still *un*certain when Chaucer stopped writing.

Only the first fragment is securely fit into place, since it starts with the General Prologue, which we know inaugurates the work. The Parson's Tale, the one story in fragment X, seems as firmly positioned as the last in the sequence. In the Prologue leading up to the Parson's story, the Host announces: "Now lakketh us no tales mo than oon" (X.16). But as we'll see later, there is reason to believe that this ending to the entire work may have also been under revision. The effect of this uncertainty could be stated in this way: while tale order *within* fragments is fixed, the order of the fragments *themselves* (and thus the arrangement of the poem) remains unstable. Put another way, we could think about *The Canterbury Tales* as a General Prologue followed by sets of tales that can be rearranged by set. We can move each set to a different place as long as its internal order is kept consistent.

This uncertainty about how to organize the fragments of *The Canterbury Tales* arises because the earliest handwritten copies of the poem made just following Chaucer's death are so different from each other. Of the eighty-one manuscripts extant, about fifty-three are complete or near

---

[6] The fact that the Cook shows up again in the Manciple's Prologue, as if he is about to be the next tale-teller, has provoked theories that the Cook's Tale in fragment I was meant to be canceled.

complete. But they are not consistently organized and suggest that Chaucer had not arranged the fragments into anything like a final form. These fifty-three manuscripts are also not of equal value: some are copies of other manuscripts, and with each act of copying the danger of corruption and wayward change grows. Neither are the manuscripts clearly related to and thus descended from one original copy: we cannot simply arrange them in their proper order of succession to find out what the earliest—ideally, authorial—copy looks like and follow that one. The complexity of the textual tradition, changing tale by tale, makes the idea of an "original" arrangement of the fragments a tantalizing mystery. The tales, which we will examine individually in the chapters that follow, are also in a state of flux. Some break off with no clue as to whether Chaucer meant to complete them later, replace them with another story, or write a link in which the break can be turned into a dramatic interruption of some kind. The versions of the tales that have survived in these various manuscripts show strong signs that Chaucer was not done moving things around; he was revising the stories themselves and even changing the tellers to whom they are assigned. While this situation makes for confusion, it's also responsible for some of the poem's mystique. *The Canterbury Tales* is a puzzle. Just enough of it is put together that its readers simply cannot stop tinkering with it.

Obviously anyone planning to print an edition must put the tales in some order. We tend to base that order on the order of the fragments in some of the best and earliest surviving copies of *The Canterbury Tales*. At least one of these copies may have been arranged by Chaucer's executors (possibly his son) shortly after his death. These two earliest manuscripts of the poem, Hengwrt (National Library of Wales, Aberstwyth MS Peniarth 392D) and Ellesmere (Huntington Library MS El 26 C 9, San Marino, CA), are also the most important for editions of the work. Between them, they determine the precise wording of each line. Ellesmere is a beautiful deluxe manuscript with illustrations of each pilgrim in the margin at the beginning of the individual tales. Its colorful borders are decorated with gold leaf. Hengwrt is a more homespun production with no such illumination and a large stain on its opening page. But they were copied by the same scribe, who clearly had access to some very good exemplars (early copies used as the basis of later ones) of Chaucer's tales—materials that may have passed through Chaucer's own hands. The two manuscripts are not, however, identical in their readings or even in the spelling of certain words, despite being copied by the same person. Ellesmere, for instance, contains a tale (the Canon's Yeoman's) that the other does not. This kind of variation, at the earliest points of textual production, has led to much speculation and hypothesizing about the conditions of the tales' creation, survival, and circulation.

The order of tales in *The Norton Chaucer*, the edition from which this handbook works and quotes, follows the now standard order for Chaucer's story collection: the one found in Ellesmere. As I have explained, that order is not Chaucer's, but it may be the closest we can ever get to his design drawing on the evidence we currently possess. But even when we follow the cues left in the manuscripts, such editorial choices about the order and layout of the tales can make the poem look more finished and stable than it actually is. For instance, the earliest editions of Chaucer's *Works*, published in the sixteenth century, did nothing to divide the fragments—what are in the Norton edition called "parts"—from each other. Those books ran the tales together in one complete circuit, making the poem look at first glance like a coherent narrative. But the printers were probably more interested in saving paper, which contributed most of the expense of bookmaking, than in thinking editorially about the poem and hiding its discontinuities. For that reason, these earliest printings of Chaucer are given the textual status of manuscripts. They preserve information about the different manuscript exemplars used (and then discarded!) as their copytext—that is, the basic model for each print edition.

Later editions used newer conventions of book design and included separations, headings, and page breaks to display the contours of the work. Many of these were insertions, fabrications, or even elisions that changed Chaucer's tale collection to suit the desires of more modern audiences. Late in the eighteenth century, scholars began comparing manuscripts to detect errors in copying and found that the best readings did not always come from the neatest copies or the prettiest manuscripts. With Thomas Tyrwhitt's 1775 edition, critical editing of the *Tales* begins in earnest. And an early high point is reached in 1894–97 with W. W. Skeat's multivolume edition of Chaucer's *Works* for the Chaucer Society, the edition that established Ellesmere as the basis for scholarly editions. That tradition persists in the vast majority of contemporary editions, including both *The Riverside Chaucer* (1987) and now *The Norton Chaucer* (2019).

The various visual layouts for editions of *The Canterbury Tales* have surely shaped understandings of the poem and could be treated at some length, but here we will consider editorial choice in tale order, as is typically read out from the table of contents. As discussed earlier, the order of fragments for any modern printed book is an important editorial choice and most now follow Ellesmere. But an influential argument made by Henry Bradshaw in the nineteenth century reordered the fragments according to the geographical references contained in the links between tales. Positing the determinism of geography along the Canterbury road, he followed no surviving manuscript's order. Bradshaw thus moved up the tales of Ellesmere's fragment VII to follow the Man of Law's Tale. If we use letters to signify fragments, the "Bradshaw shift" turns fragment VII into fragment B². While that reorganization aligns the comments in the Man of Law's Epilogue with those that open the Shipman's Tale, both of which feature a female speaker who mentions her "joly body," it has since been abandoned—even though it was adopted by the Chaucer Society, which produced Skeat's monumental edition, and thus appears in his Ellesmere-based text. *The Norton Chaucer* uses the standard numbering of fragments (relabeled "parts") I–X, but other editions also indicate fragments by letter parenthetically for comparison with other texts. This duplication facilitates cross-referencing with essays written by authors using older editions.

This context is intended to make the order of tales on the table of contents of any modern edition understandable, even interesting. A long tradition of labor hides behind the clean pages of modern print editions of

The Canterbury Tales, which mask the messiness and complexity of the text's history and speak to the need to reset our expectations of this "book." In many ways modern editions obfuscate the text's real allure. For Chaucer has left us enough of his evolving plan to let us feel that we can see him rearranging things at his writing desk. In this way, his own continual efforts as a writer provoke our continued interest in his last, unfinished work.

A Note on Using This Handbook

Like other guides to *The Canterbury Tales,* this one proceeds serially, working tale by tale. There is a chapter devoted to each of Chaucer's stories, covering its genre, major sources, and thematic expectations. In many ways, they are essays on style and offer basic information to make that style more apparent. The early chapters on the General Prologue and the tales of fragment 1 set out more self-consciously than later ones the process of close reading using the OED and the labor of translation to help novice readers see in slow motion what is done more intuitively later on. The General Prologue chapter, particularly, charts the interpretive method that the rest of the book follows. Later chapters invariably comment on strategies and topics sounded in earlier ones, as they are repeated or reinvented as the dramatic play of the *Tales* evolves. As such, the earlier chapters are slower, more deliberate, and somewhat longer; they may be better digested bit by bit. Some students will find Chaucer's text easier to read with the handbook as introduction, others might like it as after-commentary. While it's a personal choice as to whether to read the text or the handbook first, I imagine both improve upon re-reading.

THE GENERAL PROLOGUE

The General Prologue is one of the best-known parts of *The Canterbury Tales*. It introduces the pilgrimage occasion, the game of telling stories to pass the time, and the various narrators supposedly responsible for the tales. But the General Prologue is also more complex. While it pretends to simplicity—an objective set of observations about the physical features of a group of people and their occupations—this prelude manages to include information that is more than just a look at surfaces. In many ways, the General Prologue is Chaucer's first tale, not merely a background for the stories it supposedly prefaces.

The First Day and the First Sentence: Lines 1–18

This initial encounter with the text always seems to be heavily focused on language, working through the means by which we can "translate" Chaucer into modern terms. But remember, such translations already exist.[1] So, if all we wanted to do was to modernize the work, we could read one of the translations already published and be done with it. We seek to do far more than that. We want instead to read and enjoy Chaucer's Middle English poetry, and to reach that goal we must think about language

---

[1] A word about good and bad translations. Bad translations are ones we are overly dependent on, often without realizing it. I urge my students to use a translation at the beginning of the semester, and really for as long as they feel they need it, to get the plot down for each assignment. As they will quickly realize that plot is not meaning, this does no harm. Read the translation once and then hide it under the bed. Do NOT keep it open while reading Chaucer. It will become a crutch that you won't be able to do without.

change and mutation as well as other formal features of the poems: the genres, styles, conventions, and sources that the poet relies on and often transforms. These will create our horizon of expectations as we read the different parts of the larger work and appreciate all that it weaves together.

It may sound strange to call special attention to the first sentence of *The Canterbury Tales*, for every literary work begins with one. But Chaucer's first sentence is famous and has been memorized by generations of students working on their Middle English pronunciation and prosody— that is, the sound of the poetic line as it bounces along. We often read Chaucer aloud because doing so enables us to appreciate his stories *as poems*—to hear their melody and their rhyme—and, even more importantly, because it often helps us understand their meaning. Many of Chaucer's words look like their modern English equivalents. But some foreign-looking words actually *sound* like their modern counterparts or have a telltale sonic root. Using both sight and sound to aid comprehension is especially important early in the semester.

My introductory class on *The Canterbury Tales* works on analyzing the first sentence because it's an important opening and it does a lot of different things at once, prefiguring Chaucer's techniques throughout. It's also terrifically long and a little forbidding to new readers. So it's important to get a handle on the different questions and concerns that this intentionally lengthy sentence raises. Though you may have worked on it in your first class, I'm going to review the first sentence here. For one thing, this approach enables us to begin on the same page, as it were. For another, you will also find it helpful to have this discussion written down to be reviewed later, perhaps before a first exam or paper.

If we boil this sentence down to its simplest point, which is too often all we are interested in doing, it tells us that it is spring and, therefore, people are going on pilgrimage. Perhaps we are just willing to accept that as a historical fact, grateful that we have reached the period with an understanding of that declaration. But the sentence operates across 18 complicated lines of description that introduce far more than this spring

setting and occasion. Most of Chaucer's simple descriptions are loaded:
they are ambivalent claims that can be taken more than one way.

For a single sentence to be 18 lines long is pretty extraordinary, and
we must pay attention to the many cues it subtly offers and the potential
issues it raises. The first thing to note is its tone or tenor. It begins the
poem in the style and with the matter of elegant court poetry of a slightly
classical temper:

> Whan that Aprill with his shoures soote
> The droghte of March hath perced to the roote,
> And bathed every veine in swich licour
> Of which vertu engendred is the flour;
> Whan Zephryus eek with his sweete breeth
> Inspired hath in every holt and heeth
> The tendre croppes, and the yonge sonne
> Hath in the Ram his halve cours yronne,
> And smale foweles maken melodye
> That sleepen al the night with open eye—
> So priketh hem Nature in hir corages—
> Thanne longen folk to goon on pilgrimages,
> And palmeres for to seeken straunge strondes
> To ferne halwes, couthe in sondry londes;
> And specially from every shires ende
> Of Engelond to Canterbury they wende,
> The holy blisful martyr for to seeke
> That hem hath holpen whan that they were seke.   (I.1–18)

Beautiful gardens and soft climates are the stuff of Continental love poetry,
of the kind Chaucer had previously written before he wrote this "local"
story. Chaucer's concerns and vocabulary are highly poetical, as well as
calendrical and meteorological: we are in early spring, and it's raining
after a long drought. But in this opening, April and March are personified,

as are the Ram (the constellation Aries) and Zephyrus (the mild west wind). They are made into actors coordinated with each other and affecting the natural world.

To show how much is going on it this sentence, and to expose some of our tendencies to oversimplification, I use an exercise to reveal the different ways we can work to understand Chaucer's Middle English.

Summary, Paraphrase, Translation

Try to render this single 18-line sentence into these three different forms, each of which gets increasingly lengthy and detailed.

A summary boils the 18 lines into one quick statement: *When the wet spring arrives, people desire to go on pilgrimage.*

A paraphrase adds more detail but avoids the repetition to get at essentials. It might reduce the sentence by half, and puts it in your own words: *When the weather turns fine and spring rains arrive, and the lovebirds and plant life respond to the sweet season, people desire to go on pilgrimage, both overseas to foreign lands, as well as all over England to Canterbury.*

A translation seeks to render each and every word where possible, leaving out nothing. A translation of these 18 lines would produce 18 lines of modern English.

It is helpful to differentiate between paraphrase and translation, especially if you will be taking quizzes in class to help assess your progress and reading fluency. A paraphrase offers the passage in your own words, typically many fewer than Chaucer's, which a translation seeks to reproduce faithfully. As this assignment reveals, Chaucer is using very elevated diction to make a relatively simple statement. The presence of rain is clear enough ("showres soote"), but its work is more refined: it "bathed every veine in swich licour" and "perced to the roote" the drought of March. These sweet showers not only bathe (a term that suggests actions both cleansing and soothing) and pierce (a penetrative gesture) but also possess the "vertu" (power, excellence) that engenders the collective "flour." Rain, or mere water, is here rendered as "licour"—a concentrated distillation of liquid that can sometimes be intoxicating. "Licour" is not as specific as our modern *liquor*, but denotes more generally a liquid. Such terms make the rain both gentle ("soote," "bathed") and powerful ("licour," "perced," "engendred") at the same time, engaging our senses beyond the mere dampness that the words denote.

The distinction just made between *denotation* and *connotation* is worth pausing over, for it will form the basis of our reading of *The Canterbury Tales*. Denotation is what we are after when we look a word up in the dictionary or the glossary. In its simplest form, it is the word's "meaning," what might be substituted in a modern English translation. Denotation is literal. Connotation is trickier, depends on experience, and often suggests ways in which we ought to expand our understanding of the literal. Connotations are the "senses" that come with one particular word choice or word grouping over another. We are always shifting between denotation and connotation when we read. We want to know what a word means but also what a particular word choice in any given instance suggests. What does Chaucer say? Why does he choose to say it in that way? English is a language with a large vocabulary and lots of synonyms, and it also borrows heavily from other tongues. Getting the connotation right is important and often tells us a good deal more than denotation might reveal on its own. In this first half of the sentence, the denotation of many of these words and expressions is the same: "it is raining" or "everything is wet." But the connotation of the words is vastly different. It's raining in a rather elegant and literary way that makes us think of other places, mentioned in other texts, rather than the local environment literally being described.

Chaucer here is aggrandizing England in the style of some Continental precursors.

We tend to ask what something "means" in order to reduce complexity to something manageable. While this is a natural thing to do, especially for those trying to learn Middle English, we need to be careful that we are not being reductive where Chaucer is intentionally trying to be expansive. As we struggle to figure out what a particular line or phrase "means," we have to avoid discarding the less determined suggestiveness that the poet offers, which renders the situation more ambivalent than we would (at this stage) wish it to be. For help in registering these connotations, a vital tool is the *Oxford English Dictionary*, or *OED* for short. Your institution's library likely subscribes to its online version, so you can open the *OED* page on your computer while you are reading at home. The *OED* is more than a mere dictionary; it's a historical tool that records first usages, contains many obsolete forms of words, and offers a history of the English language as terms come into and fall out of use. Its many differentiated "senses" for a particular word show an array of connotations rooted in the different kinds of contexts in which the word has been used. It also contains extended information on the various forms, spellings, and etymology of words that are useful for reading Chaucer's Middle English (ME), a language complicated by a lot of borrowing from others, including Latin and French, and a variable spelling practice. It's the *OED* that will enable you to think about the uses of "licour" and "vertu" in the opening sentence—it's not something you are supposed to know before reading the poem. And it will show you examples from various kinds of early texts, so that you can see how sometimes a word emerges from a particular type of discourse. The *OED* reveals that these ME terms have broader senses than their modern English (ModE) equivalents, "liquor" and "virtue," to which they are related but not identical.

The initial sentence's elevated discourse continues with a description of the wind on the heath and the birds in this early spring season. They not only sing but "sleepen al the night with open eye," meaning that they fail to sleep, because nature "priketh hem . . . in hir corages." The birds are not merely reacting to the season: "Nature" (another personification that aggrandizes this force) is acting upon them violently, stabbing at their hearts. So too does Zephyrus's sweet breath "inspire" the woods and fields ("every holt and heeth"). The ME pronunciation of "inspired" (in-spear-ed) makes us take the meaning of that word more literally than we do now. To *inspire* is to "in-spirit" or to breathe life into something. It's what God does to Adam in the Judeo-Christian creation story. The wind thus acts much as the rain does to regenerate and renew the growth of the natural landscape's "tender croppes" (tender shoots or stems—what we recognize from the ModE word *crops*, seen and heard beneath the ME spelling). But there is an aggressive tone to this invigorating eroticism: piercing, pricking, inspiring, and engendering are all penetrative actions. The terms of the General Prologue's rainy spring season may be natural, but they can hardly be called neutral. Instead, they imply a masculine sexual force acting on a feminized landscape, depicting more than a simple seasonal rainfall.

But we have not even arrived at the main subject and predicate of this sentence, in which humans will make their appearance on the scene. Chaucer has elegantly built up our expectations with the sentence's conditional structure ("whan" . . . , "whan" . . . , "thanne"), which pivots on the (inverted) central subject and main verb: "longen folk" (people desire). In the context of the burgeoning natural world, human desire emerges as the telos of its development, but a human desire for a religious journey is *not* what the erotic gestures of this framework necessarily lead us to expect. We find ourselves somewhat deflated. The energy of springtime—birds singing, plants shooting, flowers blooming, people longing—collapses a bit in the face of pilgrimage. Rather than erotic, the human plane is rendered exotic: palmers seeking foreign shores and world-famous distant shrines ("ferne halwes"—"hallows" or "holies," holy places, as we might recall from the title of the seventh Harry Potter book), represented more locally by Canterbury, the major pilgrimage site in medieval England. We can reconcile the opening of the sentence to its latter half, of course, with a little historical thinking. The church's calendar of saint's feasts and high holy days would have structured conceptions of time in late medieval

England, so that the alignment of spring rebirth and Easter renewal would have made a "natural" kind of sense.

Easter may conjoin seasonal and spiritual aims, but it does not fully contain them. The analogy between physical and spiritual rebirth neither completely accounts for the ideas unleashed in this opening nor reconciles their potential conflict. And that's why the opening sentence is so important. It sets the stylistic tone, and its complexity strikes a note of ambiguity that we will hear again and again. For pilgrimage may be what one does in the spring, when the roads are newly passable and the Easter season is upon us, but that hardly explains why anyone is on the pilgrimage. Instead, it affords the pilgrims we are soon to meet an entirely legitimate form of movement and congress without saying anything specific about them. Are they ordinary travelers looking for some social respite after the harsh winter, or will their motives be deeper? Is this a devout group of individuals, or are they sinners who have been sent on pilgrimage as part of their penance? Is this the longest and most meaningful journey of their lives, or an extended weekend holiday? Much has been suggested but little can be absolutely known. We end, perhaps, with more questions than when we started.

Setting up a central ambivalence never fully resolved, this sentence also introduces a wide variety of discourses—meteorological, mythological, seasonal, scientific, sexual, and courtly, among others—that continually shift the tenor of this aestheticized description. That same kind of shifting will recur between tales, among narrators, and within a story's language itself to keep the terrain continually changing under our feet. It's not entirely surprising, then, that the second sentence of the General Prologue offers a contrast to the first, as it turns local and familiar. No longer far off with "palmeres" or even thinking about "every shires ende," we are in Southwark, just across the Thames "at the Tabard," greeting a group "by aventure yfalle" together (I.20, 25). This localizing gesture leads to the individual pilgrim descriptions offered by our narrator, "so as it semed me" (I.39)—as their circumstances and dress appear to someone who has just met them that evening. It's a quite realistic-sounding gesture for this narrator to pause over the figures who will be the individual narrators of the collection's stories. But it's not mere realism, or verisimilitude, or what he calls "resoun" (I.37) that governs Chaucer's decision to situate the pilgrims before he gets any further into "this tale." It may seem like common sense but there's a specific method, or rather a genre, to his madness, which is known as "estates satire."[2] In this particular type of literature, writers (generally clerical ones) offer a descriptive catalogue of society, exposing the failings and corruptions of all kinds of professions. While Chaucer's social catalogue both imitates and resists estates satire, it's thus important to see that Chaucer is invoking a set of literary conventions, not merely in the opening sentence where his style is flowery and elevated but also in the turn to the familiar, where he seems to be describing people just the way he sees them. He so smoothly transitions from one kind of writing to the other that it's hard to see what he's doing as anything more than simple observation. We'll return to this narrator and his abilities later in this introduction, as well as to the conventions of estates satire, which will help us ask questions about what is presented to us and how it is presented.

In Southwark: Lines 19–42

Your instructor most likely assigned the opening of the General Prologue up to a certain pilgrim's description for the second class. Typically, I ask my students to read through the Friar's portrait. This first assignment is sometimes the hardest—readers tend to breeze through it quickly, getting the gist of the material but not really knowing what each word means. Before diving into the first few pilgrim descriptions, think about the fiction of observation Chaucer sets before us: the estates satire masquerading as a chance event.

---

[2] The definitive account of the influence of estates satire can be found in Jill Mann's seminal *Chaucer and Medieval Estate Satire* (Cambridge: Cambridge UP, 1973).

Though Chaucer uses the genre rather deftly, his writing hardly conforms to it. Order and orderliness are central to estates satire, part of its ideology. The given order of Chaucer's pilgrims is as follows:

Knight (with the Squire and Yeoman)
Prioress (with another Nun and three Priests)
Monk
Friar
Merchant
Clerk
Sergeant at Law
Franklin
A Haberdasher, a Carpenter, a Webbe (i.e., weaver), a Dyer, and a
   Tapister (often referred to as the Five Guildsmen)
Cook
Shipman
Physician
Wife of Bath
Parson
Plowman
Miller
Manciple
Reeve
Summoner
Pardoner
The Narrator himself

Medieval society was commonly understood as composed of three "estates": those who fought, those who prayed, and those who worked. Chaucer's pilgrims can be considered in these terms, of course. But he does not offer a balanced set of estates in his Prologue, nor is its hierarchy stable. Some have called this arrangement a "roughly descending" social order, a claim mostly justified by the anchors provided by the aristocratic group at the opening and the rogues at the end. The middle is more of a mixed bag of figures who work, some within the church and others in civil society. Most are from the mercantile ranks and thus are far from the agrarian class that the estates model posited as "workers." Many professions also blur the division between secular and clerical. The Summoner, for example, works for the church, delivering summonses to those who must appear in ecclesiastical court. But he is not a cleric, nor has he taken religious vows of any kind. By contrast, the Doctor of Physic is someone who is chided for his study being "but litel on the Bible" (I.438), not exactly what we might consider the expertise of a physician. What has a doctor to do with the biblical learning of clerics? What these professions show is that secular and clerical concerns are muddled together all the workweek. Religion is not relegated to one holy day out of seven.

The internal arrangements of these figures are as interesting as their overall disposition. The Knight and the Prioress do not travel alone, and the small entourage supported by each tells us something about their status. The Prioress is a woman and in some position of authority within her religious house. She may be the second in charge of a large convent or the head nun of a smaller house, so it is decorous for her to travel with companions; together with a Second Nun (her secretary) are three priests, who serve her spiritual needs and ensure her safety. But there are other, less formal, groups organizing the arrangement of the General Prologue. The Parson and the Plowman are brothers. Five guild members travel together with their Cook. Unlike the rest of the pilgrims (some seem to be ideals of their professions, others flawed examples), the final five are a group of thieves, with occupations so fully corrupt that we have entirely different expectations of them. Interestingly, Chaucer groups himself with this last set, explicitly adding himself to their number. There is just enough arrangement here to make matters intriguing without making them dogmatic. The narrator, in fact, apologizes for "nat set[ting] folk in hir degree" (I.744), spurring us to wonder what that "degree" (order) might have looked like. What kinds of "rank" might he have imposed on these mostly worldly, mostly working-class figures? Would it necessarily be social rank? What about ethical or moral orders, or other measures of success? Which of these figures is the most successful at what he or she does? Does that success always imply virtue?

Before finishing with the pilgrim descriptions, Chaucer also describes the Host, the hosteler or innkeeper who provides their food and lodging for the evening. The overarching story of the pilgrimage and contest begins at the end of the General Prologue when the pilgrims' host at the Tabard Inn turns into the Host of the pilgrimage, traveling with them to Canterbury and acting as "governour, / And of oure tales juge and reportour" (I.813–14). While he won't himself tell a tale, the Host actively generates the linking material between tales by responding to the pilgrims' stories and often anticipating them. He sometimes successfully navigates from one tale-teller to the next; at other times his intended plans go awry and the pilgrimage takes its own dramatic turn. Over the course of the poem we find out his name, Harry Bailly (I.4358), and he becomes a more individualized participant; he often thinks of his wife, Goodelief (VII.1891–96), whom he has left behind to mind the shop.

Two larger structures are at play in these otherwise mundane concerns with order and the Host's ordering function, and they will matter for our reading of the entire *Tales*. First: Chaucer is suggestive but not doctrinaire. No clear hierarchy is imposed on the pilgrims. We are not sure what a complete list in descending rank would look like. The pilgrims are clutched together in little groups. In addition to the traveling companions mentioned earlier, the Summoner and the Pardoner are "frend[s] and ... compeer[s]" (I.670). The Man of Law is also in the Franklin's "compaignye" (I.331). Many of the pilgrims are from London and seem to be acquainted, or at least to know about each other's haunts. It has been suggested that the Miller and the Reeve are professional rivals. These associations make for some compelling nodes within the larger structure and, in some sense, compete with it as a way of managing the larger group; the subgroups leave the overarching order more uncertain and make it more nebulous, which seems to be how Chaucer likes it. Second: the situation in the *Tales* is set up for almost immediate disruption.

The Host no sooner arranges the rules, a plan engineered both to get him out of the house and to return to the Tabard with twenty-nine repeat customers, than those rules are broken or at the least bent by the bossy Miller and obstreperous Reeve, who respond to his preferential treatment of others. In both cases, Chaucer sets the stage for a drama meant to move and change. His pilgrim portraits fit into this structure perfectly, since they fail to tell us in any determinate fashion about the figures described; instead, he allows them to perform their own self-revelation through their tales, against the background he provides in the Prologue.

And Pilgrims Were They All: Reading Lines 43–269

In the fiction of the General Prologue, Chaucer talks with each of the pilgrims gathered at the Tabard that evening and becomes part of their group, which is why he presumably knows so much about them before the journey even gets started. He gives his audience the basic information on figures whom he has lately joined, turning to one randomly—the Knight—in order to begin. The fiction of such happenstance drives much of this work. These are the folks who just happened to be at that inn on that day. This is the random order in which he happened to meet them or thought to describe them. But the more we think about it, the less does happenstance seem to govern this opening. Chaucer, the writer of the poem, appears increasingly distinct from the fictional version of himself who meets these other pilgrims at the Tabard. The work's writer has certainly ordered and organized his fictional counterpart's experience to look the way it does. It will be much easier to see the difference between the Chaucer who writes *The Canterbury Tales* and the Chaucer who inhabits the poem and experiences the journey once we meet some of the other pilgrims through the descriptions he offers. But first, we might consider what these figures *as pilgrims* purportedly have in common.

Pilgrims are wayfarers, travelers on a spiritual journey carried out over the course of a geographic one. Such a journey might be internally motivated or imposed by some authority, but the physical voyage always implies a kind of inner movement as well. Because pilgrims are always implicitly in search of something, voyaging and pilgrimage are especially fertile metaphors for all kinds of human exploration, of both the universe and the self. Pilgrimage thus structures a variety of literary works and not just those depicting a physical journey, including *The Vision of Piers Plowman,* by Chaucer's near contemporary William Langland. Langland's narrator describes a dream—more accurately, a series of dreams—in which he finds himself dressed in the habit of a hermit, wandering a field full of folk. He sees pilgrims who have returned from their journeys with stories. But he himself also travels like a pilgrim, collecting stories, as he seeks out the figure of Piers, the virtuous plowman, who is on an allegorical voyage to save his soul. Chaucer's literal pilgrimage is clearly related and perhaps indebted to Langland's more figurative one.

In the General Prologue, establishing these figures collectively as pilgrims equalizes them to a degree; we meet them on a level playing field, or at least Chaucer does, having "spoken with hem everichon / That I was of hir felaweshipe anon" (I.31–32).[3] But almost immediately, these portraits individuate them, with rather little to say about the immediate pilgrimage context. In the next two sections, we examine what we can tell about these figures from how they appear and what they have told him, and we'll note the ways the portraits often work in excess of this seemingly simple function.

---

[3] I typically spend about four class periods on the General Prologue (or about two weeks of the semester), a total that includes the first, introductory class on the opening sentence of the poem. This structure allots two days to the portraits and then one to the situation and setup of the contest. Your instructor may go faster or more slowly, but the comments here are intended to help you along as you work on your own to prepare for class. Your first assignment is likely ask you to read a third to a half of the portraits in the General Prologue. (My students are typically asked to read up through the Cook but to prepare carefully up through the Friar, which gets them used to rereading, a practice that is both helpful and necessary.)

The Portraits

We tend to take the portraits of the pilgrims at face value, a bit like the way we initially read the opening sentence of the General Prologue. It is given to us in that way. We don't know how to question it or if we should. We'll need some guidance to think through what we have been told and in what way, as well as what has been kept from us. Chaucer's pilgrim descriptions begin with the Knight, who is traveling with his son (the Squire) and a servant (the Yeoman). These three are part of a dynamic portrait of aristocracy that depicts its ideals, its social niceties, and its accoutrements as distributed into three separate figures, each presenting a particular aspect of the aristocratic life. The Knight and Squire make for a contrasting pair that offers a coherent yet varied picture of a masculine ideal. In fact, together they make for a complete aristocrat, at once fearsomely heroic and brave while intensely courtly and genteel.

To get a handle on what is before us, we can count and compare the lines describing this father–son pair to see how Chaucer crafts contrasts to produce a more complex shading *within* the picture of knighthood that he paints. Both portraits are drawn around action, appearance, locale, and behavior. The most often used word in the Knight's portrait is "worthy" (and its permutations "worthiness" and "worth"). Its repetition creates his reputation as deserving of the praise and success he has attained: riding farther than any other man in Christendom and winning fifteen mortal battles (as well as slaying his foe "in listes thries" for "oure faith"; I.62–63). Here it seems as if Chaucer is doing the numbers for us by counting and thus accounting the Knight's worth: "And evermore he hadde a sovereign pris" (I.67), a phrase often glossed as "outstanding reputation." "Pris" here means "esteem, estimation, (high) regard" (*OED*, s.v. "price" n. I.4.a) and might be considered an obsolete form of the modern word "prize," itself "a token of commendation, esteem, or honour" (*OED*, s.v. "price" n. I.1.a), which we recognize more easily as "a reward, trophy, or symbol of victory or superiority" (*OED*, s.v. "prize" n.[1] A.1.a). Both are etymologically connected to the earlier "price" as well as "praise." The complicated (and at distant points conjectural) etymologies of these words suggest that they all derive from the same gesture: the expression of one's worth and the compensation for it are intimately related. One's price and one's prize are signs of one's value, the symbolic and ethical here approaching the economic closely. For one's value (as a comrade, or a soldier) might very well materialize in some payment or material rewards, whether those take the form of goods, titles, or fame. Seeking to determine which one of these Chaucer means is a bit of a fool's errand. He's using a word with a very different set of resonances in ME than the narrow meaning we would now ascribe to the very same term. The term "pris" came into English more than 100 years before Chaucer used it; it is quite common in romances and other forms of aristocratic discourse, as we can see from the *OED*'s array of textual citations under this headword. So it's no oddity or particular irony that Chaucer would use it about the Knight or that he'd keep emphasizing the Knight's "worth." Neither "price" nor "prize" is primarily economic, as today; indeed, the broader, more philosophical origins of the connection between the two words are in play throughout the portrait.

Next to his son, the Knight is all military action, and a large part of his description concerns the faraway places in which he's fought: Lithuania, Prussia, Morocco, Turkey, and so on. These exotic locales are meant to be impressive, just as his crusading "in his lordes werre" signifies his love for "chivalrye, / Trouthe and honour, freedom and curteisye" (I.47, 45–46). The phrase "lordes werre" can equally refer to a secular or a religious enterprise, as the Knight is situated in a vertically hierarchical feudal system in which he owes military service to the overlord he serves (a line that ultimately traces back to the king). But given the description of his riding far into "Cristendom as hethenesse" (I.49), we can assume that his campaigning might be religious as well as temporal. Thus, his "lord" is a bit indeterminate, but his obedience to him (or Him) is not.

While the Knight is idealized for fighting in *his lord*'s war, his son, by exquisite contrast, works "to stonden in *his lady* grace" (I.88). Their chivalric efforts are directed toward different goals, but both are associated with noble behavior and courtly service. The Knight has traveled to far-off lands, principally to the east; his son has fought mostly in France and Flanders for worldly glory. In his youth Chaucer himself fought in Artois and Picardy as a squire. In Chaucer's time these would be rather familiar campaigns, given England's near continuous state of war with the French for territorial gain on the Continent. The Squire's activities seem more refined than his father's gritty battles and are certainly more worldly than any of the Knight's spiritual fighting.

Even in attire, these two are somewhat in contrast. The Squire's ornate clothing, "Embrouded . . . as it were a mede, / Al ful of fresshe floures, white and rede" (I.89–90), draws far more attention than his father's filthy tunic, "Al bismotered with his haubergeoun" (I.76), the rust from his chain mail having stained the cloth beneath. The contrast between the dress of youth and of maturity is revealing, for of course these two would have been licensed to wear a similar kind of finery by the sumptuary laws governing dress at the time. (Such laws were designed to prevent rich merchants and other social upstarts from dressing as well as aristocrats.) The General Prologue spends 9 lines detailing the Squire's appearance (his clothes, his hair) but only 4 on the Knight, and one of them is about his horse. Similarly, the Knight's courtly manners can be summarized in one sentence, "He was a verray, parfit, gentil knight" (I.72), whereas the narrator details the younger man's courtly occupations across the description, "singing . . . , or floiting, al the day[.] . . . He coude songes make, and wel endite, / Juste and eek daunce, and wel portraye and write" (I.91–96). I like to ask my students to compare these two portraits by finding different ways to account (by counting lines in each description) for the contrast between mature Knight and youthful Squire. Schematizing the weight (as determined by number of lines) given in these two descriptions to different aspects of "knighthood" gives us purchase on what might otherwise seem undifferentiated acclaim.

Comparisons like this one don't suggest themselves everywhere; we have to strive more deliberately to yoke together a different set of pilgrims and then assess the ways in which they were described. In fact, one reason such effort becomes necessary is Chaucer's clever avoidance of proscription.

Where he might have resorted to rhetorical principles to offer somewhat standardized descriptions of the pilgrims, he instead varied his techniques widely. Some portraits are long and some rather short, giving the impression of his narrator's idiosyncratic interest in the different figures he encountered. To assess the qualitative differences, we might initially rely on a quantitative measure, simply counting the number of lines in each description to see where attention is drawn and by what extent portraits differ. The Friar's description, at 63 lines, is the longest, while the Cook is given a mere 10. How might we categorize the details offered within these variable descriptions? Do they allow for or prohibit comparison? What might sharp differences suggest? This mathematical approach is only a beginning, but it does provide a starting point from which we can begin asking more searching questions, and it offers a solid base for any claim that one description "seems" more or less outwardly focused, internally revealing, emotive, objective, and so on.

The Yeoman traveling with the Knight and Squire is not an aristocrat but a servant, so he isn't directly comparable to them. How might we consider the details of the Yeoman's portrait both alone and in relation to those he accompanies?[4] What is he able to do or to suggest about them that they do not say themselves? Just like the Knight with his attendants, the Prioress appears next with a retinue of people to serve her. This is not her only similarity to the Knight. She too has genteel manners and an aristocratic appearance. The Prioress throws into relief the other portraits because hers contains a near textbook example of the rhetorical figure known as *effictio*: a head-to-toe presentation of physical detail. She has a small nose, gray eyes, and a rosebud mouth, much like a romance heroine, even though she's wearing a "wimpel" (I.151), that part of a nun's habit that covered her neck and head. This view of her face is followed by an account of her clothing, adornment, and stature: "she was nat undergrowe" (I.156). Given that the description began with an account of her table manners and her

---

[4] For a lively reading of the Yeoman's description and its function, see my essay "Yeoman Services: The Knight, His Critics, and the Pleasures of Reading Historically," *Chaucer Review* 45.2 (2010): 194–211.

elegant speech in the insular French of "Stratford at the Bowe" (I.125), how might we interpret the idea of not being undergrown? While some have thought that this negation is intended to describe a large woman, others have argued that Chaucer's narrator instead gestures toward her upbringing in a wealthy family that was able to nourish her well. That is, the Prioress has suffered no deprivation, whether imposed from without or by her own piety. So too the Monk appears to be well fed. Indeed, the Prioress's table manners occupy our attention because they mark her efforts to appear "estalich of manere, / And . . . digne of reverence" (I.140–41). They are courtly affectations, not particularly religious ones. The Monk's eating habits and tastes are also foregrounded but to different effect. While we are told directly "a fat swan loved he best of any rost" (I.206), the Monk reveals to us (indirectly, through Chaucer's description of him) that he tends to think in terms of food:

> He yaf nat of that text a pulled hen
> That saith that hunteres been nat holy men,
> Ne that a monk, whan he is recchelees,
> Is likned til a fissh that is waterlees—
> This is to sayn, a monk out of his cloistre;
> But thilke text heeld he nat worth an oystre.   (I.177–82)

The hints of free indirect discourse heard here in the narrator's description—in which we hear the idiom of the Monk himself through the objective account Chaucer presumes to give—puts his most basic thinking into foodstuffs: plucked hens, fish, oysters. The proverbial tone, in turns of phrase such as "a fish out of water," is belied by the narrator's closing remarks, which are four independent claims:

> Now certaynly he was a fair prelat.
> He was nat pale as a forpined gost:
> A fat swan loved he best of any rost.
> His palfrey was as broun as is a berye.   (I.204–07)

"Now" suggests a causal summation of what from the previous description has made him a "fair prelat." But little of it had anything to do with the prelacy or his spiritual work. Instead, it mostly concerns his hunting equipment and fine clothing. Attention to such spiritual matters, in fact, *is* what would make him "pale as a forpined gost"—which he emphatically was not, as his appetite seems to suggest. We end, again, with admiration expressed in terms of edibles: roasts and berries. The way these four individual statements are arranged as a summary account of unsubordinated (and thus completely independent) claims is highly characteristic of this narrator, who accrues a lot of detail but refuses to draw conclusions for us.

Both well-dressed members of the regular clerical orders, the Prioress and the Monk, appear to be displaced aristocrats. Neither seems devoted to the cloister for spiritual reasons, yet both are well positioned in it. The Prioress is the second in command of her nunnery, behind its abbess. The Monk is "a manly man, to been an abbot able" (I.167). Yet despite these abilities, neither seems to have left the secular world far behind—as the Prioress's brooch, inscribed *Amor vincit omnia*, or "Love conquers all" (I.162), compellingly suggests. The phrase might refer to Christ's love, which of course does conquer all, or to romantic love, the motto's sphere before the church adopted it. We are not sure how to take it or how the Prioress takes it, and Chaucer does not say. Instead he does something more subtle. Positioning the well-bred Monk and Prioress just after the Knight, Chaucer slyly aligns the pilgrims of higher-class origins in ways that the "estates" obfuscate, thereby potentially undermining the order of society offered by the estates model.

Measuring Chaucer's Style

Comparisons can help us identify Chaucer's signature style. In order to see the light touch of Chaucer's comedy, we might compare the General Prologue to the Prologue to *Piers Plowman*, which also employs the conventions of estates satire. We would not be surprised to find Langland's poem initially more difficult to understand than Chaucer's. There is no verisimilitude of situation, such as Chaucer's chance meeting of a group of pilgrims in the Tabard Inn, in *Piers Plowman*'s episodic presentation of society—sometimes quite realistic and sometimes allegorical, in the guise of a dream. But comparisons can be difficult when one is new to this kind of historical material, whether Chaucer's or Langland's or both. In such cases it is often helpful just to go by the numbers—by which I mean specifically to count things.

The box contains a handout I give my students so that they can prepare to discuss the Prologue of *Piers* after we have finished working on the opening setup of the General Prologue.

Count and Compare

Compare the General Prologue of Chaucer's *Canterbury Tales* to the Prologue of *Piers Plowman*, a contemporary text that also relies on the genre of estates satire, by "doing the numbers":

Simple math

How many full-stop sentences are there in the first 20 lines of each poem? In the first 50?

How many lines does the first sentence take up? Can you quickly calculate an average sentence length in lines?

What does this tell us about the relative simplicity/complexity of each poem's syntax?

Compare texts

For each of the two texts, perform the following calculations:

Count and list the nouns in the first 20/50 lines of each.

Count and list the verbs in the first 20/50 lines of each.

Count and list the adjectives and adverbs in the first 20/50 lines of each.

Analyze and summarize

Which poem has more nouns—and thus brings in more concrete detail, or which changes subjects more often?

Which poem is more descriptive and ornate?

Which poem is more verb-heavy and "active"?

What can we conclude about their relative styles based on these observations?

This set of questions will enable us to generate data independent of any previous experience with premodern texts. Counting parts of speech and ways of organizing sections (by lines, sentences, or passages—even when governed by modern punctuation conventions) gives even inexperienced readers equal footing when they are trying to wrestle with the style of these works. No matter how odd or hallucinatory Langland's poem might seem—with its "thoughts" on Kingship and Kind Wit giving way to the allegory of belling the cat—we will see that Langland's sentences are far simpler than Chaucer's, his condemnation of various occupations much more clear and direct. For instance, Langland, like Chaucer, spends some time on friars. And the Friar, we will recall, gets Chaucer's longest pilgrim description (at 63 lines) in the Prologue. Langland writes more economically:

> I found friars there—all four of the orders—
> Preaching to the people for their own paunches' welfare,
> Making glosses of the Gospel that would look good for themselves;
> Coveting copes, they construed it as they pleased.
> Many of these Masters may clothe themselves richly,
> For their money and their merchandise march hand in hand.
> Since Charity has proved a peddler and principally shrives lords,
> Many marvels have been manifest within a few years.

Unless Holy Church and friars' orders hold together better,
The worst misfortune in the world will be welling up soon.

(Pro.58–67)[5]

The disdain in which Langland holds the friars is palpable and their corruption by monetary profit absolutely explicit—no matter to which order they supposedly belong. Those orders—the Gray Friars (Franciscans) and the Black Friars (Dominicans) among them—could be identified by their clothing, as their nicknames suggest. But here Langland seems unable to identify them as one kind of friar or another, their habits no longer indicating their avowed poverty as mendicants (professional beggars), and that is telling. Instead, these men "clothe themselves nicely," because their strategic manipulation of the gospel in their preaching results in "copes," fine cloaks (which they get or buy with the monetary gifts they receive from those whom they serve, especially those whom they confess, putting "their money and their merchandise . . . hand in hand"). While it may take us a moment to see how the fine cloaks earned by these friars signify so much for Langland, he is absolutely clear about their visible connection to the corruption of their profession—which he calls "marvels" of the recent past, portending the "worst misfortune in the world." It is declared on the surface, in Langland's description of them.

For Chaucer, friarly behavior poses no such impending doom. He does not speak, or perhaps even think, in such apocalyptic terms. Instead, he finds the humor in such practices, understating with some irony what Langland condemns openly. Chaucer's far longer description is full of approval:

For ther he was *nat lik* a *cloisterer*,
With a *thredbare* cope, as is a *povre* scoler,

---

[5] *Piers Plowman* is quoted from E. T. Donaldson's translation, reprinted in *The Norton Anthology of English Literature*, general ed. Stephen Greenblatt, 10th ed. (New York: W. W. Norton, 2018), A:392–93.

But he was *lik a maister or a pope.*
Of double worstede was his semicope,
And rounded as a belle out of the presse.

(I.259–63; my emphases)

Both writers focus on what the friar is wearing and how much nicer it is than what we might expect of a poor beggar or hermit cloistered away in his monastery, but they do so in markedly different ways. Working somewhat by negation, Chaucer approvingly tells us what this friar is *not* like: a cloisterer or a threadbare scholar (an example of which appears elsewhere in the General Prologue in the form of the Clerk). But he never says if the friar should be like them or not; rather, he seems impressed with the fine "double worstede" as round and well-formed as a newly cast bell out of its mold. Such fine clothes make this friar look more like a master or a pope than like some random beggar. And given his comforting penance and pleasant preaching, it comes as little surprise that he should exhibit the material signs of success: "His purchas [income] was wel bettre than his rente [pay]" (I.256). Where Langland may tell us with certainty *what*'s wrong with the friars, who have sold out their profession "principally shriv[ing] lords," Chaucer describes in approving detail *how* this work has been done: sweetly, pleasantly, virtuously, and lispingly on the tongue.[6] But he never says it should not be done that way. Both writers indicate the profitability of the friars' actions, but Langland openly condemns it where Chaucer appears impressed by the marks of their success. Moral judgments are left for his audience to make—or to miss. Thus, Chaucer *writes more* than Langland does (56 lines vs. Langland's 10), offering us a great deal of detail about what someone like the Friar habitually does and how he speaks, but he often *says far less.*

---

[6] "Vertuous" in the General Prologue (I.251) signifies the powerful and effective way he preaches—Chaucer is not invoking virtue in the modern sense, except perhaps ironically, since this is what we might expect of a friar's potent preaching.

Saying less also comes in the form of some relatively brief pilgrim descriptions: the Clerk, the Merchant, the Sergeant of Law, and the Shipman each garner about 20 to 30 lines, and none of these portraits captures the individual voice that we hear in the Monk's or the Wife's descriptions. What impresses us the most about them is the variety they offer, the nonformulaic nature of their detail. In other words, Chaucer injects individuality through a kind of informative idiosyncrasy and a plain lack of knowledge. The opacity suggests depth. The Clerk's hesitance to speak, the Sergeant's writing, the Franklin's tastes, the Shipman's safe havens form minute areas of expertise for each but seem so distinct from each other that they forestall comparison, instead provoking the desire to know more. Included among these distinctive details are a number of questions Chaucer can't answer. The Reeve may be riding a horse named Scot, but the pilgrims' personal names are often unavailable. About the Merchant Chaucer feels forced to admit, "I noot how men him calle" (I.284). Such measures keep us from identifying the pilgrims as complete individuals in the modern sense of literary characters, but they are certainly more than mere allegorical types. Chaucer's figures are nestled somewhere between those two extremes.

Contest and Conflict: Lines 542–858

Another class on the General Prologue affords an opportunity to reread it yet again. Arrangement seems to be emphasized in this part of the poem:

> Ther was also a Reeve and a Millere,
> A Somnour, and a Pardoner also,
> A Manciple, and myself—ther were namo.   (I.542–44)

Chaucer has nowhere else grouped pilgrims in advance of their individual descriptions. These are collectively a set of professional thieves, whose occupations are a bit notorious. But like all the others, they are exceptionally good at what they do and thus impressive to the Prologue's narrator. The Miller, for instance, has the proverbial "thombe of gold" for his ability to "stelen corn and tollen thries" (I.562–63). So too the Summoner was a "gentil harlot and a kinde" (I.647) for taking a quart of wine in exchange for overlooking a man's guilt. Despite their moral failings, which are baldly claimed in near Langlandian fashion, this is a superlative group of men working in less than honorable professions. Chaucer appears to recognize their crookedness openly and to be oblivious to its implications, particularly by placing himself among them: "and myself—ther were namo." Given that this narrator's lack of full comprehension of what he so blithely describes has been a source of critical debate, the self-positioning here is intriguing. By including "himself" in this odd way, is Chaucer, the author of the entire collection, once again nodding at the assumptions of status and "degree" that he has refused to employ but still manages to invoke in this situation? Does his persona's placement in the rogues' gallery align his narration in some way with their open deceptions and make him honest about his dishonesty? He makes such questions relevant by drawing our attention to his control, or lack of it, when he apologizes for his plain speaking on these matters. Worried in advance over the kind(s) of language he'll be using to report the stories he heard, Chaucer disarms his audience, preventing them from attributing his speech to his "vileinye" (I.726) by explaining his limitations: "My wit is short, ye may wel understonde" (I.746). Understand, indeed!

The portraits conclude with one given in the immediacy of the moment, when Chaucer describes the Host's entrance. He arrives in the morning to make his "rekeninges" (I.760) but stays to accompany the pilgrims to Canterbury and organize their journey and entertainment. His impromptu participation has a slightly coercive edge to it, as he gets this group to agree to his plan before he even tells them what it is:

> Ye goon to Canterbury—God you speede;
> The blissful martyr quite you youre meede.
> And wel I woot as ye goon by the waye
> Ye shapen you to talen and to playe,
> For trewely, confort ne mirthe is noon

To ride by the waye domb as stoon;
And therfore wol I maken you disport
As I saide erst, and doon you som confort;
And if you liketh alle, by oon assent,
For to stonden at my juggement
And for to werken as I shal you saye,
Tomorwe whan ye riden by the waye—
Now, by my fader soule that is deed,
But ye be merye I wol yive you myn heed!
Holde up youre handes withouten more speeche.   (I.769–83)

One can hear a soothing, convincing, and increasingly excited tone as Harry moves from beginning to end—but he never tells them exactly what he has in mind. A fiction of spontaneity is produced by the Host's cascade of ideas that interrupt each other and prevent logical disclosure. They are going "to talen and to playe" anyway, the Host avers, why not work in the way that he proposes? Sheepishly the pilgrims agree: "Us thoughte it was nat worth to make it wis, / And graunted him withouten more avis" (I.785–86). This first act of agreement makes the motley assemblage into a "compaignye" (I.764)—a company or, more loosely, companions. It also places them under the Host's control, which will later be called his "yerde" (IV.22) or yardstick, an instrument of measurement as well as correction. It's what men beat the Prioress's dogs with (I.149). This scene (I.777–840) includes a variety of words for "agreement" (as both noun and verb: "assent," "othes," "vouchesauf," "accorded," "forward," "composicioun") and judgment ("juggement," "voirdit," "ruled"). Each of these terms changes the connotation of the pilgrims' consent ever so slightly. They range from rather legalistic jargon ("voirdit," "forward") to more general agreement ("composicioun," "avis"), and they will be invoked along the journey as the Host's control, over both the group and the order of tales, waxes and wanes. But the welter of this language overwhelms us and the pilgrims, driven by Harry's enthusiasm for his plan: he'll bet his (dead) father's soul that we'll enjoy it.

Chaucer's Narrator

Chaucer's previous poetry to varying extents cultivated a narrative voice only partially in control of its story. His Canterbury narrator is no less partial and indeed just as "naïve" or uninformed as the rest of Chaucer's narrating personas. But in *The Canterbury Tales*, Chaucer's narrator repeats individually voiced stories, emphasizing even further the distanced narrative style that is his signature approach. In his earlier works, Chaucer often appeared as a dreamer recounting a vision, not fully aware of its significance, or a reader of an old, traditional history, unable to change the matter he was recounting. These are both poses, of course, taken by Chaucer's fictional representative within his own work, rather than any "real" representation of the poet and his (lack of) authorial control. As is true of the Canterbury narrators he invents in this work, Chaucer assumes authority as a writer by ceding it as a narrator. The more his fictional self-projection demurs, the more visible is the author's hand behind him. Chaucer's invention of the Canterbury pilgrims is thus a kind of narrative apotheosis in his development of individuated voicings and their compromised (because subjective) authority.

These issues have animated critics for some time, prompting one to argue that we ought to address the narrator of the General Prologue not as "Chaucer"—as if he were continuous with the author behind the fiction—but as "Chaucer the Pilgrim," acknowledging his fictive status inside the poem.[7] By this logic, readers are to measure the distance between Chaucer's writing and his narrator's observations, which are often charmingly naïve. Chaucer thus creates a sense of ironic distance, which can encourage the reader to see the foibles that the narrator describes but fails to recognize. This pose enables us to recognize Chaucer's resistance to dogma of all kinds, leaving acts of judgment to others. But it also has led to misinterpretation. For too long this ironic distance was taken as itself the ultimate point of narration, as if Chaucer were enjoining us by its means to see each

---

[7] E. Talbot Donaldson, "Chaucer the Pilgrim," *PMLA* 69.4 (1954): 928–36.

of his narrators as deeply flawed characters revealing their sins via the narrator's naïve understatement. His innocence was thereby turned into a mechanism of condemnation that tied each General Prologue description tightly to the guilty speaker of each tale. What one influential early critic called the poem's "roadside drama"[8]—the interactive banter between the traveling companions and sometime rivals—turned into a tyranny of the frame narrative over the individual stories. There has long been a kind of chicken-and-egg logic to this problem: Which exists for the sake of the other? Do the stories create the pilgrims, giving us the sense of who they are and what they are made of, or do the intentions of the General Prologue's pilgrims precede and determine the tales they tell? Because the General Prologue introduces the tales, readers felt entitled to use its descriptions to assess the pilgrims' fictions, thereby sometimes placing a limit on what those stories can mean. But when we remember that the Prologue is the first tale, simply one among the other fictions told by the pilgrims, it loses its privileged status and becomes just another story, albeit a prefatory one.

Paradoxically, the General Prologue sometimes makes sense only *after* we get to know the pilgrims and hear their tales. Like other prefaces, it is meant to be read first but can be fully understood only last, at which point its limited perspective can be taken into account. The Wife's deafness, which "was scathe" (I.446) in the Prologue and suggested other types of limitation in her understanding, is later explained in her own story as the effect of being beaten by her husband. By contrast, the Prioress's romantic and delicate affectations don't prepare us at all for the violent tale she tells, and perhaps that's the intended effect. The General Prologue might prepare the groundwork for our future surprises as much as it guides our expectations.

The narrator ends this first tale with the departure from the Tabard and the means by which the first teller is chosen. Stopping at "the watering

---

[8] See George Lyman Kittredge, *Chaucer and His Poetry* (Cambridge, MA: Harvard UP, 1915).

of Saint Thomas" (I.826), the Host calls forth the Knight, the Clerk, and "my lady Prioresse" to "draweth cut" (I.839, 838), a rather egalitarian way to choose the first speaker:

> Anon to drawen every wight bigan.
> And shortly for to tellen as it was,
> Were it by aventure, or sort, or cas,
> The soothe is this, the cut fil to the Knight[.]   (I.842–45)

Despite the emphasis on chance or luck ("aventure," "sort," "cas"), are we really surprised that the Knight has won and will open the tale-telling game? It seems far more likely that the Host engineered things this way, handing the Knight the short straw when he gave him the first draw. And so it would likely go if the pilgrims ever made their way back to London at the end. Harry Bailly is not going to let a lesser man speak before the Knight, nor would he be likely to allow anyone else to take the prize. The contest has been judged before it ever begins. But by never finishing *The Canterbury Tales*, Chaucer has left the game open and in our hands.

THE KNIGHT'S TALE

The first of Chaucer's tales is one of his best, but it is not what you might expect. *The Canterbury Tales* has a reputation for presenting short, risqué stories, full of irony and wit. As a stately, serious romance narrative full of philosophical interrogation and set in classical Athens, the Knight's Tale disrupts these expectations—which were formed, mostly, by readers long after Chaucer's time.[1] But it's also somewhat different from what Chaucer's contemporary audience might have expected of a medieval romance, as the pages that follow will discuss. For now, we might simply note that the story, and thus the story collection, defies our expectations from the start.

While the Host perhaps engineered the straw-drawing contest to begin with the Knight, setting the bar high, so too does Chaucer open with a serious contribution to the collective discourse, a tale whose assumptions and themes can be mined for various purposes in those that follow. I've introduced this tale as something surprising, but in many ways it's just what we might expect from the Knight. As a model representative of those who fight, the Knight offers us a story displaying the ideals of his class and its courtly concerns with honor and love. Genre is a literary type, and the genre of romance often emphasizes perfection and the ideal. The Knight's audience would have been guided by a set of assumptions and expectations based on their experiences of romances from before Chaucer's time.

---

[1] In the Renaissance, when Chaucer's works were first put into print and collected in a single folio, he was revered largely as a love poet and less as a social satirist.

The Knight's story transports us in both place and time from its very first line: "Whilom, as olde stories tellen us" (I.859). Rooted in the Knight's present concerns with courtesy, chivalry, honor, "and al that longeth to that art" (I.2791), the story is set in the distant past. Theseus's ancient Athens and the larger historical arc of Theban history provide the background for what will essentially be a medieval romance. Theseus is the romance's main character, but he is not central to the erotic triangle within its romance narrative. Instead, at the heart of the Knight's story sits a romantic rivalry between two knights, Palamon and Arcite. These maternal cousins and sworn brothers-in-arms are taken in battle by Theseus at the beginning of the story, and both fall in love at first sight with Theseus's wife's sister, Emelye, whom they see from their prison window. They wind up competing for her in a tournament in which the victor accidentally dies, leaving her (eventually) to the other cousin. The difficulty presented by this romance plot is immediately obvious. Knights are supposed to win their ladies through heroism and prowess on the field, not as a consolation prize. Furthermore, knights win a lady by fighting for her honor as well as their own, defeating threatening villains (whether monsters or other men) who stand explicitly against their chivalric values. As a romance, then, the Knight's Tale's biggest problem is its lack of a villain. Instead, each knight acts as the other's antagonist, making the narrative a far more psychological and philosophical enterprise.

But its style also makes the Knight's narrative a challenging first tale for new readers of Chaucer. Style goes hand in hand with the expectations of genre and must also be considered historically. Given our familiarity with action films—even those that have adapted historical matter, as the Knight's Tale does—Chaucer's story tends to disappoint readers who expect more to happen. Little action drives this story and certainly none that justifies its length. It instead contains a lot of talk, and especially self-talk, in externalized monologues. These set pieces are at the epicenter of the tale, which works through them. For an example of the way that description works as action in the Knight's story, consider the following.

At the beginning of part 2, Arcite has been living in banishment in Thebes, far away from his beloved Emelye:

> Whan that Arcite to Thebes comen was,
> Ful ofte a day he swelte and saide allas,
> For seen his lady shal he nevermo;
> And shortly to concluden al his wo,
> So muchel sorwe hadde never creature
> That is or shal whil that the world may dure.
>   His sleep, his mete, his drinke is him biraft,
> That lene he weex and drye as is a shaft;
> His eyen holwe and grisly to biholde;
> His hewe falow and pale as asshen colde;
> And solitarye he was and ever allone,
> And wailing al the night, making his mone[.]   (I.1355–66)

The static description of the lovesick Arcite contains a wealth of action: fainting, wailing, and complaining, as well as sorrowing, starving, and desiccating—generally, dying for love. Describing his sleepless, meatless, appetite-less state, the passage makes us see him growing lean and dry, pale and sallow, right before our eyes. This description of Arcite's wasted appearance embeds action within its lines. An important part of reading Chaucer involves experiencing and enjoying these descriptions, despite their repetitiveness. In fact, their repetition is part of the charm—literally, as if this material were an incantation designed to mesmerize its audience with the images it evokes: his bodily wasting because he is bereft of "his sleep, his mete, his drinke," or the sorrow "that is or shal whil that" the world simply goes on. Part of the torment is experienced in the poetic rhythm, the pulsing beat of these lines as they break upon the body of Arcite, not merely in *what* they say. (This is yet another example of how simple translation cannot capture Chaucer's artfulness.) Competing declarations of love for Emelye, prayers to the gods in their temples, death-bed commendations, and conciliatory summations make up the major "events" in this story. These speeches are, of course, ornate and stately. The pacing of the narrative lends it seriousness and dignity. But these speeches are often where the action is.

Unlike most of the other tales, the Knight's is divided into four parts, and the division helps us make our way through the story more easily. But I still would urge you to read a translation before embarking on Chaucer in Middle English. It is no fun trying to read in a number of different ways at one time. When you are still learning the language and stopping to look things up, it's helpful to know the plot as you work through the text. Some students like to read only the day's assignment before working on Chaucer's language itself. Others want to know the entire story before they go back to the beginning and work with the original. Either way is fine. Spoiler alert: there are *no* spoiler alerts in this book—as you may have already gathered. I am going to assume that you know what happens, and therefore I won't hold anything back. Also, unlike other chapters in this handbook, I am going to begin each section on the Knight's Tale with a summary of what happens in it. But even these summaries are no substitute for reading a translation first (and I would recommend a verse rather than a prose translation). You need to get a feel for the texture, the set speeches, and the difference between dialogue and the Knight's narration before you encounter them in Middle English.

Insofar as the Knight's Tale offers a pageant of the noble life and of heroic efforts to keep the gloomy forces of chaos at bay, it appears to come from the depths of the Knight's professional identity and experience. But, of course, the tale comes from Chaucer (who was not a knight) and, like nearly all medieval stories, it has a traceable source. This story is not something the Knight could have made up on the fly nor one he'd have likely heard before, even though that's the fiction. In fact, it's an unusual story, originally told in an Italian love epic written by Giovanni Boccaccio, Chaucer's near contemporary. Chaucer likely encountered Boccaccio's works (as well as Petrarch's and Dante's) on one of his official trips to Italy on business for the royal government. This exposure to Italian poetry was highly significant for Chaucer's writing, at a time when Italian literature had little influence on other English authors. Chaucer's Knight's Tale is a radical reduction of Boccaccio's epic *Il Teseida*, and he likely wrote it as a separate, stand-alone poem sometime before *The Canterbury Tales* was even conceived.[2]

Part 1

On his victorious journey back to Athens with his Amazon bride, Hippolyta, Theseus is interrupted by a convoy of mourning Argive widows. They plead with him to avenge the treatment of their husbands, who died in battle against Creon, now king of Thebes. After avenging these widows and dethroning Creon, Theseus returns with two captives: the young Theban princes, Palamon and Arcite. From their tower window, Palamon and Arcite spy Emelye, Hippolyta's younger sister, roaming in the garden below, and both instantly fall in love with her. Declaring themselves struck by her beauty, the two immediately begin to argue and become sworn enemies. At the request of Theseus's best friend, Pirithous, Arcite is released and banished from Athens, while Palamon is left to languish in prison.

If we could imagine a screenplay of the Knight's Tale, how much of the script would be devoted to the battles of part 1, especially the campaign against Creon and his "tyrannye" (I.941)? My guess is quite a lot. The backdrop for this part of the story entails epic action, invoking the story of the Seven against Thebes and the tragedy of Oedipus, yet almost none of the tale itself concerns those matters or Theseus's revenge, cursorily treated here.[3] His fight with Creon is passed over in a few lines:

---

[2] In the prologue to *The Legend of Good Women*, Chaucer mentions "al the love of Palamon and Arcite," a story that is "knowen lite" (lines 420–21).

[3] *Seven against Thebes*, written by the Greek tragedian Aeschylus, dramatizes the mythic events after the fall of Oedipus. His two sons, Eteocles and Polyneices, agree to serve as king of Thebes in alternate years; but when Eteocles refuses to give up the throne, his brother (joined by seven chieftains) wages a war that leaves them both dead. Creon, Oedipus's brother-in-law, becomes ruler as next in line.

> But shortly for to speken of this thing,
> With Creon which that was of Thebes king
> He faught, and slow him manly as a knight
> In plain bataile, and putte the folk to flight;
> And by assaut he wan the citee after,
> And rente adoun bothe wal and sparre and rafter[.]   (I.985–90)

The details of "manly" fighting and "plain" battle would make up half our imagined film, yet these are the least interesting, most formulaic features of the Knight's narration. Damage to Creon's person is traded for one line announcing the destruction of the city of Thebes, as the pulling down of its beams, roofs, and signature walls forms a synecdoche (a figure of speech in which a part stands for the whole) for epic loss.[4] Instead the Knight focuses on the thoughts and speech of figures taking part, such as Theseus, through which these actions must be understood.

One way to begin thinking about the Knight's Tale is to turn to the question that closes its first part, which reflects on the predicaments of the captive Palamon and the banished Arcite:

> You loveres axe I now this questioun:
> Who hath the worse, Arcite or Palamoun?
> That oon may seen his lady day by day,
> But in prison moot he dwelle alway;
> That other where him list may ride or go,
> But seen his lady shal he nevermo.
> Now deemeth as you liste, ye that can[.]   (I.1347–53)

The question (as well as its mode of address to its audience) orients our reading of this opening section of the poem. The Knight poses a choice

---

[4] The importance of the Theban walls and the seven gates is emphasized in any number of the city's mythological foundation stories; in one legend, they were raised by the music of Amphion.

between two evils—seeing what you want every day but being unable to attain it *or* being given your freedom on condition of banishment from even the sight of what you want: do you prefer a physical prison or a psychological one? Though the choices may seem starkly different, they are two versions of the same frustration. This structure of similarity underlying distinctness will more generally characterize the tale, its figures, and its events.

Since the question has no real answer, how we reply tells us mostly about ourselves: which would we find worse? The question itself belongs to a genre, the *demande d'amour* (question of love), and it is typically found at the end of certain French poems designed to be debated by audience members. The question thus stylizes its audience as it is being posed: "You loveres," the Knight addresses us. There are not many we would call "lovers" among the Canterbury pilgrims to whom the Knight is speaking, but he asks them to imagine themselves as such and sets the horizon of response accordingly. And *we* too are addressed as lovers, implicitly sutured into this somewhat distant narrative and asked to empathize with the situation. Even more emphatically, the Knight forces us into the position of noble lovers—those who would not be able to decide between these two unfavorable positions—by giving us the power to "deemeth" (judge), "ye that can." The insinuation is subtle. By adding "ye that can," he suggests that the problem is undecidable, a deadlock. In directing attention to the few "that can," who *are* able, he admits that some, maybe most, cannot. But the focus here may be not only on the matter judged but also on one's ability to judge, one's sensibility to the matter at hand. From a modern perspective, we could be tempted not to care, to think that one of them can find another girl to love. But almost as though he knows that his audience is made up of potentially resisting readers, the Knight preemptively turns it into a group of lovers—courtly, aristocratic, gentle lovers—subtly persuading us to play the *demande*'s game. By addressing this question to us, he makes us into the kind of exclusive audience that is worthy of pondering such questions.

The *demande* at the end of part 1 is difficult to debate without return-ing to the events narrated earlier, the circumstances in which Palamon and Arcite fell into conflict. In many ways it's the poem's primal scene, a moment that gains its significance belatedly: only after something else happens (one of them gets released) do we see its importance in hindsight. Their argument forms an originary moment of division between the sworn brothers, which is also the moment they become distinct individu-als, and by the poem's end its effects seem determinative. They are still similar, but they are no longer inseparable, literally or figuratively. At the beginning of the Knight's story they are wearing the very same livery, found in a heap of bodies "ligging by and by" (I.1011). As two sisters' sons, they are genetically close (cousins sure of their blood relation to each other),[5] and they probably look alike. No one seems able to tell them apart until the sight of Emelye distinguishes them from one another through their speech. Of course, they have precisely the same response to seeing her, though they express themselves in sharply individualizing ways.

Our examination of the declamations of Palamon and Arcite over the sight of Emelye in the garden returns us to the issue of style. The two knights say the same thing: they are struck by love at the sight of a beautiful girl and feel completely overpowered by it. Very little divides them at the level of content; they both make the same claim. But the style of each man's speech articulates a great deal. Palamon looks out the window first and sees Emelye, whom he addresses as if the young woman were a vision of Venus herself. He essentially launches an elabo-rate metaphor in which he expresses her ethereal beauty by imagining, in fairly conventional form, that the goddess of Love must be standing before him. Thus his immediate response is to offer a prayer to her and to beg her "compassioun" (I.1110). Arcite is moved by Palamon's cry of suffering, "A!" (I.1078), before he even hears what his cousin says

---

[5] Sisters' sons are sure of their blood connection to each other because it does not depend on potentially questionable paternity.

afterward—and then he turns his head and sees Emelye too. We ought to pay attention (both here and from now on) to who's saying what, because once Arcite expresses the force of her beauty on him, both men will begin arguing about it. When he turns to the cause of Palamon's suffering, "Arcite is hurt as muche as he or more" (I.1116). We must note the physicality of love, like the chemistry of attraction, because it's responsible for the orchestration of this scene, and it is spoken in the voice of the Knight as well as by the two knights. Today we often use the expression "fall in love" to get at the unreasonable and unwilled nature of the experience. It just happens to us, without much warning and almost without our notice, in an instant. That same fall is anatomized here in more violent terms, as may be appropriate for knights. Palamon is "hurt right now thurghout myn eye / Into myn herte" (I.1096–97). Arcite similarly claims, "The fresshe beautee sleeth me sodeinly" (I.1118). The sight of Emelye wounds them ("hurt," "sleeth"), as the Knight says, in a physical way, represented conventionally as being shot by Cupid's arrow through the eyes and into the heart. Both men talk this way. And so does the narrator: the Knight tells us that Arcite is hurt, physically, as much as Palamon is, or perhaps more. This claim will disarm some of the self-serving reasoning that is soon offered by the knights.

Despite the conventionality of this representation of the power of erotic attraction, Palamon is outraged to hear that Arcite feels the same way that he does and immediately invokes his priority, using his status as "brother" to try to stake a superior claim. Their argument is ridiculous on any number of levels (beginning with the fact that Emelye doesn't know they exist), but it is also deadly serious. And their continued debate about their respective rights to love this woman further differentiates the two men. The knights' stylized self-expression, both at the moment of falling in love and in this debate, tells us about each of them. Palamon waxes eloquent as he employs terms of the religion of love, admixing elements of classical mythology into his worship of his lady. Arcite gets to "the short and plain" (I.1091) here, as elsewhere, declaring that unless he finds a way to have her mercy, "I nam but deed: ther nis namore to saye" (I.1122). Hearing these words, Palamon "despitously" (I.1124) looks and asks whether Arcite is joking. "Despitous," literally "without pity," was a term used repeatedly about Creon in the opening scene of the Knight's Tale, describing his cruel and unnatural treatment of his enemies and defining the tyranny of his rule as his having acted in "despit" (in spite). (Conversely, pity will be the feature that identifies Theseus as a just ruler.) These words deserve our attention because they are silently guiding our sense of opposition, association, and response.

As they argue, rather elaborately, with each other, Palamon and Arcite reveal themselves to be very different kinds of knight (recall the contrasting descriptions of the Knight and the Squire in the General Prologue). Like his prayer's metaphysics, Palamon's argument plays in the realm of abstraction: he argues in terms of ideals and ideas, invoking a prior promise that as sworn brothers, each would further the other's claim. Arcite is more practical and pragmatic, and sometimes downright sneaky, in the way he values the literal over the metaphorical. Arcite turns Palamon's language against him. While he may have glimpsed her first, Palamon saw not a woman but the goddess Venus. The metaphor thus amounts to a confusion. Arcite calls Palamon's state an "affeccion of holinesse," whereas, by contrast, he feels "love as to a creature" (i.e., a created thing; I.1158–59). The play on the word "false" in their debate is telling. Palamon claims that Arcite is false for having broken his promise "to forthre" Palamon, to whom he is "ybounden as a knight / To helpe" (I.1148–50). Turning the meaning of the word "false" against Palamon, Arcite claims that his cousin is false, speaking words that are literally untrue. Because Palamon did not know whether Emelye was a woman or a goddess, Arcite technically loved her as a human first.

Here Chaucer has Palamon and Arcite use the same word to different purposes, equivocating on the crucial idea of "falseness" and showing how two different meanings of the same word can work at cross purposes, how one use can be transformed into the other, and thus how one's language can be turned against oneself (hint: this will happen again later).

This verbal play is the inverse of what occurred when they first saw Emelye: then, they used completely different words to describe her and different kinds of language to say the very same thing. By playing with language in these two different ways, Chaucer is able both to draw parallels between and to differentiate the two cousins, who always seem to be collapsing into each other even as they work to distinguish themselves. In this way, Chaucer explores two very different, yet equally important, aspects of knighthood: the thoughtful paralysis of the lovelorn (Palamon) and the clever activity of the heroic (Arcite). Such friction opens up, rather than decides between, differences in heroic identity.

Part 2

The Knight begins with Arcite, now in Thebes, suffering in the absence of Emelye to the point that he is unrecognizable to his friends. Again, the torment of love is physical. Arcite's "face was so disfigured / Of maladye the which he hadde endured" (I.1403–04) that he is able to return to Athens, disguised as a poor laborer, to be near Emelye. In the meantime, Palamon decides to break out of prison and flees to the woods, where he runs into Arcite. The two plan a private combat; there they are found by Theseus, who by chance has gone to the very same grove to hunt. Persuaded to show the knights pity, Theseus decides to satisfy one of them instead of killing them both on the spot. He decrees a tournament and offers marriage to Emelye as its prize.

In this part of the Knight's Tale, Theseus moves into the foreground; he thereby distracts our attention from the three young lovers and realigns our perspective with his. Much of what has happened involving Palamon and Arcite now appears as preparation for Theseus's stately arrival to the hunt—an activity reserved for the aristocracy, and one that has long been used as a metaphor for amorous pursuit. That is, Palamon and Arcite are drawn to the grove precisely so that Theseus can find them. The Knight's turn toward Theseus is worth a closer look:

> The destinee, ministre general,
> That executeth in the world overal
> The purveyance that God hath seen biforn,
> So strong it is that, though the world hadde sworn
> The contrarye of a thing by ye or nay,
> Yet som time it shal fallen on a day,
> That falleth nat eft withinne a thousand yere.
> For certaynly, oure appetites here,
> Be it of werre, or pees, or hate, or love,
> Al is this ruled by the sighte above.
> This mene I now by mighty Theseus[.]   (I.1663–73)

Part 2 emphasizes its coincidences pretty well; indeed, we are asked to understand such accident—one moment that will "falleth nat eft withinne a thousand yere"—as "purveyance," or providence, seen from a higher perspective. Destiny is the agent that executes such providence, and in this text that agency is equated with Theseus, the figure who controls decision making in this world. Palamon and Arcite arrive coincidentally in the same grove. Compounding that happenstance, Theseus decides to hunt there as well, only to find the knights fighting without any judge or official.

The central gesture of this part of the story is Theseus's turn from angry lion (at finding his two enemies in defiance of his law) to sympathetic lover. As in the first part of the story, in which the grieving widows beg him to interrupt his homeward journey to avenge their dead kinsmen, Theseus is here persuaded by the emotions of women—Hippolyta, Emelye, and their entourage—to change his mind:

> And on hir bare knees adoun they falle,
> And wolde have kist his feet theras he stood,
> Til at the laste aslaked was his mood—
> *For pitee renneth soone in gentil herte*—
> And though he first for ire quook and sterte,

He hath considered shortly, in a clause,
The trespas of hem bothe and eek the cause
And, although that his ire hir gilt accused,
Yet in his reson he hem bothe excused[.]

(I.1758–66; my emphasis)

Even though we might focus on the fight between Palamon and Arcite, the crucial element of the scene is this mood change—the *pity* that Theseus can experience and that alters his behavior because of his "gentil herte." The Knight offers a representation of what Theseus thinks to himself (I.1773–81), as well as what he says to the offenders (I.1785–825) and what he officially decrees (I.1829–69). As the central action of this part of the story, these speeches model for us the thinking that the audience should apply to these circumstances. Theseus recalls his own experience as a lover and the power that Cupid holds over all earthly creatures, spurring him to forgive Palamon and Arcite their "trespas." Once he gains their allegiance, he grants each man the opportunity to "have his destinee" (I.1842). But Emelye can't be married to both of them, so instead Theseus proposes a tournament in which one of them might "darreine hire by bataile" (I.1853). What Theseus plans is much more grandiose than the private fight he interrupted: they are to return in a year, each with a hundred men to assist in this endeavor. One will end up with Emelye "to wive" (I.1860); the other will die in a glorious effort to attain his desire. This section ends with their ecstatic happiness and their praise of Theseus for his generosity. But Theseus has also orchestrated political stability, as Emelye's marriage to either man will secure Thebes' allegiance to Athens. The disorder of Palamon and Arcite's fight has been quelled and redesigned—what we might call sublimated—into a higher form.

Part 3

In this section of the poem the Knight describes the amphitheater built to host the Theban battle for Emelye; it contains separate temples devoted to the gods Venus, Mars, and Diana. Palamon prays for possession of Emelye in Venus's temple, Arcite for victory at Mars's. Emelye, who here speaks for the first time in the tale, asks for peace so that she might remain a virgin devotee of Diana at her temple. Venus and Mars assent to these prayers by sending (variously) incomprehensible signals. Venus and Mars then run to the god Saturn to help them work out how they can both accomplish their goals. Saturn promises a solution.

From the tale's opening gestures, we know *not* to expect an elaborate battle scene. What do we get instead? The Knight continues to focus on Theseus (and somewhat on himself) in this section of the poem, beginning with the extravagance of the amphitheater, purpose-built for this event. The Knight worries that we will think him negligent if he does not detail Theseus's expenditures on the tournament lists or the details of their construction, paying close attention to the temples visited by each lover within the amphitheater. Doing so gives us opportunity to see what each of the characters sees in approaching those places. But it also shows us how we should interpret and appreciate them. Theseus should be recognized for his generosity and idealism in paying for the construction of the amphitheater. It is conspicuously extravagant and artful, hardly what we'd call a practical expenditure. Its construction remains a highly symbolic act and its lengthy description provides yet another symbolic action, ascribing value to the Knight's story. Moved by the plight of the lovers, Theseus identifies with them and works to help satisfy their desires, making marriage to Emelye possible. He is the only figure legally able to do so. Theseus also recognizes that Emelye has no awareness of their suffering for her. As he put it when he first learned of their conflict in the grove:

> But this is yet the beste game of alle,
> That she for whom they have this jolitee
> Can hem therfor as muche thank as me:
> She woot namore of al this hote fare,
> By God, than woot a cokkou of an hare.   (I.1806–10)

This situation creates a signal difficulty for today's readers of the Knight's Tale, provoking various incomprehensibilities about its definitions of "love." On the one hand, that Theseus finds Emelye's obliviousness to their "hote fare" to be the biggest joke of all seems like a shockingly modern observation that we might share, reducing the pretension of their private battle and their "dying" in love for her to trite anticlimax. On the other hand, we tend to find it strikingly cold regarding Emelye herself, because no sooner does Theseus point out this irony than he is arranging a legitimate tournament in which marriage to her is offered as the prize. Emelye "woot namore" of Theseus's thinking than she does of Palamon and Arcite's strife. Her knowledge of and consent to such matters is centrally important to the competitive game between the two knights but not to the solution that Theseus devises.

Matters are complicated in this part of the Knight's Tale when its three principals head to different gods' temples in order to make their devotions. Both the gods they choose and their prayers are highly revealing. Up to this point, Emelye has been a cipher, an object on which others have been able to project their desires and needs: she has not revealed anything of herself. So far she's had no self to reveal—until she reaches Diana's temple and finally speaks. We then find that Emelye desires no part in the romance plot in which she finds herself: "Chaste goddesse, wel woostou that I / Desire to been a maiden al my lif, / Ne never wol I be no love ne wif" (I.2304–06). This moment is something of a relief to modern readers, who tend to be frustrated by the formulas of courtly love and their tendency to provoke a kind of disbelief in the emotional states that the tale is at pains to illustrate. For instance, the response to love does not depend on "knowing" the object of desire or on attaining any kind of reciprocity. Moreover, this genre's portrayal of women is also a problem. There is nothing like equality between the sexes—far from it. Romance operates by other rules: women generally stand aloof until they are won over (and sometimes, as here, just won) by knightly means, including strength, gentility, and a general sense of "worthinesse." Palamon and Arcite each manifest a certain aspect of knighthood at the expense of

another so as to allow the tale to ask, essentially, whether is it more important to be a lover or a hero. But that question ignores the desires of the
woman, here articulated pointedly in opposition to the romance assumptions upon which the story is founded. Emelye's desire for perpetual virginity in this romance context is cast as a childish and immature wish.
Like the rule of Amazons Theseus had to correct, hers is an unnatural
and unproductive state in need of remediation—just the kind Theseus's
tournament is designed to provide. In this complex way Emily sub-
verts, even as she is constrained by, the courtly conventions that the tale
examines.

Palamon and Arcite are further differentiated in the story by their
visits to the amphitheater's temples and by the gods to which they devote
themselves.[6] It is important to note that each temple represents the power
of the god to which it corresponds, and that in each case those powers are
formidable. Covered with depictions of and allusions to classical myth,
the temples portray human suffering as a mark of the gods' power. None
seems to offer a devotee much comfort. Venus's temple portrays the suffering of love in images that we are not quite sure of but that we recognize: "The broken sleepes and the sikes colde, / The sacred teres and the
waymentinge, / The firy strokes of the desiringe" (I.1920–22). So too
appear images of

> Plesance and Hope, Desir, Foolhardinesse,
> Beautee and Youthe, Bawderye, Richesse,
> Charmes and Force, Lesinges, Flaterye,
> Dispence, Bisinesse, and Jalousye,
> That wered of yelowe goldes a gerland,
> And a cokkou sitting on hir hand[.]   (I.1925–30)

---

[6] Each god is associated with a planet, which (according to astrological lore) has the
most power during the hour when it is in ascendance. Therefore the three visit each temple
at the time when its god (planet) can have the greatest effect.

The description of Jealousy (traditionally associated with the color yellow rather than green) surrounded by the iconography of cuckoldry suggests that these abstractions are painted as personifications, as in one of Chaucer's important French precursors, the allegorical *Roman de la rose* and its walled garden of idleness. While they may be figured as attractive bodies, their effects on others are not so very attractive. The stories of Hercules, Medea, Turnus, and Croesus that the Knight mentions celebrate not so much the joy of love as its destructive power: "Lo, alle this folk so caught were in hir las / Til they for wo ful ofte saide allas" (I.1951–52). Venus's power is measured by the grief of the people she touches. Making one's offering would be no less terrifying in this temple than in the others.

"Terrifying" is a good word for the description of Mars's temple. In a romance that exalts heroic behavior, we might expect to see a representation of the nobility of war and righteous battle. Instead, the temple depicts Mars's power in gruesome images of destruction:

> The cruel Ire, reed as any gleede,
> The pike-purs, and eek the pale Drede,
> The smilere with the knif under the cloke,
> The shipne brenning with the blake smoke,
> The treson of the mordring in the bed,
> The open werre, with woundes al bibled,
> Contek with bloody knif and sharp manace[.]   (I.1997–2003)

Cruel anger and burning ships remind us of Homeric epic, but little is heroic in pickpockets and deceptively smiling murderers. Even more strikingly than in the temple of Venus, the distinctly homely images of cruelty and destruction depicted in the temple of Mars seem far from the glories of the battlefield:

> The sowe freten the child right in the cradel;
> The cook yscald for al his longe ladel.

> Nought was forgeten by the infortune of Marte
> The cartere overriden with his carte—
> Under the wheel ful lowe he lay adoun[.]   (I.2019–23)

Not only are those touched by Mars unlucky (note what Chaucer calls "the infortune of Marte"), but there is something distinctly ironic in their misfortunes: they come because of the very precautions being taken.

Diana's temple, too, is not immune from violent contradictions in powerful representations. Emelye may seek her protection as the virgin goddess of the hunt, but Diana is a goddess also associated with the changeable moon, whose different aspects (as Hecate and Proserpina) yoke virginity to childbirth and death through the same changeability to which women are uniquely subject. The stories painted on Diana's temple show her angry transformations of those who were most devoted to her: Callisto into the constellation Ursa Major, Daphne into a laurel tree, Acteon into a deer. Most arrestingly, Emelye sees the statue of Diana staring down into Pluto's underworld at "a womman travailling . . . hire biforn" (I.2083), who is praying to "Lucina" (Diana as goddess of childbirth; I.2085) to help deliver her baby. What might Emelye learn from a careful reading of these various images?

The effect of all three temples is the same despite the seemingly wide variation in their imagery: the gods are ambivalent, with powers that are far more extensive and multidimensional than any of the lovers seems to realize. They can grant humans' prayers, but who knows what else they may do in the process? Palamon prays to Venus in the most self-abnegating, indeed unheroic, of terms:

> I keepe noght of armes for to yelpe,
> Ne I ne axe noght tomorwe to have victorye,
> Ne renoun in this cas, ne vaine glorye
> Of pris of armes blowen up and doun;
> But I wolde have fully possessioun
> Of Emelye, and die in thy servise.   (I.2238–43)

By contrast, and characteristically, Arcite's appeal to Mars is more direct: "Yif me the victorye—I axe thee namore" (I.2420). Both are given signs that their prayers have been favorably received. Between the two men's requests, Emelye makes a more benign prayer to "sende love and pees bitwixe hem two, / And fro me turn away hir hertes so" (I.2317–18). But while Emelye can imagine a peaceful solution by which their hot love for her is "queint or turned in another place" (I.2321), she also acknowledges that her desire to remain a virgin might not be attainable:

> And if so be thou wolt noght do me grace,
> Or if my destinee be shape so
> That I shal needes have oon of hem two,
> As sende me him that most desireth me.   (I.2322–25)

Emelye is certainly the most disappointed (and, for some, disappointing) of these three figures, but she is also the one with the most complex understanding of the subjected human condition in this story. Palamon and Arcite are continually given speeches whose complete significance they do not know, whereas Emelye fully understands the limitations under which she lives. She is the first of a host of female figures in *The Canterbury Tales* (and throughout all of Chaucer's works, really) who bear the burden of human knowledge and its limitations.

Part 4

Just before the battle, Theseus decides to blunt the weapons so that no one will be killed. It's an extremely humane and noble gesture to tame the violence that the tournament legitimates. In the melee, Palamon is captured in battle and thus loses the contest. During Arcite's victory lap around the amphitheater, a fury sent by Saturn startles his horse, which falls on him and mortally injures him. On his deathbed, Arcite recommends Palamon to Emelye as a worthy servant in love. Following a grandiose funeral and a year of mourning, Theseus suggests the marriage of Palamon and Emelye as a way to find consolation. The squabbling gods are thus able to satisfy each of the seemingly contradictory prayers offered to them.

Theseus's powers are both grossly diminished and highly aggrandized in this final episode of the story, which is the tale's longest part. Despite his careful reorganization of the tournament rules "to shapen that they shal noght die" (I.2541), things go awry. Theseus's care to prohibit the most lethal weapons, "No manere shot, ne polax, ne short knif, . . . Ne short-swerd" (I.2544–46), fails to protect the participants in the way he intends. The tournament produces its victor and then brings him down almost immediately. Arcite gets just what he asked for—"victorye—I axe thee namore"—almost to the point of ironic literalness. Palamon ends the story, eventually, in "possessioun / Of Emelye," which is just what he requested. And because Emelye receives both men, she is certain to have received the one who desires her more. All prayers have been answered, but has anything been decided?

As in the other parts of the story, the plot absorbs little of our attention. The general fighting is described in a mere 20 lines (I.2601–20) before we reach the crucial moment, the "ende ther is of every deede" (I.2636). Palamon is captured, and in short order Arcite is declared winner and mortally wounded. All that happens in the first 200 lines, leaving us quite some way from the tale's end. Much of the story's close is about making order out of this chaos, which has turned the variously elegant, generous, and politically advantageous efforts of Theseus into a philosophical mess. Saturn's solution to the squabbling of Venus and Mars cannot be seen at the level of the human actors, nor does it seem to be rational: it is simply expedient. It solves the logical contradiction between the promises of two gods, but it does little to address the key questions at hand: Who loved Emelye best? Who deserved to win? Which aspect of knighthood was more important? This final section of the tale instead takes on higher questions, as the meaning of life is contemplated from the

vantage point of Arcite's untimely death. Like many of his citizens, Theseus cannot find solace after this event:

> No man mighte gladen Theseus
> Saving his olde fader Egeus,
> That knew this worldes transmutacioun,
> As he hadde seen it chaungen, bothe up and doun,
> Joye after wo, and wo after gladnesse,
> And shewed hem ensamples and liknesse:
> "Right as ther died never man," quod he,
> "That he ne lived in erthe in som degree,
> Right so ther lived never man," he saide,
> "In al this world that som time he ne deide.
> This world nis but a thurghfare ful of wo,
> And we been pilgrimes passing to and fro:
> Deeth is an ende of every worldly sore."   (I.2837–49)

This rumination on life's changeability—what the Knight calls "this
worldes transmutacioun"—participates in the tale's larger philosophical
meditations on what seems an inscrutable universe. Such questions were
asked early in part 1, when the two knights found themselves facing
changes in the fortune that they thought they wanted. Both men interro-
gate their circumstances by pointing to the workings of the "cruel goddes
that governe / This world" (I.1303–04). They ask: "What is mankinde
more unto you holde / Than is the sheep that rouketh in the folde?"
(I.1307–08); "What governance is in this prescience / That giltelees tormenteth innocence?" (I.1313–14); "Allas, why plainen folk so in commune
/ On purveyance of God, or on Fortune, / That yiveth hem ful ofte in
many a gise / Wel bettre than they can hemself devise?" (I.1251–54).
These questions articulate the limited perspective and diminished agency
of individuals who—as pagans, from the perspective of the Knight's
audience—lack the faith in the benevolent Providence that their language
unknowingly invokes. But they also speak to a frustration with what

seems "a tyrannical world of fate which leaves no room for the exercise of the human will or the realization of human desires."[7] In fact, the tale questions the very nature of those desires and the ability to understand them when Arcite concludes: "We witen nat what thing we prayen here" (I.1260).

Cast as the agent of destiny from the start (I.1663–69), Theseus suggests the plan to join Palamon and Emelye in an effort to end civic mourning and turn to a celebration of Arcite's heroic life. In the most famous speech in the tale, Theseus invokes the "Firste Mevere," an Aristotelian articulation of causation—here Jupiter, the king of the gods, who set up a fair chain of love that links temporally bound created forms to eternity. Influenced by Boethius's neoplatonic *Consolation of Philosophy*, which he was translating at the time he was composing this tale, Chaucer gives Theseus a philosophical view on the vagaries of the world, as the ruler urges a kind of stoic acceptance of what cannot be altered:

> Thanne is it wisdom, as it thinketh me,
> To maken vertu of necessitee,
> And take it wel that we may nat eschue,
> And nameliche that to us alle is due[.]   (I.3041–44)

Suggesting a change in perspective—to see Arcite as heroically departed out of life's wretchedness rather than as meaninglessly killed—and a celebratory response to "make of sorwes two / O parfit joye, lasting evermo" (I.3071–72), Theseus completes the gods' plans with his own ministrations, making virtue of necessity. And this last part's elaborate description of Arcite's funeral works to that purpose. We should note that while the Knight's story ends with a wedding, its attention is devoted to the funeral

---

[7] These are the words of Jill Mann, whose excellent essay "Chance and Destiny in *Troilus and Criseyde* and the *Knight's Tale*," in *The Cambridge Companion to Chaucer*, ed. Piero Boitani and Jill Mann, 2nd ed. (Cambridge: Cambridge UP, 2003), 93–111 (quotation, 96), explains the Boethian philosophy underwriting these classical stories.

and to accounting for the "certayn yeres" (I.2967) of mourning that necessitate the political union that brings the tale's events to a close.

The recourse to the idea of a "First Mover," of course, reminds the Knight's medieval Christian audience of the heavenly Mover of all things, whose plans we cannot read openly and whose goodness is the basic assumption of faith. Chaucer keeps the discourse of the tale classical while invoking ideas that provide comforting answers to the tale's larger and complex questions—even if they are not fully available to the tale's characters. The Knight thereby wraps up his tale much as does Theseus, turning sorrow to happiness in a celebration of human ambition through aristocratic forms.

THE MILLER'S PROLOGUE
AND TALE

When the Knight finishes his noble story, the Host turns to the Monk for "somwhat to quite with the Knightes tale" (I.3119). The choice is not so random as the phrase might suggest, for the Host's unspoken agenda for the contest emerges in this turn. Given his clothes, his pastimes, and his prominent position in the General Prologue, the Monk shows signs of attachment to a social order from which he has supposedly removed himself. These details suggest that he might have once been an aristocrat before entering his religious order, and the Host—like any good innkeeper— seems fully aware of the submerged signs of rank in his appearance. In asking for something to "quite" (to requite, to repay [the kindness or gift of]) the Knight's Tale, the Host establishes tale-telling as a form of gift exchange. A story's "sentence" (meaning or moral) and "solas" (enjoy-ment) are the forms such gifts can take; and these, we will remember from the General Prologue, are the elements that will determine the contest's winner: "Tales of best sentence and most solas" (I.798). But no sooner does the Knight offer a story that may bear both gifts than the Host's plans are derailed. As if seeing where this scheme of polite requital will leave him, the Miller interrupts: "By armes and by blood and bones, / I can a noble tale for the nones, / With which I wol now quite the Knightes tale" (I.3125–27). Drunk, almost falling off his horse, the Miller defies the Host's ideas of who might be the "bettre mann" (I.3130) and turns the first fragment of the *Tales* away from the Host's emerging plan. This kind of disruptive gesture is Chaucer's signature move. Rather than construct an orderly or tight structure, he implies one, furtively, in the very act of dismantling it before it gets too far along. He will do this again and again in the poem, offering us glimpses of a set of plans that change before they can solidify.

The Miller's effort to repay the Knight similarly changes the meaning of "quite," taking polite repayment—a little more aggressively—to the level of retaliatory payback. If we look at the closely associated meanings of *quit* in the *OED*, we'll see an array of more and less aggressive connotations to this word for requital. One could say that there is always something aggressive about gifts, no matter how selflessly they seem to be given. A gift is, by definition, something given freely. But once given, it entails a kind of debt. At the same time, the order in which the Host seems to call forth the pilgrims to deliver their gifts distributes power among the group, with "some bettre man . . . tell[ing] us first another" (I.3130), in ways that the Miller here resists. The Prologue to the Miller's Tale is rife with such resistance. Not only does the Miller detect and resist the privilege the Host assumes for pilgrims of certain rank and status (like the Monk), the Reeve resists the Miller before he ever gets going with his story. As part of his boisterous intrusion "in Pilates vois" (I.3124)— that is, with the loud, ranting voice of the character of Pontius Pilate from the cycle of mystery plays in which he may have himself participated—the Miller introduces the kind of tale he plans to tell:

> I wol telle a legende and a lif
> Bothe of a carpenter and of his wif,
> How that a clerk hath set the wrightes cappe.   (I.3141–43)

The story sounds innocuous enough: a tale of trickery involving a student and a carpenter, about as different from the lofty Knight's Tale as one can get. But the Reeve reacts rather forcefully to what he calls "lewed dronken harlotrye" (I.3145). What does the Reeve know that we don't?

One of the things the Reeve perhaps knows is genre, and two are in play here. The tale's married workman ("wrighte") and a tricky student ("clerk") invoke the broad outline of a fabliau. This is a genre, quite popular in French literature, which often takes its energy from the conflict between intellectuals and townsmen. Fabliaux are comic tales centered on a sexual trick, typically played on an older husband by a young cleric or student who sleeps with the man's wife. They are located in the everyday world of medieval towns and cities (not faraway places like classical Athens) and invoke the town–gown rivalries between working-class and university men. Common features of the fabliaux are trickery, deception, and adultery, as well as a compensatory motif called "the biter bit" or "the trickster tricked," in which the tale's trickster gets ahead of himself and becomes the partial victim of his own prank. Fabliaux mock various aspects of social life, notably the acquisitive desires of workmen and the sexual desires of clerics, priests, and women.

Unlike the Knight's Tale, which he adapted from a longer Italian work, there is no single source for the Miller's Tale. Instead, Chaucer seems to have interwoven the plots from three different fabliaux-like stories into a seamless whole. He weaves the motif of the "misdirected kiss" with that of the "prophesied disaster" and the "hot rod" (i.e., branding iron) to create something greater than any of the short vindictive tales he mines.[1] But these are not the genres or kinds of story that the Miller mentions in his preface to his tale. Instead, he aligns his story with saints and their life narratives, a genre known as hagiography.

When the Miller calls his tale "a legende and a lif," he makes an obviously parodic link to a saint's life. It provokes the Reeve into protesting the Miller's prospective tale on moral grounds: "It is a sinne and eek a greet folye / To apairen any man or him defame, / And eek to bringen wives in swich fame" (I.3146–48). The Reeve's recourse to sin jars with the Miller's comic invocation of the saint's life, suggesting

---

[1] See the materials on the Miller's Tale in *Sources and Analogues of the Canterbury Tales*, ed. Robert M. Correale with Mary Hamel, vol. 2 (Cambridge: D. S. Brewer, 2005), as well as Larry D. Benson and Theodore M. Andersson, comps., *The Literary Context of Chaucer's Fabliaux* (Indianapolis: Bobbs-Merrill, 1971). These books contain examples of the fabliau episodes that Chaucer wove together into the Miller's story.

that he is overly moralizing, a killjoy impervious to the Miller's come-dy.[2] But we might also think about the kinds of popular religious genres invoked in this opening: the plays signaled by "Pilates vois" and the popular lives of the saints called to mind here. Whereas modern culture tends to separate secular and sacred completely, in the Middle Ages religion played a greater role in everyday life. It was not merely reserved for Sundays and holidays. The result, unexpectedly, is not just a more moral view of the world, as some have framed it, but a more ribald discourse of religion. We'll return to these interconnected ideas throughout this handbook.

In the short space of 78 lines of prologue, Chaucer has launched an entirely different poem than the one we thought we were reading only moments earlier. The different class conflicts in this opening complicate the stylized romantic or philosophical conflict that the Knight had portrayed in socially sophisticated ways. It is no surprise, then, that Chaucer takes this opportunity to apologize for his representation of the Miller's language:

> And therfore every gentil wight I praye,
> Deemeth nought, for Goddes love, that I saye
> Of yvel entente, but for I moot reherce
> Hir tales alle, be they bet or werse,
> Or elles falsen som of my matere.
> And therfore, whoso list it noght yhere,
> Turne over the leef, and chese another tale,
> . . . .
> Blameth noght me if that ye chese amis.   (I.3171–81)

---

[2] The Miller's response to the Reeve, "Why artou angry with my tale now? / I have a wif, pardee, as wel as thou" (I.3157–58), implies that the Reeve may be more personally insulted than morally outraged by such a story. He doesn't want to imagine that his wife could be plotting and planning against him.

Speaking less as the naïve narrator of the General Prologue than as the writer of the entire collection, he advises us to "turne over the leef, and chese another tale" if we are disturbed by the Miller's "harlotrye" (I.3184). The conversation begun here about telling tales verbatim or else "falsing" (a word that implies both fictionalizing and misrepresenting) material will continue, as will a discussion of speaking broadly versus slavish imitation—matters that make a difference both within particular stories and between them in the linking material in which the pilgrims engage with each other and the Host. These engagements form some of the most compelling parts of Chaucer's collection and have sparked much debate about their importance to the project as a whole. Scholars who were at one time intensely interested in the links between tales for geographic clues they might supply to their proper order and perhaps to the evolution of Chaucer's overall plan were fond of noting the "roadside drama" in these interstitial pieces, in which various affiliations and arguments among the pilgrims took place.[3] The narrative of the *Tales'* roadside drama has at various times received as much attention as the pilgrims' stories themselves.

The Miller's Tale rebuts the Knight's romance with a comic tale of desire and its fulfillments. This tale is more squarely located within the ordinary world and its tangible goods, far from the Knight's abstractions. We can see the shift from ideal to real in the feminine object of desire in each story, a movement from the ethereal Emelye to Alison, the carpenter's wife. Emelye is described in the Knight's Tale in the conventional terms of courtly romance (I.1035–55). The Miller presents his desirable heroine in a parallel rhetorical form, from head to toe, but at greater length and in quite different terms (I.3233–70). Everyday items—animals,

---

[3] By "roadside drama," scholars mean those dramatic interactions among the tales' pilgrims that underwrite their narrative contributions to the storytelling contest. The term, which often refers to what is read into or out of the links between the tales, is associated with the influential early criticism of George Lyman Kittredge, who saw the poem as akin to a Shakespearean "Human Comedy." See his published lectures, *Chaucer and His Poetry* (Cambridge, MA: Harvard UP, 1915).

details of dress, domestic commodities, money—replace those of courtly value. Where Emelye sings "as an angel hevenisshly" (I.1055), Alison's song "was as loud and yerne / As any swalwe sitting on a berne" (I.3257–58). Hers does not make you think of a world beyond this one but sounds loudly within it.

Too many readers new to Chaucer want to detect moral insinuation in Alison's description, even as they attempt to read the tale from the Miller's point of view, as we are being asked to do. Remember, the Miller's goal is to requite the Knight's romance with a story of "real" desire, and to do so he has to invent a heroine who generates that kind of desire. Such a figure would not be a woman of questionable repute—how would that put the Knight in his place? We need to read Alison's description carefully but not judgmentally. Like the tale itself, she is drawn in amoral rather than immoral terms.

Alison's clothes are described in detail, and they point to her rich husband's care for her welfare. She wears white trimmed with black, perhaps conveying both a sense of her innocence and the darker edge it has in this story's not-so-idealized world. But her dress more overtly shows us how little household labor she does and thus how much money she has to spend on finery. Another wife might be dressed in darker colors because they would show soiling less easily. Alison has no such worries, either because she has many outfits or because she has a servant (the Gille we hear about later). Much of her attire is decorated with silk: her belt, her collar, her headband, and her purse's tassels. She is both decorated and herself a decoration, "ful more blisful on to see / Than is the newe perejonette tree, / And softer than the wolle is of a wether" (I.3247–49). Alison engages all the senses of the observer, including the sense of touch. We are told what she feels like to the hand (softer than a ram's wool), rather than just what she looks or sounds like. Perhaps we should recognize that what we are experiencing are those aspects of her appearance that are important and meaningful *to the Miller* from his specific social and gendered location: "She was a primerole, a piggesnye, / For any lord to leggen in his bedde, / Or yet for any good yeman to wedde" (I.3268–70). This statement is typical of the Miller, who has no patience for the Knight's overrefinements and presumptions. Alison is not a cultivated rose but a wildflower, a beauty who springs up out of the dung, good enough for any aristocrat to want to bed or any good yeoman (a free man and not a serf) to marry. This is high praise precisely for the ways it cuts across class lines and installs Alison as a proper object of desire for both sets of men: for one, a mistress; for another, a wife.

The Miller's comic story therefore has far different priorities than the Knight's romance. He replaces the slow-paced, elevated narrative of courtly ideals with the quick, economical plot of appetite and clever practicality. In the Miller's story, too, two men will compete for the love of a woman, but not in the sublimating and thus largely disembodied terms of romance that the Knight used. Instead, the wily Nicholas will plot with the carpenter's wife in order to cuckold her older, doting husband. In the process, yet another lovelorn clerk, Absolon, will be tricked as well, and he will wind up inadvertently giving Nicholas his partial comeuppance. Valuing healthy, animal appetite over empty romantic gestures, the Miller's story locates its energy in the "natural" attraction of Nicholas and Alison, its two young lovers (despite—or, more accurately, because of—her marriage to the older John). The fabliau's allegiances are with cleverness and natural appetite, not with morals. By convention its plots are adulterous, as fabliau husbands tend to be more concerned with their business than their wives, and they are made to pay for their priorities.

These comments might suggest two things: (1) the Miller's Tale bears little relation to the Knight's since its priorities are so different, and (2) being amoral, the Miller's story has little to do with religion. Both claims are untrue. Consider first the relation of the Miller's Tale to the Knight's. With a kind of symmetry that could not be achieved by an impromptu tale told on horseback just after the Knight's was heard, the Miller offers a stunning structural repetition of this previous story. To wit: Both stories contain a central amorous triangle (two men of the same occupation in love with one woman) and an older, controlling male figure standing behind them. The Miller replays the Knight's story with a different set of assumptions that drives the narrative in another direction. Perhaps we were not ready for the parallel formation and the ironic swerve it will take, but the Miller's rehearsal of the Knight's opening shows us what we are in for. The Knight began:

> Whilom, as olde stories tellen us,
> Ther was a duc that highte Theseus:
> Of Atthenes he was lord and governour,
> And in his time swich a conquerour
> That gretter was ther noon under the sonne.   (I.859–63)

The Miller's imitation is unmistakable:

> Whilom ther was dwelling at Oxenford
> A riche gnof that gestes heeld to bord,
> And of his craft he was a carpenter.   (I.3187–89)

Formally echoing the Knight's opening, the Miller fills it with a bathetic content that reduces its formal tone. The term *bathos* (and the adjective *bathetic*) refers to the anticlimactic reduction gestured at here—the sudden appearance of the common in an otherwise elevated situation. Describing a figure who stands in parallel status to Theseus, the sound of "gnof" (*guh-nawf*, whose hard *g* makes for some awkward pronouncing) tells us nearly all we need to know. Glossed as "churl," this word, which apparently originated in the Scandinavian languages, is first deployed in English here by Chaucer. The *OED* tells us to "compare East Frisian *knufe* lump, *gnuffig* thick, rough, coarse, ill mannered" (s.v. "gnoff"), and these associations certainly align with the Miller's characterization of John the carpenter, unlike the slick students in his town. Though both stories introduce their wise older men first, those men hold different positions of authority in each. Theseus is the noble conqueror and just ruler of the Knight's story; John holds his wife "narwe in cage" because she is much younger and "he was old / And deemed himself been lik a cokewold" (I.3224–26). Lest we be confused about his status, the Miller openly states that since John was ignorant ("his wit was rude"; I.3227) and did not know his Cato (the practical Roman philosopher who would have taught him about the conflicts between youth and age), "He moste endure, as other folk, his care" (I.3232). He deserves what's coming to him. From the start, there is little sympathy and absolutely no admiration for John.

In the Miller's Tale, our attention quickly shifts to its real protagonist, Nicholas. This student takes a room in John's house "allone, withouten any compaignye" (I.3204), a strange detail to note until we realize that the phrase is adapted from the Knight's Tale. On his deathbed, Arcite ponders the changeability of life that leaves a man, "Now with his love, now in his colde grave, / Allone withouten any compaignye" (I.2778–79). That expression of the fundamental futility of human planning and understanding is starkly at odds with its mundane context here, as the Miller describes Nicholas's housing situation. But it is precisely this bathetic reduction of the grandiose and philosophical to the quotidian and ordinary that characterizes what the Miller does to the Knight's story more generally. He takes the wind out of it—sometimes, as here, with its own language.

We can also see this strategy in the scene of Nicholas's wooing of Alison. Deploying the traditional language of courtly love to more physical ends, the Miller transforms the quotations of the Knight's Tale that he cites into more literal urgings. As Nicholas grabs Alison "harde by the haunche-bones," she coyly pushes him away (I.3279). His declaration at this moment is, like Arcite's words, in concise and plain language: "Ywis, but if ich have my wille, / For derne love of thee, lemman, I spille" (I.3277–78). *To spill* means to die, because one spills blood or metaphorically spills one's life at the moment of death. But Nicholas is in danger of spilling another vital fluid in his excited state. The Miller even more directly quotes Arcite's line "I nam but deed" (I.1274) when Alison explains that they must be carefully secretive around her jealous husband (I.3296). In both instances, the romantic hyperbole of the Knight's discourse is rendered more literal and material in the Miller's usage, illustrating how Chaucer starts with the metaphorical and then reduces to the literal—a trajectory that we might find counterintuitive, because we generally view the literal as naturally preceding the metaphorical.

One of the most famous puns in all of *The Canterbury Tales*, contained in this very scene, may exemplify the importance of reading Chaucer in his original language rather than just in modern translation: the play on "quainte" (I.3275). This word evolved into our modern English *quaint*, which now means attractively unusual or old-fashioned; but it once had a large range of meanings from which these more quaint ones descend. Derived from a French term (*cointe*, "clever, astute, expert, experienced") and ultimately from the Latin *cognitus* (literally, "known"; in postclassical senses, "wise, clever, sensible"), here "quainte" similarly means clever, able, artful, or cunning, which are all attributes of students (*OED*, s.v. "quaint," adj.). When this term is used of things, it denotes objects that are cleverly made, artful, pleasing, or elaborate. The ingeniousness of the Miller is shown when he uses the same adjective as a substantive noun to designate a particular part of Alison's body: "And prively he caughte hire by the queinte" (I.3276). Grabbing her between the legs, Nicholas catches her by the elegant, pleasing [thing or part]. Translations of the Miller's Tale struggle to render this double use of the same word in two different ways—in what is known as a *rime riche*—as idiomatically as Chaucer does. But they resort either to something vulgar and coarse ("privately he caught her by the cunt") or to euphemism ("privately he grabbed her where he shouldn't"). Neither renders Chaucer's extraordinarily "quainte" method of speaking literally without speaking coarsely.[4]

---

[4] Students who work with the *OED* will note that the definition of the noun *quaint* has recently changed. In the dictionary's latest update, the word is more explicitly linked to the female genitals—this appearance in the Miller's Tale being of course one of its earliest citations—and to the development of *cunt*, a term of Germanic origin that seems to have preceded it. The *OED* claims that Chaucer's use of "quainte" here follows "punningly" the Germanic word or is "a euphemism for" it. But it is *how* Chaucer does so with the rime riche that is most impressive.

The Miller's Tale is a funny and irreverent story, but it becomes a comic tour de force in its intelligent replaying of the Knight's Tale. In this parodic deformation of the Knight's romance, the Miller's Tale rewrites the grand narrative of fate and fortune, played out at the planetary level of the gods, into a story of domestic trickery deploying the fiction of a second flood. The cosmic forces at play in the Knight's Tale are reduced to the "astromye" (I.3451) to which Nicholas devotes the time he should be studying theology at university. The carpenter mocks him for such useless, esoteric interests and tells him about the philosopher who fell into the "marle-pit" (I.3460) because he did not look where he was going. But John's cocksure practicality disappears when Nicholas draws on his astrological endeavors to predict an impending flood. John quickly falls under his spell.

The particularities of this plot to hoodwink the gullible husband bring us to the topic of religion in the Miller's Tale, a serious subject we don't expect to find in an amoral fabliau. The trappings of medieval Christianity are all over the Miller's story; they pervade the everyday world of the Miller's Oxford. Front and center is the flood story used to terrify Alison's superstitious husband. Nicholas even cites the biblical narrative of the Flood and the story of Noah's ark in describing the imminent danger. By listening to Nicholas, the carpenter will be able to prepare for the catastrophe. John must make three "kimelins" or wooden tubs (I.3548) to hang in the rafters of the barn. John, Nicholas, and Alison will each await the flood in an individual tub (so that there will be no temptation to "sin" between the spouses as they try to save themselves from God's punishment). When the flood waters come, they will cut themselves down and float away in their individual arks. Nicholas's scheme depends on John's being both familiar with the Noah story in general and ignorant of its specific details.

The Noah story that John knows is not the biblical narrative from Genesis (or its exposition in sermons) but its more comic representations from the cycle plays. In the plays, poor Noah is a henpecked husband with a recalcitrant wife, who does not fully believe in his foreknowledge of the coming flood. The difficulties of getting his wife aboard the ark are played for comic effect. Nicholas capitalizes on this aspect of the story, telling John that he'll need to be convincing to get Alison to join in their plan to save themselves. He sets John, a carpenter like Noah in the cycle plays, to work building their mini-arks so that he can put into action his other plan—to have Alison "sleepen in his arm al night" (I.3406). On the evening of the supposed flood, they climb into their tubs, wait for John to fall asleep, and then climb down to spend the night in each other's arms.

Nicholas's parodic use of the Noah story preys on John's ignorance. The carpenter vaunts his unlearned state over the useless intellectualism of students like Nicholas who have their head in books all time: "blessed be alway a lewed man / That noght but only his bileve can" (I.3455–56). John here cites the Beatitudes from the Gospel of Matthew in order to claim an "innocence" that rests simply on the power of faith, his "bileve" (literally, "belief, creed"). Such belief does not need complex rationalization or explanation or theory. But John's unlearned innocence is shown to be mere ignorance, a kind of willful blindness that redounds on him. He likewise does not understand much of his faith. When he finds Nicholas gaping upright in bed, supposedly in a stupor caused by his alleged vision of the flood, John blesses the house against spirits and demons, reciting "the White Pater Noster" (I.3485). This is not the behavior of the faithful but the antics of the superstitious. And John's ignorance of the flood story is even more damaging. At the end of the Flood narrative in Genesis, God sends the rainbow as a promise never to destroy the earth with water again. John appears unaware of this crucial detail, which arguably explains the story's purpose: the reestablishment of the covenant between God and man.

Chaucer's joke in the Miller's Tale depends on a presentation of religious matters in popular cultural forms: the cycle play of the Flood, the play of the Nativity (in which Absolon has clearly played Herod and the Miller has perhaps played Pilate), the play of the Annunciation in which the angel Gabriel "seduces" the virgin with the word of God and impregnates her, as celebrated in Nicholas's song *Angelus ad Virginem* (I.3216). But religion is located in the quotidian happenings of the Miller's Tale not merely via the civic drama and the way it permeates the thought and casual metaphors of the everyday world. The interpenetration is also seen in behaviors such as Absolon's "cencing" of the ladies of the parish (I.3341), an activity during which he clearly (and inappropriately) checks them out. Again, the conflation of what we would separate as secular and sacred is fundamental to this medieval world as well as to its parodic representation in the Miller's Tale, where religious "knowledge" becomes the mechanism of the prank. As someone who had seen the plays, and as a carpenter who might have worked on the Flood play directly (the story of Noah was typically staged by the guild of shipwrights, who were carpenters), John ought to know the story better than he does.[5] Instead, he gets caught up in Nicholas's plot, both its promises and its threats, and these turn out to be his undoing. He reveals himself as far more ignorant than innocent, and his instincts for self-preservation, which emerge over and against his supposed faith, do him in.

This story would be funny enough, but Chaucer also develops an underplot that coalesces into an elaborate finale. As in the Knight's romance, here there are two rival lovers for a single woman. But outside of courtly romances, women tend to know whom they desire. For the setup, we might again turn to the opening descriptions. Absolon, who is given the name of an Old Testament figure famed for his beauty,[6] is described last among the characters. Though he is interested in the women of his parish, Absolon is a foppish figure, feminized by his clothes, curled hair, and squeamishness about farting (a metonymy for other bodily functions) and "daungerous" about speech more generally (I.3338).[7] He is the opposite

---

[5] The mystery plays were dramatic representations of Bible stories performed and financed by members of the craft guilds for holidays such as the Feast of Corpus Christi.

[6] See 2 Samuel 14:25.

[7] Here Chaucer's syntax can be confusing. In modern English, we'd think that "daungerous" was an adjective modifying "speeche" and that the two words together stood parallel to farting—i.e., "he was squeamish about farting and dangerous speech." But that

of quick-witted Nicholas, whose ability to play with words and manipulate the language of courtly love to his own erotic ends is his strength. Like Palamon and Arcite, then, Absolon and Nicholas are distinguished by their ways with words.

But whereas Palamon and Arcite are always so closely balanced in the Knight's story that we cannot decide between them, the difference between "hende Nicholas" (I.3199) and jolly Absolon is sharper. Chaucer's repeated use of "hende" as an epithet for Nicholas is telling. Meaning both "attractive" and "nearby," this word descends from the root for *hand*; dexterity and cleverness are implied in being both good with one's hands and "at hand" to make things happen. All of these senses are relevant to Nicholas, who manipulates the language of courtly love as his hands roam over Alison's body. Absolon takes the behavior of courtly love more seriously and is mocked for doing so. His lovesick behavior and wooing strategies (singing under Alison's window, primping his attire, proffering gifts, hamming it up onstage) are entirely out of place in the social class depicted by this comic literary genre. Like the Miller, Nicholas understands the gestures of courtly love to be a cover for the erotic energies below the surface. Absolon does not seem to know anything beyond kissing, and he is not even very proficient at that.

At the tale's climax, John snores away in his tub awaiting the flood while Alison and Nicholas frolic in bed. Along comes Absolon, who wants to confess his love for Alison at her window while he thinks her husband is out of town. After an open rebuke, he begs a kiss, "For Jesus love and

---

is not what this line means. The editor has inserted a comma after "farting" to help clarify the sentence's structure: its main verb is "was," and "squaimous" and "daungerous" are parallel. Thus a better translation reads "he was somewhat squeamish about farting and [was also] fastidious about speech." Because Absolon tries to woo Alison by the traditional means of singing under her window only moments later, it's hard to see how he'd be squeamish about "speeche daungerous," which we could also translate as "flirtatious speech": he seems to flirt with her just fine. But if we double the main verb in the sentence and see "was" as governing both parts, the result is a squeamishness about the body and a fastidiousness or extreme carefulness about his speech that makes some sense in light of future events.

for the love of me" (I.3717). It's a line without much meaning, intended simply to move the plot along, but it suggests the complete ineptitude of Absolon in this situation. He is all form and no content, enjoying the mannerisms of loving far more than the act of love itself. Were he more in tune with the physical energies of his genre, he'd have long ago slunk away to develop a better strategy to reach his goals. But we are not sure that Absolon has goals or even knows what the goals of such lovemaking really are. He would much rather play an extravagant part in the dramatic spectacle of love, with its display of unrequited love-longing, than do what Nicholas does: direct the fiction to his own physically satisfying ends. This difference is played out at length in the tale's closing episode and is perhaps hinted at in Absolon's turn "play[ing] Herodes upon a scaffold hye" (I.3384) as part of his wooing strategies. He is all performance.

In the face of Absolon's irritating request, Alison sticks her buttocks out the window, giving him a cheek to kiss. He gets more than he bargains for:

> Abak he sterte, and thoughte it was amis,
> For wel he wiste a womman hath no berd.
> He felte a thing al rough and longe yherd,
> And saide, "Fy, allas, what have I do?"   (I.3736–39)

Absolon has been chasing Alison's tail for the entire tale; yet when he gets a mouthful of what he's ostensibly been after, he is disgusted. His response reveals his inappropriateness for the lover's role in the fabliau, which Alison instinctively knew all along. With his hot love now "cold and al yqueint" (I.3754), Absolon seeks out the blacksmith for a weapon of hot revenge. He returns to the window for another kiss with a blade right out of the smith's fire, ready to vent his ire on Alison's body. Instead he gets Nicholas, who has gone to the window to "amenden al the jape" (I.3799). By adding something to Alison's prank, Nicholas hopes to make the joke even better—and he does, but he pays for it. When he sticks his buttocks out the window for a second kiss,

> This Nicholas anon leet fle a fart
> As greet as it hadde been a thonder-dent
> That with the strook [Absolon] was almost yblent,
> And he was redy with his iren hoot,
> And Nicholas amidde the ers he smoot.   (I.3806–10)

Burned across the buttocks "an hande-brede aboute" (I.3811; note the return to "hande" with regard to this "hende" figure), Nicholas cries out for water. His shouts awaken John, who thinks that the flood has come and cuts himself down from the barn roof. In all the fracas, the neighbors come running to find that John has fallen out of the rafters and broken his arm. Nicholas and Alison blame the situation on his inordinate fear of Noah's flood and his kooky plan to escape, whereby they "turned al his harm unto a jape, . . . no man his reson herde" (I.3842–44).

By this point in the story we have almost forgotten John, because the antics of Nicholas, Alison, and Absolon are so engrossing, the comedy of their actions augmented by the fine wordplay of the exposition. But in the closing gestures of the tale, all is measured: John's foolishness is openly acknowledged by the entire town, as is Absolon's fastidiousness and Nicholas's overweening confidence. Each is punished in precisely the right way, with a kind of poetic justice that replays the cosmic justice dealt out in the Knight's Tale—only in the fabliau register. No need for any philosophical "First Mover" speech to make meaning out of the events here. The Miller wraps everything up in a few lines:

> Thus swived was the carpenteres wif
> For al his keeping and his jalousye,
> And Absolon hath kist hir nether eye,
> And Nicholas is scalded in the toute:
> This tale is doon, and God save al the route!   (I.3850–54)

This thrifty ending deals out its justice simply; as in the Knight's Tale, the desire of each of the male figures is satisfied. (Alison goes unpunished, or perhaps has already been punished by being married to John in the first place.) Whereas the logic of the gods rested on the literal meaning of the prayers they received, here each gets what he asks for in a more figurative sense. The Miller's Tale is excellent comedy. It is also a far more brilliant counterpoint to the Knight's Tale than the ostensibly drunken Miller could possibly understand.

THE REEVE'S PROLOGUE
AND TALE

Most Canterbury pilgrims, like most modern readers, laugh broadly at the Miller's story. Only Oswald the Reeve fails to enjoy it, "Bycause he was of carpenteres craft" (I.3861). Identifying with John, the Miller's humiliated husband, the Reeve takes the tale as an insult directed personally at him. He uses his age as an excuse for his anger and frustrated condition, promising to quite the Miller himself (rather than his tale) in due course. The polite repayment structure of this opening fragment has taken a sharply aggressive turn.

In his retaliation, the Reeve sets out to best the Miller by humiliating him at every turn "with blering of a proud milleres eye" (I.3865). In doing so, he tells a similar story—yet another fabliau, going the Miller's trickery one better at each and every opportunity. His story replays the Miller's (and thus, in a distant way, the Knight's) in a heightened key of violence and revenge. Once again, we have a story of two clerks and a townsman who are at odds from the start. The local setting is Trumpington near Cambridge, the other great English university town. We are introduced to the older man, a miller named Simekin, whose description echoes that of the Miller in the General Prologue with his flat "camuse" (I.3934) nose and an array of handy blades. More nasty than comic, the Reeve's story begins by describing this thieving miller and his haughty wife, who is the illegitimate daughter of the town parson. They both take pride in her convent upbringing and the wealth that the parson hoards to bestow on their daughter, Malin, a girl of twenty whom they plan to marry into the aristocracy to raise the family's social status. To round out this irregular family, a baby of six months lies in his cradle, a "propre page" (I.3972). He will later provide the means of the tale's trick. The portraits of these figures are darkly satiric and openly condemnatory. We are told of Simekin's wife that

> Ther dorste no wight clepen hire but "Dame."
> Was noon so hardy that wente by the waye
> That with hire dorste rage or ones playe,
> But if he wolde be slain of Simekin,
> With panade, or with knif or boidekin,
> For jalous folk been perilous evermo—
> Algate they wolde hir wives wenden so.   (I.3956–62)

This opening offers little that is attractive or playful. At the beginning of the Miller's Tale, John the carpenter goes off to nearby Osney, and Nicholas "fil with this yonge wif to rage and playe" (I.3273). But there is no "rage and playe" with Simekin's wife, who holds herself superior to everyone around her. Her husband stands ready to ward off such attention with his array of weapons, which (as the Reeve reveals) is a show mostly to intimidate *her*. The use of "dorste" (dared) twice in this passage is telling. The Reeve's Tale is full of such daring: the word appears six times in all. But such daring is neither heroic nor clever; it is simply challenging. Everyone in the Reeve's story is spoiling for a fight. Simekin fancies himself much smarter and more cunning than those around him, and certainly would tout his superiority to the jealous husband of the Miller's story, who is duped, at least in part, because of his doting love for young Alison. The Reeve's miller would fall into no such "snare" (I.3231). Instead, he has married strategically "to saven his estaat of yemanrye" (I.3949), shoring up his position as a free man (neither villein nor serf).[1] Given Simekin's excessive concern

---

[1] "Saven" means, literally, "to preserve or maintain" (*OED*, s.v. "save" v. I.5.a.), but remember this is a tale full of threats. Simekin's precautions are possibly necessary and the Reeve's description thus a bit ironic.

for this marital blood alliance and what it means for his status (I.3945), it is more than ironic that he focuses only on her dowry and convent education. He seems unaware of any moral stain belonging to the parson's illegitimate daughter. The Reeve thereby depicts Simekin's limitations in more widely damning terms than the Miller presents John's. He aligns them with the parson's deeply flawed understanding of his moral function, which takes too literally the aphorism "For holy chirches good moot been dispended / On holy chirches blood that is descended" (I.3983–84; literally: "For holy church's good [goods; goodness] should be spent / upon those descended from holy church's blood"). Properly understood, it speaks not to one's literal genealogy but to spiritual inheritance: those "descended" from the holy church are its members in Christ's blood. But this parson uses the offerings (or goods) collected by the church to enrich his own blood descendants, which, being a celibate priest, he should not have.

Going back to our counting strategy, we might note how much shorter the Reeve's Tale is than the Miller's, which is itself considerably shorter than the Knight's. Exclusive of their prologues, the Miller's Tale, at 668 lines, is more than 50 percent longer than the Reeve's mere 404. Both stories are "thrifty"—economic narratives that waste little time and gesture and are themselves concerned with waste and profit, making us attend to the details on which they lavish their limited attention. But the Reeve's is stingy by comparison, making the descriptions that it does offer even more surprising. We expect his tale to depict its principal characters (miller, wife, clerks), but we also hear about others: their daughter, the parson her grandfather, even the college warden who must be coaxed to let the students go to the mill on the manciple's behalf. Yet instead of enriching the world of the story, these descriptions tend to impoverish it by emptying the human relations they depict of any substance or meaning. There is no relation here that is not based on selfish gain or unwarranted conflict. The clerks are antagonistic toward their college's manciple, and for no particular reason tell the miller that they "hope he wil be deed" (I.4029); "hope" here might be literally rendered as "expect," but their use of the word points to a kind of wish for his death, as it would seem to give them something to do. They are also antagonistic toward each other; their assault on the women in the story is performed in competition, so that "whan this jape is tald another day" one won't "be halden a daf, a cokenay" (I.4207–08). No healthy appetite stirs these young men into action: in this story, desire is pure aggression.

In place of a frisky young wife, this fabliau presents Simekin's haughty "dame" and a sexually frustrated daughter, whom the Reeve begrudgingly describes as half attractive. She has an odd mix of qualities: gray eyes and "brestes rounde and hye" (I.3974–75) are attributes typical of romance heroines, but others are less appealing. Camuse-nosed like her father, she has the broad hips of a broodmare—"But right fair was hir heer, I wol nat lie" (I.3976), the Reeve admits. Where the Miller finds the humor in each of his characters, the Reeve hates his. They are not human creatures with foibles and limitations; they are corruptions through and through. This focus is central to the Reeve's story: the tale is designed to incriminate its miller and thereby condemn *the* Miller. Every one of its details is chosen to reflect poorly on the miller in his tale, no matter what that does to the story or to the other figures in it. The Reeve's agenda ignores the story-telling game; he is stalking different prey than the Host's free dinner back in Southwark.

Simekin's reputation for thievery precedes him, and the clerks in the Reeve's Tale arrive at his mill in a preemptively antagonistic mood. Their patterns of speech—especially the pronunciation of certain vowels—introduce them as a pair of bumpkins from way up in the north who attend Soler Hall. By using some unusual spellings, Chaucer creates the first representation of regional speech in English writing. Because the manciple of their college is sick, Simekin has been stealing outrageously; this situation forces the manciple to allow the clerks to go to the mill to supervise the grinding of the college's wheat. It is not something he wants them to do, but he has little choice. These two think they can prevent Simekin's thievery, but Simekin sees their intent from a mile away and is ready for them.

> This millere smiled of hir nicetee,
> And thoughte, "Al this nis doon but for a wile.
> They weene that no man may hem bigile,
> But by my thrift, yet shal I blere hir eye
> For al the sleighte in hir philosophye.
> The more quainte crekes that they make,
> The more wol I stele whan I take:
> In stede of flour yet wol I yive hem bren.
> The gretteste clerkes been noght the wisest men,
> As whilom to the wolf thus spak the mare.
> Of al hir art ne counte I noght a tare."   (I.4046–56)

Simekin holds the clerks' learning, what he calls their "philosophye," in little regard, much as John held himself above Nicholas's studies on "astromye" (I.3451). Undergirding John's disdain for such study is a genuine concern that Nicholas has fallen ill or "in som woodnesse" (I.3452), but Simekin is simply competitive. He measures his "sleighte" against the "sleighte in hir philosophye" and even boasts about stealing more from them the harder they try to prevent him. We might note the reappearance here of "quainte," meaning "clever," but in no such clever way as it was used in the Miller's story. The Reeve's story instead generates multiple terms for trickery itself ("wile," "blere hir eye," "crekes," "stele"). The name of his profession is also a word for theft (*OED* s.v. reave, v.1).

The two clerks feign interest in the workings of the mill and stand watching the grain go into the hopper and come out the other end as flour. While they are occupied in this way, the Miller lets loose their horse, which they must then chase down in the fens (marshes) where it is running after the wild mares. During that time, the miller's wife and daughter bake half the flour into a cake (so that the clerks cannot reclaim it). When they return exhausted, they must ask the miller for "herberwe"— or to buy his hospitality for the night (I.4118–19). Not only has the miller been able to steal their grain, he now stands to make a profit on the meat and drink he procures for them (and shares) as they spend the night at his house.

In his anger at the Miller, whom he thinks has insulted him with a tale of an ignorant, beguiled carpenter, the Reeve tells a version of the Miller's story in which a miller proves too clever for his own good. The comedy of the fabliau is compromised as revenge replaces sexual desire as the tale's primary motive. In the Miller's fabliau, the clerks concoct schemes by which they seek to procure the carpenter's wife; but in the Reeve's fabliau, his clerks scheme to have sex with the miller's women in compensation for the goods they have otherwise lost because their flour was taken and used up. The erotic ends of the Miller's story have become the violent means of the Reeve's, producing a much more disturbing kind of comedy that makes hardly anyone laugh, besides the completely wasted Cook. The intelligent trick on the Miller's carpenter involving the Flood is replaced with a cold law of "esement" (I.4179) by which Alain calculates what he has coming to him:

> Som esement has lawe shapen us:
> For John, ther is a lawe that says thus,
> That gif a man in a point be agreved,
> That in another he sal be releved.
> Oure corn is stoln soothly, it is no nay,
> And we han had an ille fit today,
> And sin I sal have nan amendement
> Again my los, I wil have esement.   (I.4179–86)

Of course, the language of the Reeve's characters, being Chaucer's, is far more intelligent than they know. The idea of *easement* is here used in subtle and subtly calculating ways. One meaning of "esement" is relief, in the sense of relief from hardship or a complaint (*OED*, s.v. "easement" 3.a., "Redress of a grievance; compensation, recompense"). Alain is looking for some redress according to a law of substitution that will enable him to exact relief ("be releved") for his grievance ("be agreved"). A kind of tit-for-tat logic is at work here to arrive at "the flour of ille ending" (I.4174) for Simekin, who has stolen their flour. Because Alain is explicitly planning to jump into bed with the miller's daughter as recompense, the "esement" he here claims for himself is also a literal and bodily kind of relief—the comfort of sexual relief or release.[2] In being willing to take something in exchange for the flour that he has lost, he turns the terms of compensation into a pun as he finds his equivalence in Malin's "flower," her virginity. Alain speaks at the level of metaphor (flower for flour, sexual easement for legal redress), but his actions operate in one sense at the level of the (punning) literal.[3]

It is important to remember that every detail of the Reeve's story is focused on humiliating the miller figure: not only through what the Reeve says about this miller directly, which is pretty bad, but also through the actions of others in the story. For instance, while Simekin's combative dishonesty speaks poorly of him, the fact that he's tricked in return by two rather unintelligent students and then punished by his own wife and daughter is even more damning. The clerks are able to revenge themselves on him by taking advantage of his greed as well as his brash self-confidence. In response to their request for "herberwe," for example,

> The millere saide again, "If ther be eny,
> Swich as it is yet shal ye have youre part;
> Myn hous is strait, but ye han lerned art:
> Ye can by argumentes make a place
> A mile brood of twenty feet of space.
> Lat see now if this place may suffise,
> Or make it rowm with speeche as is youre gise."   (I.4120–26)

---

[2] The *OED* specifies this action as "relieving the body by urinating or defecating" (s.v. "easement," 3.b), but "ese" is used in the Wife of Bath's prologue repeatedly to mean "pleasure" or "ease" in just such a sexual sense.

[3] These are not puns marked by the *OED*. In fact, the *OED* cites this line from the Reeve's Tale only to support meaning 3.a, "recompense"; it does not acknowledge the other senses Chaucer teases out of the word when it is repeated in this passage.

With false modesty he admits his house is small for guests, but their philosophical methods are sure to enlarge it by "art." Mocking them even at their most vulnerable, he fails to hear what they have said:

> "[M]en sal taa of two thinges,
> Swilk as he findes, or taa swilk as he bringes;
> But specially I praye thee, hoste deere;
> Get us som mete and drinke and make us cheere,
> And we wol payen trewely atte fulle:
> With empty hand men may none hawkes tulle.
> Lo, here oure silver, redy for to spende."   (I.4129–35)

The Reeve's Tale is full of aphorisms and soothsaws, little sayings of commonsense wisdom that license certain behaviors and opinions. They are not always easy to understand. Here John seeks to put Simekin at ease, by proclaiming their need: "Men must take one of two things: such as he finds or such as he brings." It seems like an admission of weakness, something like "Beggars can't be choosers." He tries to make the situation attractive to Simekin by pronouncing another aphorism—"Men can lure no hawks with an empty hand"—and showing some silver coins to his would-be host. This moment seems pivotal. Simekin hosts the students in his small one-bedroom house with a dinner of roasted goose and ale that he himself shares. He seems to have them completely at his advantage and under his watchful eye—until the snoring begins and Alain hatches his plan for recompense.[4] Simekin hardly realizes that he has become the lured bird, the one who will be paid back "atte fulle" in ways he cannot yet imagine.

Whereas the Miller brought the Knight's grand conflicts waged on the fields of ancient Greece into a single household, the Reeve compresses

---

[4] The snoring also closely links the Reeve's to the Miller's Tale in ways fashioned by Chaucer, not the Reeve. Both of the tales' schemes begin to be put into action as the husband snores loudly, John in his kimelin and Simekin and his wife in their bed.

matters even further into a single room. There the clerks gain access to Simekin's family and particularly his daughter, a treasure he has been hoarding for some time. Thinking to repair his losses, Alain creeps into Malin's bed: "And shortly for to sayn, they were at oon" (I.4197). Worried that he'll look bad back at college if he does not get something for his "harm" (I.4203), John moves the cradle so that the miller's wife (who had gotten up "to pisse," I.4215) mistakes the configuration of the room in the dark and climbs into his bed: "And on this goode wif he laith on soore. / So merye a fit ne hadde she nat ful yoore: / He priketh harde and deepe as he were mad" (I.4229–31). She is not alone in being confused by this "cradle trick": when Alain tries to return to the clerks' bed, he finds the cradle, and so he moves over to Simekin's bed, bragging about his night "swiv[ing]" Malin (I.4266). Simekin awakens the whole house in a violent outburst that only leaves him beaten and bruised. In the dark, his wife mistakes his nightcap for the clerk's tonsure, and she knocks him out with her distaff. The clerks grab their flour, cake, and horse and return to college.

The Reeve ends his story just as the Miller did, by tallying up its actions:

> Thus is this proude millere wel ybete,
> And hath ylost the grinding of the whete,
> And payed for the soper everydel
> Of Alain and of John that bette him wel.
> His wife is swived and his doughter als.
> Lo, which it is a millere to be fals!   (I.4313–18)

But unlike the summation at the end of the Miller's Tale (I.3850–53), where everyone gets a kind of poetic justice—just what they have been "asking for" all along without realizing it—the Reeve's summary is extraordinarily focused on the miller himself. He is beaten and has lost his profit (on both the milling of the wheat and the supper he arranged). And he has had his wife *and* his daughter "swived," a term usually glossed (rather politely) as "copulated with" but should be more idiomatically translated as "screwed," to convey both its sexual sense and the injury involved. *Swiving* is not a neutral term for sexual intercourse (itself a rather sterile gloss for this act) but rather connotes illicit behavior of some kind. Husbands don't swive their own wives but find their wives swived by other men, like Nicholas, and the injury for such an act is suffered by the husband. Simekin has had his wife and his daughter swived, and they have both enjoyed it. The daughter interprets the clerk's sexual attention as love, weeping at his departure from her in the morning in a parody of the aubade (dawn song) associated with parting lovers and found in romances like Chaucer's own *Troilus and Criseyde*. Malin has been raped and doesn't know it, perhaps because at 20 she's been hoping for a "lemman" (I.4240) to release her from her family's designs. When the Reeve tallies the tale's events, Malin does not count except as a marker of injury that can be done to her father's social aspirations in an ending that is neither poetic nor just.

In focusing the punishments of fabliau on his miller, the Reeve has forgotten the broader social comedy of his story and the storytelling contest more generally. We can calculate his neglect in some of its surprising detail. His tale features a number of pilgrim occupations—not just a miller and two clerks but a wife, a parson, a manciple, and even some nuns (implied by the nunnery). The clerks call Simekin "hoste deere," recalling the Tabard Host. No other tale contains so many of the pilgrim professions mentioned in the General Prologue. Little wonder, then, that there's no universal laughter at the end of his story and no diversity of opinion. In the course of the Reeve's revenge on the Miller, everyone listening has been insulted.

In a final irony, the Reeve may even provoke sympathy for his fictional miller. In punishing him so completely through the malice, anger, or stupidity of everyone around him, the Reeve has left us with little to hold on to and with a resounding echo of revenge ringing in our ears. While he may hope we now "know" something about the camuse-nosed Miller whose tale he found so personally insulting, we mostly know about the choleric Reeve's anger, vindictiveness, and self-loathing. Thus, despite the Reeve's intent, which is so outwardly focused, this tale reflects mostly on the Reeve himself.

THE COOK'S PROLOGUE
AND TALE

The last of the tales of fragment I is itself a fragment, broken off just as we are told the bare outline of the story. It promises to be quite rowdy, with a "joly prentis" (I.4399) and his friend who "hadde a wif that held for countenaunce / A shoppe, and swived for hir sustenaunce" (I.4421–22). No one is sure what this tale would have looked like had it been completed. The outline does not conform to any identifiable source. Nor do we know why Chaucer stopped writing. In the Hengwrt manuscript, the scribe has written in the margin "Of this Cokes tale Chaucer writ namoore." Since the relatively recent identification of that scribe as Adam Pinkhurst, who copied the Ellesmere manuscript and perhaps is the man immortalized in the scolding lyric known as "Adam Scriveyn," we are now a bit more confident in connecting that marginal statement to Chaucer himself.[1] If Chaucer's personal copyist says he wrote no more of the Cook's Tale, we can assume that Chaucer never finished this story—the exemplar was not simply misplaced.

The London Cook finds the miller's comeuppance a funny "argument of herbergage" (I.4329) about the dangers of guests "brought into [one's] privetee" (I.4334), and it inspires a local tale of "oure citee" (I.4343). These terms suggest the professional familiarity of those in the London victualizing trades. If they don't particularly know each other, they know each

---

[1] Linne R. Mooney, "Chaucer's Scribe," *Speculum* 81.1 (2006): 97–138.

other's circumstances. The Cook's prologue advertises a kind of full circle back to the General Prologue and its originary setting: a "tale . . . of an hostiler" (I.4360) in which, he tells Harry Bailly, "er we parte, ywis, thou shalt be quit" (I.4362). Perhaps the Miller is not alone in wanting a bit of revenge for the Host's attempted arrangement of tales and tellers?

While many have lamented the unfinished nature of the Cook's Tale, others have waged strong arguments that it is intentionally left incomplete. Yet another tale of two men and a woman, the Cook's fragment implies an even more debased form of "love" in the wife's professional "swiving." The working-class world that provides the basic milieu of the fabliau is reduced here to a sham. The apprentice, Perkin Revelour, corrupts his master's business, stealing from his strongbox, and the wife only pretends to have a shop as a cover for prostitution. What more needed to be said?

By this logic, the tale is over before it ever gets started. The only thing it manages to describe is the kind of revelry and work avoidance that Perkin practices to get himself fired—more accurately, released from his indenture as an apprentice—through his gambling ("dis"), drinking, and riotous "revel" (I.4391–414; quotations, 4391–92). His love of dancing and music bodes poorly for any master who will "it in his shoppe abye" (I.4393; "abye" is literally "abide, put up with, allow," but also "a-buy, pay for"). Indeed, the few details sketched by the Cook's Tale suggest a story chock full of "paying for it" in rather literalized ways.

Whatever romantic sublimations or erotic desires dominated the first two tales are by now long gone. Such desires are debased into other kinds of transactions that have payment as their goal. In the Reeve's story, that payment is violent "atte fulle" (I.4133). In the Cook's, it's cold cash. This kind of crass reductiveness has prompted some to argue that Chaucer never meant to finish this scurrilous story, intending only to write some kind of link to the next, whatever that might eventually be. But we might look to the Prologue again, and to the relation between "revel and trouthe" (I.4397) there and in the tale proper, to discern the broad outline of a tighter connection between the nascent Cook's Tale and the collection's larger concerns.

Perkin is a dangerous apprentice because his partying and spending lead to theft. The Cook extemporizes a bit on this wisdom:

> For sikerly a prentis revelour
> That haunteth dis, riot, or paramour
> His maister shal it in his shoppe abye,
> Al haue he no part of the minstralcye.
> For thefte and riot, they been convertible,
> Al conne he playe on giterne or ribible;
> Revel and trouthe, as in a lowe degree,
> They been ful wroothe alday, as men may see.   (I.4391–98)

Even in this brief snippet of story—the entire Cook's Tale is only 58 lines long—one hears music everywhere, if not literally then by implication. His talent for dancing gives him his name "Perkin Revelour" (I.4370–71), for "at every bridale wolde he singe and hoppe" (I.4375). Any procession going through Cheapside (the retail part of London) causes him to dance right out of the workplace, "To hoppe and singe and maken swich disport" with a "meinee" of companions (I.4381–82). As elsewhere in *The Canterbury Tales*, and particularly in the Miller's Tale, music carries a salacious connotation. Nicholas plays the "gay sautrye" (I.3213) in his hostel room; and when he seals his plot with Alison, "He kiste hire sweete, and taketh his sautrye / And playeth faste, and maketh melodye" (I.3305–06). Making melody is typically associated with, if not a euphemism for, sexual activity. Here that music carries no euphemistic meaning but is fully "convertible" to theft—even if the master of the shop knows how to "playe on giterne or ribible" but refuses to take part in the minstrelsy. Neither knowledge or mastery can protect his business if his apprentice indulges. These entertainments will have a way of corrupting work from below. Such wisdom draws sharp distinctions between play, diversion, and game on one side and earnest work and its truthfulness on the other.

In this opening, the Cook uses singing, dancing, and minstrelsy making to signify the riot and revelry that opposes truth and honesty. The

Prologue also displays a similar opposition between truth and game that seems to be related to the local conditions of the tales of fragment I. The Host has mocked the Cook, here named Roger of Ware, for some shady practices in handling food: selling from his fly-ridden shop stale goods that have been reheated twice (I.4346–52). He wants Roger's story to be better than his usual wares and implies that truth sometimes comes through a person's jokes: "A man may saye ful sooth in game and play" (I.4355). Admitting the truth of that claim, the Cook has a balanced rejoinder: "But 'Sooth play, quaad play,' as the Fleming saith" (I.4357), at the very moment he identifies the Host by his given name, "Herry [Harry] Bailly" (I.4358). This is difficult stuff and easy to skim over because it doesn't seem integral to the story, which hardly goes anywhere anyway. The familiarity that the Reeve presumes in his response to the Miller is being picked up by these two Londoners in the Cook's Prologue, men who work in the same hospitality business. The Host is regaining control of the pilgrimage after the scuffle between the Knight and the Miller, and the Miller and the Reeve, with a mild commentary on the devolution of the storytelling into pointed ad hominem attacks. The Host and Cook here play at the kind of local reference that was attempted all too seriously in the Reeve's story. In doing so they raise counterclaims for the game of fiction making: games, jokes, and stories may contain truths under the guise of play. Conversely, a true jest is a bad one, which is what "sooth play, quaad play" means—a teller can hit too close to home. Striking just the right balance between bald truth and meaningless game is a challenge; they are "ful wroothe alday," particularly when working "in a lowe degree"—that is, outside the ranks of the idealized representatives of the estates and in the real world of most of the Canterbury pilgrims. The Cook's Tale may end abruptly, but it is fully engaged with the terms of tale-telling and character developed early in *The Canterbury Tales*.

THE MAN OF LAW'S
INTRODUCTION, PROLOGUE,
AND TALE

Fragment I relies on a tight set of connections, both thematic and formal, reproduced nowhere else in *The Canterbury Tales*. The second fragment, by contrast, contains only one story: the Man of Law's Tale. Its introduction marks what seems a new beginning through the Host's calculation of the date and time, "the eightetethe day / Of April, that is messager to May" at "ten at the clokke" (II.5–6, 14).[1] A new start to a new day is fitting after the antics of fragment I. But some have suggested that this introduction might represent an even more momentous beginning: an abandoned opening to the collection as a whole, one that was superseded when Chaucer invented the rivalrous "quiting" game and reworked fragment I around it.

The structural uncertainties of the *Tales*' in-progress state can be seen not only in the discontinuities between fragments I and II but also in the differences between parts of the Man of Law's Tale, both in form and content. Written in the same rhyming couplets as everything placed before it (and the vast majority of the tales to come), the Man of Law's Introduction is followed by a prologue in a new verse form, rhyme royal

---

[1] Especially because it mimes a similar calculation of the date and time found in the Parson's Prologue, this opening seems to envelop a different frame for *The Canterbury Tales* as a whole.

stanzas, which it also shares with the tale itself. These are seven-line units combining concatenating rhymes and couplets (*ababbcc*) that Chaucer advanced as an English response to French octosyllabic verse and Italian ottava rima. He used rhyme royal for two earlier works, *The Parliament of Fowls* and *Troilus and Criseyde*. In *The Canterbury Tales*, this verse form is reserved for stories of pious moral sentiment: the Clerk's Tale, the Prioress's Tale, and the Second Nun's Tale, in addition to the Man of Law's. Compared with couplets, rhyme royal stanzas are more difficult to write (three *b* rhymes), and they "feel" different to the ear. The stanzas tend to support complete ideas and to be more self-contained than the riding rhyme (heroic couplets) of Chaucer's pentameter, which can go on for any number of lines.

The five stanzas of the Man of Law's prologue constitute an abbreviated translation of part of Pope Innocent III's treatise *De miseria condicionis humane* (*On the Misery of the Human Condition*), written in the late twelfth century. In Chaucer's handling, its denunciation of wealth is transformed into praise of merchants, who are, incidentally, the first movers of his story. It begins with merchants circulating goods in the Mediterranean, and the Man of Law will shortly claim to have learned the tale from "a marchant, goon is many a yeere" (II.132). But the Prologue is also suggestive in the way that it *dis*connects from the tale that follows and what that disconnection might imply about Chaucer's practices of composition. At the close of the Introduction, the Man of Law claims to speak in prose (II.96), though in his tale he clearly does not. This inconsistency may suggest that what followed was in an earlier version a prose tale better aligned with the moral attitude struck by the Introduction's rhetoric—prompting some to suggest that story now known as Chaucer's Tale of Melibee, an allegorical moral treatise extolling female counsel and urging patience in adversity, was once attributed to the Man of Law. But that proposed revision does not explain the continuity between the Prologue and the present tale in their shared verse form. Clearly Chaucer was still at work on this material and had not yet finished smoothing the transitions either between or within fragments.

Despite these signs of revision in Chaucer's developing plan for *The Canterbury Tales*, there is some indication that these materials were collected with the Man of Law (and what he could do for the ongoing frame narrative) in mind. For example, the Host addresses him using the language of his profession:

> "Sire Man of Lawe," quod he, "so have ye blis,
> Telle us a tale anon, as forward is.
> Ye been submitted thurgh youre free assent
> To stonden in this cas at my juggement.
> Acquiteth you now of youre biheeste:
> Thanne have ye doon youre devoir atte leeste."   (II.33–38)

Reverting to the language of contract first uttered in the General Prologue ("forward," "assent," "juggement"), the Host reestablishes his control by addressing the Man of Law in legal terms ("submitted," "acquiteth," "devoir"), giving purpose to his selection as the next narrator. By these means Chaucer puts the frame narrative in motion, depicting the Host's power waxing and waning, lost and regained, as the journey progresses. Gestures like these will sporadically reappear in the links throughout *The Canterbury Tales*.

The Man of Law responds in a like manner that links the language of legal contract to the economics of Harry Bailly's mercantile milieu and again recalls the General Prologue: "To breken forward is nat myn entente: / Biheeste is dette, and I wol holde fain / Al my biheeste. I can no bettre sayn" (II.40–42). The reciprocity of law ("For swich lawe as man yiveth another wight, / He sholde himself usen it by right"; II.43–44) impels him to offer a "thrifty" (II.46) tale, one that wastes no one's time and cancels his debt to the other tale-tellers and the Host, without engaging in the kind of ad hominem quiting seen earlier. The Man of Law's idiom, like the quasi-legalistic jargon in the General Prologue, helps the Host regain control over the proceedings.

One particular point of comedy deserves our attention before we get to the serious matters in the story told by the Man of Law—one of

Chaucer's signature moments of authorial self-reflexiveness. Before telling his tale, the Man of Law complains about a writer named "Chaucer" who has told so many stories (and not particularly well) in English that he has nothing new to offer (II.46–56). He then gives a questionably competent list of Chaucer's works that manages to insult, with some humor, the contemporary poet John Gower for telling the incestuous story of Apollonius of Tyre,[2] a romance of peregrinations and lost children that is related through some shared source materials and tale types to the story that the Man of Law eventually tells. The Man of Law's frustration is registered, of course, with comic obliviousness to the fact that a member of this current fellowship is named Chaucer. These deep connections and subtle ironies suggest that Chaucer is thoughtfully at work in this section of the *Tales*; it is not the mere hodgepodge of materials that the changing verse form might suggest.

Somewhat unexpectedly, given the terms and ideas set forth in the Prologue and Introduction, the tale offered by the Man of Law is a pious narrative of female suffering cast in the adventurous plot of romance. With its generic hybridity and starkly Christian thematics, it also differs from the tales we have encountered thus far. Combining features of the romance and the saint's life, it is the first of a series of Canterbury tales—the others are the Clerk's Tale, the Physician's Tale, and the Second Nun's Tale—celebrating feminine constancy. The Man of Law's Tale focuses on a figure named Custaunce and her travels; she first goes to Syria to be married to its newly converted sultan, but she is then cast out to sea by her enemies who seek to expel the Christian religion she brings with her. Her three sea voyages separate cyclical patterns in the narrative of exile and

---

[2] John Gower was a slightly older contemporary of Chaucer's who wrote poetry in Latin, French, and English. His tale collection, *Confessio Amantis*, ended with the lengthy story of Apollonius of Tyre (known to modern audiences as the source of Shakespeare's *Pericles*). Mentioned in the dedication at the close of *Troilus and Criseyde*, Gower was clearly one of Chaucer's closest friends and poetic rivals in late medieval England. Their story collections contain a number of the same narratives, including the one in the Man of Law's Tale. The Man of Law's omission of *Troilus* in this list of Chaucer's works is a comic (and slightly damning) representation of his literary taste.

return, joy and woe, sin and repentance. Her first voyage ends in massacre and exile; her second includes a trial for murder and ends in marriage; her third returns her home. Custaunce's son, Maurice, is a historical figure whose story can be found "in th'olde Romain geestes" (II.1126), giving the Man of Law's Tale a claim to being a semi-historical account detailing the return of Christianity to Saxon England. But it includes materials both fantastic and miraculous that defy a modern sense of history.

The tale's historical features come from a more proximate source, Nicholas Trivet's fourteenth-century Anglo-Norman *Chronicle*, which tells a story of ancient British history that ends with the ascension of the emperor Maurice to Roman rule. Like Trivet's story, the Man of Law's Tale is also related to the folktale narratives of the "accused queen" and "exiled princess" found in a number of romances, among them *Emaré*. Such romances were not the purely secular genres we now take them to be but were also concerned with morals and miracles, placing them closer than we might expect to the genre of saint's life, also known as hagiography. The protagonists of both romances and saint's lives must endure trials of similar kinds that test their virtue and fortitude. Custaunce's travails at sea certainly place her in that role. But unlike the romance, whose "hero" is typically male, the saint's life can also valorize the heroism of women, which is depicted in terms of passive suffering.

The female saints of hagiographies bear witness to their faith, typically under extreme and violent pressure to renounce it, before a scene of martyrdom—a death that always implicitly rehearses the sacrifice of Christ for humanity. Custaunce is neither a martyr nor such a witness. Instead, she is a quiet example of faith and a vehicle for Christ's heroism and thus for the spiritual conversion of those around her. Exiled twice in a rudderless boat, Custaunce is miraculously saved by her faith in God and devotion to Mary (*the* exemplar of passive maternal suffering), proving that Christ is the best of champions one can have. The tale emphasizes the Marian archetype in Custaunce's appeal to Mary as a suffering mother (II.841–54) in a similarly "rewful" situation. This mixture of hagiography and romance adventure in tales such as the Man of Law's has made them difficult to categorize generically, as well as uncomfortable. The pathos evoked by such exemplary tales and the suffering of their virtuous female protagonists are problematic for modern readers.

The Man of Law's Tale also displays wider cultural ambitions in the adventurous story it transmits. Its rivalrous conflict between and within non-Christian cultures skirts the edges of its marriage plot, itself directed by a spiritual rather than worldly focus. Custaunce is no romance heroine, even one trapped in a situation like Emelye's; she is instead an unhappy participant in a marriage contract "in destruccioun of Maumetrye, / And in encrees of Cristes lawe deere" (II.236–37), making the marriage plot itself something other than it seems. Because the stakes of marriage here are religious conversion and cultural transformation rather than mere personal satisfaction, marriage takes on a symbolic function in the tale, much like its allegorical significance in the wider Christian tradition as a figure for the union of Christ with the church, or the soul with God. These features make Custaunce's status as a wife all the more strange and distant from the amatory concerns of romance.

The Man of Law's story will attempt to ally Custaunce with newly converted princes and will censure malicious efforts to foil those plans. She is resisted by her suitors' mothers, who wish to purge their lands of "so straunge a creature" (II.700) and find Custaunce foreign, elf-like, even "feendlich" (II.751).[3] But her dramatic (and repeated) exile affords a miraculous display, which itself occasions more widespread Christian conversion. Custaunce's trials end when she finally returns to Rome and her father's imperial court with her son, who functions as both her messenger and her message. His striking resemblance to her effects a scene of recognition and reunion with her husband and her father, both of whom

---

[3] Her alterity is experienced, by turns, in religious, linguistic, and generally cultural terms. I am conflating the two different scenes of her mothers-in-law's perfidy in this summary. The sultaness's resistance because of her adherence to her Muslim faith should be distinguished from Donegild's more general malice. We might also do more work investigating what the more generally "pagan" Northumbria signifies in opposition to Christianity and thus what Custaunce restores to Britain in this story.

presumed her dead. These recursive movements in the Man of Law's Tale mime the "exile and return" adventures of romance but also transcend them, using their moves to make much more metaphysically significant claims. Custaunce's return home is no mere "happily ever after" ending but a spiritually fulfilling resolution to worldly adversity, tracing the allegorical movement of the soul back to its point of origin, where death is celebrated as "an ende of every worldly sore" (I.2849).

The tale has been making similar efforts all along: its heroine also resembles yet transcends romance's descriptive register. Custaunce is presented in moral terms in which her beauty is found in her virtue:

In hire is heigh beautee withoute pride,
Youthe withouten greenehede or folye;
To alle hir werkes vertu is hir gide;
Humblesse hath slain in hire al tyrannye;
She is mirour of alle curteisye;
Hir herte is verray chambre of holinesse,
Hir hand ministre of freedom for almesse.   (II.162–68)

Her wealth of virtues appears in contrast to the vices she abjures ("pride," "folye," "tyrannye"). There is a chaste diffidence to the heroine of the Man of Law's secular hagiography. Her effect on the sultan—"plesaunce / To han hir figure in his remembraunce" (II.186–87)—is distinctly separated from Custaunce herself, who desires no such match. Indeed, she weeps at the news that she must travel into "the Barbre nacioun" (II.281) and abandons herself to the decisions of others: "Wommen are born to thraldom and penaunce, / And to been under mannes governaunce" (II.286–87). The desire she inspires occurs in her absence; she is merely a story the sultan has heard and therefore is not responsible for inspiring it. Unlike Emelye, glimpsed a-Maying in her garden in what might be seen as an unconsciously erotic and amorous activity, or Alison, openly flirting with the boarder in her own house, Custaunce is entirely innocent and thus the power of her virtue (and its sacrifices) is that much greater.

Chaucer's verse form, we might note, enforces this reading by separating these events, cause and effect, into distinct stanzas. There is literally no contact, either between Custaunce and the sultan or between the lines of the text dealing with each of them, that might implicate Custaunce herself in these actions and arrangements.

Romance, we should note, is already a conflicted genre and not merely the singularly courtly narrative I have been describing. It is full of the kinds of cultural and religious conflict we see in the Man of Law's Tale, and it is marked by widely differing traditions and source material. For instance, interreligious love is a concern in a number of Middle English romances indebted to French sources, among them *Floris and Blancheflour* and *The Sultan of Babylon*. In such stories Islam occupies a more cosmopolitan position in and around the Mediterranean than the remote English island might care to acknowledge. These romance effects infiltrate the Man of Law's narrative in ways his hagiographical focus may not fully account for. But they certainly account for the attractive exoticism of the story in its context and help support its bid for the prize among the other tales.

Certain aspects of the Man of Law's Tale make it seem like a rejoinder to the Knight, particularly its (lack of) patience for some of the Knight's narrative display—for example, his elaborate description of Theseus's equally involved efforts at having the amphitheater constructed ("I trowe men wolde deeme it necligence / If I foryete to tellen the dispence . . ."; I.1881–82). The Man of Law has little tolerance of such narrative extravagances:

> Me list nat of the chaf ne of the stree
> Maken so long a tale as of the corn.
> What sholde I tellen of the royaltee
> At mariages, or which cours gooth biforn,
> Who bloweth in a trompe or in an horn?
> The fruit of every tale is for to saye:
> They ete and drinke and daunce and singe and playe. (II.701–07)

In his reluctance to specify the menu ("which cours gooth biforn") or the music at the wedding ("a trompe or . . . an horn"), the Man of Law reminds us, by implication, of the "dispence / Of Theseus . . . To maken up the listes royally" (I.1882–84) detailed by the Knight. He thereby sets his tale up in counterpoint to the Knight's, as one similarly invested in important matters but one more directly and economically invested in the "corn." Even the corn and chaff metaphor itself is important. It is one of the standard exegetical tropes for separating the moral level of a story from the literal, the meaningful from the merely ornamental, or, in Chaucer's earlier terms, "sentence" from "solas" (I.798). Reminding us of the Knight's focus in the process of leaving it behind, the Man of Law gestures beyond the worldly terms of courtly romance, even as he deploys them.

These distinctions do not distance the Man of Law's Tale from the Knight's idealizing story so much as distinguish its focus and underscore its aim. Written in an equally ambitious register, the Man of Law's Tale shares the elevated diction and cosmic perspective of the Knight's Tale but works in another key. The sultan claims that he must have Custaunce or "he nas but deed" (II.209), speaking in the same idiom as Arcite and his parodic imitator Nicholas. And the tale also has a similar metaphysical grasp, echoing the Knight's when the Man of Law makes references to a "firste meving" and "cruel Mars" (II.295, 301). In addition, he gestures toward the unknown fate that attends the sultan's desire for Custaunce in a manner that could be glossed by Arcite's own lament that "we witen nat what thing we prayen here" (I.1260). The Man of Law opines similarly on the universe's inscrutability:

> Paraventure in thilke large book
> Which that men clepe the hevene ywriten was
> With sterres whan that he his birthe took
> That he for love sholde han his deeth, allas:
> For in the sterres, clerer than is glas,
> Is writen, God woot, whoso coude it rede,
> The deeth of every man, withouten drede.   (II.190–96)

A combination of the planetary influences of the Knight's story with the "astromye" furtively studied by Nicholas (I.3451), the Man of Law's "hevene ywriten" sketches a starry roadmap that humans simply cannot interpret but to which they are nonetheless subject.[4] Even more fatalistically, despite its Christian reassurances, a tragic knowledge preoccupies the Man of Law's narration:

> O sodein wo that ever art successour
> To worldly blisse, spreind with bitternesse!
> Th'ende of the joye of oure worldly labour!
> Wo occupieth the fin of oure gladnesse.
> Herke this conseil for thy sikernesse:
> Upon thy glade day have this in minde,
> The unwar wo or harm that comth bihinde.   (II.421–27)

This "tragic" sentiment, which is repeated throughout the tale, vies with the "happy" ending both its romance and its Christian heroics might lead us to expect. One could call its ending happy or comic, because Custaunce returns home safely and is ultimately reunited with her husband and father. But the tale refuses to close with happiness, pursuing its characters "til deeth departeth hem" (II.1158). Repeatedly collocating joy and woe (and not in such reassuring ways), this won't be the only one of the Canterbury tales to suggest that "this world nis but a thurghfare ful of wo" (I.2847; the speaker here is Egeus, Theseus's father, by the way). Later tales, more generically "religious" than the Man of Law's, will also suggest as much, because ultimately Christianity does not put as much value on this life as on the next. Our critical values must be reprioritized.

---

[4] Whereas the Knight questions what "purveyance" governs a world in which "giltelees tormenteth innocence" (i.e., innocence is tormented without guilt; I.1314), the Man of Law's entire goal is to show the triumph of Christian providence, a promise of security missing from the other tale.

Particularly interesting for our modern multicultural society, the tale offers more than naïve Christian orthodoxy (though it does offer plenty of that, too) in its sensitivity both to the Syrians forced into a conversion against "Makometes lawe" (II.336) and to the plight of wives. The Man of Law's Tale seems acutely aware of the demands its genre makes, especially on women. Custaunce's subjection to the power of father and pope and to her alien husband(s) is nearly as threatening as the men aroused by her along the way (the would-be rapist in the boat and the spurned Northumbrian seducer who murders Hermengild). So much so that in a tale celebrating her role as a conduit of conversion and change, the narrative voice falters over the future it propels. We are left with a plot that drives action forward but a narrative that laments what happens:

> Allas, what wonder is it though she wepte,
> That shal be sent to straunge nacioun
> Fro frendes that so tendrely hire kepte,
> And to be bounden under subjeccioun
> Of oon, she knoweth nat his condicioun?
> Housbondes been alle goode, and han been yore:
> That knowen wives—I dar saye you namore.   (II.267–73)

This won't be the only time the Man of Law dares "saye . . . namore" about what women know. His description of Custaunce's wedding night is notorious for its reticence about what wives must put up with from "folk that han ywedded hem with ringes" (II.712). It's not so much that the Man of Law is prudish about the nighttime "manere necessaries as been plesinges" (II.711) to new husbands as he is conflicted about his saintlike heroine ("wives been ful holy thinges"; II.709). The Man of Law seems rather acutely aware of what married women have to endure. Thus, gender forms one of the tale's most interesting inner conflicts, particularly given what most often follows in most editions: the Wife of Bath's Prologue and Tale.

Powerful women also manipulate Custaunce and thus complicate the gender politics of the story: both mothers-in-law set her adrift in an effort to rid their nations of her influence. The sultaness, especially, seems reasonably portrayed despite her monstrousness and vilification. Her loyalty to her own religion is touching but ultimately empty if it results in the kind of ambition that makes her murder her son. The tale thus constantly counterpoints the evil attributed only to women—as Eve's inheritors—with the good that only another woman can accomplish: the sacrificial Mary. While one woman damns all her offspring to sin and penance, the other saves mankind by bringing forth her son and then watching his crucifixion. In its condemnations and celebrations of femininity, the Man of Law's Tale has remained provocative, as the Wife of Bath's explosive Prologue perhaps attests.

THE WIFE OF BATH'S
PROLOGUE AND TALE

The Wife of Bath opens fragment III without introduction or preface. She begins in medias res—in the middle of things—challenging some implied but unspoken claim made against her knowledge of the "wo that is in mariage" (III.3). Her first word, "experience," provides the authority out of which she speaks as well as her subject matter, and it is clearly opposed to clerical *auctoritas*, or written authority. Dramatically arresting, the Wife's Prologue captures us from the start with the tenor and pitch of her voice. Its aggressive, argumentative, and somewhat defensive posture sets the tone for the rest of her performance. She has a lot to argue with, even if we don't know, particularly, what has just set her off. It might be the Man of Law's Tale, but because Chaucer wrote no link between the two, we cannot be sure. But if not the Man of Law's Tale per se, then one just like it—a tale that valorizes a kind of suffering, patient femininity and reluctantly sexual wifehood that her Prologue clearly rejects. If it was meant to follow what is currently fragment II, her Prologue turns the Man of Law's more philosophical view of human life as earthly suffering into the tale that gets it all wrong, portraying instead the particulars of female existence under patriarchy, which she knows firsthand.

As we read the Wife's long preamble, it's important to know a few things up front: women are forbidden to preach—in fact, even to speak—in church. And that silence is enjoined more broadly in theological writings about women and marriage. The model for such an injunction is Eve.

She "taught" Adam to eat the fruit of the forbidden tree, an act that, according to doctrine, got humanity expelled from paradise and brought sin into the world. Women were thought to be less rational (and thus more carnal, belonging to the body and its lower appetites) than men and, as such, were in no position to be teaching them anything. The body should not tell the mind what to do. Such thinking is only a small part of the general assumption of the inferiority of women in the Middle Ages, a topic much discussed and elaborated in both religious and social texts on female behavior and the proper regulation of women.

There is an entire history of writing that is culturally anti-female, or what has been called both misogynist and antifeminist, behind the Wife of Bath's creation. That history depicts women as illogical, libidinous creatures prone to talkativeness, self-interest, and bodily pleasure. Before embarking on her rambling, associative, and pugnacious Prologue, we must know this context, which is rooted in a set of antimatrimonial tracts by the early church fathers, particularly Jerome, and by the teachings of St. Paul. These texts form both the background and the foreground of the Wife's discourse.[1] She argues explicitly with these teachings at the same time that she implicitly demonstrates their claims about women. Thus, there seems to be no winning for the Wife from the outset.

The Wife's Prologue, accordingly, defends her experience against written authors' complaints about women, showing how the "woes" of marriage are always given, implicitly, from the male point of view. Her speech takes on a seemingly modern force, in relation to both her era and ours. This wife has been married five times and considers herself an "expert in al myn age" (III.174) on these miseries, which she is proud to have doled out to (rather than accepted from) the often-recalcitrant men she has wed. Such a turn is crucial to understanding the Wife, because she literally turns the evidence *against* her back upon itself. She makes herself

---

[1] These texts can be surveyed in the collection edited by Alcuin Blamires, with Karen Pratt and C. W. Marx, *Woman Defamed and Woman Defended: An Anthology of Medieval Texts* (Oxford: Clarendon P; New York: Oxford UP, 1992).

an agent, while women have traditionally been thought to be objects. Even the phrase "wo that is in mariage" would not have been neutral. In tracts written by male and largely misogynist writers, those woes conventionally belong to husbands. Thus her adoption of the phrase is itself revolutionary, for it upends the initial assumptions of what has for so long been a social given.

Characterizing the Wife's narration are the quick shifts and turns she makes along the way. Despite speaking so directly about sex, the body, and pleasure, the Wife is hardly what we'd call direct in style and structure; her discourse meanders—with purpose, but not always to her own advantage and in ways that, her detractors are quick to point out, are stereotypically feminine. For example, she begins by exalting her experience over written "auctoritee" (III.1). But no sooner does she dismiss clerical authority focused on biblical precedent than she turns directly to this kind of evidence, citing the example of the wedding at Cana in order to argue against its traditional interpretation. The Wife privileges the practical and material over and against the ideal. While Christ's visit to one wedding at Cana had been interpreted as an allegorical expression of the dictate "that [she] ne sholde wedded be but ones" (III.13), in practice women and men were often married multiple times. The Wife can even produce alternate biblical examples "of bigamye or of octogamye" (III.33) in Solomon, Abraham, and Jacob. She quotes St. Paul himself ("Bet is to be wedded than to brinne"; III.52) as licensing the marriage of widows (III.49–50). And, of course, remarriage was perfectly legal. In fact, the state encouraged it so that property would be returned to social circulation. Marrying a rich widow could be seen as a lucrative prospect for socially ambitious men.

But even this description of the Wife sounds a bit more logical and less digressive than her opening seems to us. The modulations of her speech (and the associative nature of her thoughts) require some attention. She derails herself more than once in the first 10 lines:

Experience, though noon auctoritee
Were in this world, is right ynough for me

> To speke of wo that is in mariage:
> For lordinges, sith I twelf yeer was of age—
> Thanked be God that is eterne on live—
> Housbondes at chirche dore I have had five
> (If I so ofte mighte han wedded be),
> And alle were worthy men in hir degree.
> But me was told, certayn, nat longe agon is,
> That sith that Crist ne wente never but ones . . .   (III.1–10)

What has happened here? These lines track the Wife's shifting thoughts, alive to various associations and modifications as she goes along. She begins directly enough, touting the advantages of her own experience of the difficulties of married life over the sterile authority of the church fathers—a bunch of celibate men exalting the status of celibacy and virginity, much to their own advantage. By contrast, her experiential wisdom is founded on her own life: five consecutive husbands beginning at age 12. She's basically been married as early as legally possible, giving her as much marital knowledge as her forty years allow. Despite how odd this sounds to modern audiences, she happily claims her more than twenty-five years of marital experience, thanking God that she's able to say as much. The way she says so tells us a good deal. Her marriages are legitimate, "at chirche dore," where the banns (or public proclamations of intent) would be posted for anyone (with anything bad to say about her) to contest. But we need to look at the next comment, offset by parentheses: "If I so ofte mighte han wedded be." The parentheses make the claim into a dramatic aside and suggest that someone, somewhere has been criticizing her or at least questioning the validity of so many marriages. It strikes us as more than a little sarcastic or at least indignant, as it implicitly recalls someone's theory of an ideal, singular marriage over and against the reality of the social, marital economy that the Wife knows and will shortly explain.

Although she may be primarily interested in emphasizing her experience as more important than the authoritative teaching ranged against her, and she may be seen as stereotypically feminine for doing so, the Wife can also debate the question of marriage on theological grounds, resisting her critics in multiple ways. In the second sentence of her Prologue she refers to the parable of the Samaritan woman at the well (from the Gospel of John), as if responding to someone who had thrown it up in her face at one point. Christ told this woman that because she had had five husbands, the man she was with now was not her husband. From there the Wife launches into a series of questions about canon law—how many spouses one may have, and where such a number is legislated "by expres word" (III.61)—citing, instead, a more "gentil text" that bids her "wexe and multiplye" (III.28–29). Much is going on here and not just in the commonsensical way it seems to be. Chaucer is playing with his sources and, more profoundly, making his creation, the Wife, knowingly play with *her* sources, thereby producing some tricky literary business.

The Wife speaks out about clerical misogyny and its logical contradictions and hypocrisy, coming from men who know little of marriage in practice and work only in theory. As she so memorably puts it: "Who paintede the leoun, tel me who?" (III.692), a rhetorical question that underscores the one-sidedness of the situation:

By God, if wommen hadden writen stories,
As clerkes han within hir oratories,
They wolde han writen of men more wikkednesse
Than al the merk of Adam may redresse.[2]   (III.693–96)

As the Wife well knows, women have their own tales of wickedness to tell about the men who have mistreated them. Such stories would be told from

---

[2] The "merk of Adam" alludes to the stain of original sin, but the Wife seems to conflate the mark of Cain with a similar sign of Adam's masculine condition. Cain receives his mark after the murder of his brother Abel (Genesis 4:11–16): it both signified his being cursed for that sin and protected him from being murdered because of it as he became a fugitive and a wanderer. By analogy, the mark of Adam, like the mark of Cain, is what both signifies his sinfulness and protects him from retribution ("redresse") for it.

what would be the lion's perspective. But even as the Wife issues some very rational (albeit self-serving) opinions about the unfairness of these anti-feminist assumptions, she herself appears to validate them. Her language and the behavior she describes confirm the claims in the very same antimatrimonial texts, like Jerome's *Adversus Jovinianum*, against which she argues.

Sometimes the Wife's behavior emerges literally from Jerome's book. For instance, at the end of her Prologue she describes what her fifth husband, the young clerk Janekin, reads to her:

> He cleped it Valerie and Theofraste,
> At which book he lough alway ful faste;
> And eek ther was somtime a clerk at Rome,
> A cardinal, that highte Saint Jerome,
> That made a book again Jovinian;
> In which book eek ther was Tertulan,
> Crysippus, Trotula, and Helowis,
> That was abbesse nat fer fro Paris;
> And eek the Parables of Salomon,
> Ovides Art, and bookes many oon—
> And alle thise were bounden in oo volume.   (III.671–81)

She mentions Valerius Maximus and Theophrastus, authors of vitriolic antimatrimonial tracts. Jerome is perhaps the best-known of these misogynist writers. His *Against Jovinian* argues vehemently for the superiority of virginity over marriage. Tertullian was a Roman rhetorician who composed exhortations on subjects such as chastity, monogamy, and adultery. "Crispus" was likely a name picked up from Jerome, where it denoted another misogynist authority. "Trotula" was a classical text on gynecology that enumerated female difference (some would say physical inferiority) in anatomical and medical terms. Heloise is the infamous student and lover of the French theologian Abelard, who was castrated in punishment for their illicit affair. Solomon is credited with writing proverbs, many of which condemned the nature of women and warned men about dealing with them. Ovid's *Ars amatoria* and *Remedia amoris*, handbooks on the "art" of seduction and its "remedy" (i.e., how to resist it), both satirized the power of love. These standard texts of antifeminist and antimatrimonial sentiment are the very sources from which Chaucer has drawn the Wife, often taking her words right out of their pages. Some might call this ironic structure a condemnation of the Wife; but for the most part, she has been read far more sympathetically as a revelation of the hypocrisy of these sources and as evidence of the biases that come from their (exclusively masculine) institutional origins.

To be sure, Chaucer gives the Wife far more attention than seems necessary, even if he is playing with irony here. He seems to delight in the havoc she wreaks on the traditions that have engendered her. The Wife exposes the systematic power structures of marriage, particularly its economics. As a wealthy clothmaker she has expertise in commercial markets, and she uses their economic structures to explain her approach to wedlock. Indeed, it is hard to know whether the Wife would have learned about economic practices first from marriage or from clothmaking. Even the church's teaching on marriage invokes concepts of debt and repayment, perfectly orthodox ways of understanding and navigating one's sexual obligation in marriage. The "debt" of marriage that the Wife repeatedly mentions prohibits a spouse from refusing sex to the one who has requested it. One's body is not one's own to withhold. She explains:

> Myn housbonde shal it han both eve and morwe,
> Whan that him list come forth and paye his dette.
> An housbonde wol I have, I wol nat lette,
> Which shal be bothe my dettour and my thral,
> And have his tribulacion withal
> Upon his flessh whil that I am his wif.
> I have the power during al my lif
> Upon his propre body, and nat he[.]   (III.152–59)

The subtle logic of the marriage debt may begin with male privilege accorded to her husband "both eve and morwe," but she quickly turns it against him. If the principle ensured that wives could not refuse their husband's desires, this wife guarantees that he will "have his tribulacion withal / Upon his flessh," exulting in the power that desire gives her. She makes his desire into his "tribulacion." This kind of language, indeed the very theory of the marriage debt, muddles categories (sexuality and religion) that we typically think of as separate. And this particular mix of economics and religion is one that the Wife always turns to her full advantage.

In the second section of her Prologue, which follows the Pardoner's brief interruption (marking the end of her sermonizing rhetoric), the Wife details the practices, schemes, manipulations, and ruses by which she managed her five marriages. When the Wife announces that "wo" and "tribulacion" are the subjects of her expertise, we might wonder about the difference between the woe she experiences and the tribulation she causes by being "the whippe" (III.175) or at the least the "purgatorye" (III.489) of the men she has married. One seems naturally to lead to the other. Is this conflation in the Wife's mind at all problematic?

Such a circular understanding of marital strife arises from the conflict between social theories of marriage, which put the man at the head of the household, and the Wife's experience of it—in which she has been able, repeatedly, to get the upper hand. It is as if the Wife knows that there is no such thing as happiness in marriage (certainly not for women) within the standard social hierarchy. There is instead only strife. Her strategies do not aim for an equilibrium of power between husband and wife; she seeks power over her husbands, as if to correct the imbalance into which she entered when she first wed as a very young girl. And in telling us of her marriages, even in the most general of terms, the Wife reveals the conditions of everyday life: old men who could be easily manipulated by their desire for her youth, younger men whom she desired and was able to attain with the wealth she accrued over the years. But there is no wisdom of Cato, as claimed in the Miller's fabliau, in the world in which the Wife lives, where man weds "his similitude" (1.3228). She shows instead how, in her lifelong experience, "youthe and elde is often at debat" (1.3230), because marriage is a business and, for her, a profession. Those who marry for love are those who can afford to do so. Everyone else makes a match based on his or her economic needs and power.

In the process of demonstrating this economically based system, the Wife also reveals much about herself, highlighting the many ruses by which she got the better of each of the men she was with:

> O Lord, the paine I dide hem and the wo,
> Ful giltelees, by Goddes sweete pine!
> For as an hors I coude bite and whine;
> I coude plaine and I was in the gilt,
> Or elles often time I hadde been spilt.
> Whoso that first to mille comth first grint.
> I plained first: so was oure werre stint.
> They were ful glad to excusen hem ful blive
> Of thing of which they never agilte hir live.
> Of wenches wolde I beren hem on honde,
> Whan that for sik they mighte unnethe stonde[.]   (III.384–94)

These lines describe a perverse form of flattery to her husbands, because, as she says, it "tikled . . . his herte" to think that she "had of him so greet chiertee" (III.395–96). This fondness (from the Old French *chierte*, derived from Latin *carus*, "dear"; *OED*, s.v. "cherte, chertee") is related to the idea of charity, which is an interesting way to think about the Wife's performance of "care" for her old husbands. The Wife tells us more here than just the means by which she drives these older husbands crazy or gets what she wants out of them. Chaucer reveals the Wife to be a complex figure, one who both admits to a dishonesty that could cast doubt on nearly everything that she tells us (including this very admission) and draws us in with her startlingly honest confession. The more she confesses to lying to them, the more we believe her—and rightly so.

One of the reasons we tend to believe the Wife's confession is her lack of bitterness. She laughs at herself and what she has managed to get away with ("O Lord . . . by Goddes sweete pine!") as she reflects back on the pain she inflicted on these older, "giltelees" men. Her tactic, in fact, is to accuse them first so that they have no opportunity to complain about her. Flattered by her false accusation of their infidelity, they were glad to defend themselves for acts they could hardly manage physically at their age (like running about with "wenches"). The Wife brilliantly manipulates these old men with her aggressive performance of jealousy, with the result that they overlook her own behavior. Accusing them first, she is able to turn their attention in the direction she wishes and away from her "gilt." Indeed, her complaining serves to distract them from her own activities. She captures this strategy with an image right out of the fabliaux: whoever gets to the mill first, gets to grind first. She has always been one step ahead of them.

This confession of her guilt, both in the way she manipulates and distracts these men and, more literally, in the behavior she hides from them ("I coude plaine and I was in the gilt"), might suggest that the Wife was engaged in the same adulterous activity of which she complains. This is a border she straddles in a number of places, but her literalness, I think, saves her from that extreme. For example, the Wife's fourth husband is a "revelour" who had a "paramour" (III.453–54), and that made her jealous. Her answer to him is to make him suffer precisely what he has inflicted on her:

> I saye I hadde in herte greet despit
> That he of any other hadde delit,
> But he was quit, by God and by Saint Joce:
> I made him of the same wode a croce—
> Nat of my body in no foul manere—
> But, certaynly, I made folk swich cheere
> That in his owene grece I made him frye,
> For angre and for verray jalousye.   (III.481–88)

Of course, no one can prove anything about the Wife for certain; ultimately, we are imagining the mental life of a literary character. But it would seem to require that we posit an entirely different level of self-deception to read the Wife as caring so much about her reputation (as an adulteress) that to save it she would fabricate a lie, which promotes the fiction that she is an adulteress. That is, the Wife would be covering up her "real" adultery by only pretending to adultery for her husband's sake. It is much more likely that the Wife is a serial monogamist, one who hews pretty closely to the letter of the law despite sometimes gross violations of its spirit. The more subtle irony of such a stance is that the Wife is so careful always to be under the protection of marriage that she commits adultery in her heart if not with her body "in no foul manere." She is so practically concerned to have a future husband at the ready that she over-prepares for a brief widowhood. Thus, we should not be surprised by the story of the young clerk Janekin, husband number five, whom the Wife lined up while her fourth husband was still alive: "For certaynly, I saye for no bobaunce / Yit was I never withouten purveyaunce / Of mariage—n'of othere thinges eek" (III.569–71). The Wife is sinless here in only the most literal and physical of senses.

The Wife has been accused of the excesses of such literality for a long time. In the example of the Samaritan woman that she raises early in her Prologue, the Wife speaks only of the story's literal meaning. But in various sermons, the story is told as an allegory of false gods and false religions. The husbands of the Samaritan woman are not real husbands at all, and, in these readings, Christ accosts her to illustrate not the appropriate number of marriages but the singular status of God. The Wife's literal understanding of this story suggests that she is a bad reader, adhering to the literal, the carnal, and the material and thus attending to the dead letter of scripture rather than to its living spirit. Such limitation has been traditionally connected with the Wife's deafness "that was scathe" (I.446). But in making her physical disability into a sign of moral failure, many have rationalized the abuse that she has suffered. Toward her Prologue's end, she reveals that her deafness was caused by her husband's blow: "For that I rente out of his book a leef, / That of the strook myn ere wex al deef" (III.635–36). The detail suggests a more cruel relation between the moral book that Janekin wields and the Wife's resistance to its teaching, a relation that has done her physical harm.

By the time we near the end of her Prologue, it is hard to believe that the Wife still has any tales left to tell. She concludes the story of her reconciliation with Janekin in her fifth marriage, ready to begin her tale proper, only to be lightly remonstrated by the Friar for the length of her "preamble" (III.831). The Friar's words incite the Summoner to respond, and the two begin an argument that will be concluded only when, at the end of her performance, they can tell stories openly criticizing each other's professions. At this point, however, the Host must step in to give the Wife the floor once more.

The Wife's tale is both more and less than we've been led to expect. Her economic expertise and anticlerical humor set up expectations for some kind of clever comic tale, such as a fabliau pitting the intellect of clerks against the savvy of wives. Indeed, some evidence suggests that the fabliau told by the Shipman was once hers, an assignment that would fit nicely with the endlink to the Man of Law's epilogue that mentions the next speaker's "joly body." It would make a lot of sense. But much to our surprise the Wife instead tells a fairy story, set in the old days of King Arthur, a tale that seems far more conventional in genre than her Prologue has led us to expect. Such romances tend to test and demonstrate the values of the nobility and reinforce fairly conservative gender roles, neither of which is an outcome that seems of much interest to the speaker of the Wife's Prologue. But the Wife's tale is no ordinary Arthurian romance exalting one of the king's well-known knights of the Round Table. It is a variation on the tale of the loathly lady and offers a particular kind of wish-fulfillment fantasy of marriage that complicates and deepens nearly everything presented in the Prologue.

The background to the story may be familiar, an illustrious court with Arthur and Guinevere at its center, but the protagonist is an unnamed "bacheler" (III.883) who behaves in an outrageous manner. With practically no preparation for the reader, this knight comes upon a girl and "rafte hir maidenheed" (III.888). The king's subjects clamor for justice, and the perpetrator is immediately sentenced to death "by cours of lawe, and sholde han lost his heed" (III.892), except that the queen begs the king's mercy. In response, he allows her to determine the knight's fate. In the place of the king's immediate punishment, the queen poses a question—"What thing it is that wommen most desiren" (III.905)— giving him one year and a day to find "an answere suffisant" (III.910) to satisfy the women of the court. In the short space of this opening, a number of structures have been set in place that will be important to our reading of the tale. Beginning with rape is uncommon in medieval romance, and modern readers are often left alienated and uncomfortable. Instead of ignoring the sexual assault or trying to historicize it away (as occurring in a different age with different understandings of rape), we need to read it carefully in the context of the tale's setup, even though we are given a skeletal account of what happened.[3]

The crime is little described or explained, but it is equated with two other things: the death sentence and the difficult question. There is an implicit echo of the "maidenheed" the knight stole in the sentence he is issued: "sholde han lost his heed." This repetition reads as talionic or Old Testament justice: the punishment of an eye for an eye, or here "head" for "head," which provides a certain kind of literal satisfaction in the letter of the law and of the text. One of the things that this repetition does—besides making some readers feel better by absolutely condemning his behavior—is to articulate an equivalence between the knight's head and the maiden's. Furthermore, that is exactly what the knight gets wrong in the crime: he is guilty of misperceiving her desire or will as less important than his. One

---

[3] A look at the word "rape" in the *OED* will produce interesting and provocative conversation, however. The word for sexual violation descends from a word for theft, aligning the assault on a woman's body with the theft of property against her father or husband. Legally, the charge of *raptus* could be used for sexual assault or kidnapping (yet another kind of theft of men's property). Remember that women had no legal personhood and could not bring charges in a court of law as men did. That the Wife's Tale begins with a sexual assault, "maugree her heed," is inarguable.

can manufacture a number of scenarios, some violent, others more seductive, between the opening lines of the tale. By not narrating much, the tale makes such leaps of imagination necessary, to a degree. But the knight took what he should not have, elevating his right, or desire, or power so far above hers that he assaulted her "maugree hir heed" (III.887). This phrase literally means "despite her head": that is, despite what she thought, or what she could do—in other words, he acted entirely against her will. Arthur's justice makes "hir heed," her will, exactly equivalent to his head, his will, and, in this situation, his life.

The queen's sentence does something similar. In posing the question to him she makes him consider women's desire—exactly "hir heed," what she thinks, precisely what he ignored and usurped. Not only does this form of punishment make the knight consider fully the other's desire that he so rudely trampled, it may be intended as an exquisite form of torture. As the knight soon realizes, he can find no "two creatures according infere" (III.924). The answer for which the queen asked may be impossible to acquire. No two women would answer the question in the same way; the question is important only to the extent that it forces the recognition that women, like men, have their own will and desires, and it makes him confront that recognition in a painful and extended way. Thus, the knight's quest to save himself may be intended as a year of contemplative penance in which he has to meditate on his sin before submitting to death.

But the queen's penance affords the knight the possibility of redemption, making her justice something greater than the king's vengeful sentence. At the end of a painful year of searching, the desperate knight sees a vision of dancing women and rides toward them. As he approaches, they disappear into thin air, leaving an old crone sitting on the grass. The scene is nearly archetypal: seduced by beauty, he is confronted with age and thus death. Isn't that a version of the knight's encounter with the maiden (a connection that, of course, he could not see) in the tale's opening? This old woman promises the answer to his conundrum if the knight will swear to do the very next thing she asks of him, submitting his will to hers. The knight strikes the lifesaving bargain and returns to the court with the answer to Guinevere's riddle: "Wommen desire to have sovereinetee" (III.1038), an answer that no woman present could gainsay. Sovereignty is not merely power but the kind of individual self-determination the knight had denied the maiden he assaulted. But the knight's joyful relief is short-lived: it vanishes when the old woman reminds him of his promise and asks him to marry her. Despite his involuntary revulsion, he has no choice but to acquiesce. The old woman has saved the knight from his plight, but her manner of doing so makes him relive his sin from the victim's perspective. "Maugree his heed," he must assent to this woman and "love" her.

The tale's set of equivalences and inversions does not end there. The old woman undertakes to teach him something with her words, something greater than she can make him experience with her power. She goes to bed with him after a short wedding ceremony and lectures him on the matters that cause him so much distress: her lowliness, age, and ugliness. This bed-time pillow lecture adduces the moral good that comes from these physical handicaps with a rather orthodox Christian set of values that hadn't seemed, up until now, the Wife's major concerns. After her lesson, she issues the knight one more test. Knowing his worldly desire, she asks him to choose whether he'd have her old and faithful to him or young and desirable with all the trouble that will come with it. This question demands that he weigh appearances, both personally and socially, against substance. Not knowing how to choose, the knight leaves it up to her:

> My lady and my love, and wif so dere,
> I putte me in youre wise governaunce:
> Cheseth youreself which may be most plesaunce
> And most honour to you and me also.
> I do no fors the wheither of the two,
> For as you liketh it suffiseth me.   (III.1230–35)

The logic of the narrative dictates that the pillow lecture has had its effect, confusing the knight, if nothing else, as to the terms of his nobility and supposedly refined understanding of these issues. He has learned the answer to the question he has sought yet again, this time in a most personal way. One might even say that in giving this response to the old woman, he has demonstrated an *internalization* of the logic of female sovereignty. For he has earlier *seen* the answer, when Arthur gives the queen the right to decide his fate, and *heard* the answer from the old woman, when she "rouned . . . a pistel in his ere" (III.1021). He now *performs* the answer in private as part of his future married life. This is no show for the court. But even more important than his really having found the answer to the question of women's desire is that answer's power to redeem and renew. After he has learned his lesson to the full, the old woman can now reward him with both beauty and faithfulness. Even more than Guinevere's, her feminine justice thus redeems rather than destroys, leaving the couple to live happily ever after.

The Wife's tale frustrates many modern readers, who tend to be impatient with the processes of teaching, demonstrating, and internalizing that she takes pains to coordinate, as well as the class categories (i.e., the natural superiority of the aristocracy) that the tale takes for granted. But it's not as if Chaucer doesn't realize he's done something extraordinary with the Wife of Bath's Tale. The story, like the Prologue that it follows, shows the superior wisdom of women and their experience in the patriarchal world that constrains them. Put to comic proof in the Prologue, this logic brings about deeper spiritual significance in the Tale that her deafness—signaling her inability to hear the spirit of the law beyond its letter—would have seemed to preclude. The Wife's magical narrative attains a heightened form of awareness, but it remains difficult to sustain the romance. We all have to return, eventually, to the everyday world.

That return is marked in this performance. While the voice of the practical, pragmatic Wife has been muted during much of this idealizing narrative of feminine redemption, it comes back with a vengeance in its close. Celebrating this couple's "parfit joye" (III.1258), she wishes for meek young husbands who are "fresshe abedde" and the "grace t'overbide hem" if they are not (III.1259–60). She ends by calling down a plague upon those who resist their wives' authority, sounding much more like the antagonist of the Prologue. Even after a superlative example of the world-changing power of romance and women's justice, the magic of the genre is fleeting. We are back to the "real world" of the Wife's experiential voice.

The Wife of Bath casts a long shadow in *The Canterbury Tales*. She is its most memorable pilgrim figure, not simply because of her uniquely human voice and feminine rhetoric but because of the effects she has in and on the larger work. For the Wife's Prologue not only prompts the return of the squabbling Friar and Summoner when her tale is done but sparks a series of stories—familiarly known as "the Marriage Group"—that continue to debate the role of women and the nature of marriage in the fragments that follow hers.

THE FRIAR'S PROLOGUE
AND TALE

The Friar's and Summoner's Tales are a close-knit pair of rivalrous satires. Taught and studied less frequently than many other Canterbury tales, they are somewhat difficult to assimilate to a coherent reading of the poem. The two dramatically follow and thematically disrupt the Wife of Bath by changing the subject. They cut off her discussion of sovereignty in marriage, deferring a conversation that later will be resumed by the Clerk, Merchant, and Franklin. In doing so, they provide a hiatus before the so-called Marriage Group. At the same time, they are also tightly connected to her story by the manuscript tradition as well as by the conversational drama in the links. That is strong evidence that they are indeed intended to follow her performance, even if they pose problems for those viewing this section of *The Canterbury Tales* as a debate on marriage. Once again, the story collection shows signs of being incomplete, its organization still unsettled in Chaucer's mind.

More crucially, their literary contribution to the collection, and thus the expectations they excite, is uncertain because they are clear ad hominem attacks. Each story registers as a sarcastic hit at the other's profession with what has been called a "satiric anecdote" in which rapacity provides the principal motive. They are mean jokes on the gullibility of the wicked and are full of tendentious verbal quibbles that are hermetically sealed from the pretense of game and play that underwrites the rest of the *Tales*.

These conditions have made it difficult for the Friar's (and the Summoner's) readers to discern a firm literary frame of reference or to name the tale's genre with confidence. The tales resemble fabliaux, because the prideful trickster in each is tricked in an ultimately self-revealing way. This structure only enhances their function as exempla illustrating a truth about each social type, even as each falls short of appealing to a wider audience by exemplifying a more universally applicable moral, as exempla are wont to do. Indeed, the Friar's closing moral—"The leoun sit in his await alway / To slee the innocent if that he may" (III.1657–58)—seems to miss the story's mark entirely. Its greedy and stupid summoner could hardly be considered an "innocent." Instead, the Friar's Tale illustrates a far more local truth: "Pardee, ye may wel knowe by the name / That of a somnour may no good be said" (III.1280–81), a claim that can be read in more than one way. His tale dramatizes both the valueless speech of summoners ("no good may be said *by* a summoner") and the valueless nature of summoners themselves ("no good may be said *about* a summoner"). But even more importantly, as Derek Pearsall notes, "The real force of the satire comes from showing the Summoner and the Friar to be gullible fools, both of them, what is more, gullible in the same way, in mistaking the surface for the reality, the literal for the inward meaning. An implication of puppet-like emptiness, even of spiritual deadness, can thus be left to attach to them, as well as stupidity."[1] An extended version of this emptiness will appear later in the Pardoner's performance. The Friar–Summoner pair is, perhaps, a sketch in preparation for the Pardoner's more fully dramatized self-presentation.

The Friar's Prologue begins its attack on the Summoner with an evasive gesture that theatrically commends the Wife on the important matters "touched" by her tale but ultimately puts the Wife in her place (in the pejorative and aggressive sense of that phrase). One might think that the Friar is alluding to the moral and ethical terms of the old woman's pillow lecture, but his response only pretends to appreciate it. Dismissing the kind of "difficultee" her tale treated in favor of "game" (III.1272, 1275), the Friar is not so gamesome; his scowl or "louring cheere" (III.1266) indicates that he is smoldering in anger, all the time maneuvering for an

---

[1] Derek Pearsall, *The Canterbury Tales* (1985; London: Routledge, 1993), 217.

opportunity to attack the Summoner. Both of them have been waiting their chance to speak and seemingly ignore much of what the Wife had to say. This kind of indirection provides *The Canterbury Tales* with some of its vitality, driving the tales in lively and unexpected directions. For it is by means of such seeming happenstance that Chaucer avoids the deadening repetitiveness or overly restrictive formulas of other tale collections. There's no deep relation between the Wife's narration and the arguments of these two figures.[2] And yet, the very shallowness of their opportunistic interruption adds a certain depth to the whole.

The Friar illustrates the corrupt nature of summoners by providing a short narrative example such as might be heard in a sermon. As a preacher and one licensed to hear confession, the Friar would know many stories like this one, which he could use as embellishment on any number of occasions. The story told in the Friar's Tale circulated in popular tradition; its earliest written version appears in a collection of exempla most likely intended for use by preachers.[3] Its two signature features also appear in the Friar's story: a meeting with the devil and the distinction between a "heartfelt curse" and words uttered in mere frustration. In these versions, an *avocatus* (an administrative figure, not a lawyer per se) meets a devil and urges that the devil claim what is offered to him when, in frustration, both a farmer curses his horse and a woman her child, verbally sending them "to the devil." But since these curses are not meant, the devil cannot act upon them. However, when one of these figures curses the avocatus, the devil has full power to claim him because that curse is sincere. A manipulator of accusation and false charges, the avocatus is undone by the charged language of those he defrauds.

Already we can see the game Chaucer makes of this exemplum by further elaborating on the similarity of the devil and the Summoner (who

---

[2] This lack of a connection has not stopped anyone from trying to manufacture one. The best of these is Penn R. Szittya, "The Green Yeoman as Loathly Lady: The Friar's Parody of the Wife of Bath's Tale," *PMLA* 90.3 (1975): 386–94

[3] Caesarius of Histerbach in *The Sources and Analogues of the Canterbury Tales*, ed. Robert M. Correale and Mary Hamel, vol. 1 (Cambridge: D. S. Brewer, 2002), 88–89.

plays the part of the avocatus), making a drama of a telling self-recognition out of their sworn friendship to one another. The devil is not merely a figure who has power in the tale (as in the prototype exemplum): he is also a revelatory source of interest to the Summoner, for the devil is a more perfect version of the "bailiff" the Summoner pretends to be. Chaucer's tale enlarges the scope of the exemplum with a detailed portrait of the system underwriting the Summoner's bad name, the corruption that makes "summonsing" a byword for extortion (III.1301–74). It is a part of the story we tend to read through quickly and not very attentively, because we take its details about archdeacons and bishops to be mere background. But the logic of corruption portrayed in this opening—in which holding back enables one to catch a larger prey—pervades the rest of the tale.

First there is the archdeacon's court and the work it does for the bishop. The church maintains an elaborate hierarchy, from the pope in Rome down to the priests who tend each neighborhood parish. Between these points we find Christendom divided into telescoping geographical sectors. Bishoprics, a subsection of this structure, were organized around cathedrals, each housing the seat of a bishop. Under each bishop were a number of deacons, headed by an archdeacon, to help him more locally administer his bishopric. The spiritual services provided by the bishop include governance over moral behavior and punishment of transgressions, some of which Chaucer lists:

> In punisshing of fornicacioun,
> Of wicchecraft and eek of bawderye,
> Of defamacion and avoutrye,
> Of chirche reves and of testaments,
> Of contractes and of lak of sacraments,
> Of usure, and of simonye also[.]   (III.1304–09)

And, most of all, of "lecchours dide he grettest wo" (III.1310). One who transgressed against the civil law faces charges in civil court; one who transgressed against moral law is summoned to ecclesiastical court. The summoner, at the lower end of this hierarchy, delivers summonses to individuals to appear before the bishop's bench. And from the catalogue of transgressions provided above, the summoner has some rather provocative material to work with and upon.

But this scheme represents only the formal structure of the ecclesiastical court. The Summoner also has his own network of colleagues and subordinates to help him get his job done: a bevy of pimps, prostitutes, and informants to tell him who is susceptible to his influence and likely to offer a bribe to keep them out of trouble. This beginning is easy to gloss over, but it sets up the rest of the story, giving us a sense of what the Summoner is looking out for when he is described as "ever waiting on his prey" (III.1376). The Summoner essentially has two jobs, an official one and one that directs the power of his office to his own personal profit—a form of manipulation rendered in terms of language and writing. Before men may be brought to ecclesiastical court, their names are written "in the erchedeknes book" (III.1318). And for a price, this Summoner will find a way to make sure that those names are struck out. In fact, he often makes that offer to individuals whose names have not even been written there. The effortlessness with which such writing is changed lures the Summoner into thinking that all language can be as easily corrupted. But there is a truth to what various figures in the tale say that remains stable, beyond the manipulations of inscription and erasure. Such truth is seen in two forms: straightforwardly, as the curses of the carter and the old woman, and more figurally, in the conversations between the Summoner and the fiend he happens to meet upon on the road.

The Friar's Tale narrates a chance meeting between two men, each pretending to be a "bailly" (III.1392), which we might remember is the Host's surname. But neither, strictly speaking, is a bailiff—that is, an estate agent who collects rents and revenue. Both use the label to hide their real occupations, which are bywords for fraud and corruption. Insofar as both "summoner" and "fiend" can be figured as "bailiffs," they are rendered equivalent, if not identical, to one another. That identification plays out in their instant recognition of each other (III.1395–96) and in the oath of brotherhood that they swear and that the summoner upholds (III.1405). Over the course of the tale, these two men will also swear to share their profits, revealing a deep equivalence between them—ultimately as fiends in Satan's company.

At first, the two are cautious because they are feeling each other out, scheming for some profit through the acquaintance. The Summoner does not recognize the demonic signs in this yeoman's attire—black-fringed hat and green jacket—nor in the location of his home "fer in the north contree" (III.1413). Both have been associated with the devil. And the Summoner pays little attention to the bow and arrows he sports, which clearly mark him as a hunter. Absorbed in hunting his own prey, the Summoner fails to recognize any danger to himself. Yet all of the yeoman's words ring with a delicious double meaning. He assures the Summoner that they shall one day see each other at his northern dwelling: "Er we departe I shal thee so wel wisse / That of myn hous ne shaltou never misse" (III.1415–16). "Wisse," from the infinitive *wissen*, "to know," implies at least two different levels of understanding in this brief statement: the first, a simple kind of information (directions to a new companion's abode), and another, more ominous foreshadowing of his similarity to the Summoner. We can read the yeoman's knowledge in two ways. He will make his house so well-known ("wel wisse") that the Summoner won't be able to mistake it, *and* the demon knows the Summoner so well that he won't be able to avoid escaping the demon's house—that is, hell. The Summoner has been preyed upon, because he is already fully known and recognized from the start.

Almost immediately, both men confide in each other, complaining of the difficult straits in which their superiors put them that force them to live by "extorcions" (III.1429). Neither has any qualms of conscience regarding their actions, and they continually reveal to each other the dishonesty by which they profit, speaking truthfully about their falsehood to other men and to their superiors. The longer the conversation continues, the deeper into the duplicity we get, until the Summoner, who would not

reveal his professional name "for verray filthe and shame" (III.1393), asks
the yeoman for his (III.1444). Here is the yeoman's blunt response:

> I am a feend: my dwelling is in helle.
> And here I ride aboute my purchasing
> To wite wher men wol yive me anything;
> My purchas is th'effect of al my rente.
> Looke how thou ridest for the same entente,
> To winne good—thou rekkest never how:
> Right so fare I, for the ride wolde I now
> Unto the worldes ende for a preye.   (III.1448–55)

Telling the Summoner exactly what he is about, this language pushes
toward metaphoricity and figurality (as in his "purchasing") even as it des-
ignates an unmistakably literal truth. He is a fiend, whose dwelling is in
hell, and he rides "now" to the ends of the earth in search of his prey, giving his yeoman's garb and weaponry the deadly meaning that did not
seem clear to the summoner before. But the language of earning (purchase and rent) is still figural, to some extent, and it seems to color the
sense of "prey." This discourse of collecting and hunting both obfuscates
and defines the trickery that the fiend typically uses and is using here on
the Summoner. The Summoner's response is perplexing, because he at
once comprehends *and* seems to ignore the meaning of what the fiend has
said. Unfazed by the idea that this yeoman is a devil, the Summoner
inquires about the logic of shape-shifting, wondering if fiends have any
natural form in hell. It never occurs to the Summoner that *he* is the prey
being stalked by the devil in the form of a companionate yeoman, who
mirrors back the shared disguise (of bailiff) which the Summoner uses and
by which he is thus deceived.

The play of literal and figurative in this story makes this scene confusing. Up to this point, the demon and the Summoner have been concealing
themselves in figural language. In metaphorizing their activities to the
work of "baillies," they have somewhat hidden their identities, even as

they have identified with each other's intent. But such metaphorizing is not what catches out the Summoner. As the tale progresses, these two "confess" to each other their extortions and their intent until the devil reveals himself. The Summoner appears captivated by the spectacular image of his own deceptive power and, in turn, inquires as to its extent and limitations. This attention comes across as a kind of comic blindness to the danger of the very thing that so enthralls him. It is both a wicked irony and a childish insult to depict the Summoner seriously pondering the shape-shifting question. In the Summoner's Tale that follows, a similarly ridiculous yet logically probing question will preoccupy the friar at the center of its story.

Despite the blunt revelation of the yeoman's fiendish nature, the Summoner continues to hold his "trouthe" to his sworn fellow (III.1525), refusing to forsake him because, it seems, doing so would be forsaking himself and his own purpose. The tale turns into a drama of intentionality, illustrating the division between meaningless and sincere oaths. In what follows, the two meet a carter, who curses his horses and cart in frustration, and an innocent old woman, Mabley, whom all along the Summoner had planned to extort. She curses him and sends him to the devil with full intent, bringing the story to its abrupt and comic close. The Summoner's oath to "holde compaignye" with the yeoman (III.1521) is also heartfelt, despite the fact that it ultimately condemns him to hell. That is an outcome that the Summoner apparently cannot help embracing no matter the guise in which he tries to conceal himself.

This attention to language derives at least in part from the practice of confession. Both the Friar's and Summoner's tales show both an exploration of and a dependence on the power of confession, a mechanism that, yet again, connects them to the Pardoner's tour de force narration. The Friar and the Summoner ask us to consider, while they deploy, the power of confession in their tales. One can even analyze their relation to each other through it. The Friar is empowered to hear confession; he's the only legitimate figure, other than a priest, who can do so. And this capability puts him into direct competition with the Summoner, who depends on the sinfulness of others for his income. For it is only in such a state of sin that the Summoner can extort his victims.

As we have seen in the General Prologue, the Friar's absolution might be so pleasant, and he might be so understanding to penitents otherwise a bit hard of heart, that some prefer him to their parish priest (I.221–30). Remember that friars live by begging for their sustenance, and that it would be customary to show one's gratitude for the absolution a friar bestows—and his understanding for one's weaknesses that he might forgive—with a small token, a donation that helps keep these beggars working in this way. The Friar described in the General Prologue understands this situation very well:

> For unto a povre ordre for to yive
> Is signe that a man is wel yshrive;
> For if he yaf, he dorste make avaunt
> He wiste that a man was repentaunt;
> For many a man so hard is of his herte
> He may nat weepe though him sore smerte[.]   (I.225–30)

Not only does the size of the gift demonstrate how well-confessed the giver is (a reflection of the worth of the Friar), but sometimes the gift itself is the sign of repentance made by those otherwise too stoic to show their emotions. The signification of the gift slides rather easily here from showing gratitude for the Friar's work (probing into one's sinfulness and bringing forth one's confession) to substituting for it. His "esy" and more "pleasant" (I.223, 222) confessional style thus makes him more powerful "than a curat" (I.219) and further makes for a rivalry with others in the business of forgiveness and its debts, such as priests and summoners. For if the Friar gets to an individual first, there's little guilt left over on which the Summoner can prey.

In the Friar's Tale, the Summoner winds up "confessing" to a devil in disguise, revealing his deep affinity with that creature and the evil he represents. But the devil met by the Summoner is a "better" version of himself in the sense that he's a more honest surrogate for the power he represents. The demon in the story works for, rather than against, Satan, whereas the Summoner only abuses his office. He defrauds the church as much as he defrauds its members, and for his personal gain. It may be too much to say summoners are no better than devils. They may, in fact, be considerably worse.

THE SUMMONER'S PROLOGUE
AND TALE

We may not find the moral of the Friar's Tale particularly apt, but the story has gotten the better of the Summoner, who at its end "lik an aspen leef . . . quook for ire" (III.1667). He shows that he is particularly piqued at the devilish, hellish aspects of the Friar's Tale by going one better in full scatological mode, with an illustration of where friars get such expertise about the devil. Not only do friars know hell better than summoners, they have a special residence there close to Satan's body: "Right so as bees out swarmen from an hive, / Out of the develes ers ther gonne drive / Twenty thousand freres on a route" (III.1693–95). These depths will be plumbed, so to speak, throughout the Summoner's story, a piece of satire that details the intellectual probing and material grasping of friars and is based in a literal exploration of the filth of avarice.

The sources for Chaucer's story are uncertain. One narrative analogue for its governing idea actually presents its inversion.[1] In that tale, a Cistercian monk taken to heaven searches for his brethren, who seem to be nowhere, only to find them nestled under the cloak of the Virgin. The vignette thus depicts the special status of friars in idealized form, which the Summoner's Tale wittily reverses. Sentiment against friars, or antifraternal sentiment, was rife in Chaucer's day, particularly in Lollard reformist writings, which are critical of the corrupt avariciousness of the

---

[1] Caesarius of Histerbach's *Dialogus miraculorum* (ca. 1223), a collection of miracle stories, contains this narrative of the friars and the Virgin.

church. And this tale, in particular, focuses its attention on the special status that friars presume as those whose relation to Christ is closest because they live in imitation of the apostles. In any case, the attribution of this elaborate and inverted exemplum to the Summoner, in careful response to the Friar's Tale, is nothing short of brilliant. It is an illustration of vice raised to the status of an extended set of double entendres, or plays (both in sense and in sound) upon words, set in a narrative in which the literal and the figurative are continually conflated.

Irate at the Friar's assault on the name of summoner, he turns his anger into the very subject of his story and its method of fictional revenge. The tale features both a sermon on ire and an angry rebuttal of its platitudes through a false and humiliating trick. Like the Friar's, the Summoner's Tale offers an extended description of its target and his unsavory practices. Here we meet Daun John, one of the most successful beggars in his confraternal house, visiting the home of one of his clients, Thomas, to try to fleece the sick man. The details of this character portrait are arranged to make this friar look greedy, arrogant, and slightly effeminate. A large part of the humor lies in the features of the friar's stereotype. Not exactly the amorous and convivial figure described in the General Prologue, the friar in the Summoner's Tale is the Friar's limp imitation, loquacious and pompously learned. He openly flirts with Thomas's wife in a greasy performance of courtly manners that are meant to show off a status he is not supposed to have.

The striking feature of a friar is his avowed life of poverty. Often called a "limitour" (III.209), a friar is limited or restricted to a particular area in which he is allowed to preach and to beg for alms. He is expected to live off such donations, sharing them with his brethren communally. Essentially, friars work for the spiritual good of others whose gifts help sustain them. They do not work directly for their own keep. In addition, friars are the only figures, other than priests, who are allowed to hear confession and prescribe penance. This function makes for some rivalrous competition for clients between the two groups. Since a friar is an itinerant beggar (in contrast to the priest, who collects a tithe from his parishioners and lives in the parish with them), his payment is more directly connected to the act of confession and the show of repentance by the individual confessing. It is a small step to making forgiveness a cash transaction. As the General Prologue narrator repeats from his conversation with the Friar, "in stede of weeping and prayeres, / Men moote yive silver to the povre freres" (I.231–32). Daun John capitalizes on this slippage.

As traveling preachers, friars were also literary performers and scholars of scripture. This tale depends particularly on its friar's pride in his learnedness despite all claims of simplicity and humility, and it will turn on some fairly intellectual concerns with various arts of language and science, at one point called "ars-metrike" (III.2222). Daun John is a familiar of the family he visits in the tale. He has certainly been to their house frequently. One detail often mentioned is John's act of shooing away the cat from the cozy bench. Cats find the most comfortable place in the house, and with this gesture the friar thus puts himself in that privileged spot. It seems like something he does often, whether visiting Thomas or others, since he considers himself an entitled guest. And it reveals his self-importance as well as his overfamiliarity, both of which mark him as a hypocrite.

This "simple" friar also speaks in three languages: not just the English they all use but also French and Latin. To both husband and wife, he responds "*je vous di*" (I say to you; III.1838) in a pretentious and affected way. He also seasons his moral wisdom with a Latin phrase from the Bible: "*Cor meum eructavit*" (my heart has uttered [lit., "erupted"]; III.1934), which foreshadows later eruptions in the story. Thus, friar John throws about both his learning and his cosmopolitanism as he pretends to quiet simplicity. Accepting the wife's invitation to dinner with a performance of concern for the death of the creatures that make up its dishes, he mentions a set of rarefied items of which he could eat but a nibble: the liver of a capon, a roasted pig's head, some fine white bread. Daun John has expensive tastes for a man who begs to get his sustenance. Such hypocrisy is of a piece with this story's general depiction of the friar, who uses the recent death of the couple's newborn baby to illustrate the importance of the confraternity. He manages to turn his neglect in their time of need into a sign of his superior worth—for, of course, his entire convent saw this child "er that half an hour / After his deeth . . . born to blisse" (III.1856–57), a vision attesting to how "oure orisons been more effectuel, / And more we seen of Cristes secree thinges / Than burel folk" (III.1870–72). Nothing, it seems, deters the friar from reminding Thomas that he could (and perhaps should) be making the friar an offering. Even Thomas's frustration that he has not seen the fruit of his generosity to "diverse manere freres" (III.1950) is turned against him by Daun John, who accuses him of faithlessness:

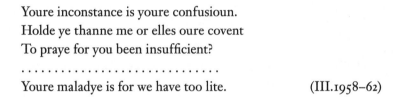

Youre inconstance is youre confusioun.
Holde ye thanne me or elles oure covent
To praye for you been insufficient?
. . . .
Youre maladye is for we have too lite.   (III.1958–62)

All conversational roads lead, eventually, to the idea of donating to the friar's house: it is the answer to all problems and concerns.

Not only does Daun John take every opportunity of enjoying himself under the guise of self-abnegation, he also lectures his hosts on the virtues of fraternal renunciation, which is what underwrites the superiority of their prayers. A sizable part of the tale involves its impromptu sermon on ire, full of illustrative examples and ending, of course, with a request for a donation. The lecture only infuriates Thomas—"This sike man weex wel neigh wood for ire" (III.2121)—which is itself ironic, given the topic of the sermon and its presumed purpose of monetary gain. Thomas's anger prompts him to humiliate the friar by rewarding the hot air of his sermon in kind and with a foul stench. Taking the opportunity to make good on the friar's language of "fundament" and "grop[ing]" one's conscience (III.2103, 1817), Thomas sends him in search of a secret gift "binethe my buttok[,] . . . / A thing that I have hid in privetee"

(III.2142–43). The tale thus makes a scatological turn, locating its discourse in excrement, anality, and the lowest of bodily functions. These terms will be made into the basest of humiliations and the substance of an intellectual problem that the friar takes astonishingly seriously.

Part of what drives the story beyond this point of having received the insult of the fart is the transfer of anger from Thomas to Daun John. Having solemnly promised to share what he gets from Thomas with all of his brethren, Daun John is full of ire, perplexed as to how "to parte that wol nat departed be" (III.2214). The answer to the problem is no less ridiculous than the problem itself, and it is solved by a child servant. The boy, Jankin, devises a scheme to have old Thomas sit atop the center of a cartwheel with each of the twelve friars of John's fraternity at the ends of its spokes, ready to share equally in both the smell and the sound made by the fart. The comedy here lies at least partially in the seriousness with which such an insult has been taken and the scholarly treatment it receives for the remainder of the tale. Not only is the friar mocked by the gift of the fart itself, a foul emission of hot air in recompense for his windy sermon, but he is further demeaned by the sham intellectualism of the debate. His status as a "maister" (III.2184), a master of arts conferred by schooling, is put in question as he grapples with this conundrum—how to divide something that is indivisible. Playing on and debasing theological questions debated in schools and universities in the Middle Ages—for example, "How many angels may dance on the head of a pin?"—this concern in the Summoner's Tale mocks esoteric questions about the infinite reach of the divine, as well as the ridiculousness of the intellectuals who pretend to contemplate such matters. Going even further in this vein, the cartwheel solution draws on the iconography of the descent of the Holy Spirit to the twelve apostles at Pentecost, "that great rushing of wind with tongues of fire."[2]

---

[2] Peter W. Travis, "Thirteen Ways of Listening to a Fart: Noise in Chaucer's Summoner's Tale," *Exemplaria* 16.2 (2004): 13. The parody of Pentecost was first identified by Alan Levitan, "The Parody of Pentecost in Chaucer's *Summoner's Tale*," *University of Toronto Quarterly* 40.2 (1971): 236–46.

It is nearly impossible to read the Summoner's Tale apart from the Friar's; the two are intertwined in theme and dramatic interaction. Both tales are concerned with language at a deep level. Their satiric figures manipulate language duplicitously. And yet in both tales terms are used ironically in ways that exceed the understanding of the figures within them. The disguised devil in the Friar's Tale certainly speaks a truth that the Summoner does not understand, as when he explains that the forms assumed by fiends are those "most able ... oure preyes for to take" (III.1472). Since the fiend in the Friar's Tale disguises himself as a "bailly" and a yeoman with whom the tale's summoner identifies, it is an image of himself that undoes the Summoner. Similarly, the figures in the Summoner's Tale have no idea of the full meaning of what they are saying. In mentioning "ars-metrike" and claiming that *Cor meum eructavit*, the fictional friar puns in ways beyond his knowledge. The nobleman at the end of the story tries to comfort the friar despite the "odious meschief" (III.2190) done to him: "Distempre you noght: ye be my confessour; / Ye been the salt of th'erthe and the savour" (III.2195–96). Although he has no idea what the "blasphemy" that has been perpetrated on the friar may be, his language is replete with scent and flavor ("odious," "salt," and "savour") and thus without his knowledge applies perfectly to the sense-shocking odiferousness of Thomas's gift. The governing intelligence here comes from outside the fiction of the story, located in the consciousness of someone who is already jaded by the rapaciousness of these clerics and who finds humor in celebrating their stupidity. Its logic might be summed up as a kind of ars-metrike, an art of measurement and calculation that wittily plays on bodily humor—here a pun sounded on "arse," from where the vengeful calculation emanates.

The self-contained nature of these two tales can be seen in the ending of the Summoner's Tale. Chaucer did not append an epilogue concluding their debate or the drama of fragment III; instead, it ends with the tale itself: "My tale is doon: we been almost at towne" (III.2294). The next story, the Clerk's, returns to thematic issues and source materials from the Wife of Bath's Prologue; and for that reason, the tales of the Friar and the Summoner (under the pressure of time) are often skipped in under-graduate classes. The comic interlude they provide is no less entertaining despite disrupting the emerging marriage debate in this part of the *Tales*. Moreover, its concerns with language, intent, and the corrupting power of money do engage with other parts of *The Canterbury Tales*. These satires may be dramatically isolated because of the ways in which Chaucer was composing, still shifting and changing the positions of his materials and revising the links, but they are thematically central to the larger work.

THE CLERK'S PROLOGUE
AND TALE

The Clerk's Tale begins a new fragment that is neither fully linked to nor sharply separated from what has come before. Its opening could be fitted to any number of situations once Chaucer decided on its immediate predecessor. But there is little doubt that the tale is meant to be closely coordinated with the Wife of Bath's performance. Harry Bailly addresses the Clerk by wittily castigating his aloofness from the game and reminding him of his earlier "assent" to its rules in the following terms:

> Ye ride as coy and stille as dooth a maide
> Were newe spoused, sitting at the bord.
> This day ne herde I of your tonge a word—
> I trowe ye studye aboute som sophime. (IV.2–5)

It may be customary to admire clerks for a maidenly demeanor,[1] but the Host's embellishment, "newe spoused," tilts toward condescension, not to mention the wifely submissions that will shortly consume everyone's attention. The Host assumes that the Clerk's silence comes from his studiousness, imagining that he's likely thinking about theological matters, "som sophime." Such academic disputes in the universities and the schools

---

[1] Helen Cooper notes "the commonplace comparison of the ideal clerk with a maiden," likely a mark of clerical humility, in her *The Canterbury Tales*, Oxford Guides to Chaucer, 2nd ed. (Oxford: Oxford UP, 1996), 185.

were both serious intellectual matters and concerns—such as the difficulty presented by the Summoner's Tale "to parte that wol nat departed be" (III.2214)—that practical businessmen like the Tabard Host might find a wasteful expenditure of time. This simple opening to the Clerk's Tale thus forms loose connections to the preceding fragment through some difficult "impossibles," a concept that reminds us not only of the fraught questions of the Friar's and Summoner's Tales but also of the Wife of Bath's challenge. Here is what she posed, specifically in terms of clerical authority:

> For trusteth wel, it is an impossible
> That any clerk wol speke good of wives,
> But if it be of holy saintes lives,
> Ne of noon other womman never the mo[.]   (III.688–91)

The Clerk's Tale offers precisely what the Wife called "an impossible": a story that speaks well (i.e., "good") about a wife, indeed one that depicts an impossibly good wife. It is the story of patient Griselda. Emerging from the folktale sources behind Boccaccio's *Decameron*, where it holds pride of place as the final tale of the last day, the Griselda story was widely popular. Petrarch so admired it that he translated it into Latin (thereby exalting it), a version that Chaucer follows closely.

We've seen quite a few clerks in the preceding tales, especially the fabliaux, and these young men have hardly restricted themselves to scholarly pursuits. The fabliaux clerks as well as those characterized by the Wife in her Prologue have had decidedly worldly interests. Perhaps with such precedents in mind, the Host mocks the Clerk for his lack of conviviality; he does so by characterizing him as a newly married girl, one who sits frozen "at the bord" (the wedding dinner table)—waiting, that is, for the momentous first night with her new husband. The metaphor is not only effeminizing but also aggressive. There are other images the Host might have used for the Clerk's studious reticence. The Host's aggression here makes for just the kind of challenge the Clerk's Tale is designed to address.

The story that follows has been almost universally recognized as one of the best of the Canterbury tales (even if one of the most frustrating for modern readers), an extraordinary exemplum that exalts women, and specifically a wife, by figural means. It is another of the rhyme royal tales, set in that elevated metrical form to convey its solemnity and seriousness, or what the Clerk will call "sadnesse" (IV.452). His story indeed relays a rather sad tale of feminine suffering, but that is not what the Clerk means by using that word. "Sad" is one of the central terms of his tale, where it means "grave" and "serious," not merely "unhappy" (*OED*, s.v. "sad," adj. 3.b). But over the course of the Clerk's Tale, the emotional toll of Walter's tests, "hir sadnesse for to knowe" (IV.452), probes the limits of Griselda's emotional as well as ethical endurance. And the Clerk accounts for it in affective terms, too, wondering what "merveilous desir" (IV.454) drives a husband to put his wife to so much unnecessary suffering. Our frustration with Walter's tests does not arise merely out of that narrative or out of our historical and cultural difference from its moral certainties but is actively fueled by the Clerk himself, such as when he asks:

> What needed it
> Hire for to tempte, and alway more and more,
> Though some men praise it for a subtil wit?
> But as for me, I saye that yvele it sit
> T'assaye a wif whan that it is no neede,
> And putten hire in anguissh and in drede.   (IV.457–62)

These first-person statements on the narrator's part have garnered a great deal of critical attention. The Clerk alerts us to what Griselda emphatically cannot: the sadistic unfairness of Walter's tests. For Griselda has promised never to gainsay any of Walter's decisions by verbal recrimination or even "frowning countenaunce" (IV.356). Much to the Wife of Bath's chagrin, one would imagine, the Clerk narratively revels in the suffering ("anguissh and . . . drede") of Griselda, at the same time that he distances himself from it. Since Griselda is forbidden to show any dissent or emotion because of the vow she made to Walter at their wedding, the Clerk is the only means by which Griselda's anguished emotional life is ever known. Just as Walter does within the tale, the Clerk gets to enjoy exactly what he disavows.

Like the Wife of Bath's Tale and perhaps in direct response to it, the Clerk's Tale is also about sovereignty in marriage, but here that power is configured in starkly different ways. The wife in the Clerk's story does not want sovereignty except insofar as she can give it away, ceding it completely to her husband:

> But as ye wol yourself, right so wol I:
> And here I swere that never willingly
> In werk ne thought I nil you disobeye,
> For to be deed, though me were looth to deye.   (IV.361–64)

These are Griselda's terse wedding vows, which make up the most succinct form of her promise to Walter. Such claims to obedience become longer and more elaborate each time he tests her: when he orders his sergeant to take her infant daughter from her (presumably to be killed), and then her son (to meet the same fate), and finally when he divorces her to marry another, returning her to her father's house.

In the face of these humiliations, Griselda remains steadfast to her word:

> "I have," quod she, "said thus and ever shal:
> I wol nothing ne nil nothing, certayn,
> But as you list; noght greveth me at al
> Though that my doghter and my sone be slain—
> At youre comandement, this is to sayn.
> I have nat had no part of children twaine
> But first siknesse and after wo and paine.
> . . . .
> And certes, if I hadde prescience

Youre wil to knowe er ye youre lust me tolde,
I wolde it doon withouten necligence.
But now I woot youre lust and what ye wolde,
Al youre plesaunce ferm and stable I holde.
For wiste I that my deeth wolde doon you ese,
Right gladly wolde I dien, you to plese."   (IV.645–65)

Griselda's own language addresses the broader meanings of the action, and particularly of marriage, embedded in this story. The first thing to notice here is that in this tale, marriage is far more than a union of a man and woman, or mere "romance." It stands as a figure of more important relationships, guaranteeing duty, obedience, submission, and service—on Walter's part as well as Griselda's. Neither Walter nor Griselda comes to marriage via a conventional route. Walter marries not for his personal pleasure but to satisfy his subjects, who are concerned for the future. Marriage is desired to produce political stability in the form of an heir, who will ensure that no "straunge successour sholde take / [Walter's] heritage" (IV.138–39). Similarly, Griselda has no personal desire to marry and remains entirely unaware she is being considered as a bride for the marquis.

Walter's proposal is itself a set of "demandes" (IV.348), an unproblematic set of questions that make particular demands of her:[2]

[B]e ye redy with good herte
To al my lust, and that I freely may,
As me best thinketh, do you laughe or smerte,
And never ye to grucche it night ne day?
And eek whan I saye "Ye" ne saye nat "Nay,"
Neither by word ne frowning countenaunce;
Swere this, and here I swere oure alliaunce.   (IV.351–57)

---

[2] In calling these questions "demandes," Chaucer reminds us of the *demandes d'amour* of French debate poetry—one of which appears at the close of part one of the Knight's Tale, while another ends the Franklin's Tale.

Her only promise to Walter is a promise of radical obedience: no "love," no "cherish," no "till death do us part." In the demands made of Griselda in these questions and, more emphatically, in her response (quoted earlier) in which she offers her death as the ultimate gift to Walter's pleasure, we can see what forms the assurance of her absolute obedience to him and what the tale calls "love" (IV.667).

The stark contrast between the impersonal nature of this marital union—joining a ruler and his lowest, most humble subject for the sake of his people—and the personal, nearly whimsical characterization of the behavior prohibited in it (grouching, laughing, frowning, smarting, and talking back) disrupts any secure sense of the tale's plot and orients us toward its symbolic function. Drawing on well-known stereotypes of quarrelsome wives, the tale operates in a symbolic economy in which marriage is a figure for more perfect relationships governed by consent.

The marital relationship works as an important metaphor in theology and grounds an understanding of Christ's relationship to the church, figured as his bride by the exegesis written on the biblical Song of Songs.[3] But even in the world of Saluzzo depicted in the tale, the marriage of Walter and Griselda means something beyond what the two of them "feel." Marriage is a political act, a truth that the Knight's Tale knows as well. Theseus's bride is the captive queen of the Amazons; Emelye is the spoils of a tournament, and her marriage cements a peace between Athens and Thebes. The Knight's Tale struggles to overwrite the political exigencies of marriage with a story of personal desire and fate-altering love. So too does the Wife of Bath's Tale recast the aristocratic privilege of its rapist-knight into an ethical problem. Both tales "know" that social class and politics override almost anything else, and the fantasies that they produce over and against social reality only ever reinforce the political status quo, a sure demonstration of subversion

---

[3] The Song of Songs or Song of Solomon is part of the Hebrew Bible. The poems were read as an allegory of Christ's loving relationship to the church and God's relationship to the soul.

and its containment. Marriage is equally a part of this system in *The Canterbury Tales*.

Walter's marriage is not merely a political act designed to assure his subjects, it's a drama produced and arranged for them. Walter's subjects so earnestly desire for him to wed and produce an heir that they offer to choose him a wife "born of the gentileste and of the meeste / Of al this land" (IV.131–32). But when Walter assents to their request that he marry, he releases them of that burden by exacting yet another promise from them:

> Lat me allone in chesing of my wif:
> That charge upon my bak I wol endure.
> But I praye you—and charge upon youre lif—
> That what wif that I take, ye me assure
> To worshipe hire whil that hir lif may dure,
> In word and werk, bothe heer and everywhere,
> As she an emperoures doghter were.
>
> And ferthermore, this shal ye swere: that ye
> Again my chois shal neither grucche ne strive.
> For sith I shal forgoon my libertee
> At youre requeste, as evere mote I thrive,
> Theras myn herte is set, ther wol I wive.
> And but ye wol assente in swich manere,
> I praye you speketh namore of this matere.   (IV.162–75)

Walter's assent to the wishes of his subjects amounts to a challenge to them—to accept whatever wife he chooses without complaint. In warning them not to grutch or fight against his decision, he uses the same logic and some of the same language as appear in his "demandes" to Griselda when he gains her consent. The parallelism of the scenes is important, showing the marital metaphor in action. In taking a wife, Walter marries his people. Aligning the consent and subjugation of citizens and wife in the same act and with the same language, Chaucer reveals the metaphorics of marriage-as-political-formation all the more clearly.

But the drama in Walter's behavior is more literal too, for he performs his marriage for his subjects, and they watch as his audience. Having gained their assent to his choice, he picks the lowest-born woman in the village to wed in a spectacle designed to surprise and delight. Walter literally stage-manages a dramatic production for them, with costuming, props, and music arranged in advance:

> But nathelees this markis hath doon make,
> Of gemmes set in gold and in asure,
> Brooches and ringes for Griseldis sake;
> And of hir clothing took he the mesure
> Of a maide lik to hir stature,
> And eek of othere ornementes alle
> That unto swich a wedding sholde falle.
> . . . .
> This royal markis richeliche arrayed,
> Lordes and ladies in his compaignye,
> The whiche that to the feeste were yprayed,
> And of his retenue the bachelrye,
> With many a soun of sondry melodye,
> Unto the village of the which I tolde
> In this array the righte way han holde.   (IV.253–73)

The wedding procession marches to Griselda's cottage, surprising both its inhabitants and the "richeliche arrayed, / Lordes and ladies in his compaignye" who have followed it there. All are spectators and unwitting performers in Walter's play of reciprocal obedience to his "lust," which is exhibited here in his "chois," for a wife. "Lust" merely means "desire," not the morally questionable urge to which we reduce the word today. Yet there is certainly something whimsical about Walter's "lust" in choosing Griselda as his bride: she is not the "emperoures doghter" that one might expect a marquis to select for his match. The play he orchestrates cements the political function of marriage by making everyone a willing participant in its contracts and implicated in its terms. Insofar as Griselda accepts Walter, the people also accept Griselda, she "that standeth here." He then demands, "Honoureth hire and loveth hire I praye / Whoso me loveth. Ther is namore to saye" (IV.369–71).

In hindsight, we will see that Walter has here constructed a test, or at least a challenge, for his people as important as the one he will inflict upon his wife. In fact, the tale somewhat justifies what Walter does to Griselda by having his subjects fail to keep their part of the bargain. In this triangulated marriage-as-political-arrangement, Griselda's patience stands in sharp contrast with her subjects' faithlessness, their willingness to trade her for a younger, more noble wife. They fall into a trap, set by Walter, meant to catch out disobedience—what seems to appear as resistance to him rather than assent. That is, if Walter's subjects were true to their promise to worship Griselda, they would rebuke and resist his desire to remarry. His people thus become responsible for his continued testing of his wife. Only by designing their roles in relation to one another does Walter make bearable his own actions in the tale. For the wavering of his subjects gives him, in retrospect, the justification to test his wife, making his behavior to Griselda part of that more elaborate scheme and a kind of necessary cruelty.

These rational apologetics for Walter's actions have not sat well with the Clerk's readers. At the end of the tale, the Clerk makes an allegorizing gesture that generalizes Griselda's exemplary endurance:

> For sith a womman was so pacient
> Unto a mortal man, wel more us oghte
> Receiven al in gree that God us sent.
> For greet skile is he preve that he wroghte;
> But he ne tempteth no man that he boghte,
> As saith Saint Jame if ye his pistel rede:
> He preveth folk alday, it is no drede[.]   (IV.1149–55)

The problem with reading the Clerk's Tale as an allegory is not with Griselda but with the rest of it, especially Walter, who can in no way approximate God. Walter is a poor figuration of the divine here, tempting his wife so that he can "know" the limits of her endurance. God would already know it and would, moreover, exhibit no such "lust" to know more. The Clerk himself implies the comparison to Job, who was similarly tested. But in that story, God allows the devil to tempt Job; he does not undertake the test himself. Walter is a better devil figure, to be sure, but that is not what the Clerk's allegorization calls for. He invokes allegory as a simplifying gesture, as if it would help generalize the tale's reference beyond its narrow (and frustrating) application to women and to wives, which the Clerk claims we should resist. In the end, the Clerk fails to make his analogies stick, leaving us with a compromised conclusion, which perhaps helps explain why the Clerk does not stop speaking when he's "done." He feels the need, as he tells us, to offer "a song to glade you" (IV.1174) and to turn our attention away from such serious matters.

Continuing beyond the tale's ending, he closes with something traditionally called the Clerk's "envoy" (from the French *envoi*, itself derived from *envoyer*, "to send")—a kind of writing that sends the tale out into the world, in effect addressing it to that audience. Its status is somewhat questionable and its purpose not all that transparent, despite being fairly easy to understand. After what could be a sober ending to his "sad" story, the exhortation "Lat us thanne live in vertuous suffraunce" (IV.1162), he turns to address the Wife of Bath directly. It would be "ful hard" (IV.1164) to find two or three Griseldas nowadays, he says. Shifting to a distinctly commercial, economic register he has not used before, he speaks the Wife's language: if women were put to such a test now, "The gold of hem hath now so badde alayes [alloys] / With bras, that though the coine be fair at eye, / It wolde rather breste atwo than plye" (IV.1167–69). The envoy is thus written "for the Wives love of Bathe . . . and al hir secte" (IV.1170–71) and composed in a different verse form, the double ballade—a singsong metrical pattern that picks up the pace of Chaucer's regular riding rhyme after the stately rhyme royal—to turn to the literal level that his tale had purposefully avoided. These measures directly addressing the Wife would seem to give the lie to the Clerk's stated intent. He wants to be sure, that is, that the Wife (and thus, in some sense, we too) read Griselda *as a wife*, not merely as a figuration of the human soul.

This song grows more acerbic as it progresses, imagining the ways "ye archewives" (IV.1195) should, in the real world rather than the ideal world of Griselda, provoke their husbands to "care and weepe and wringe and waile" (IV.1212). It is full of the behavior advocated by the Wife in her Prologue: complaining, nagging, and answering back. Tone is hard to distinguish, but the verse form of the envoy clearly changes the tempo of the stately Clerk's Tale. Its stanzas rush to get their words out, creating a kind of crescendo of admonished complaint and urged argument, as the suppressed anger and frustration of the tale are finally released.

The Clerk has answered the Wife back, but he's perhaps gone too far. He's certainly worked himself up in this roaring conclusion. And it's definitely a stylistic inversion of the tale's tone of calm superiority. Somewhat ironically, it mirrors the end of the Wife of Bath's Tale: there, at the happy end of her redemptive romance, the Wife also loses it, returning to the overbearing voice of the Prologue. We are not quite sure what Chaucer may be doing with these outbursts. But it's certainly something of a surprise that two such different tales and tellers should end in so similar a fashion.

THE MERCHANT'S PROLOGUE
AND TALE

The Clerk ends his envoy in a lather, urging wives to lash out at difficult husbands and make them "care and weepe and wringe and waile" (IV.1212). The Merchant finds this song familiar and responds directly by repeating its refrain: "Weeping and wailing, care and other sorwe / I knowe ynough, on even and amorwe" (IV.1213–14). Such a fluid transition between tales obviates any need for the Host's intervention. Picking up on the Clerk's satiric terms, the Merchant repeats them in dead earnest to produce an organically motivated transition.

Offering his fellow pilgrims what might be the darkest picture of the life of married men, the Merchant complains of his wife's "passing cruel-tee" (IV.1225), as different from Griselda's mild humility as possible. He's been married only two months (IV.1234), but it's been such a nightmare so far that although he could tell tales, he refuses to talk about what he calls his "owene sore" (IV.1243). Thus the Merchant as narrator is in the unusual position of speaking out of a *denial* of his own experience, rather than its authority. So we might expect the Merchant to change the subject. Instead he returns almost compulsively to the Wife's topic, the "wo that is in mariage" (III.3)—now offered from a husband's point of view (not his own, of course!). For in refusing to talk about his own personal "sore," he tells of another man's, a man far more foolish than he. Given the contrary relations of the Wife and Merchant to their own experiences, their performances bear an uncanny likeness, even if their attitudes toward marriage are starkly opposed. The Merchant draws on many of the same sources as the Wife in yet another examination of the issues of sovereignty and mastery in marriage. But unlike the Wife—or the Clerk, for that matter—the Merchant seeks not to construct an ideal so much as to disclose, with some bitterness, the more painful blindness of love: "For Love is blind alday and may nat see" (IV.1598). Despite such attempts at deflection, the Merchant's Tale bears an uncanny resemblance to what seems his own humiliating marital situation, drawing on the authority of an experience he might otherwise like to forget.

In the overall structure of the Marriage Group, the Merchant sets the debate back a step or two. His anti-matrimonialism would seem a return to what the Wife originally argued against in her Prologue. Why retreat to that point? The answer may lie in genre. He gives his tale, structured like another ribald fabliau, a setting a level above its typical bourgeois or even clerical environment and thus far from his own mercantile class. Its sources are various and not strictly of the same kind as other fabliaux in the *Tales*.[1] His protagonist is a knight of Pavia in Lombardy— an Italian like the Clerk's Walter, who also like Walter begins the story a bachelor. Older than the marquis by a good measure, this knight's attention is also "on his lust present" (IV.80), here spelled out in more explicit terms: he "folwed ay his bodily delit / On wommen theras was his appetit" (IV.1249–50). In an ostentatiously self-gratifying gesture, this knight, the aptly named Januarye (befitting his hoary white hair), suddenly decides to marry. He explains:

> Frendes, I am hoor and old,
> And almost, God woot, on my pittes brinke:
> Upon my soule somwhat moste I thinke.
> I have my body folily dispended—

---

[1] Like the Miller's Tale, the Merchant's Tale seems to be a compilation of episodes from different sources woven into a seamless whole. A good book sampling these sources is the compilation by Larry D. Benson and Theodore M. Andersson, *The Literary Context of Chaucer's Fabliaux* (Indianapolis: Bobbs-Merrill, 1971).

> Blessed be God that it shal been amended!
> For I wol be, certayn, a wedded man,
> And that anon, in al the haste I can,
> Unto som maide fair and tendre of age.   (IV.1400–07)

Voiced by this aged figure, the spiritual benefit of marriage takes center stage to correct a life "folily dispended." Folly, even more than marriage, is on display in Januarye's performance of repentance here. His concerns for his "soule" are an excuse to continue enjoying a behavior made less frequent by his age. Even more, those supposedly greater moral concerns make a spectacle out of Januarye's desires. We quickly realize that the Merchant has nothing but bitter disdain for this sixty-year-old who has spent his life getting his pleasure wherever he could and who now, toward its end, pretends to more refined concerns. Such details may afford some distance from the Merchant's own unhappy situation, but one senses too that it also allows him to indulge his self-loathing and disdain in displaced form.

Citing again the very materials invoked by the Wife of Bath's Prologue, specifically Theophrastus on marriage, Chaucer crafts yet another response to her performance (and to the Clerk's as well) in the voice of a disillusioned husband. The opening of the tale is complex, as the Merchant's narrative voice blends with Januarye's own; we are not always sure who is speaking. That's because after clearly citing Januarye's newly acquired opinions on marriage—"'Noon other lif,' *saide he*, 'is worth a bene'" (IV.1263; my emphasis)—the Merchant continues by more generally adopting Januarye's perspective, reveling in its selfish irrationality and delusion. Not only does this mean that the story as a whole adopts Januarye's point of view and follows the course of his thinking, but it more actively argues against authorities like "Theofraste" (IV.1295) in ultimately myopic ways. The Merchant's Tale is very unusual in offering a narrator who speaks not only from a certain social location and cultural perspective (as happens with other Canterbury tale-tellers all the time) but from one he finds ridiculous. The Merchant narrates at some distance from his past self and previous opinions in one of the most self-ironizing performances that *The Canterbury Tales* offers. We will return to this narrative performance after looking at the Merchant's story.

As a fabliau, the Merchant's Tale is another story of "tendre youthe . . . wedded [to] stouping age" (IV.1738). The genre's town–gown rivalry is replaced by a purely generational one. Januarye is tricked by his young wife, May, and his squire, Damian, whose romance begins at the wedding. There is nothing elaborate or intellectual about the antics in the Merchant's Tale. Since the husband and the lover come from the same knightly profession, the rivalry between them differs from the seemingly "natural" friction between working men and students. As a squire, Damian aspires to Januarye's position, and thus his attention to Januarye's wife is framed as rivalry within one social class. Unlike other fabliaux, most of the tale's attention is directed toward the mismatched marriage itself: Januarye's decision to marry, his efforts to engage his brothers to help him procure a wife, and the advice of friends about matrimony. Such material appears as an elaboration of the comic logic driving tales like the Miller's, whose narrator acknowledges the way "youthe and elde is often at debat" and leaves its old lover to "his care" (I.3230, 3232) as a matter of course. The Merchant's Tale instead examines what the other fabliaux take for granted—what the Reeve says about old men: "For in oure wil ther stiketh ever a nail / To have an hoor heed and a grene tail" (I.3877–78). Doubling down on this impatience with the romantic aspirations of old men, the Merchant seems excessively focused on what Januarye has coming to him.

The Merchant's Tale, in fact, dwells on the flawed and self-deluded thinking of this old lover. Its narrative indulgently tracks Januarye's analogously self-indulgent thought processes, which are often carried forward into conversation with others. Januarye counters and reframes the arguments of the antifeminist writers to his own benefit in order to convince himself of how profitable the state of marriage will be with a young, pliable, and obedient wife, and he congratulates himself on making such a smart decision and justifying his careful choice. He makes much of her youth and its importance. An older woman will be too crafty, he surmises, but a young girl will be innocent, easily molded into an ideal spouse who can care for all his needs. Not only does Januarye cite the same authorities as the Wife at certain points, he sounds much like her. For example, he compares the learning of wives to students: "For sondry scoles maketh subtile clerkes: / Womman of manye scoles half a clerk is" (IV.1427–28).[2] The Wife had similarly claimed "of five housbondes scoleying am I" (III.44f). Moreover, Januarye echoes the Wife in happy antipathy to living as a chaste bachelor, a prospect that makes him proclaim, "But sires, by youre leve, that am nat I" (IV.1456).[3] A later reference to her as an authority (discussed in what follows) also connects the two.

For much of his narration, the Merchant allows Januarye to revel in his deluded fantasy. Consider the image of the marketplace mirror he uses to conjure for himself an imagined parade of available, nubile girls:

> Many fair shap and many a fair visage
> Ther passeth thurgh his herte night by night;
> As whoso tooke a mirour polisshed bright,
> And sette it in a commune market-place,
> Thanne sholde he see ful many a figure pace
> By his mirour; and in the same wise
> Gan Januarye inwith his thought devise
> Of maidens whiche that dwelten him biside. (IV.1580–87)

---

[2] Compare the lines added in some manuscripts of the Wife of Bath's Prologue that strike a similar chord:

> Diverse scoles maken parfit clerkes,
> And diverse practikes in sondry werkes
> Maken the werkman parfit sikerly:
> Of five housbondes scoleying am I. (III.44c–f)

[3] Compare the Wife's similar response to the "greet perfeccion" of virginity: "And lordinges, by youre leve, that am nat I" (III.105, 112).

This is an image of his mind ("inwith his thought") contemplating the young women who live in the vicinity, from whom he clearly can freely choose. But in making it a "commune market-place," the tale does two subtle things at once. First, in a way it democratizes Januarye's situation. He's not choosing a wife from his own social class in some elaborate kind of negotiation, as Walter's subjects propose. He is thinking in broader, "common" terms. But, more nefariously, it also suggests that Januarye is buying his wife. We may or may not have ever considered why Alison marries John, the Miller's carpenter. But the suggestion here is that Januarye is procuring his young and impressionable wife on the open market. The image belies the moral reasoning behind his decision to take a young bride and implicitly raises the reciprocal question that Januarye could never imagine on his own: what does a pretty young girl see in him? The Merchant will show us, in stomach-churning detail, precisely what she sees on their wedding night.

Once Januarye chooses one of these girls, the fresh young May, "of his owene auctoritee" (IV.1597), he cannot be dissuaded. But he goes further, asking his friends to confirm his decision and assist in negotiating the match. The braggart claims that his only regret in taking such a bride is that he might be *too* happy in his earthly life, thereby endangering his immortal soul:

> For sith that verray hevene is bought so deere
> With tribulaciouns and greet penaunce,
> How sholde I thanne, that live in swich plesaunce
> As alle wedded men doon with hir wives,
> Come to the blisse ther Crist eterne on live is?
> This is my drede, and ye, my bretheren twaye,
> Assoileth me this question, I preye.   (IV.1648–54)

Claiming to be afraid of having his "hevene in erthe here" (IV.1647), Januarye rubs everyone's nose in what he perceives as his good fortune and reveals his true intent.

His brother Justinus ("the just one") can hardly stand Januarye's self-serving performance of "folye" (IV.1655) and answers his question much as the Wife of Bath might: "Despaire you noght, but have in youre memorye / Paraunter she may be youre purgatorye" (IV.1669–70). Justinus echoes how the Wife of Bath spoke about the ways she was forced to take the upper hand with her husbands and answer their charges. In a surprising gesture that has been extensively discussed in the scholarship on the tale, Justinus even refers to the authoritative teaching of the Wife of Bath by name:

> The Wif of Bathe, if ye han understonde,
> Of mariage which ye han on honde
> Declared hath ful wel in litel space.
> Fareth now wel. God have you in his grace.   (IV.1685–88)

Knowing that Januarye will heed no advice from him, Justinus gives up and sarcastically indulges his brother's hopes that a wife will be his saving grace. The other brother, aptly named Placebo ("I will please"), has always told Januarye just what he wishes to hear: "'I saye it is a cursed man,' quod he, / 'That letteth matrimoigne, sikerly'" (IV.1572–73). Between the two of them, they allow Januarye to fall into the snare he has set for himself.

The wedding itself is a spectacle, part of the long, slow process leading up to what will be the fabliau's rivalrous triangle and adventurous trick. The marriage and enfeoffment (that is, legal installation) of May in Januarye's property are not as compelling as the celebration that follows. For one thing, it's where Damian falls in love with her as she sits upon the dais at the feast. Both husband and lover are struck by her beauty, each of them "ravisshed" by her look (IV.1750, 1774). The evening after the wedding is a lengthy scene of male desire. Januarye's gaze upon his beloved object turns swiftly into a threatening desire for possession: "in his herte he gan hire to manace / That he that night in armes wolde hire straine / Harder than ever Paris dide Elaine" (IV.1752–54). By contrast, Damian is wounded by love of May and takes to his bed. While the other guests are getting the wedding chamber ready and taking their leave, Damian is retreating into illness.

The Merchant treats this point at length in the narrative, lamenting the treason of Damian, Januarye's own squire, "lik to the naddre in bosom, sly, untrewe" (IV.1786), and considering the shifting thoughts of Januarye himself. He is at one moment straining to get the guests out of the house so that he can get his wife to bed and at another bewailing the harm he might do her with his sexual urgency. May's own perspective provides one of the most disturbing images in the tale. On her wedding night, May lies under Januarye as he rubs his bristly face on hers, his neck skin flapping just above her:

> He lulleth hire, he kisseth hire ful ofte—
> With thikke bristles of his berd unsofte,
> Lik to the skin of houndfissh, sharpe as brere,
> (For he was shave al newe in his manere),
> He rubbeth hire aboute hir tendre face,
> And saide thus, "Allas, I moot trespace
> To you, my spouse, and you greetly offende[.]"   (IV.1823–29)

And after their night together,

> He was al coltissh, ful of ragerye,
> And ful of jargon as a flekked pie.
> The slakke skin aboute his nekke shaketh
> Whil that he song, so chaunteth he and craketh.
> But God woot what that May thoughte in hir herte
> Whan she him saugh up sitting in his sherte,
> In his night-cappe and with his nekke lene—
> She praiseth nat his playing worth a bene.   (IV.1847–54)

May's point of view throws into sharp relief the self-absorption of Januarye, who has a hard time thinking about matters beyond his own desires. Even here, when he seems to consider the "delicacy" of his new bride, he does so from a corrupt perspective. He imagines himself too potent and forceful for the young girl he's married. His concern about "offending" her suggests that (at least in his mind) she's an inexperienced and possibly reluctant lover. Of course, he assumes a certain amount of modesty on her part, an assumption largely shaped by his ideas of ideal maidens-cum-wives. But he has little idea of what May really wants. Lest we too quickly conclude that the Merchant is sympathetic to the woman in this story, we ought to remind ourselves of the parts of the tale that suggest otherwise. Think of the Merchant's ironic quotation of the Knight's Tale, "Lo, pitee renneth soone in gentil herte!" (IV.1986; cf. I.1761), after Damian writes his complaint to May. This sentiment may be worthy of a knight's situation, but the Merchant delivers it with disgust. The tale is also full of sordid detail and expressions that lower our opinion of young "love." The antics of Nicholas and Alison were worthy of some admiration because they were rooted in healthy, natural desire, in which the phrase "maketh melodye" (I.3306) can be read as a joyous metaphor for erotic play. No such elation energizes the Merchant's Tale. Instead, the attraction of Damian and May is represented as a courtly commonplace and the height of treason.

In the context of its genre, the attraction of these two young lovers amounts to a fait accompli. Their youth draws them together and apart from Januarye, no matter what legal relations (as squire and wife) they bear to him. Damian's lovesickness gives him a chance to express himself to May. A good courtier, he writes "al his sorwe, / In manere of a complainte or a lay" (IV.1880–81), and wears it in a purse hung near his heart. When Januarye sends May to a sick Damian's bedside with the other ladies of the household, the visit gives Damian the opportunity to pass his letter to her. So far, so good, as their actions conform to the genre's imitation of courtly niceties. But then the Merchant's narration swerves away from anything subtle. Not only does May retreat to a private realm to read it,

> She feined hire as that she moste gon
> Theras ye woot that every wight moot neede,
> And whan she of this bille hath taken heede,
> She rente it al to cloutes at the laste,
> And in the privee softely it caste.   (IV.1950–54)

We might imagine the latrine to be the only place where May can find privacy in her house, but the Merchant's inclination to specify the excess detail is striking. Perhaps the action is logical; Januarye hardly gives her a minute to herself in the tale (and once he becomes blind, his hand is literally always upon her). But saying such things is by no means necessary. Women may retreat to their closet in order to do what "every wight moot neede" but there's no need to mention it aloud, nor for May to make strategic use of this privacy to destroy the evidence, casting the "cloutes" away. The logic of privacy aside, it also suggests something foul and dirty about her feelings for Damian, which is appropriate neither to romance nor fabliau. Such a conflation of the private with the privy can only be the Merchant's, and it is thus colored by his affect.

Similarly uncourtly, unromantic, unsympathetic representations of their lovelorn behavior appear when May returns a letter to Damian with a kind of violence:

> To visite this Damian gooth May,
> And subtilly this lettre doun she threste
> Under his pilwe: *rede it if him leste.*
> She taketh him by the hand and harde him twiste,
> So secreely that no wight of it wiste,
> And bad him be al hool, and forth she wente[.]
>
> (IV.2002–07; my emphasis)

Furtive and violent, May both twists and thrusts at her target to make her meaning known. It won't be the only thrusting done in this tale. The Merchant's begrudging remark, "rede it if him leste," explains May's intent, but more emphatically conveys the Merchant's annoyance and dissatisfaction.

Damian and May deceive Januarye by making a copy of the key to the pleasure garden he has crafted for his own delight. It is the place where "he wolde paye his wif hir dette / In somer seson" (IV.2048–49); but even more cagily, "thinges whiche that were nat doon abedde, / He in the gardin parfourned hem and spedde" (IV.2051–52). It is not clear, exactly, what activity Januarye performs in the garden that can't be done in bed. The retreat itself is a figuration of the "Paradis terrestre" (IV.1332), the earthly paradise that Januarye was imagining his wife to embody and thus a version of the garden of Eden, with all its attendant implications of enclosure, temptation, and sin. The proximate literary source for the garden and its wicket gate is the allegorical French poem *Roman de la rose*, a source that also marks it as a potentially dangerous place of self-delusion as well as intense pleasure.

We should pause here to note that Januarye's garden is governed by Pluto and Proserpina, who have been reduced from their role as rulers of the classical underworld. Unlike the forbidding planetary gods of the Knight's Tale, here they are transformed into the king and queen of "fairie." As such, they act in a more benign fashion as a distorted mirror image of Januarye and May themselves, an older husband who has manipulated a younger girl into marriage and who possesses her against her will. The aggressive competition between Pluto and his wife foreshadows the conflict in store for Januarye. Whereas Januarye once compared the idea of a young wife to "warm wex" that men "with handes [could] plye" (IV.1430), May has copied the key to the garden by taking its impression in warm wax (IV.2117). His image of her literally becomes the means by which she deceives him, and the same is true more figuratively. For Januarye has been duped all along by his ideal image of a wife: seeing her purely instrumentally—as the key to his happiness, as it were—he has never considered things, as the Merchant does repeatedly, from her point of view. But this perspective is connected less to revisionism than to the Merchant's loathing of his former self, which he cannot help displaying from such critical points of view within the tale. May happens to have one of the most effective perspectives for conveying such a portrait.

The high point of Januarye's misunderstanding occurs in the garden itself, to which May has summoned Damian; there she gives him signs to climb a pear tree where she will scheme to meet him. Climbing upon her husband's back to satisfy a craving for pears common to "a womman in my plit" (IV.2335), May meets her lover in the tree: "And sodeinly anon this Damian / Gan pullen up the smok and in he throng" (IV.2353–54). This is perhaps the most direct expression for sex in all of Chaucer's works. It forms the denouement of the fabliau, like the cry for water in the Miller's Tale or for help in the Reeve's that brings the entire scheme crashing down upon the cuckolded husband. This act of thronging prompts Pluto to restore Januarye's sight at that very instant. But Proserpina has decreed that May will have "suffisant answere"[4] (IV.2266), and she immediately responds that his newly restored sight must somehow be imperfect: "As me was taught, to hele with youre eyen / Was nothing bet to make you to see / Than strugle with a man upon a tree" (IV.2372–74). Refusing to admit what he saw, how "in it wente" (IV.2376), May arouses his skepticism about his healed sight, suggesting that in a day or two it will be "ysatled" (IV.2405): for "he that misconceiveth, he misdeemeth" (IV.2410). Given that May is pregnant (recall her "plit" that causes a craving for pears), the idea that proper conception and judgment are important to each other is also ironic. Januarye has already misconceived and misjudged; in fact, he has misconceived *because* he has misjudged. He has chosen the wrong woman to marry, and her child is likely not his but Damian's.

In these closing movements of the Merchant's Tale, I have been suggesting, we see a scorching of the conventions of romance even as the Merchant deploys some of them in his fabliau. He shows a hate for his own tale because it likely rehearses, no matter how much he changes the social class of the characters, his own self-delusions and errors of judgment. The Merchant's Tale, we might say, is a tale of avoidance: both thematically, as it showcases what one ought to avoid, and narratively, as it tries to avoid saying something it only winds up repeating.

---

[4] Such an "suffisant answere" is just what the old woman gave to the knight to satisfy the queen in the Wife of Bath's Tale.

THE SQUIRE'S PROLOGUE
AND TALE

An unfinished tale broken off just as it is about to take an expansive turn, the Squire's Tale has subsequently both piqued the interest of readers and suffered from critical neglect. It is nowhere near a central tale in terms of the critical reception of Chaucer's collection, yet it was deeply interesting to Renaissance readers. In 1616 John Lane, lamenting that the Squire never got to finish his exotic story, wrote a continuation.[1] The very fact that the tale is unfinished and breaks off just as a new section is beginning has lent it a kind of mystique. Did Chaucer intend to flesh out this multi-plot romance and extend the materials that appear only in nascent form in its opening, or is it meant to be left deliberately tantalizing in its inter-rupted state? The suggestiveness of the Squire's Tale has always been its principal feature, even if we have been unsure how to take it.

In the tale's rather short prologue of 8 lines, the Host commands the Squire to "say somewhat of love, for certes ye / Connen theron as muche as any man" (V.2–3). This opening heads a new fragment, but it fails to link the tale to any previous story. Like many of the other links in *The Canterbury Tales*, these lines assert the control of the Host by showing each pilgrim's willingness to follow his rule. The tale breaks off two lines into a third part. Some manuscripts leave the rest of the folio sheet blank and begin the next page with a heading designating "the wordes of the

---

[1] *John Lane's Continuation of the Squire's Tale* was first published in 1887, by the Chaucer Society.

Frankelyn to the Squire, and the wordes of the Host to the Frankeleyn." These comments are often presented as an introduction before the short Prologue to the Franklin's Tale and as such can appear to be an intentional disruption of the Squire's performance, which threatens to go on for some time. In it we meet the ambitious Franklin, whose own story follows and thematically refers back to the marriage tales of fragments III and IV.

His own introduction may be short, but the Squire's Tale looks as if its expansive romance narration might overtake the rest of Chaucer's poem. It tells a story of the king of the Tartars, Cambiuskan, and his daughter Canacee. Twenty years into his reign, Cambiuskan is visited by a stranger bearing magical gifts: a brass horse, a ring, a mirror, and a sword. Each of these gifts is powerful. The horse transports its rider anywhere, appearing and disappearing by the twist of a pin in its ear. The sword inflicts biting wounds that only a counterstroke of its own can heal. The mirror predicts adversity, revealing friend and foe, especially to ladies in love. The ring allows communication with birds as well as intimate knowledge of plants. This mirror and ring are sent purposefully to Canacee and thus portend a romance plot of some kind in which they will be of use.

Not only are the details of the Squire's story elaborate, but the narration follows suit. Much of the Squire's Tale is devoted to a conjunction of rhetoric and what we'd call science. We should remember that Chaucer had an interest in scientific knowledge. He produced a treatise on a device used to take astronomical measurements, the astrolabe. Many of the Canterbury tales make recourse to such scientific matters: Nicholas's "astromye" in the Miller's Tale (I.3450), the "magik naturel" (V.1125) in the Franklin's Tale, and alchemy in the Canon's Yeoman's Tale, which will be discussed later. There is talk in this story about the technologies behind the magical gifts and their exotic sources, both the places from which they came and the ancient books that may be able to explain their operations. They are the gifts of the "king of Arabe and of Inde" (V.110), and they make the people of Cambiuskan's court nervous—their origin appears to be "fairye" (V.96), or even something more sinister:

> Of sondry doutes thus they jangle and trete,
> As lewed peple deemeth comunly
> Of thinges that been maad more subtilly
> Than they can in hir lewdnesse comprehende:
> They deemen gladly to the baddere ende. (V.220–24)

But their means of trying to understand these fantastical objects seems less "lewed" than this narrator suggests. They "speke of Alocen and Vitulon, / Of Aristotle, that writen in hir lives, / Of quainte mirours and of perspectives, / As knowen they that han hir bookes herd" (V.232–35). Aristotle is widely known today. But the other two—Alhazen, an Arabic authority on optics, and Vitello, an Italian expert on perspective—are less so, and their names would also have been less familiar to Chaucer's English audience.

While these details seem appropriate to the exotic nature of the tale and its location in the Tartar court, they belong to the Squire's narrative style, a style that matches the genre he has chosen. For example, the Squire uses a fittingly "scientific" means of denoting time, elaborate in its astrological and mythological references:

> Phebus hath laft the angle meridional,
> And yet ascending was the beest royal,
> The gentil Leoun with his Aldiran,
> Whan that this Tartre king, Cambiuskan,
> Roos fro his bord theras he sat ful hye[.]
> . . . .
> Now dauncen lusty Venus children deere,
> For in the Fish hir lady sat ful hye
> And looketh on hem with a frendly eye. (V.263–74)

The stylization of these lines sharply contrasts with the trope of modesty consistently deployed by the Squire throughout the tale ("I wol nat taryen you, for it is prime," V.73; "I can nat sowne his style," V.105; "I saye namore," V.289; etc.).

Eastern and globalized, the Squire's Tale also uses a Western romantic standard of comparison. When the foreign knight first arrives, the Squire comments on his self-presentation at court:

> With so heigh reverence and obeisaunce,
> As wel in speeche as in countenaunce,
> That Gawain, with his olde curteisye,
> Though he were come again out of fairye,
> Ne coude him nat amende with a word.   (V.93–97)

And disparaging his own descriptive power, he says:

> Who coude telle you the forme of daunces,
> So uncouthe, and swiche fresshe countenaunces,
> Swich subtil looking and dissimulinges
> For drede of jalous mennes aperceivinges?
> No man but Launcelot, and he is deed.   (V.283–87)

These comparisons with Western romance archetypes make up the larger fabric of the story, both its simple plot and its complex narration. The point is not merely that the Squire aspires to ideals of chivalry and romance (and romance telling) appropriate to figures such as Lancelot and Gawain, but that the exotic tale itself operates by a comparatist logic. Thus the members of the Tartar court interpret the magic horse by proposing similitudes:

> They murmured as dooth a swarm of been,
> And maden skiles after hir fantasies,
> Rehersing of thise olde poetries,
> And saiden it was lik the Pegasee,
> The hors that hadde winges for to flee,
> Or elles it was the Greekes hors Sinoun,
> That broughte Troye to destruccioun,
> As men in thise olde geestes rede.   (V.204–11)

In describing the new and unfamiliar, the strange and magical that some align with the dangerous, the tale's characters as well as its narrator take recourse to a set of Western European literary figures that the Squire's audience will know: Lancelot, Gawain, Pegasus, the Trojan horse crafted by Sinon. The startlingly new relies on the classically old—that which has to be exceeded, but that without which nothing can be known.[2]

The image of the swarm of bees (to illustrate the sound of the murmuring crowd) is part of a soundscape that makes the Squire's Tale quite distinct from other stories in Chaucer's collection. This tale is chock-full of noise—whispering, talking, hypothesizing, and arguing: the verbal effects of the wonder inspired by the events and the locale. The term *wonder* is used excessively in the Squire's Tale both as a noun, to classify the objects and their powers that have not been seen before, and as a verb, to express the confusion, amusement, and curiosity that they cause. And the extent of this wonder, paradoxically, can be expressed only in its inexpressibility. Indeed, much of part 1 of the Squire's multiplot story intends to generate these effects through the acknowledgment of its insufficiency to do so.

Part 2 of the tale focuses on a different soundscape by concentrating on the story of Canacee and the peregrine falcon she befriends. Walking out in her garden (because of a dream that awakened her early) with the magic ring on her finger, Canacee finds that she understands birdsong: "For right anon she wiste what they mente / Right by hir song, and knew al hir entente" (V.399–400). This central episode is engrossing. Our attention turns to the peregrine, who tells the story of the false tercelet who swore his love only to betray his mate with a kite. The Squire gives us something wholly new and mysteriously familiar with this tale. It's as if he is revising Chaucer's *Parliament of Fowls*—a dream vision that centers on the romantic choice to be made by a formel eagle among three suitors

---

[2] See Patricia Clare Ingham, *The Medieval New: Ambivalence in an Age of Innovation* (Philadelphia: U of Pennsylvania P, 2015), esp. the introduction, "Newfangled Values," 1–20.

on Valentine's Day—along the lines of *Anelida and Arcite*, a poem that laments the betrayal of a noblewoman by her false lover.

Ultimately, the story breaks off only 2 lines into part 3. The peregrine has told her sad story to Canacee and fainted into her lap. The princess carries her home and makes a mew where the bird can recover. But before he ends this section, the Squire forecasts how matters will turn out:

> How that this faucon gat hir love again,
> Repentant, as the storye telleth us,
> By mediacioun of Cambalus,
> The kinges sone, of which I you tolde.
> But hennesforth I wol my process holde
> To speke of aventures and of batailes,
> That never yet was herd so grete mervailes.   (V.654–60)

He may not get to finish his tale, but the broad outline is sketched for us. The laws of genre are invoked in the contours of what seems to be inter-laced romances moving between narratives of Canacee and her brothers and likely involving the magical gift-objects to suggest how these matters end: how Algarsif "wan Theodora to wif" (V.664), how Cambalo "fought in listes with the bretheren two" (V.668), and so on. Both the extensive-ness of the Squire's prospective narration and its foregone conclusions have led readers to see the Franklin's response as an intentional interrup-tion. The Franklin's "praise . . . [of his] wit" (V.674) shortens the Squire's romance at the same time that it compliments his efforts at such an elabo-rate tale, surely too long for the space of the pilgrimage frame. Thus, the Franklin pretends that he thinks the Squire finished and, possibly inspired by the Squire's contribution, proffers his own.

The Franklin seems to admire the Squire, even if he's not paying all that much attention to his tale. The younger noble learned his eloquence and gentility from his father, the Knight, and his "gentilesse" inspires a kind of paternal envy in the Franklin, who "hadde levere than twenty pound worth land" (V.683) that his own son, who is something of a libertine, could learn from him. Harry Bailly finds this complimentary (and self-deprecating) discourse a waste of time, interjecting "Straw for youre gentilesse!" (V.695) and forcing the Franklin to "tel on [his] tale withouten wordes mo" (V.702). Perhaps because he had been looking for an opportunity to seize the floor all along, the Franklin is only too happy to oblige.

THE FRANKLIN'S
INTRODUCTION, PROLOGUE,
AND TALE

The Franklin's story has long been read as the conclusion to the debate on marriage generated from the Wife of Baths' Prologue. This tale begins where most romances end, with a wedding. Arveragus and Dorigen design a marriage contract so as to "lede the more in blisse hir lives" (V.744). Arveragus promises to obey his wife in everything "as any lovere to his lady shal" (V.750), while Dorigen swears never to be the cause of "werre or strif" between them (V.757). The two thereby intend to live married by the dictates of courtly love: Arveragus will keep only "the name of sover-einetee" (V.751), leaving Dorigen free of his "maistrye" (V.747). The tale, of course, tests the possibility that such a private agreement can govern marital affairs, even as it contributes to the debate on marriage. The agreement eventually may prove flawed, but the Franklin's confidence in its underlying patient passivity is what ultimately saves the day.

By aligning his story with the genre of a Breton lay (V.709–15), the Franklin signals some magical intervention in his tale of love. Lays (from the French *lais*) are short narratives, typically about love, and they originate with Marie de France's *Lais*, a collection of purported French translations of ancient Breton tales that circulated orally. Marie wrote in the Anglo-Norman dialect of twelfth-century Britain, at a time when the island was ruled by French-speaking nobles in the wake of the Norman conquest. Thus, the Breton lay is a "native" genre despite being in what seems a foreign language. But the Franklin's effort is nostalgic and performative (as are many of his rhetorical flourishes), because no such Breton or even French source seems to lie behind his tale. It is instead an adaptation of a story from Boccaccio's *Filocolo*, in which a married lady rashly promises herself to an unwanted suitor if he can produce a May garden in January—thereby intending to put him off.[1] The genre invoked by the Franklin is thus a kind of literary affectation that tells us more about his aims than about its source. He likewise sets the tale in the days of "thise olde gentil Britons" (V.709), presumably before Christianity regulated "oure bileve" (V.1133), to suspend any disbelief in its fantastic events. The Breton lay's pagan magic provides the unfalsifiable logic that drives the tale. But otherwise, with its knight, squire, lady, and clerk, the story's setting appears not too distant from the Franklin's aspirational world.[2]

The story begins in earnest when Arveragus leaves for England "to seeke in armes worshipe and honour" (V.811), as knights are wont to do. In his absence, his wife Dorigen frets and makes herself sick worrying about his safe return, fastening on the danger posed by the "grisly rokkes blake" (V.859) off the coast of Brittany. They become a physical projection of her "derke fantasye" (V.844), her fear that her husband will die even as he tries to return home. Because her friends are concerned for her mental health, they take her, as a distraction, to a party where she falls into conversation with her neighbor, Aurelius, a squire who has secretly

---

[1] That the story concerns a *May* garden in *January* invokes the principal figures from the Merchant's Tale and their pleasure garden in a displaced form, which suggests a rather unusual kind of inspiration, sourcing, and intertextuality for this section of *The Canterbury Tales*.

[2] Much critical attention has been spent on the precise social class and possible gentry status of the Franklin, a wealthy landowner (in medieval Latin, *francolanus*). He too is rather concerned with such class matters, paying much attention to "gentilesse" in his tale, which ends with the implied debate on what kind of behavior was the most "free" (in French, *franche*) or generous. Peter Coss offers a full account of the debate and relevant historical information in his chapter on the Franklin in *Historians on Chaucer: The 'General Prologue' to the* Canterbury Tales, ed. Stephen H. Rigby (Oxford: Oxford UP, 2014), 227–46.

loved her for years. When Aurelius blurts out his affection, Dorigen is horrified and tells him in no uncertain terms that she'll never return his love. Emphasizing the point, she says "in play" (V.988):

> Looke what day that endelong Britaine
> Ye remoeve alle the rokkes, stoon by stoon,
> That they ne lette ship ne boot to goon.
> I saye, whan ye han maad the coost so clene
> Of rokkes that ther nis no stoon yseene,
> Thanne wol I love you best of any man—
> Have heer my trouthe—in al that ever I can.   (V.992–98)

Even her rebuff of a rival suitor is shaped by her anxiety about the black rocks. She cannot help dwelling on them. This addendum to Dorigen's flat-out refusal, "Take this for final answere as of me" (V.987), has led many readers to accuse her of heartlessness or vindictiveness or both, and thus to blame her for the events that ensue from this rash statement.

How are we to understand Dorigen's words here and why she utters them? The answer is certainly overdetermined, given the tale's attention to language, intent, and form—particularly as told by this socially conscious and rhetorically sophisticated pilgrim who pretends to modest simplicity. For example, he claims:

> Colours ne knowe I noon, withouten drede,
> But swiche colours as growen in the mede,
> Or elles swiche as men dye or painte;
> Colours of rethorik been too quainte[.]   (V.723–26)

That's a rather dramatically rhetorical way of disavowing any claim to rhetorical sophistication. As one aware of the way "some people" are able to speak elegantly, then, the Franklin gives us a few different ways to think through the rhetoric of Dorigen's refusal. We might begin with the last line, "have heer my trouthe." These are the words that make play into promise or oath, and they are the same ones used when Dorigen and Arveragus exchange their wedding vows ("Have heer my trouthe—til that myn herte breste"; V.759). Dorigen formalizes this playful language with her "trouthe," and thus plights her troth with these words. Of course, Dorigen thinks she's promising, yet again, *never* to love Aurelius, and she means it. This is what she thinks she has said. Little does she know that with the help of a clerk of Orleans steeped in "magik naturel" (V.1125), hell might indeed freeze over.

Her answer to Aurelius is also cast in the language of her neurosis. Dwelling on the black rocks to the point of madness, she seems unable to speak in any other way. Her language, here "in play," is thus part of her same fixation, and perhaps a sign of some incapacity. Such limitations might make her play with Aurelius a sign less of her cruelty than of compulsion. But if we are moved to think about compulsion, we might also consider the constraints of Dorigen's social position, indeed of the courtly love marriage in which Arveragus has set her. We've heard many other tales in which love and marriage are separate. While a distinctly literary phenomenon, courtly love is essentially an extramarital affair. There is nothing particularly odd about Aurelius's loving another man's wife (even if Dorigen scolds him about it in her refusal). In fact, by agreeing to conduct one's marriage in terms of courtly love— in which the husband will "folwe hir wil in al, / As any lovere to his lady shal" (V.749–50)—the attention of a rival suitor has in a sense already been invited.

The conventions of courtly love invite other things as well, including a suitor's resistance to any "final answere." Rejected lovers or those ignored by their ladies do not leave off loving and find another object of affection—witness Arcite in the Knight's Tale. Instead, they turn their attention to earning the lady's love. Indeed, this is just what Arveragus did in the opening of the tale, "er she were wonne" (V.733). What might Dorigen know about this situation? How can she convey a convincing refusal within a courtly genre that reinterprets resistance as coy flirtation? If we take the constraints of genre seriously, we can perhaps understand why Dorigen might feel compelled to give Aurelius an impossible task *precisely as* the only effective form of rejection. She uses courtly convention to her own ends, if not quite to her own advantage.

In the various ways we are compelled to read Dorigen's words "in play," then, the Franklin's Tale turns to the complex, even competitive, operations of language: the things we say, missay, and fail to say. Few other tales go as far as the Franklin's in making us consider how our words speak against us even as they declare what we want.[3] In fact, he begins with the following observation:

> For oo thing, sires, saufly dar I saye:
> . . . .
> Pacience is an heigh vertu, certayn,
> For it venquissheth, as thise clerkes sayn,
> Thinges that rigour sholde never attaine.
> For every word men may nat chide or plaine:
> Lerneth to suffre, or elles, so mote I goon,
> Ye shul it lerne, wherso ye wol or noon.
> For in this world, certayn, ther no wight is
> That he ne dooth or saith somtime amis[.]   (V.761–80)

As an opening gesture, the Franklin's lecture on patience might seem to strike a strange note. It comes just as the couple's marriage has been arranged as a mutual renunciation. It thus answers the other tales of the Marriage Group with a private rewriting of patriarchal privilege and an effort to denounce "maistrye": "Whan maistrye comth, the God of Love anon / Beteth his winges and farewel, he is gon!" (V.765–66).

Declaring this ethic in advance of the story may be somewhat self-defeating, as it augurs the violation of the ideal it has only just proposed.

---

[3] For a broader discussion of this aspect of language and the Franklin's Tale's role in displaying it, see my *Desire in the* Canterbury Tales (Columbus: Ohio State UP, 2015), 9–13.

That is, it suggests that even under these ideal conditions, a certain amount of patient understanding will still be necessary. The Franklin links mutual obedience ("frendes everich other moot obeye"; V.762) with liberty, a freedom desired by both men and women: "Love is a thing as any spirit free" (V.767). Both Dorigen and Aurelius are, in a sense, trying to renounce their privilege. Arveragus strives to follow Dorigen's will rather than leading with his. Dorigen promises that no strife between them will be caused by her. These are mild versions of Griselda's more powerful renunciation of will and, being mutual, may avoid the spectacle of domination provided by the Clerk's Tale. But this prefatory material does more than comment on the couple's intended goals: it also forecasts the impossibility of such precaution. No relationship can be arranged in perfect terms, because error is inevitable. The Franklin's Tale turns its audience toward Griselda's patience but in milder and more balanced form.

But back to Dorigen's rejection. Aurelius leaves this encounter with Dorigen heartbroken and in full comprehension of the "impossible" (V.1009) condition she has given him. There has been no misunderstanding here. But after a year or more of lovesick madness, his brother turns to an old schoolfellow, a clerk of Orleans, who might know how to save Aurelius's life. The clerk is a magician who says he can make the rocks disappear for a week or two, for an exorbitant sum. Enchanted by the various things he sees in the magician's study, "theras his bookes be" (V.1207), Aurelius agrees to the bargain—"Fy on a thousand pound!" (V.1227)— and returns home to await this miracle. Only a short while later, a high tide washes in and makes it seem that "for a wike or twaye / . . . the rokkes were awaye" (V.1295–96). Dorigen must now leave her safely returned husband and become Aurelius's lover. When she tells her husband about her promise, he forces her to go to Aurelius and hold to her word, saying, "Trouthe is the hyeste thing that man may keepe" (V.1479). Where he could have refused to recognize the promise (because it was made by a woman and a married one at that) or could have physically threatened Aurelius for having designs on his wife, Arveragus upholds Dorigen's words, taking her independent action seriously. She goes off rather sadly to keep her pledge. But once Aurelius hears what Arveragus has done and notices Dorigen's sadness, he immediately relents, releasing her from her bond. Arveragus's gentle deed inspires Aurelius to imitate him. The squire then goes to explain to the magician why he needs more time to repay him. Hearing the story, the clerk quits the debt immediately: "But if a clerk coude doon a gentil dede / As wel as any of you, it is no drede" (V.1611–12).

The circuit of forgiveness and generosity now complete, the Franklin asks his audience to judge "which was the moste free, as thinketh you?" (V.1622). "Free" (in our modern sense of the word, but typically glossed as "generous") is a curious word here, for of course it signals largesse. He wants to know who was the most generous: the man who gives up his wedded wife (and thus his rights as a husband); the man who gives up what he strives toward, earns, and pays for (and thus his rights as a lover); or the bourgeois who gives up his profit on work performed—even if the tale obscures precisely how that happens. There is a sense that Arveragus and Aurelius, as nobles, have behaved according to the dictates of their class and thus much as we might expect. Indeed, Aurelius (as a squire) is already expected to imitate the noble behavior of a knight like Arveragus, but the clerk is not. The magician is bound by no such class identity or aspiration, so perhaps his generosity is more impressive, earning him the title of most "free." At least that might be the assessment of the Franklin, another figure who imitates the nobility of the gentry from a location technically outside its bounds.

Yet the more modern sense of "freedom" is also in play here, for our analysis above of the relative merits of male generosity depends on the constraint placed on these figures by social class. More tellingly, we might question what it is that each man presumes to give up and whether he possesses or has earned that which he relinquishes, and such a query implies a constraint. Were these men "free" (in the more modern sense) to be "free" (generous)? We can think about freedom in terms of its opposition to constraint, something underwriting our evaluation of the behavior of these men. The two nobles are constrained by their class status to behave in the ways that they do, and for that reason we might not account either the most generous. The clerk is unconstrained; his generosity comes purely from himself, and it would seem to fly in the face of his own interests. Because there is nothing to be gained by his generosity, it is genuine, whereas Aurelius and Arveragus get to experience and enhance their status by their generous acts. Since the tale returns to them what they gave away, it rewards those who began with the most: Arveragus keeps his wife, and Aurelius keeps his "heritage" (V.1584).

But what about Dorigen in this economy of constraint? As a woman, she is the most constrained figure in the tale, and the weight placed on her makes us consider precisely what each of the men gave up and whether they had a right to it in the first place. Arveragus gives up his wife, whom he has sworn to obey in everything. But when he swears her to silence and forces her to go to Aurelius to keep her promise, he does not sound like an obedient lover. Similarly, Aurelius did not remove the rocks "stoon by stoon" (V.993) from the coast of Brittany but paid for an illusionist, who seems merely to have pulled an almanac off his bookshelf to reliably predict the tide. Neither of these men technically did what they claimed to have done. And by what right do they so presume? Aurelius should know better, according to Dorigen, than to "love another mannes wif, / That hath hir body whan so that him liketh" (V.1004–05). But Dorigen herself gives the lie to their freedom, showing that their generosity is dependent on something else—an obligation, perhaps even submission, that she understands better than they.

In the end, the Franklin tells a story in which everyone's renunciations turn out to everyone's profit in the ethical economy, undermining the debate about mastery and sovereignty begun in the Wife of Bath's Prologue. The answer that the Franklin offers is that no one should have mastery (which we might define as control over another person or being) and everyone should have sovereignty (or control over themselves). He thereby disambiguates two terms that have been used synonymously at times in various stories in the Marriage Group, which elides self-determination and control over another.[4] He does so by endorsing patience with the speech of others:

> Lerneth to suffre, or elles, so mote I goon,
> Ye shul it lerne, wherso ye wol or noon.
> For in this world, certayn, ther no wight is
> That he ne dooth or saith somtime amis[.]   (V.777–80)

Language is very much at the heart of the Franklin's Tale, almost as centrally as mastery. Indeed, we may not be able to think of the two separately.

This observation returns us to the matter of "entente," which is everywhere under consideration in this story of various kinds of promises, as well as to the Franklin's strategic misidentification of the tale as a Breton lay. This detail about genre could be connected to the Franklin's other rhetorical displays as part of his effort to perform with narrative skill. Few other Canterbury narrators announce their genres so overtly, as if to impress the pilgrim audience. The Franklin's intent appears at such points as this description of the end of the party:

> But sodeinly bigonne revel newe,
> Til that the brighte sonne loste his hewe,
> For th'orisonte hath reft the sonne his light—
> This is as muche to saye as it was night.
> And hoom they goon in joye and in solas[.]   (V.1015–19)

He chooses an excessively elaborate way of saying "it got dark and everyone went home." The Franklin similarly describes changes in season and weather in ornate terms (V.1245–55), to the point of perhaps forgetting—"And 'Nowel!' crieth every lusty man" (V.1255)—the pagan setting he otherwise

---

[4] For a discussion of this difference between sovereignty and mastery in the Marriage Group, see my essay "Desire in the *Canterbury Tales*: Sovereignty and Mastery between the Wife and Clerk," *Studies in the Age of Chaucer* 31 (2009): 81–108.

takes pains to historicize. In both form and content, then, the Franklin attends to the ways things get said and to their radically transformative effects. This is nowhere more evident than in his explanation of what the magician does to make the rocks disappear. His speech is a litany of books and tables consulted "in thilke dayes" (V.1293) to produce a subtle calculation: "But thurgh his magik, for a wike or twaye, / It seemed that alle the rokkes were aweye" (V.1295–96). The Franklin's terms explaining the calculation are as much an illusion as the magician's work. His use of language transforms the coast—or at least its perception by everyone, both in the tale and in the tale's audience.

While such explanatory "scientific" language is responsible for the magical transformation of the black rocks in the tale, language of another kind moves the rest of the story to its conclusion. The Franklin emphasizes the way that the characters in the tale must retell its prior events. Consider, for instance, how Dorigen confesses to Arveragus:

> "Allas," quod she, "that ever was I born:
> Thus have I saide," quod she, "thus have I sworn—"
> And tolde him al as ye han herd bifore:
> It needeth nat reherce it you namore.   (V.1463–66).

Aurelius takes a similar approach in explaining his situation to the clerk at the tale's end:

> Aurelius his tale anon bigan,
> And tolde him al as ye han herd bifore:
> It needeth nat to you reherce it more.   (V.1592–94)

In using the very same words, the Franklin calls attention to the need to summarize and rehearse the story. Such a statement sounds like a critique of language's failures, but the tale might instead be viewed as demonstrating language's stunning success. In both cases the retold story provokes a form of generosity and forgiveness for words' unintended effects. Rather than faltering at each juncture, the speaker's language has been all too powerful and transformative. Is this what the Franklin, who is trying to win a storytelling contest among some of his social betters, secretly intends? Perhaps. Inaugurating a more overt debate on language and intent,[5] the Franklin's Tale concludes the Marriage Group and transforms itself into something spectacular.

---

[5] Language and intent were, of course, implicit subjects of the Friar's and Summoner's Tales. Here we see that the Franklin's Tale picks up themes other than marriage, such as class and "gentilesse," from the Wife of Bath.

THE PHYSICIAN'S TALE

After the lively debate of the Marriage Group, it's easy to be let down by what follows. The Physician's Tale hardly disappoints on that count. Typically defined as an *exemplum*, or a literary example, it concerns Virginia, who was killed by her father in order to protect her purity. Modern readers have found it perplexing in both form and content. But rather than suggest that the story is some kind of intentional failure (on Chaucer's part or the Physician's), we might see the tale as provocatively experimental. Such experimentation would align the Physician's Tale with much of Chaucer's often provisional poem, in a fragment that ultimately offers a meditation on death.

The Physician begins his story with the authority of Livy's history of Rome: "Ther was, as telleth Titus Livius . . ." (VI.1). We've seen exempla deployed in *The Canterbury Tales* before (in the Friar's and Summoner's Tales, for instance). Exempla are short, illustrative stories, often providing descriptions or definitions, and they appear in longer works that provide an interpretive frame. In that larger context, they illustrate a particular point or truth: exempla *exemplify* something. In Livy's *Ab urbe condita* (literally, "from the founding of the city"), the Virginia story sits as an example—like that of the chaste wife Lucretia, with which it is often paired—justifying the political response to tyranny and legitimating the civic revolt at the origin of the Roman Republic. Like the other medieval redactions that seem to have been more immediate sources for the poet than Livy himself, Chaucer's version retrofits this example to match the ethics of medieval Christian culture.[1]

---

[1] These other medieval adaptations of Livy include the French *Roman de la rose* as well as Gower's retelling in the contemporaneous English *Confessio Amantis*. For a fuller

Opening with an encomium praising virginity, Chaucer aligns the Physician's Tale with others that glorify purity and chastity in women. In *The Canterbury Tales,* many of these bear an explicit relation to the genre of hagiography, or saint's life. As a popular genre with the Physician's Christian audience, hagiography provides the tale's local grid of intelligibility, making sense out of sacrifice. Walking to the temple one day with her mother, Virginia is seen by the corrupt judge Apius. Struck by her beauty, he concocts a scheme to declare her his stolen slave to separate her from the protection of her family and take her into his possession. Her father, Virginius, pleads his case in court against this trumped-up accusation, but, since the judge presiding over the case is Apius himself, the legal result is a foregone conclusion. The father must turn her over to Apius's agent, Claudius, who had brought the charges before the court. But before this order can be enforced, Virginius takes Virginia's life to save her from the consequences of this illicit desire.

One can see the attraction the girl holds for medieval storytellers. A beautiful young heroine whose virtue is purity (read right out of her name), Virginia's "martyrdom" seems easily adaptable to the moral assumptions of a medieval audience. Conforming the classical example to the contours of a saint's life, the Physician attempts to render its moral and ethical allegiances intelligible. The conflation of classical and hagiographic genres is augmented by some explicitly Christian references inserted into the story that perhaps helped make its brutal outlines seem more familiar and maybe more palatable. The most obvious of these references is the biblical one to Jephthah's daughter, from Judges 11. In a gesture unique to the Physician's version of the story, Virginia asks her father to delay her execution in order "my deeth for to complaine a litel space. / For pardee,

---

discussion of the way Chaucer's tale departs from Livy and more closely follows the *Roman* and Gower, see my "Disfigurements of Desire in Chaucer's Religious Tales," chapter 4 of *Desire in the* Canterbury Tales (Columbus: Ohio State UP, 2015), esp. 173–78. It is worth mentioning that the French story is the one that first makes Virginia's death not a stabbing but a decapitation, as in the Physician's Tale.

Jepte yaf his doghter grace / For to complaine'er he hire slow, allas"
(VI.239–41). Directly afterward,

> She riseth up and to hir fader saide,
> "Blessed be God that I shal die a maide!
> Yive me my deeth er that I have a shame;
> Dooth with youre child youre wil, a Goddes name." (VI.247–50)

Such changes to Chaucer's story render its focus entirely different from
Livy's. Virginia is killed in her home, in a manner planned in advance,
whereas in Livy judgment is rendered in the Forum, where Verginius
stabs his daughter with a knife grabbed from a butcher's stall. The threat
to Verginia in Livy's history is a threat to every Roman citizen, and her
father's act "asserts her freedom" in the only way available to him.[2] But no
abstract virtue of virginity is at stake there. Thus, when Virginia accepts
her fate, glad that she can die a "maide," her death becomes a self-sacrifice
to virginity. And it is in this respect that she resembles the virgin martyr
saints, who often professed their faith by refusing to marry according to
their pagan parents' wishes. The bodily integrity of the female saint, and
especially her sexual purity, was the ultimate sign of her faith and of her
dedication to Christ.

Given the historical shift in contexts outlined above, we are licensed
to read the Physician's focus on Virginia in a new light. Like other medieval redactions, his story is at pains to put her at its center and to reframe
the virtue it exemplifies accordingly. But it does so only imperfectly. Part
of the problem with this medieval "modernization" of the classical exemplum lies in some of the material the Physician adds to the story: the
description of the heroine in the opening as a crafted object of Nature
(VI.9–29), as well as the details about the good governance of children
(VI.72–102). Nothing is particularly wrong with including such detail or

---

[2] See Livy 3.48, as translated in Robert M. Correale and Mary Hamel, eds., *Sources and
Analogues of the Canterbury Tales*, vol. 2 (Cambridge: D. S. Brewer, 2005), 546–47.

commentary, except their failure to cohere into any governing theme. The Physician drops them as easily as he picked them up. Though we might expect the exemplum to end with some kind of moral about the danger of natural beauty or lax parental supervision, the tale itself turns instead to focus on the immoral behavior of the men involved. The audience is left surprised (and not for the first time) by the closing moral attached to the example.[3]

Hagiography provides the language of female heroism that medieval culture most clearly understood, underwriting the Physician's adaptation. Such a strategy would nicely align with the historical parameters of the Physician's own profession. Today we tend to think of a physician merely in terms of medical science and the cure of bodily disease, but in Chaucer's era those practices were steeped in spiritual pursuits to a degree that would probably surprise us. When the General Prologue narrator says, "His studye was but litel on the Bible" (I.438), the claim raises important questions about matters relevant to being a "Doctour of Physik" (I.411), which include astronomy, "magik naturel" (I.416), and diet. In the humoral understanding of health as a balance of substances—the four "humors" being black bile, or melancholia; yellow bile, or choler; phlegm; and blood—the body can be affected by planetary influences, weather, emotional strain, and digestion. A physician might consult the heavens for an auspicious time to administer his medicine and would look to the Bible as an authoritative text on creation and the natural world, which formed the basis of his field of expertise. The moral principles underlying biblical knowledge would be an integral element of the Physician's practice and thus inform his tale.

We'd be hard-pressed, however, to use this medieval understanding of "medicine" to read the Physician's Tale as unproblematic. Even if we take for granted his shift of attention from the heroic Virginius to the virtuous Virginia in these historical terms, the tale remains full of difficulties and

---

[3] The Summoner's Tale also ends with a moral problematically fitted to its exemplum. The Manciple's Tale makes it into an art form.

seeming contradictions. Most significantly, by the time we reach the end of the story, our attention has shifted from Virginia to Apius, whose punishment and suicide end the story. In his summation, the Physician applies a moral for his audience's benefit:

> Heere may men seen how sinne hath his merite:
> Beth war, for no man woot whom God wol smite,
> In no degree and in no manere wise.
> The worm of conscience may agrise
> Of wikked lif, though it so privee be
> That no man woot therof but God and he.
> For be he lewed man or elles lered,
> He noot how soone that he shal been afered.
> Therfore I rede you this conseil take:
> Forsaketh sinne, er sinne you forsake.   (VI.277–86)

While morals are meant to generalize, making the force of a narrative more widely applicable, this particular "moral" has confounded Chaucer's readers. It seems to be inspired by Apius's death and "wikked lif," for the story ends with the way "sinne hath his merite." Somewhere in the middle of this short narrative, we moved from an example of virtue to a frightening portrayal of vice.

Once the central interest of the story, Virginia is rendered a mere tool for understanding how our secret vices (known to only God and ourselves) will eventually lead to our end—a gesture that aligns "us" with Apius. This conclusion of the tale appears devoted to inspiring a certain fear— hence the lingering image of the trembling worm of conscience. The closing injunction to forsake sin before it forsakes us thus seems unduly reductive. Having forgotten Virginia and possessing no means to heroize her in the pre-Christian world she inhabits, the story swerves to a different end. Her virginity can be praised, but sublime martyrdom is unavailable to her. Instead, Virginia is merely killed by a father who himself has begun to resemble a domestic tyrant. No scene of miraculous endurance or frustrated torture projects her virtue as would occur in a saint's life. And neither does her death or her father's imprisonment inspire civic revolt, as the classical exemplum did. Because Virginia has nowhere to go in the Physician's Tale, it turns to a moralization that is overly focused on Apius's sin and its possible infection of a wider audience.

THE PARDONER'S PROLOGUE
AND TALE

The Pardoner offers one of the tour de force performances in *The Canterbury Tales*. As he did for the Wife of Bath, Chaucer gives the Pardoner a lengthy prologue in which the pilgrim professes, confesses, and otherwise complicates the scene of tale-telling: in this way he offers a dramatic production in the place of a simple story, or what the Pardoner calls "som honeste thing" (VI.328). The word "honest" here does not mean exactly (or only) what it does today; rather, it refers to something honorable or respectable.[1] Such propriety is a concern because the pilgrims collectively recoil from the Host's request for "som mirthe or japes" from the Pardoner (VI.319). They are afraid he'll infect them with "ribaudye" (VI.324).

In his thoughtful response, the Pardoner promises a kind of honesty more in line with our modern sense of the term: truthfulness. As we will see, his narrative power lies in the honest disclosure of his dishonesty, even the depths to which he is willing to expose himself in this manner. The Pardoner's discourse is not only a confession of the extent of his deception but a performance of his deceitful script, an example of how he operates "al by rote" (VI.332). The only reputable story the Pardoner can offer is the one he uses all the time as his illustrative moral example of his theme: *radix malorum est cupiditas*—"avarice is the root of evil." He thus prefaces this story with another "honest" one, a truthful confession of his

---

[1] *OED*, s.v. "honest," adj. and adv. 1.b and etym. From the Old French *honté*, "honor," "respect."

intent in telling it—his own personal avarice—the ironic contours of which turn any sense of "som honeste thing" on its head.

As a fundraiser for the church's charitable causes, the Pardoner is another pilgrim (like the Wife of Bath) who benefits from the confusion proliferated by an elaborate theology of debt. The Wife exploited the doctrine of the marriage debt, whereas the Pardoner traffics from the other side of the spiritual economy through the system of indulgences he sells as part of the apparatus of penance. *Selling* is not exactly the right word for what he should be doing, but it accurately characterizes how he offers his pardons to his clients, a method that we will consider at some length. His performance in his Prologue and his Tale cannot be fully appreciated without a clear understanding of the official system of confession and penance, and the related practice of indulgences. Because he intentionally obfuscates matters (mainly by conflating his office with that of a ministering priest), he threatens to turn Chaucer's readers into his sermon audience. Both could be easily misled by his claims about his authority and his office, caught in his nets of ambiguity and deception.

Pardoners are figures licensed by ecclesiastical authority to publish—literally, "to make public"—indulgences, which were more familiarly called "pardons" in Middle English. These were part of the elaborate machinery of official forgiveness, contrition, and penance. Indulgences were complex affairs and, as one recent scholar explains, might "be understood as the remission—or better, the payment by others—of a sinner's debt of punishment (*poena*; lit. 'pain') for sins already forgiven through the sacrament of penance, wherein moral guilt (*culpa*) was removed."[2] The system therefore depends on the distinction between forgiveness *a poena* (from the pain of punishment) and forgiveness *a culpa* (from guilt of one's actions or intent—what we might think of as the "real" forgiveness of sin, which only an ordained priest can offer). As we will see, the Pardoner, who can offer the first but not the second, continually conflates his office with that

---

[2] Alastair Minnis, *Fallible Authors: Chaucer's Pardoner and Wife of Bath* (Philadelphia: U of Pennsylvania P, 2008), 74.

of the priest. In the painted miniatures of the pilgrims decorating the Ellesmere manuscript, the Pardoner is dressed boldly in red, not because pardoners necessarily had to dress that way but, more emphatically, as a visual sign of his discursive disguise and deception. He dresses like the Parson, who is also depicted in red, a color often worn by priests at the time. The Ellesmere artist thus signals in this visualization the Pardoner's efforts to confuse listeners into substituting the kind of pardon he sells for divine forgiveness itself, a confusion that would reduce the apparatus of penance to an easy financial transaction.

The indulgences that the Pardoner hawks are complicated "goods," tied to satisfaction, the performance of which was part of the sacrament of penance. Those seeking to be forgiven had to demonstrate sincere contrition (true sorrow) for their sin, which they then confessed openly and freely to a priest (or friar licensed to hear confession) and for which they repented. As a final gesture, it was necessary to make satisfaction—that is, to perform work that might be carried out in this world as well as in the next, in purgatory. As its name suggests, purgatory is the place where individuals are purged of the stain of sin before entering heaven. Satisfaction is thus a form of remediation, of making good on one's faults and making up for them. It might take the form of prayer or even pilgrimage. But graver sins might be harder to purge and were more difficult to satisfy in these ways, necessitating divine intervention. Such a heavy debt might be paid only out of the "treasury of merit," the superabundance of goodness produced by the works of Christ and the saints. For that payment against the pain caused by such sins, a formal indulgence was needed.

Indulgence often took the form of material donation—say, to a hospital or to a church—and was meant to be a sign of repentance for a confession already made in full. But various ecclesiastical injunctions to action (crusades, for example, or charitable building efforts) promised plenary indulgence, which "could easily be mistaken as a release *a poena et a culpa*."[3] The confusion became widespread and made indulgences easy

---

[3] Minnis, *Fallible Authors*, 77.

targets of reformist criticism. An important aspect of indulgences was their function within a system of display, in which sinners openly perform their repentance. But the system was also constructed to offer a kind of hopefulness. One could do something for oneself (or others) in aid of purgatorial penance: good works could remediate bad ones. The system was simply too easy to abuse and too difficult to defend against confusion and thus corruption.

Chaucer's Pardoner carries seals, patents, and bulls that supposedly guarantee his authority. The seal and patent constitute his worldly credential to raise money for the hospital "of Rouncival" (I.670), a locale just outside the city of London. But the bulls are also spiritual credentials, "the documents which announce and describe the indulgences he will dispense as his clients give alms to one or more of the various charitable causes for which he is collecting."[4] As we can see from this definition, the generosity that was part of contrite satisfaction was supposed to come first; the indulgence (the time off from a future stint in purgatory) was the reward of such generosity. The Pardoner, however, purposefully confuses cause and effect to make a simple cash payment the basis of forgiveness.

When the Pardoner turns from the inn, at which he has momentarily paused, to begin his story, he opens with a preamble organizing his tale. In fact, he tells the tale of his tale, complicating any simple story he might offer. He announces that he will tell the same story he always tells his listeners and potential donors. The prologue explains the sermon context in which he typically delivers it. Beginning with a direct address to the other pilgrims, the Pardoner orates about his usual oration:

> Lordinges—quod he—in chirches whan I preche,
> I paine me to han an hautein speeche,
> And ringe it out as round as gooth a belle,
> For I can al by rote that I telle.

---

[4] Minnis, *Fallible Authors*, 100.

My theme is alway oon, and ever was:
Radix malorum est cupiditas.   (VI.329–34)

From the beginning, the Pardoner's Prologue repeats the story and the scene of its telling that he supposedly describes. When he seems to speak about the kind of preaching he does in church, he does so by using those very same techniques on the Canterbury pilgrims. He delivers his prologue in the same "hautien speeche" as he claims to use on his clients and rings it out "by rote" for them as well. For instance, just after he announces his perennial theme "*Radix malorum est cupiditas*," he tells us how he "in Latin . . . speke[s] a wordes fewe / To saffron with my predicacioun, / And for to stire hem to devocioun" (VI.344–46). Isn't that just what he's done to us?

It's therefore hard to tell the difference between the Pardoner's description of his habitual behavior and his actual performance of it, into which he seems to slide so smoothly. Performing his description as he describes his performance, he recalls the Wife and her gendered ventrilo-quism. In both cases, self-consciously autobiographical prologues compli-cate the scene of narration. Their tales fit into a larger story of themselves that acts out or acts against what they've confessed. Given that the Par-doner's occupation is based in the business of confession and forgiveness, his prologue and tale are doubly entwined. The Wife may have been hon-est about her dishonesty, but the Pardoner is a walking Cretan liar's paradox—when a man says, "I always lie," is he lying or is he telling the truth? From his first utterance about "som honeste thing," the Pardoner has had us off balance. For the respectable story the pilgrims insist on hearing is also his inner truth: "I preche of nothing but for coveteise" (VI.424). His hypocrisy underwrites his honesty and poisons any truthful claim that he might make.

The source of Chaucer's Pardoner is the character Faux Semblant, or False Seeming, from the *Roman de la rose*, who is a figure of exquisite verbal deception. In that allegorical work, the figure's name proclaims his duplicity as well as the effect he has on others. He is a vice figure, who announces his hypocrisy as he demonstrates it. The *Roman* provided medieval vernacular writers with a textbook on self-consciously ironic literary deception. In Faux Semblant, Chaucer found a mesmerizing figure whose narration was at the same time engrossing and dangerously vertiginous.

The Pardoner's Prologue contextualizes the tale that he eventually tells—a story of three rioters in search of Death—with details about its environment and purpose, a story, in effect, about the way the Pardoner uses the story. Like the Wife of Bath's Prologue, the Pardoner's is also an autobiographical narrative and a confession of sorts—complicated, of course, by his professional role in the "business" of repentance. He reveals his methods of extortion and his tricks. He drives listeners to participate in his deceptions by accusing those who resist him of being most shamefully "envoluped in sinne" (VI.942). In addition, he tempts them with the promised benefits of his relics (good harvests, healthy flocks), which he reveals as a mere "gaude" to deceive the gullible and "lewed peple" (VI.389–92). Even further, he confesses his full intent in these deceptions:

> I preche of nothing but for coveitise;
> Therfore my theme is yet and ever was
> *Radix malorum est cupiditas.*   (VI.424–26)

He knows that by these means he may "maken other folk to twinne / From avarice, and sore to repente" (VI.430–31). However, he follows this claim with an open admission: "But that is nat my principal entente" (VI.432). It may not be his intent, but it is his narrative strategy. For he introduces his tale by acknowledging,

> For though myself be a ful vicious man,
> A moral tale yet I you telle can,
> Which I am wont to preche for to winne.   (VI.459–61)

The Pardoner's earnings rest upon the morality of a tale that he tells for immoral, avaricious purposes. In this way he raises the question of

whether a tale can be fully separated from its teller, a question as important to reformist theology as it is to modern Chaucerian critics worrying
about the limits of "roadside drama."

The Pardoner's Tale seems simpler than the Prologue, but it will in
the end complicate matters even further. An exemplum illustrating his
sole theme, that avarice is the root of all evil, his tale incidentally depicts
the sins of the tavern (gluttony, gambling, and swearing), which is where
we find the three rioters at its opening. For a moral anecdote, it's full of
interesting local detail. The story is located in Flanders, a part of the Low
Countries that had various trade connections to England. Flemish styles,
like the Merchant's beaver hat, were seen in London, and resident alien
businessmen from Flanders were the particular targets of violence during
the Peasant's Revolt of 1381, to which the Nun's Priest will expressly refer
in his tale when he mentions the hullabaloo made by rebels "whan that
they wolden any Fleming kille" (VII.3396). Moreover, the Pardoner's Tale
takes place in a time of plague, a disease that ravaged England repeatedly
over the previous century. The pestilence might have a kind of symbolic
value for the tale, representing the malaise of sin hanging over its decayed
world, in which "yonge folk . . . haunteden folye" (VI.464). But it also has
a timely resonance for Chaucer's contemporary audience, which likely has
vivid memories of the plague—popularly called "the Death."

In this exemplum, three men respond to the predations of pestilence
upon their kin by swearing an oath to slay Death. In the tavern "er prime"
(before 9 A.M.; VI.662), these men are drunk and overhear the plague being
characterized as "a privee thief men clepeth Deeth, / That in this contree al
the peple sleeth" (VI.675–76). The tavern boy speaking these words is
ostensibly repeating the explanation of his mother, who enjoins him to
"beth redy for to meete him evermore" (VI.683), but his figurative language
is grossly mistaken by these sinful and inebriated adults, who thereby make
a ludicrous effort to perform an impossible task that blasphemes the heroics
of the crucifixion. In their quest for Death, the three meet an Old Man
upon the way, whom they berate for his age and infirmity. Himself a
memento mori (a reminder of death), the Old Man claims that "Deeth,

allas, ne wol nat have my lif" (VI.727), a statement that leads the three rioters to believe he is Death's "espye" (VI.755). We might note the game being
played by the Pardoner's Tale. Like his characters, his readers must understand his Tale's language figuratively, beyond its literal signification, at the
same time that it can be playfully reduced to the literal. For despite the way
that these rioters have undertaken "an impossible" (III.688), mistaking the
idea of death for a proper name, they have also undertaken a quest for death,
a goal they will most surely achieve. In fact, they may have already done so.
The Old Man directs them toward what they seek:

> "Now sires," quod he, "if that ye be so lief
> To finde Deeth, turne up this croked way,
> For in that grove I lafte him, by my fay,
> Under a tree, and ther he wol abide[.]"   (VI.760–63)

But under the tree, the three rioters find a wealth of gold florins. They forget all about their quest as they begin to plot how to transport their treasure safely home. Drawing straws, they send the youngest of the three to
town for provisions (bread and wine), while the other two ready the gold
to be moved under cover of night. Once the youngest departs, the elder two
begin to scheme against him: a treasure split in half is greater than one
divided by three. Meanwhile, the youngest procures bread, wine, and poi-
son, in order to do away with his co-conspirators and keep the fortune for
himself. He poisons two bottles of wine and returns to his fellows. Upon
his arrival, they slay him just as they had planned. Once the deed is done,
one of the rioters shares a poisoned drink with his brother, "For which
anon they storven bothe two" (VI.888). And thus, the three rioters find
the death they were seeking.

A story in which three men seek Death can end in no other way than
this, with the three men dead. Their quest makes literal what they do figuratively from the start. The Pardoner's discourse demands that we differentiate literal and figurative, as well as worldly and spiritual meanings.
Such pertain even to "life" itself and the everyday existence of the figures

in his story. These men occupy its center, but they are spiritually dead before it even begins. That deadness is figured in a number of ways, including their literal understanding of the "privee thief" who comes in time of plague. As the child explains:

> And maister, er ye come in his presence,
> Me thinketh that it were necessarye
> For to be war of swich an adversarye;
> Beth redy for to meete him evermore:
> Thus taughte me my dame. I saye namore.   (VI.680–84)

Instead of seeking any moral or spiritual readiness to confront death, they respond to the challenge of confronting Death as if undertaking a physical endeavor, opposing someone they could conquer. They understand the threat at the wrong level. Even worse, their misunderstanding amounts to blasphemy. Not only do they continually swear by various parts of Christ's crucified body—the "armes," "blood," and pinioning "nailes" mentioned at various times (e.g., VI.651–54)—but their efforts to slay Death amount to a ridiculous parody of Christ's death and resurrection, the heroic action that conquered the finality of death for humankind.

Everywhere we look in the Pardoner's Tale, we find a scene of parodic inversion of this central miracle of Christianity. For instance, the rioters are sent by the Old Man "up this croked way" to a tree under which they will find Death. The crooked way leads to tree at whose roots they find gold rather than to a tree of life, the true cross, at whose base they would find salvation. The treasure at the base of this tree proves false, igniting the avarice that is the fundamental cause of their demise. Similarly, when the two rioters send the youngest one for their provisions, the bread and wine he obtains become the means to a last supper of a decidedly deadly nature, a wicked inversion of the communion celebration.

From the beginning, they eat and drink so much that "they doon the devel sacrifise / Withinne that develes temple," both in the tavern and within their own bodies (VI.467–68). This drunken, gluttonous behavior, too, is a mockery of communion. It inspires the Pardoner to deliver a sermon within the Tale on these tavern vices (VI.481–658): in it he decries cooks, "how they stampe and straine and grinde, / And turnen substance into accident" (VI.536–37), a dramatic reversal of the miracle of transubstantiation itself by which the "accidents" of bread and wine are turned into the "substance" of Christ's body and blood.

The most perplexing figure in this simple tale of life and death is the Old Man who directs the rioters on their way. His significance has been much debated, since he is pivotal in their quest. But he is not the grim reaper figure that many take him for. He is instead an unrecognized image of the rioters' desire. Wishing to slay Death, they seek a perpetual living that is a perversion of eternal life, a withering age that would leave them without direction. The Old Man appears in order to provide a contrast to these young men, who are oblivious to what they want or seek in asking to find Death. For the Old Man himself, knowingly, pursues the same thing, though Death will not have him. Looking for a man to exchange youth for his age and knocking at his "modres gate" (VI.729) with his staff, the Old Man appears to be an image of the knowledge lacked by the rioters: life on earth is merely a prison, turning man into a "restelees caitif" (VI.728). Not only do the rioters fail to understand the child's words, they do not know what it is that they desire. They do not know the extent to which they are already dead. As the Pardoner concluded earlier in his sermon: "But certes, he that haunteth swiche delices / Is deed whil that he liveth in tho vices" (VI.547–48). The Old Man personifies this living death, which the Pardoner, at some level, must understand.

Once the rioters have met their end, the Pardoner wraps up his story quickly, looking to cure his listeners of avarice by working as the conduit for their generosity. He narrates the script he habitually uses:

> Boweth your heed under this holy bulle!
> Cometh up, ye wives, offreth of youre wolle!
> Youre name I entre here in my rolle: anon
> Into the blisse of hevene shul ye gon.

> I you assoile by myn heigh power,
> Ye that wol offre, as clene and eek as cler
> As ye were born.—And lo, sires, thus I preche.   (VI.909–15)

Still conflating his power to wash them "clene and eek as cler" with that of the priest who forgives sin itself, the Pardoner ends his performance of his performance: "And lo, sires, thus I preche." But what follows is even more arresting:

> And Jesu Crist that is oure soules leeche
> So graunte you his pardon to receive,
> For that is best; I wol you nat deceive.   (VI.916–18)

For a hot minute the Pardoner seems to be telling the absolute truth. But that truth unravels the entirety of his discourse, for it exceeds the avarice that has everywhere else been the ground and source of what he has to say, both its meaning and its intent. Thus the Pardoner's immediate retreat into his sales pitch: "But sires, oo word forgat I in my tale: / I have relikes and pardoun in my male" (VI.919–20). Immediately after demonstrating the way he offers false goods to the "lewed" people inside his tale, the Pardoner turns to the Canterbury pilgrims and does the same to them. What is happening here?

One might say that the Pardoner narrates as an automaton, performing his script with sheer unconscious force. Once he starts, he simply goes to the end, which always includes offering listeners an opportunity to donate to his causes and purchase pardon. However, his turn from the tale of his performance to his present audience pivots on the recognition of Christ's pardon as "best," offering a flash of self-recognition for the limitation of his intention—what G. L. Kittredge long ago called "a very paroxysm of agonized sincerity."[5] The Pardoner here reveals a

---

[5] George Lyman Kittredge, *Chaucer and His Poetry* (Cambridge, MA: Harvard UP, 1915), 217.

desire for a kind of pardon beyond his own power to grant that he has found otherwise unavailable to him and that he has generally resisted acknowledging. This momentary flash of sincerity is more than diffuse comedy on the part of the congenital hypocrite: it enacts a drama of despair, the one unforgivable sin. To despair, to set oneself apart from the rest of humanity as being beyond redemption, is to fail to believe in God's forgiveness and amounts to a denial not of one's own power but of God's power.

This momentary self-recognition has provoked wide debate about what the Pardoner is and is not, focusing on the privation at the heart of his discourse and his character. After spending so much time talking about his greedy acquisitiveness, the Pardoner for once acknowledges the lack driving everything he says and does. But it's not merely Christ's forgiveness that the Pardoner may lack or that is so different from the kind of pardon that he deceptively deals to people. The Pardoner himself is lacking from the start. In the General Prologue, Chaucer describes the Pardoner's duplicitous appearance by alluding to a physical privation that seems to signify his spiritual one: "I trowe he were a gelding or a mare" (I.691). He thereby points to the absence of marks of normative masculinity—the beard that looks lately shaven but never grows—as a sign of a deeper evil. Refiguring his sin in the features of secondary sex characteristics (his voice, his hair, his skin) that liken him to such emasculated creatures has provoked much debate about the Pardoner's so-called sexuality and the possibility that he is a eunuch, one who is either literally or figuratively castrated for God. Such a condition would be embraced by the devout wishing to cut themselves off from the enjoyments of the world and the body. But this does not describe the Pardoner, leaving us to wonder whether his physical resemblance to a eunuch is a sign of yet another form of sinfulness, which his friendship with the Summoner in the General Prologue suggests. Chaucer makes it both impossible to ignore the Pardoner's sexuality, whatever it might be, and difficult to discuss it with any certainty. It becomes a figuration for the unknowable and inscrutable in him.

THE SHIPMAN'S TALE

Providing the opening of the longest and most generically various fragment, the Shipman's is the last of the four fabliaux in *The Canterbury Tales*. Hardly connected at all to the pilgrim who is its teller, it is far less dramatically circumscribed than any of the other three. It plays no part in any narrative "quiting," as the Miller's and Reeve's do; nor is it part of some elaborate disavowal and denial of its narrator's misery, as the Merchant's Tale seems to be. In fact, we are hardly sure the Shipman is meant to tell this tale, since its opening suggests it is voiced by a married woman. Describing a merchant and his wife in its opening, the Shipman's Tale laments the case of the "sely housbonde" (VII.11) who does not seem to understand what the real cost will be if he resists paying for what his wife requires:

> He moot us clothe, and he moot us arraye,
> Al for his owene worshipe, richely—
> In which array we dauncen jolily;
> And if that ne noght may, paraventure,
> Or elles list no swich dispence endure,
> But thinketh it is wasted and ylost,
> Thanne moot another payen for oure cost,
> Or lene us gold—and that is perilous. (VII.12–19)

The narrator here speaks of "we" and "us" wives in relation to these naïve husbands, men held to be "wis" because they are "riche" (VII.2) and who think they have full control over the household economy. This description forecasts the tale it precedes, a story that shows how this merchant-husband, in the end, "payen moot for al!" (VII.10). But this voice sounds nothing like a shipman or any other kind of man. Rather, it sounds a lot like the Wife of Bath, whose Prologue exhibits similar wisdom about husbands, husbandry, and the politics of debt and payment in the household. The Wife, of course, is the only secular woman on the pilgrimage who could refer to herself in these terms. This fact has led most scholars to read the Shipman's Tale as Chaucer's first attempt at a story for the Wife of Bath, a fabliau whose concerns he eventually replaced with the current Prologue's sermon and autobiographical confession. The Shipman's Tale and the Wife of Bath's Prologue do similar things and take a similarly economic approach to marriage, and both seem informed by the Wife's skill in the commerce of the cloth-making industry, which infuses this rhetoric. Both performances support and are supported by a sense of keen business acumen.

Like the Wife of Bath's Prologue, the Shipman's Tale tells the story of an unusually canny wife, a woman who is on the lookout for her own "good"—a term with a range of meanings having to do with her profit or benefit, including both goods and pleasure[1]—and who can keep one step ahead of her husband in such matters. Like other fabliaux, it is full of verbal trickery and sexual deception, but in this particular story the wife manages her situation brilliantly. She dupes her husband, enjoys a lover, and gets away with a great deal of money, through a punning equivocation on "taile" (VII.416), implying the interconnected meanings of tail/tally/tale in play throughout the story. None of the other fabliaux in the collection end so happily or celebrate the ingenuity of a clever (if unfaithful) wife. From its very beginning, the Shipman's Tale seeks to tell the "repair" (VII.21) one is forced to endure when one marries such a woman "of excellent beautee, / And compaignable and revelous" (VII.3–4). "Repair" can be

---

[1] "Good" appears repeatedly in the Shipman's Tale. Its husband demands his wife "to keepe oure good . . . / And honestly governe wel oure hous" (VII.243–44) in his absence. The Wife of Bath uses a similar expression for a knowing wife, who "can hir good" (III.231). What one does with one's goods (possessions) is intimately related to what's beneficial to one's status, reputation, and comfort.

glossed as "visitors" (those who repair to one's home), but it also has a more general meaning of "return," as in the return on one's investment or what returns to one in the end. It is used in the second sense later in the tale. The merchant's return home is marked with this very term: "To Saint Denis he gan for to repaire" (VII.326). These senses are not unrelated, since the "repair" that this husband must endure comes from the many guests he receives in his home, an effect of his showy hospitality that includes parading his pretty wife around. The term cuts both ways.

One such guest is a monk, Daun John, who enjoys the merchant's "largesse," or generosity, which is on display through his fair wife as much as anything else (VII.20–24). Born in the same village as the merchant, the monk claims "cosinage" (VII.36), or kinship, with him. The familial term is used to invoke their close friendship. But *to cozen* is also to trick or to deceive (*OED*, s.v. "cozen" v. 1), and the tale plays liberally with this meaning as a connotation of their kinship. As we will see, the monk's familiarity with his friend, the merchant, is expressed through the merchant's wife: his family, his familiar (a word sometimes spelled "famulier" in ME), and his *mulier* (Latin, "wife") are lexically intertwined. The familial is slightly ironized by these other related terms. Kinship (cousinhood) is tainted by deception (cosinage), and marriage troubled by frequent proximity and overfamiliarity. We can take neither their status as cousins nor their familiar friendship at face value.

The tale witnesses a set of exchanges based on these relations between characters. Technically the husband and wife are the only familial relations, but the monk stretches the familiar into the familial whenever he can. The husband and monk are not blood or even legal relatives. But these two "cousins," monk and merchant, swear brotherhood to one another (as many pairs in various Canterbury tales do): "Thus been they knit with eterne alliaunce, / And ech of hem gan other for t'assure / Of bretherhede whil that hir lif may dure" (VII.40–42). Similarly, Daun John addresses the wife as "nece" (VII.100, 125), even as she calls him "cosin" (VII.114, 143). Such terms of address are what make matters familiar and familial. They do not reflect a status prior to the one they seek to forge.

The exchanges between monk and merchant or monk and wife are not merely verbal but are also financial. The monk borrows a hundred franks—an amount hard for us to calculate, but certainly a considerable sum—from the merchant (supposedly for his own need) and lends it to the wife so that she can pay off an earlier debt that threatens her life. We might wonder about that: is this threat merely a bit of dramatic embellishment on her part? These stories put the merchant's money into circulation within the confines of his house, where it remains. For when the merchant meets the monk on his return from a business trip, he is told that John has already returned the money to the wife, "Upon youre bench—she woot it wel, certayn" (VII.358). The wife claims some confusion:

> For God it woot, I wende withouten doute
> That he hadde yive it me bycause of you,
> To doon therwith myn honour and my prow,
> For cosinage and eek for bele cheere
> That he hath had ful ofte times heere.   (VII.406–10)

We are clearly in a benign version of the Merchant's Tale, with a wife who can, like May, lie to her husband and make him believe her. He stops chiding her once he sees there is "no remedye" and charges her "ne be namore so large: / Keep bet my good, this yive I thee in charge" (VII.427, 431–32). This merchant hardly understands what he says, since the wife is quite competent in keeping her "good" (her goods as well as what's good for her) and working with the conditions of generosity and the freedom to perform it.[2]

The Shipman's Tale is a virtuoso performance of the power of language to change (and maybe even shortchange) the world. As already noted, the wife produces the happy ending to the potential conflict in the story with a pun. Finding herself duped by Daun John into a confrontation

---

[2] We might remember (and compare the usage of) such terms from the Franklin's Tale. See above, pp. 171–81.

with her husband about the hundred franks she took as her lover's gift, she sidesteps trouble by playfully telling him to "score it upon my taile" (VII.416). By asking him to mark the debt on her tally (her account as his wife), she proposes that he take the debt out in trade (i.e., sexually). "Taile" can also literally mean "tail," and this sense of the word more bluntly poses the physical nature of the wife's account with her husband and their system of tracking debt. She explains: "Ye shal my joly body han to wedde. / By God, I wol noght paye you but abedde" (VII.423–24). This simple play with the language of marriage and economic pledging ("wedde") reveals the equivalencies that are everywhere else made more subtly in the story. When money is exchanged, so is sex—most of the time—but the transaction is often hidden under the polite cover of language, what we might call in the words of the Shipman's Tale "certayn tokenes." For when the monk explains that he returned the franks to the wife "upon youre bench . . . by certayn tokenes" (VII.358–59), we are privy to two different ways of comprehending such tokens or signs, while the merchant understands just one.

The monk means, literally, that he went to the merchant's counting-house (or home office), where the merchant keeps the bench at which he does his "rekeninges" (VII.218), and paid her back in cash, the hard proof of repayment. Benches (in French, *banques*) were set up for the money-lenders to change currencies at a region's borders, a historical circumstance that led to our modern term *bank*. Thus, going to the merchant's bench means going to his "counting-bord" (VII.83), and the "tokenes" he used would apparently be coins, markers, or other evidence that the debt was repaid. But given the secret relationship between the wife and the monk—which has all the while depended on various "tokenes"—a clandestine meeting upon the merchant's bench takes on a more salacious meaning, particularly because the monk claims he needs the money "for certayn beestes that I moste beye" (VII.272). It is not merely the merchant's comprehension here but ours that is being tested. Put simply, we are listening to private conversations that rescript other private conferences in terms that both reveal and conceal. The monk would wish, of course, to keep his affection for the merchant's wife private. It is hardly something he can share with his sworn brother, and thus he claims to need the loan to purchase livestock. *We* know what the money is for, however, and for us the fabricated excuse is all the more telling as it at once covers and expresses the monk's true intent. Such animal husbandry is hardly related to what seems at first the real reason he wants the cash: to satisfy the wife's desire and obtain her love. But in a cruder sense, it is precisely what he wants the money for: to buy a living creature whose sexual labor he wants to enjoy for the short period the merchant will be away in Bruges. The monk's excuse both hides and expresses—what Freud would say "screens," in that it both obscures and projects—his intent. Moreover, his crude language also participates in the economic drama of exchange and commodity transformation that the tale everywhere presents.

The Shipman's Tale is a short, tight narrative that ends with the wife getting more money out of her husband by some sly and underhanded means—in the words of the tale's opening, making him "pay" for his frugality. But importantly, his punishment does not hurt him. Like the Miller's Alison, she is in on the scheme. Even more than Alison, though, she is its central mover. By begging the hundred franks from John, she begins the circuit of deceit and secret tokens—language that works in a number of different ways simultaneously—effectively asking the monk to pay for her sexual favors and, perhaps, even provoking him to use her husband to do so. Her claim that her life is in danger because of a previous debt becomes a bit suspect in hindsight. What might be a total lie might also be euphemism. Who knows how many times the merchant's wife has turned this trick before?

The language and logic of business and Lombard banking—"chevissaunce" (VII.329), "chapmanhede" (VII.238), and "creance" (VII.289; see 303)—permeate this story, showing us the power of the symbolic economy that goes far beyond a simple trade in goods.[3] The circulation of terms

---

[3] See Diane Cady, "The Gender of Money," *Genders* (2006), available online, www.thefreelibrary.com/_/print/PrintArticle.aspx?id=179660978.

in this story creates a kind of surplus value in language and narrative. Each word and expression comes to mean more than one thing and enriches those who can wield them. Hence the Wife's winning pun on "taile" at the end of the story. Her account is not only economic and sexual, it is also her story, the fictions she can create within the confines of the Shipman's Tale itself. The circulation of money is a trade in narratives as well—telling sad stories to the monk and making excuses to her husband, the wife is the most successful of the lot.

THE PRIORESS'S
INTRODUCTION, PROLOGUE,
AND TALE

The Shipman's Tale may begin in an uncertain state of revision with its ostensibly female speaker, but Chaucer locks the tale securely into place at its end. The story closes firmly attached to this "gentil maister, gentil mariner" (VII.437), in a link that further sharpens matters by drawing a contrast to "my lady Prioresse" (VII.447), to whom the Host turns next, expecting something soft and decorous.

We may not be the only ones surprised, then, by the Prioress's Marian miracle story and its murderous violence. While we are not familiar with the genre into which she ventures, it seems to defy the Host's expectations of her, too. But we should not therefore conclude that the Prioress's Tale is unsuited to her. On the contrary, her choice of a miracle of the Virgin appears closely coordinated to her status as a nun and indicates pious aspirations, which we did not quite realize she had. Yet another tale extolling feminine virtue, it does so through a blood libel narrative—a story of the ritual murder of Christians by Jews told and retold throughout the medieval period, in which the blood of the victim cries out for vengeance and accuses the murderer. Its feminized victim is a young schoolboy. The Prioress's Tale seems, at certain moments, a sentimental story, full of emotional energy directed at the child at its center. It is told by a nun who thereby performs her devotion to the Virgin, the agent of the story's miracle. But it's also a gruesome narrative about murder and the retributive punishments meted out to hateful assassins. Few tales exhibit more of a contrast between form and content, its aesthetic architecture and its horrifying detail, a division that has troubled the Prioress herself from the start.

In the General Prologue, the Prioress's aristocratic beauty belies her spiritual devotion and complicates our perception of her station. She has the form of courtly behavior down cold: she reaches "semely" at the table for her meat and wipes her lip clean so that no residue is left on her cup (I.133–36). She would thus make a fine dinner companion, with whom one might need to share one's plate. Further, she "pained hire to countrefete cheere / Of court, and to been estalich of manere" (I.139–40). Taking pains to imitate the good manners of courtiers is important in such social situations, even for the avowedly religious. But behind the forms of her behavior, the Prioress shows what might be called ethical limitations, which return us to her status as a nun. We understand as much from the General Prologue's description of her "conscience and tendre herte" (I.150), feelings lavished on pets or other small creatures instead of on the poor and needy. Such human objects of sympathy or concern are never mentioned, of course. The General Prologue narrator merely speaks of animals to illustrate her charitableness and pity (I.143), despite their not providing entirely appropriate examples. We get the impression that the affections of this cloistered woman are displaced. Some have taken that impression so far as to argue for a frustrated maternalism on the Prioress's part. More conservatively, however, we might remember that the cloistered life has removed her from the world. Could the awkward conflation of sympathies for pets and people be an effect of her reclusive experience, removed from the real world? That might be a generous reading, but all such conjecture is necessarily speculative. The effect on her story (and on our expectations, like the Host's) may be more relevant. Since she weeps even for a mouse's distress "if it were deed or bledde" (I.145), we are led to expect a more delicate narrative from her, perhaps even a romance of some kind. For a nun named "Eglentine" (I.121), which is a species of cultivated rose, and who wears a brooch inscribed *Amor vincit omnia* (Love conquers all), who was taught to speak Anglo-Norman French, and who shares features with the typical gray-eyed romance heroine (I.124–62), such an assumption seems nearly compulsory. And yet, the Prioress offers no such refined story and shows no squeamishness about death or bloodshed. She instead proffers a disturbingly self-reflective tale, both beautiful and chilling—a bit like the Prioress herself. That very combination has left audiences as wonderstruck as are the Canterbury pilgrims at its end, when "every man / As sobre was that wonder was to see" (VII.691–92). The Host reacts as he did at the end of the Physician's Tale (VI.317), when, feeling "pitee" for Virginia, he breaks the silence by turning explicitly to some "mirthe or japes" (VI.317, 319). He here seeks a similar change of pace by beginning to "japen" with Chaucer at the end of the Prioress's Tale (VII.693). A pattern has formed that makes these tales of pitiful suffering and moral fervor a prelude to or even a license for levity.

The formal beauty of the Prioress's story might be harder for modern readers to appreciate, but its aesthetics are written into its elegant rhyme royal stanzas.[1] These are seven-line stanzas with three interlocked rhymes (*ababbcc*), a form that, "like the theme of transcendence to which Chaucer attaches it, implies completion and finality in ways that the riding couplets of most tales cannot."[2] As in the Man of Law's Tale and the Clerk's Tale before hers (and later in the Second Nun's Tale, to which hers is related), the Prioress's rhyme royal is Chaucer's chosen vehicle for serious stories of human pathos, feminized suffering, and Christian heroics. The formal connection between these four tales is important and demands that we take the Prioress's story seriously, despite its virulent anti-Semitism.

---

[1] See Barbara Nolan, "Chaucer's Tales of Transcendence: Rhyme Royal and Christian Prayer in the *Canterbury Tales*," in *Chaucer's Religious Tales*, ed. C. David Benson and Elizabeth Robertson (Cambridge: D. S. Brewer, 1990), 21–38.

[2] Nolan, "Chaucer's Tales of Transcendence," 23.

Even more than these other stories with serious moral content, the Prioress's Tale is fully conscious of its aesthetic difference from other Canterbury performances. It is aware of its status as song and as prayer. The Prioress frames her tale of a young "clergeon" (VII.503), literally "a little clerk" and thus a schoolboy, who eschews his Latin lessons so that he might learn an antiphon (a short chant sung as a refrain) in praise of the Virgin, as itself a song. Both her tale and the clergeon perform *O Alma redemptoris mater* (O blissful mother of the redeemer), a song in praise of Jesus's mother, "the white lilye flour / Which that [Christ] bar, and is a maide alway" (VII.461–62). The clergeon obviously performs the song literally. He practices singing it as he walks to and from school each day. The Prioress performs it figuratively in a song about the singing of this song. The entire tale is, in fact, a prayer to the Virgin and a remembrance of her role as vehicle and mediator who brings Christ to humanity, both literally as his mother and more figuratively as the supreme intercessor between heaven and earth. Prayer to Mary is the most effective means of reaching her son.

That intercessory role is figured by the "grain" that she places on the clergeon's tongue. Once he is found, he explains:

> This welle of mercy, Cristes moder sweete,
> I loved alway as after my conninge;
> And whan that I my lif sholde forlete,
> To me she cam, and bad me for to singe
> This antheme verraily in my dyinge,
> As ye han herd; and whan that I hadde songe,
> Me thoughte she laide a grain upon my tonge.
>
> Wherfore I singe and singe moot, certayn,
> In honour of that blissful maiden free,
> Til fro my tonge of taken is the grain;
> And after that thus saide she to me,
> "My litel child, now wil I fecche thee

Whan that the grain is fro thy tonge ytake:
Be nat agast, I wol thee nat forsake."   (VII.656–69)

The object of much debate, the grain both signifies a promissory gift and functions as a kind of talisman to achieve the miracle, the song beyond death, that enables the child to be found. While its symbolic function for the Prioress's story is clear, its precise symbolism in Christian culture is not and has generated much speculation. No other such Marian miracle features a grain of this kind. Full of symbolic meaning, it has been identified with various biblical referents, including seeds of paradise and pearls of redemption. It seems a small and insignificant object, and yet it is the miraculous sign of Mary's intervention. But despite its apparent valuelessness, the grain is emphatically the answer to the child's prayer. And it entices critics with the allure of its uniqueness. They hope (so far in vain) that the grain will identify the miracle text that provided Chaucer's source for the story.

It is hardly surprising that the Prioress wants to identify with the child in the story. His innocence and blind devotion makes him a favored subject and ultimately brings him to Christ's presence through the Virgin's intercession. The Prioress presumably desires the same thing. Her tale makes the analogy between herself and the innocent child even stronger. Before the Virgin's innumerable virtues, the Prioress likens herself to "a child of twelfmonth old or lesse, / That can unnethes any word expresse" (VII.484–85). In five beautiful stanzas addressing Christ and his mother, the Prioress has praised Mary by situating her beyond the Prioress's abilities to speak, thereby directing all praise of the Virgin back to the Virgin herself, the song's ultimate source. The Prioress thus offers the ultimate modesty trope, paradoxically expressing the inexpressibility of the Virgin's goodness.

But while, out of modesty and humility, the Prioress will accept no praise for this hymn to the Virgin, she conversely wishes to avoid being assigned any blame for the story. That is why she compares herself to the twelve-month-old, who cannot express himself in language. These are the innocent babes of the Prioress's very first stanza, who perform Mary's praise "by the mouth . . . on the brest soukinge" (VII.457–58). It's an idea that will need further exploration, since her tale features a child singing a song he is unable to translate, and who thus knows not the meaning of the words that he sings but only their intent. The Prioress's clergeon provides a nice contrast to the Pardoner, who also knows his Latin "al by rote" (VI.332). Whereas the rote memorization of his Latin theme, together with the story it illustrates, is a sign of the Pardoner's emptiness and corruption, here it is a sign of the child's devoted naïveté. This idealized image of youthful innocence is particularly tied to a language only innocently understood, and it's an image that the Prioress cultivates for herself in the story as she draws the analogy between herself and the schoolboy martyred for his love. The relationship forces us to examine our understanding of innocence and its virtue. For, of course, the story presupposes an audience far less innocent and thus more knowing than the figures within it.

The tale's aesthetic considerations are not merely formal: metrical, rhetorical, or poetic. They are also cultural, part of how the tale participates in liturgical structures and historical remembrance. The Roman Catholic Church calendar was organized in recollection of important events in Christian history, the lives of Christ and the saints. Feast days celebrated Christmas, Easter, Pentecost (the descent of the Holy Spirit on the apostles), and various commemorations of the saints—usually their martyrdom. The mass celebrated on these days included special songs, prayers, and scriptural readings. We should recall the performative aspect of the Catholic mass: readings, hymns, responses, and songs literally rehearse the past by recalling its events and their emotive force through artful reenactment and repetition. The celebration of the Eucharist is the most literal of these performances: Christ's bodily sacrifice is remembered as the priest re-performs his actions at the Last Supper, in which, through the miracle of transubstantiation, bread and wine are made into the body and blood of the Savior and then shared.

As the Prioress's Tale relates its story of the discovery of the murdered boy through his miraculous song, it recalls the Feast of the Holy Innocents, also known as Childermas. Celebrated on December 28, the feast commemorates the deaths of those children condemned by Herod in his search for the prophesied new king, following an edict that caused the holy family to flee to Egypt. The opening psalm for that mass is Psalm 8:1–2:

> O Lord our Lord, how excellent is thy name in all the earth! who hast set thy glory above the heavens.
> Out of the mouth of babes and sucklings hast thou ordained strength because of thine enemies, that thou mightest still the enemy and the avenger.

That commemoration not only explains the occasion for such a story, and its focus on children, childhood, and innocence, but also creates the mood generated by the tale and the echo of maternal lamentation it continually sounds. Like the church service that it recalls, the tale indulges in the sorrows of inconsolable women who have lost their sons, as did Mary and Rachel, the iconographic sorrowing mother of the Old Testament.

These allusions to contemporary feast days and holidays are augmented by references to prayers like the Little Office of the Virgin (or the Hours of the Virgin)—a liturgical devotion (or set of prayers, hymns, and readings used for a special service or for matins, the morning prayers) to the Virgin Mary, who was a particular object of veneration for medieval Christians and especially for women. The references and allusions interwoven into the Prioress's story are part of its aesthetic design and make an implicit claim to sophistication, though perhaps one it would disavow (as the speech of a child). But its frame of reference is also more local: it alludes to "yonge Hugh of Lincoln" (VII.684), a child martyr whose shrine in Lincoln Cathedral commemorates his supposed death at the hands of the Jews before their expulsion from England in 1290.

Modern readers find the grossly anti-Semitic sentiment of the Prioress's Tale disturbing. The Jews in the story are assigned an automatic villainy: they are viewed as responsible for the murder of Christ, on which the analogy of the child's mother to the suffering Mary trades. Throughout the tale, the innocence of the boy and the pitifulness of his mother are emphasized to produce an affective response to his ritual murder similar to that for the crucifixion. Its intent is to incite anger, among other strong emotions. The tale is not an allegory of the crucifixion per se, but it draws on that event's emotive force in shaping its central action and audience response. Like the antiphon that the boy learns, the Prioress's Tale *as song* calls for a response: "*O Alma redemptoris mater,*" a refrain we hear again and again that itself recalls Mary's role as the mother of the crucified redeemer and, arguably, sutures the audience into its song.

While the child cannot translate the song (because, ironically, he skips his Latin lessons in order to memorize it), he knows that it's sung "of oure blisful Lady free, / Hire to salue, and eek hire for to praye / To been oure help and socour whan we deye" (VII.532–34). The tale's plot makes literal this promise, by helping and succouring the child upon his death. Further, it demonstrates the power of the innocent devotion of this child as it stresses his diminutive size: "This *litel* child his *litel* book lerninge" (VII.516; my emphases). The Prioress uses the word "litel" no fewer than eleven times, ensuring our affection for one "so yong and tendre . . . of age" (VII.524). But even more importantly, she reports his earnest desire to learn the song despite the cost to him (in his own words, he "shal be beten thries in an houre"; VII.542), thereby aligning his innocence with his devotion, a childlike acknowledgment of his own sacrifice.

Practicing the song as he walks through the Jewish ghetto on his way to and from school, the clergeon has little awareness of any danger he creates for himself; the Prioress leaves it to Satan to point out his offense and incite the Jews to violence:

> O Hebraic peple, allas,
> Is this to you a thing that is honest,
> That swich a boy shal walken as him lest,
> In youre despit, and singe of swich sentence,
> Which is agains oure laws reverence?   (VII.560–64)

The suspense created by the tale depends on an audience understanding precisely what the child does not: that his song might offend others, particularly the Jews, who would find it "agains [their] laws reverence." Also opaque to him is the way in which his willingness to be beaten "thries an hour" can be seen as a prefiguration of his willingness to die for his devotion.

This kind of innocence or unknowingness stands in sharp contrast to the audience's superior knowledge, and it causes us some pause. A bit like the reaction of the sultan's mother in the Man of Law's Tale, who refuses to let "Makometes lawe out of [her] herte" (II.336), here the cultural Other's resistance is imagined as a legal bind. Can such a recognition of others' religious dilemmas amount to a kind of sympathetic understanding of them, even if as a by-product of their demonization? The tight relation between the aesthetics of devotion and the cruelty of its bigotry has been, of course, recognized, but it has also paralyzed thought about the tale, making it hard to read and nearly impossible to enjoy. But we might benefit from a sharper deconstruction of the oppositions (transcendence/bigotry) that this tale propounds, helping us to calculate the cost of its enlightenment (or lack thereof). The Prioress's Tale pays for its manner of potentially forward thinking.

The Prioress's is one of the shortest of the Canterbury tales; both its plot and its stylized methods of representation are highly compressed. So too is the murder of the child, which occurs in two stanzas of graphic description that impresses us with its terse elegance as well as its foul detail:

> Fro thennes forth the Jewes han conspired
> This innocent out of this world to chace:
> An homicide therto han they hired
> That in an aleye hadde a privee place;
> And as the child gan forby for to pace,
> This cursed Jew him hente and heeld him faste,
> And kitte his throte and in a pit him caste.

I saye that in a wardrobe they him threwe,
Wheras thise Jewes purgen hir entraile.
O cursed folk of Herodes al newe,
What may youre yvel entente you availe?
Mordre wol out, certayn it wol nat faile,
And namely ther th'honour of God shal sprede:
The blood out cryeth on youre cursed deede.   (VII.565–78)

Insofar as the tale seems appropriate to the Prioress, there are a number of things to say. The elegance of the rhyme royal and her reliance on rhetorical apostrophes seem appropriate to her social affectations. But the elegant stanzas are belied somewhat by their content, which the Prioress is careful to detail. The boy is not merely killed but has his throat cut, and he's cast into a "pit" that she identifies as a latrine, "wheras thise Jewes purgen hir entraile." This specificity is not ladylike, but it goads her supposed audience into violent indignation.

While much of her tale appears naïvely indignant and retaliatory—hers is not one of the Virgin's miracles that ends with conversion of the Jews but instead one that concludes in an equally violent retribution, a turn to the old law rather than the new that we'd hope she'd espouse—it remains in no way unique. There are plenty of Marian miracles that neglect the possibility of conversion and thus forgo the narrative of redemption they might tell, instead focusing on the blunt satisfactions of talionic justice (seeking an eye for an eye). We might compare our response here with those to the Wife of Bath's Tale and its opening scene of rape and trial, which produces exactly the opposite desire in modern readers. Whereas we want sympathy and redemption for the Jews in this story, many want a simple retaliatory death for the knight in the Wife's Tale. We have to examine those responses. For Chaucer is consistent, at least, showing the greater tendency of women to embrace redemptive justice throughout. The Prioress, however, lacks it: "And al was conscience and tendre herte" (I.150), indeed.

It has been difficult for Chaucer's readers to come to terms with the Prioress's Tale. The anti-Semitism of the story is entangled in the quasi-allegorical narrative it wants to tell and is entirely formulaic, integral to the genre it reproduces. Two insertions into the narrative that remind us that the Prioress (rather than Chaucer) is speaking, the repeated "quod she" (VII.454, 581), have been emphasized by some scholars to distance her voice from the narrator's rehearsal of it. These insertions are a bit unusual and might be evidence of previously written material that has been reworked into the Prioress's Tale. Such distancing is not the same thing as a full-blown ironizing of the Prioress's aggression, which has also been proposed. Something in the middle may be called for. Chaucer, it seems, understands full well from experience that the naïveté of innocence can be seen and understood only after it has been lost. This is the postlapsarian human condition. And it is certainly a condition that the Prioress, in expressing her desire to speak as an innocent before the Virgin, must understand—otherwise, there would be no desire for that lost innocence in the first place. But how Chaucer is implicated in the knowledge of the experience that the Prioress pretends to lack is another question.

CHAUCER'S TWO TALES:
SIR THOPAS AND MELIBEE

Fragment VII has long drawn critical attention for the six tales it contains, which make it the longest of the fragments and the most generically ambitious. With its fabliau, Marian miracle, tail-rhyme romance, prose treatise, set of tragedies, and animal fable, it feels like a miniature version of *The Canterbury Tales* itself, full of narrative variety. At its center are two tales told by someone almost wholly forgotten as a potential storyteller because he's been effaced by the voices he ventriloquizes: the pilgrim Chaucer. Here again, as in the Man of Law's Introduction, Chaucer reminds us of his authorial status in the act of disavowing it. He offers "a joke performance where the author tells tales guaranteed to lose the contest posed by Harry Bailly."[1] But this time, instead of having one of his fictional creations disparage his poetical works, he becomes part of Harry Bailly's roadside banter—even by trying to avoid it—when the Host suddenly turns to him for some comedy.

This gesture is structurally similar to that in fragment VI after the story of Virginia, where the Host felt his heart "lost for pitee of this maide" (VI.317). Here again, he turns to someone to "japen" following a tale of intense emotion that has nearly killed the tale-telling game with the silence it elicits: "Whan said was al this miracle, every man / As sobre

---

[1] This lovely formulation comes from Seth Lerer, "'Now holde your mouthe': The Romance of Orality in the Thopas-Melibee Section of the *Canterbury Tales*," in *Oral Poetics in Middle English Poetry*, ed. Mark C. Amodio (New York: Garland, 1994), 181.

was that wonder was to see" (VII.691–92). But here the Host himself does the joking, and at the pilgrim Chaucer's expense:

> "What man artou?" quod he.
> "Thou lookest as thou woldest finde an hare,
> For ever upon the ground I see thee stare.
>
> Approche neer, and looke up murily.
> Now ware you, sires, and lat this man have place!
> He in the wast is shape as wel as I—
> This were a popet in an arm t'enbrace
> For any womman smal and fair of face;
> He seemeth elvissh by his countenaunce,
> For unto no wight dooth he daliaunce.
>
> Say now somewhat, sin other folk han said.
> Tel us a tale of mirthe, and that anon."   (VII.695–706)

The portrait of the artist contained within this fictional sighting is doubly comedic, as it trades on a physical resemblance to the historical poet— short and slightly portly—that we find mocked in other poems, notably *The House of Fame,* and that also is consistent with the figure in the author portraits of some manuscripts.[2] This pilgrim Chaucer is, then, akin to the real Chaucer at the same time as he mimes the poet's fictional self-representations, who are nothing like what we imagine the real Chaucer (well-read, perceptive, deft) to be. We see this familiar caricature in the Host's slight to the reporter of tales as a quiet and somewhat taciturn fellow, staring at the ground and hoping to go unnoticed.

---

[2] The eagle that carries "Geffrey" aloft in the dream vision poem *The House of Fame* comments obliquely on the dreamer-poet's heft when he notes "thyn abstinence is but lite" (660).

Chaucer's tales form a diptych, a two-panel picture that generates its meaning from the interrelation of its two parts. The first, he claims, is the only tale he knows (VII.708–09), but he never gets to complete it. Instead, Harry Bailly interrupts what he labels Chaucer's "rym dogerel" (VII.925), and the poet has to petition to finish with another kind of offering, something in prose. The Host may have felt Thopas to be a waste of time, but Melibee, by contrast, consumes a great deal of it, occupying a considerable number of manuscript pages. No other pilgrim is allowed two stories. The others who are interrupted, the Squire and the Monk, never attempt a second tale.

The tales of Thopas and Melibee are often considered in oppositional terms, and there are good reasons for taking this approach. As a tail-rhyme romance, Thopas is all mirth and almost no sense, pure "solas" (I.798) divorced from any meaning. The tale has always been understood as a literary joke and a parody of a Middle English romance form whose use by a serious writer like Chaucer is unimaginable. Some of these source texts are mentioned by name in the tale itself, which cites

> romances of pris,
> Of Horn Child and of Ypotis,
> Of Beves and Sir Gy,
> Of Sir Libeux and Pleindamour—
> But sire Thopas, he bereth the flour
> Of royal chivalry.   (VII.897–902)

Into the catalogue of popular romance heroes and their texts, Chaucer has wittily inserted his own Thopas.

Tail-rhyme was a popular romance form native to fourteenth-century England.[3] Its singsong rhythm comes from its shortened tail line (following

---

[3] Tail-rhyme originates with Latin hymnody, and pious tail-rhyme texts precede the romances in both Old French and Anglo-Norman. But tail-rhyme romance is a distinctly English product. The first recorded Middle English tail-rhyme romances are inscribed in

either rhymed couplets or triplets within the stanza) with a different rhyme, often used by Chaucer for comic deflation (*aabccb* or *aaabcccb*, for instance). The tail line is where he locates some of the stanza's most formulaic filler. In Chaucer's Thopas, he also sporadically includes what Rhiannon Purdie memorably dubs "rogue bob-lines"—two-syllable additions at the end of some stanzas for even further comic, and often ironic, effect.[4] The form, as Chaucer deploys it here, tends to dangling afterthought as it pushes the nearly empty narrative forward. Divided into parts labeled "fits," these sections get progressively smaller as the poem moves along. Its structure diminishes, even as its content attempts to aggrandize and expand, until the Host stops it altogether because it is going nowhere.

Composed of borrowed rhetorical tags as well as stock phrases and plot elements from the romance and ballad traditions alike, Thopas has earned a number of its own stock descriptors, including "a hodgepodge," "derivative," and "stereotypical," in the negative sense. Research has proven how important medieval romance is to Chaucer's writing, but that has not at all lessened our sense of Chaucer's "scorn" in presenting Thopas to his audience.[5] A number of smart readers have noticed the childish and childlike nature of Sir Thopas. As a knight, he seems hardly ready for the adventure he seeks. His tale reads as something of an *enfance*, medieval romance's version of a prequel. Not only the protagonist, then, but Chaucer's literary effort itself has been characterized as child's play—and bad play at that.[6] The imitation of adult, aristocratic material amounts to bad parody.

---

the famous Auchinleck manuscript (ca. 1330–40). They were out of vogue by the end of the century, and after Chaucer parodies the genre here the tail verse becomes associated with irony and trickery in fifteenth-century drama. See Jessica Brantley, "Reading the Forms of *Sir Thopas*," *Chaucer Review* 47.4 (2013): 416–38.

[4] Rhiannon Purdie, *Anglicising Romance: Tail-Rhyme and Genre in Medieval English Literature* (Cambridge: D. S. Brewer, 2008), 69. The best-known example of the bob completes each long alliterative stanza in *Sir Gawain and the Green Knight*.

[5] Purdie, *Anglicising Romance*, 11.

[6] See Lee Patterson's "'What Man Artow?': Authorial Self-Definition in *The Tale of Sir Thopas* and *The Tale of Melibee*," *Studies in the Age of Chaucer* 11 (1989): 117–75.

Importantly, the tale shows a consistent undercutting of its own aristocratic genre with various details from outside those generic bounds.
While Thopas might not seem old enough for his intended adventure,
neither does he seem adequately genteel. His innocent youthfulness might
be signified by the color of his armor, shield, and horse, which are all
white. Pure and virginal, perhaps, but they are also thus essentially empty
and blank precisely where his hereditary status and identity ought to be
inscribed. His origin is in Flanders, a European center of trade and trades-
men, many of whom were alien businessmen in London during Chaucer's
time. The bourgeois terms of his description contribute to his problematic class standing. Juggling "hosen broun" (VII.733) and "cordewane"
(leather, VII.732) with "siklatoun" (cloth of gold, VII.734), Thopas mixes
up commercial products with more aristocratic goods, which are usually
not measured by the "jane" (or half-penny, VII.735).

The tale's heroic content is not any more impressive. Thopas is less
the subject of well-known adventures in need of retelling than a very
young and inexperienced seeker of them who wishes for his life to turn
into a book. In one of the romance sources to which Chaucer may allude,
a knight named Lanval, neglected by the Arthurian court, is discovered
by a fairy mistress, and his high status is confirmed by the fact that she
takes him as her lover. The romance is about the very construction of a
realm of privacy beyond the public life of the court, which seems both
to generate and to confirm the fairy's power, and Lanval's struggle to keep
her existence a secret.[7] Showing signs of familiarity with just such a story,
Thopas seeks "an elf-queene" (VII.788) as his lover, forsaking *the idea* of
all other women before he ever encounters one. We are not quite sure that
he ever will. The romance precepts he seeks to live by look as if they will
stymie rather than aid any such experience.

---

[7] See Marie de France's *Lanval*, trans. Dorothy Gilbert, in *The Norton Anthology of
English Literature*, ed. Stephen Greenblatt, 10th ed. (New York: W. W. Norton, 2018),
A:171–85. Chaucer probably cites the contemporary Middle English version of this story
told by Thomas Chestre, *Sir Launfal*.

While Thopas's varied romance sources have been extensively detailed, Chaucer also offers a scene in his own *Tales* out of which the joke of Thopas was possibly generated. Turning back to the end of its Prologue—still in the rhyme royal stanzas of the preceding Prioress's Tale—we find Harry Bailly feeling a bit self-satisfied with the "daintee thing" (VII.711) he has gotten Chaucer to promise the company. The parodic terms of Thopas come right out of the Host's falsely complimentary description of Chaucer already quoted above:

> This were a popet in an arm t'enbrace
> For any womman smal and fair of face;
> He seemeth elvissh by his countenaunce,
> For unto no wight dooth he daliaunce.

Chaucer turns these words against the Host, giving him (in the tale) exactly what he claims to see in Chaucer. The ineptitude with which the Host subtly charges Chaucer here reappears in the story, in the doll-like, feminized, "elvissh" features that make Sir Thopas incapable of the "daliaunce" welcomed by other knightly—both more mature and more masculine— heroes. The entire tale appears as an expansion of this one stanza of mock-derision and thus becomes a high-level piece of literary artistry at the blockheaded Host's expense. He can hardly be expected to see his own (mis)perceptions of Chaucer as the origin of his doggerel performance. The Host's frustration with the Tale of Sir Thopas places him outside the jest.

By contrast, the Tale of Melibee is serious stuff, a "sentence"-packed narrative in which more authorities are quoted than anywhere else in *The Canterbury Tales*.[8] Chaucer's "litel thing in prose" (VII.937), as he calls it, is an allegorical narrative about good governance. Its protagonist,

---

[8] See Christopher Cannon on the citations in Melibee and its proverbs in "Proverbs and the Wisdom of Literature: *The Proverbs of Alfred* and Chaucer's *Tale of Melibee*," *Textual Practice* 24.3 (2010): 407–34. For "sentence," see I.798.

Melibee—"that is to sayn, a man that drinketh hony" (VII.1410)—is a figure of the spiritually distracted individual, one drunk on the sweet pleasures of worldly things. The narrative opens with Melibee's having been wronged. While out playing in the fields, his old foes break into his house and beat his wife, Prudence, and wound his daughter, Sophie, leaving her for dead. As an allegorical figure, Prudence is easy enough to understand. Sophie represents wisdom (in Greek, *sophia*). She is wounded through the five senses: in her hands, feet, ears, nose, and mouth, with some confusion arising between "feet" (*piez*) and "eyes" (*oiez*) in the French manuscripts that provide the tale's immediate source.[9]

The tale is composed of a dialogue between Melibee and Prudence, in which she argues for patience and forgiveness over and against Melibee's vengeful anger. Prudence marshals an impressive number of texts and authorities to her cause, citing Seneca, Cicero, and Solomon among others drawn from the various medieval compilations of wisdom and proverbs known as *florilegia*. Differently from the Tale of Thopas but no less extensively, Melibee is a tissue of references containing little to no action. Part of the tale's enjoyment is in its sheer accumulation of citations and authorities. A number of Chaucer's favorites, used elsewhere in *The Canterbury Tales*, appear here, though often with less imaginative force. The immediate drama of the tale also plays on the fabliau comedy of many of Chaucer's other stories of marital friction, as a stubbornly angry husband resists the calm logic of his wife. Thus, in the middle of a debate about proper governance and punishment, we find a discussion about the value of women and the governance of wives of the sort that could provoke the Wife of Bath. Melibee is a very competent, edifying story, making a nice riposte to the burlesque of Thopas that Harry Bailly judged to be "drasty ryming" not worth a "tord" (VII.930).

Chaucer's two offerings would seem to divide the terms of judgment for the storytelling contest between them and to play on the sterility of opposing them in this way. It certainly confounds the Host's ideas and

---

[9] David Lawton, *The Norton Chaucer* (New York: W. W. Norton, 2019), 400, n. 5.

undercuts any presumption that sentence and solas will together occupy a single story. But too often this recognition has devolved into neglect of these stories, especially Melibee, as another "ironization" of their function or their teller.[10] We might consider what these two efforts allow Chaucer to include in his *Canterbury Tales*. All tales that get cut off (the Monk's, Thopas's, and perhaps the Squire's) proceed with no end in sight. Each of these has inspired arguments that their truncation is part of a design to include longer genres in the storytelling collection without fully committing to one that might threaten to overshadow the rest of the pilgrims' stories. But the Tale of Melibee and later the Parson's Tale give the lie to that position. Both are rather lengthy prose texts, and neither seems to have relied on any strategy of abbreviation to ensure its inclusion. Perhaps their status as prose gives them a latitude not allowed to others.

A final word about performance and the productive tension between oral and written forms. These two tales raise the issue of oral and written form and the drama of performance in *The Canterbury Tales* in specific ways. As has often been noted, the prose of Melibee appears more appropriate to private reading than to verbal recitation. Can we even imagine someone having memorized this long tract, with all its cited authorities, and then performing it to the company? More than anything else heard to this point, it gives us the impression of a text meant to be read. The same is true of Thopas. In a significant number of early and authoritative manuscripts of *The Canterbury Tales*, Thopas comes marked with brackets that call attention to the tale's metrical form. These features, according to one recent critic, make visible that which is audible in performance, thereby calling attention to the drama of oral delivery supposedly underwriting the entire Canterbury fiction.[11] Because he works so hard to perform an

---

[10] Cannon's "Proverbs and the Wisdom of Literature" offers (in a corrective to this opinion) a particularly detailed account of the medieval pleasure in such compilations of even contradictory wisdom, such as the Tale of Melibee.

[11] Brantley, "Reading the Forms of *Sir Thopas*."

act of underperforming, it is perhaps unsurprising that the tales Chaucer ascribes to "himself" in the fiction of the poem should address performance as such. He reminds us of the performance's success precisely by dramatizing and self-consciously inscribing its failure, as judged by the Host.

THE MONK'S PROLOGUE
AND TALE

Surely one of the least considered tales in the Canterbury collection, the Monk's Tale is itself a tale collection in miniature. Its sixteen "tragedies" have defined the genre for the medieval tradition in sharp contrast to the later Renaissance tragedy, a dramatic production of distinctly secular and often psychological concerns. The Monk's tragedies are instead narratives of Fortune, "the harm of hem that stoode in heigh degree" (VII.1992), and monitory examples "trewe and olde" of why men should never "truste on blind prosperitee" (VII.1997–98). Striking a similar chord again and again, they come to an abrupt end when the Knight cuts their teller off, afraid that the Monk will actually narrate the complete "hundred in my celle" that he brags about possessing (VII.1972).

The fatal stories of hubris and decline told by the Monk vary in length and historical disposition. He begins easily enough with the Christian beginning of history, the fall of Lucifer, which he dispatches in a single stanza in near aphoristic fashion. By the time the tale is brought to its close, he's telling more proximate histories, known to scholars as the Modern Instances, about relatively contemporary figures such as Bernabo Visconti and Pedro the Cruel of Spain.[1] But the trajectory is not

---

[1] The so-called Modern Instances are four tales of recent historical vintage: in addition to Bernabo Visconti and Pedro, they feature Ugolino and Peter of Cyprus (Pierre de Lusignan). In some manuscripts, these four stories are located at the end of the Monk's Tale. The movement of this block has suggested to some scholars that the Modern

linear, nor is it progressive. The final tale the Monk narrates is actually of Croesus, the legendary king of Lydia known for his immense wealth. Interspersed are various classical and biblical figures in no particular order and of no regular length.[2]

Chaucer's immediate (and thus most recognizable) source for the series is Boccaccio's *De casibus virorum illustrium* (*On the Fall of Illustrious Men*), which is mentioned in some of the manuscripts in a heading separating the tale from "The murye wordes of the Hoost to the Monk," often printed as a prologue. *De casibus* also tells a series of stories, as its Latin title suggests, chronicling the downfall of prominent figures. Yet Boccaccio's work does not use the generic term "tragedy." Instead, the "tragic" approach to Fortune in the Monk's Tale comes from the influence of Boethius's *Consolation of Philosophy*, a text that, as was mentioned in the discussion of the Knight's Tale, Chaucer translated into English; it had a strong impact on his early works, such as *Troilus and Criseyde*, as well as on the Knight's Tale itself. While Boethius's influence on the Monk's Tale is deep, his Christian-friendly philosophy, advocating an intellectual distance from the things of this world, is not consistently applied. Some of the Monk's figures are wicked and deserve the fall coming to them (Lucifer, Adam, Nero); some others do not deserve it (Hercules, Zenobia). A number are neither good nor bad, and a few seem to be subject to malicious designs against them (Samson). We end with a sense of Fortune's fickle changeability but are given no glimpse of a "grand design" of Christian ethics and thus receive no consolation.[3]

The Monk narrates in a metrical form unique among the tales. His eight-line stanzas of hexameter poetry distinguish the various individual

---

Instances were later insertions to a story begun before *The Canterbury Tales* took shape in Chaucer's imagination.

[2] The manuscripts show some variation in the placement of the Modern Instances, but nowhere is the order of episodes strictly chronological.

[3] Derek Pearsall's explanations of the Boethian limitations on the Monk's stories are particularly helpful. See *The Canterbury Tales* (1985; London: Routledge, 1993), 280–85; quotation, 283.

tragedies from Chaucer's other poetic tales, which are written in continuous couplets or rhyme royal stanzas. Helen Cooper calls this metrical form "the most elaborate of the whole Canterbury series."[4] But for most readers the repetitive drive of each episode prevents the form from registering as anything particularly elegant or aesthetic. In addition, the regular metrics are marred by the stories' irregular lengths. Zenobia (the only woman treated in the tale) is the longest of the Monk's tragedies at sixteen stanzas. Many are much shorter, around five to seven stanzas long. A few occupy a single stanza, blunting the metrical form's overall effect.[5]

The most interesting element of the tale, by far, is its dramatic context. We might remember the Monk from the General Prologue, "an outridere that loved venerye" (I.166). The narrator's description leads us to expect a different kind of story than the repeated formula we get from him here. Harry Bailly certainly has different expectations. When the Knight interrupts the Monk's litany of tragedies, the Host offers him the opportunity to tell a more entertaining story: "Sire, saye somwhat of hunting, I you praye" (VII.2805). But the Monk refuses: "I have no lust to playe. / Now lat another telle, as I have told" (VII.2806–07). This disgruntled prelate hardly resembles the worldly hunter and rider so interested in food whom the narrator described earlier, and he certainly differs from the flirtatious and manipulative Daun John of the Shipman's Tale.[6] What are we to make of such sharp shifts and inconsistencies?

---

[4] Helen Cooper, *The Canterbury Tales*, Oxford Guides to Chaucer, 2nd ed. (Oxford: Oxford UP, 1996), 334. Chaucer also uses the form in his "ABC to the Virgin," but nowhere else in his corpus. There too it links 26 verses, one for each letter of the alphabet, connected by their common praise for Christ's mother.

[5] Cooper notes the sentences' length and complex structure: "The syntax tends to be complex, with only one or two sentences per stanza, and there is usually a strong syntactic link across the fourth and fifth lines where the verse might otherwise break. This in itself gives an impression of high style, of spaciousness and rhetorical elaboration" (*Canterbury Tales*, 335).

[6] Much as the Clerk responded to the antics of clerks depicted in the fabliaux, the Monk appears to be a corrective to the Shipman's monk, Daun John.

An earlier generation of critical readers would have ascribed these differences to the insertion of unrevised or insufficiently adapted material written earlier for some other purpose. (And that may well be true.) But such claims rely on the assumption that the tales are always more sophisticated versions of a prior design. I would suggest instead that we pay attention to what the fiction of divergence from a previous design produces. As we have seen, especially in the Prioress's performance, Chaucer appears as interested in defying audience expectations as in setting them up. Much of fragment VII could be read as a series of upended assumptions, including those we might have entertained about the sophistication and literary talent of Chaucer-the-narrator himself.

The Prologue to the Monk's Tale even dramatizes a fiction of such disappointed expectations, presenting the usually robust Harry Bailly as a henpecked husband when he notes, at some length, that his wife is nothing like the patient Prudence of the Tale of Melibee. Harry's comments start out as criticism of his wife, but they soon become more self-revealing about himself as a husband. The Monk's Prologue contains the lengthiest presentation of the Host's marital life and offers a scene of self-deprecating comedy in which he recalls the violence of his wife, named Goodlief, who rules his roost with an iron claw.[7] These comments square with and develop similar remarks following the Merchant's Tale, even if they paint the normally formidable Host as a bit of a shrimp (VII.1955) in the face of his wife's ire.[8] When he would simply "bete my knaves" (VII.1897), she

---

[7] In some editions, including *The Norton Chaucer*, "Gode lief" is read not as a proper name but as an address to an absent friend, or to the abstract idea of such a friend. According to Jacqueline de Weever's *A Chaucer Name Dictionary: A Guide to Astrological, Literary, and Mythological Names in the Works of Geoffrey Chaucer* (1987; New York: Garland, 1996), Godelieve was the name of a Flemish saint known for wifely submission and obedience, so naming the Host's wife after her might be seen as ironic (158). For historical records of the fourteenth century that attest to the use of the name in England, see Edith Rickert, "'Goode Lief, My Wyf,'" *Modern Philology* 25.1 (1927): 79–82.

[8] These sentiments have appeared in a number of places in the links among the tales, sometimes verbatim, and the repetition seems to reveal incomplete revision—the manuscripts are not at all clear as to which lines were meant for cancellation. Though the duplication is

orders: "Slee the dogges everichoon, / And breke hem bothe bak and every boon!" (VII.1899–1900). The turnabout witnessed here is not merely contradictory or relevatory; it demonstrates self-exposure made possible by the depth of conversation and comfort among the group reached at this later stage of the Canterbury game. These in no way feel like comments that could have been made early in the journey, before a considerable familiarity with the pilgrims had grown through their fictions—which are always a form of self-revelation. If we take the fragment's telltale disruptive structure seriously, then the link's comical marital violence, forming a preface to two stories to be told by celibate men (the Monk and the Nun's Priest), participates in its logic precisely because it is the last place we might expect to hear about such domestic matters.

One striking tendency within the Monk's Tale is its narrator's consistent coordination with the Knight—as if the Knight and the Monk were somehow deeply conjoined in Chaucer's imagination. We might remember that these two figures were described within 90 lines of one another in the General Prologue, suggesting a certain proximity (either in spatial arrangements in the Tabard Inn or in the narrator's memory) that I have largely presented in terms of estate. For while the Knight and the Monk are now members of separate estates—the aristocratic and the clerical—there are subtle signs that they once were not, which may be how the Monk became so well-positioned in his monastery in the first place. Such a background would account for the Monk's rather aristocratic tastes for hunting and riding, at table and in costume. And the deep class affiliation also seems to affect others' perceptions. When the Host seeks an appropriate "bettre man" (I.3130) to requite the Knight's Tale, his first instinct is, like Chaucer's in the General Prologue, to turn to the Monk.

The alignment of Knight and Monk is not merely hereditary; it is also intellectual and thematic. While the Monk's "tragedies" emerge from the literary effects of a version of Boethian stoicism, the Knight's Tale also

---

often blamed on the scribes (who may have misread the indications for cancellation as they copied the manuscripts), perhaps Chaucer had not yet decided where to cut.

locates its philosophical energies in the same tradition. Put another way, their tales can be seen as different approaches to similar questions about chance and destiny, action and predestination. Both tales might also be seen as analogous narrative wills-to-power for their high-ranking and ambitious narrators. That claim might seem to apply more obviously to the Knight, who seeks his image of power in the world-shaping control of a figure like Theseus, the tale's prime mover. But we could read the Monk's tragedies in much the same way. His tragic narratives of fortune stalk their naïve prey as relentlessly as this hunter fells his victims in the greenwood. Both men explore their own power and potency through the lengthy stories with which they dominate the other pilgrims. It's less of a surprise, then, that the Knight interrupts the Monk's Tale. In some ways he's been presented as the only man who could take on such a responsibility and tempt the ire of the Host. That's not to say that the scene reveals a full-blown antagonism, only to acknowledge that a fairly restrictive class consciousness has dictated some of Chaucer's imaginative choices from the start.

THE NUN'S PRIEST'S
PROLOGUE AND TALE

Fragment VII—what has been called the "literature group" of *The Canterbury Tales* for its generic variety[1]—ends with the tour de force narrative of Chaunticleer and the fox, told by the unassuming Nun's Priest. The acclaim is nearly universal for this story, which has been labeled the "best and certainly the most inimitably 'Chaucerian' of the *Tales*."[2] But it's not immediately apparent why that is so, especially to a novice reader of the work for whom the Nun's Priest is an unusually shadowy figure among the Canterbury pilgrims. In the General Prologue, the Prioress and her companion nun travel with "preestes thre" (I.164). More a set of accessories to the Prioress's status than characters themselves, the priests are neither described nor differentiated from one another. We don't know if they will participate in the game or not. When, by fragment VII, the group is further reduced to a single Nun's Priest, our expectations are not very high and neither are the Host's. The lean horse on which he rides provokes the Host's "rude speeche and bold" (VII.2808) to this cleric, who has been asked to provide merriment after the Monk's unexpectedly gloomy performance. Such meager expectations set up a delightful surprise.

---

[1] Alan Gaylord was the first to label fragment VII the "literature group" in his essay "Sentence and Solaas in Fragment VII of the Canterbury Tales: Harry Bailly as Horseback Editor," *PMLA* 82.2 (1967): 226–35.

[2] Derek Pearsall, *The Canterbury Tales* (1985; London: Routledge, 1993), 230.

Fables are the stock-in-trade of preachers and parish priests, so it seems fitting that the Nun's Priest would turn to this genre. But the tale he tells is something more than the simple moral story that we would anticipate from a fable. The tale of the cock and the fox is as old as Aesop,[3] and in most versions it displays the familiar turnabout logic of the fabliau in which those who practice deception tend to be paid back in kind. Chaucer's immediate source is a version of the fable retold by Marie de France, "Dou Coc et dou grupil" ("The Cock and the Fox").

Like the Nun's Priest's Tale, Marie's story focuses on the rooster at its center. It tells a brief story of practicality and good sense, without any particularly "moral" (in the sense of doctrinal) meaning. But the Nun's Priest's fable is much longer than is typical. Something more elaborate happens here, owing to the influence of a different source of animal literature: the beast epic, which itself developed out of the fable of the fox and wolf. This development can be seen most clearly in the cycle of tales known as the *Roman de Renart*. The main protagonist is always Raynardus, the fox, who contends with his enemy, the wolf, at the court of the lion king.[4] Like the beasts of this tradition, the Nun's Priest's animals are rhetorically excessive, turning the instinctual behavior of roosters and their predators into complex philosophical and linguistic affairs. The ordinary world of animal impulse is aggrandized into epic, world-shaping action. Decentered in the Nun's Priest's mock-epic fable and domesticated as the English-sounding "Russel" (VII.3334), the fox displays a rather mundane hunger that is translated into realms of betrayal, deception, and apocalypse (when the birds shrieked in despair, according to the Nun's Priest, "It seemed as that hevene sholde falle!"; VII.3401). Whereas both

---

[3] The fullest account of the classical sources that circulated under and associated with the name "Aesop" can be found in Jill Mann's *From Aesop to Reynard: Beast Literature in Medieval Britain* (Oxford: Oxford UP, 2009).

[4] Jill Mann helpfully differentiates the popular animal literatures, while delineating their strong connections, in "Beast Epic and Fable," in *Medieval Latin: An Introduction and Bibliographical Guide*, ed. Frank Mantello and A. G. Rigg (Washington, DC: Catholic University of American Press, 1996), 556–61.

simple beast fable and elaborate beast epic portray animals speaking as humans in order to point out their limitations while celebrating their cleverness and dexterity, the epic takes the connection further than the fable. It makes possible a more grandiose portrayal of the pretension of the animal characters and thus a more sharply comic critique of human weaknesses.

To visualize what's at work in the Nun's Priest's Tale, we can take a colored pencil to the text and box the lines relating the fable's plot. By bracketing the elaborately descriptive discourse of the narrator and the various textual authorities cited by the animals—anything that might be classified as a digression—we can winnow rhetorical flourish from basic story line and action to keep matters clear. Returning to the narratological distinctions made elsewhere, between mere plot (the sequence of events) and narrative (the way such events get presented to us), we can see how this preacher's tale makes its comedy out of the elaboration of plot and narrative—indeed, far more narrative than the genre of fable typically warrants.

We are alerted to the conflation of animal genres early, for a simple widow's farm has never been so rhetorically described, nor her unpretentious diet praised in such detail. The Nun's Priest's narration colludes with the aims of the genre, creating a mock-epic presentation that calls attention to the difference between style and subject matter. Thus a bunch of chickens are turned into some rather aristocratic poultry that make the widow's barn into their "halle" (VII.2884). This kind of excess also appears in the opening depiction of Chaunticleer and his wives. Drawing on the idioms of courtly romance, the narrator elaborates on the rooster's features with terms borrowed from three different traditions—the heraldic (relating to heraldry, the art of coats of arms), lapidary (pertaining to gems and precious stones), and bestiary (relating to books about animals and imaginary beasts):

> His comb was redder than the fin coral,
> And batailed as it were a castel wal;
> His bile was blak, and as the jeet it shoon;

> Like asure were his legges and his toon;
> His nailes whitter than the lilye flour,
> And lik the burned gold was his colour.   (VII.2859–64)

We may miss the gem tones carefully chosen here (coral, jet, azure, gold) in place of their more mundane equivalents (red, black, blue, yellow), but a refined courtliness is also inscribed in the very terms of comparison: the bird's coxcomb seems to be furnished with battlements, like a "castel wal." The aristocracy of the barnyard fowl literally appears in these details as well as in the rhetorical trope of the Nun's Priest's head-to-toe description. Similarly, Pertelote deports herself much like a courtly mistress:

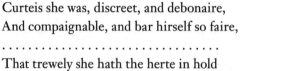

> Curteis she was, discreet, and debonaire,
> And compaignable, and bar hirself so faire,
> . . . .
> That trewely she hath the herte in hold
> Of Chauntecleer, loken in every lith.   (VII.2871–75)

The Nun's Priest is well aware of the elevation created by his rhetoric, and, in typical mock-epic fashion, he often lets the air out of this high-flown discourse, at various points reminding us that we are talking about chickens. For instance, in the midst of the hen's description above, the Nun's Priest includes a detail, "Sin thilke day that she was seven night old" (VII.2873), disrupting the courtly elegance with a reminder about a hen's life span. The Nun's Priest uses this kind of comic introduction of the commonplace, known as *bathos*, throughout the story, mixing courtly manners and deportment with normal poultry behaviors: clucking, pecking, feathering, and treading (a polite word for chicken sex). Part of the tale's delight lies in the rhetorical excesses of and about these creatures, which the Nun's Priest takes to new heights. These are precisely the parts of the story that do not drive its plot and that contribute little to the action, which in any case is minimal. Instead, the learned digressions, debates, and internal examples obfuscate the barnyard drama but become, suddenly, a central feature of the tale and the butt of its narrative joke.

Whereas the Knight's Tale compressed its action into the elaborate speeches of its characters, the Nun's Priest's Tale comically arrests any forward motion with its language. No sooner are his principal figures, Chaunticleer and Pertelote, introduced than they begin an argument that derails the fable's skeletal plot. These chickens might be the aristocrats of their barnyard, but they argue like any other husband and wife—and we have seen plenty of squabbling couples in *The Canterbury Tales* thus far. Their marital strife is part of the Renart tradition, but Chaucer's version of it is more exquisite than any precursor's. He not only has his chickens squabbling like men and women, he has them deeply invested in human concerns—for example, the cock's damaged sense of his own masculinity.

The story begins when the rooster awakens from a frightening dream, which the sources use as a means to have the wife interpret the impending danger of the fox in practical ways that her arrogant husband can ignore. The Nun's Priest turns this scene into an affair with deep (reverse) psychological motivations, replete with the kind of intellectual display worthy of a well-beneficed cleric. Typically a mere prompt for marital disagreement, the episode becomes something more in the Nun's Priest's hands. Chaunticleer finds himself needing to save face in front of his wife, who "can nat love a coward" afraid of a mere dream (VII.2911). In dressing down her husband for his fearfulness, Pertelote sounds a lot like the Wife of Bath:[5]

> For certes, what so any womman saith,
> We alle desiren, if it mighte be,
> To han housbondes hardy, wise, and free,
> And secree, and no nigard, ne no fool,
> Ne him that is agast at every tool,

---

[5] Pertelote especially recalls the early version of the Wife of Bath's discourse that eventually became the Shipman's Tale.

> Ne noon avauntour. By that God above,
> How dorste ye sayn for shame unto youre love
> That anything mighte make you aferd?
> Have ye no mannes herte and han a berd?   (VII.2912–17)

Part of the confusion wrought by the tale comes from this lengthy episode of squabbling spouses before the fox ever makes it on the scene. For Chaunticleer has to reestablish his "mannes herte" with his wife, who has called his avian virility into question, and he does so by rather elaborate means.

Pertelote doesn't think much of Chaunticleer's dream, which she attributes to physical causes that she would cure with herbs. Not only does Chaunticleer take apart her practical feminine wisdom, grounded in sources on digestion and humoral balance like Cato (here cited as a practical philosopher), he has to put her back in her place under his domestic authority. The hen prescribes a laxative for what she diagnoses as a "superfluitee / Of . . . rede colera" (VII.2927–28) that caused his dream of a black-tipped, red adversary. The rooster amasses more authoritative sources than Cato for his counterargument on the importance of dreams. (If we return to our practice of counting lines, his speech is three times longer than hers. And in these circumstances, particularly, length does matter to him!) Citing Macrobius, St. Kenelm, the Old Testament, and Homer, he also retells two exempla from "oon of the gretteste auctours that men rede" to show "that dremes been to drede" (VII.2984, 3063). This litany of classical lore and textual citations out of the mouths of chickens is comic enough, but the conclusion to their argument is funnier still.

Chaunticleer has spent a considerable amount of time telling his wife how much she does not know, whipping himself up into something of a froth of intellectual superiority:

> Shortly I saye, as for conclusioun,
> That I shal han of this avisioun
> Adversitee, and I saye ferthermore

That I ne telle of laxatives no store,
For they been venimes, I woot it wel:
I hem defye, I love hem neveradel.   (VII.3151–56)

Chaunticleer's fervor comes across in this statement of defiance—"I hem defye, I love hem neveradel"—in his own words, an explicit lack of "love." He may have no love for laxatives, but as in this case they are his wife's suggestion, his avowal serves as a rejection of her too. Or so it seems. He has to do some backpedaling or quick subject-changing, injecting some flattery to sweeten his corrective:

Now lat us speke of mirthe and stinte al this.
Madame Pertelote, so have I blis,
Of oo thing God hath sente me large grace:
For whan I see the beautee of youre face—
Ye been so scarlet reed aboute youre eyen—
It maketh al my drede for to dien.
For also siker as *In principio*,
Mulier est hominis confusio.
Madame, the sentence of this Latin is,
"Womman is mannes joye and al his blis."   (VII.3157–66)

How did we get here? This is often what first-time readers find themselves saying. We have not yet left the opening description of the barnyard with its aristocratic poultry, a set of well-read and opinionated creatures that, we continually have to be reminded, are chickens. Hence the inserted comment "ye been so scarlet reed aboute youre eyen." Otherwise, the beauty of her face that surely seems the great gift of God could easily lead us to forget that the conversation here is between birds. This combination of conventionally courtly (and thus human) language with the details of avian physiognomy is both ridiculous and the punch line.

But this banter takes the usual beast-epic joke even further. Establishing both the domestic hierarchy of our barnyard fowl and the kind of bookish wisdom upon which it is based, the tale also rehearses a debate between the sexes that we have heard before—and does something more with it. Pertelote has called her husband's masculinity into question, and he turns to the Bible and the wisdom provided "In the beginning" (*In principio*), at creation, to respond: *mulier est hominis confusio* (literally, "woman is the confusion [ruin] of man"). Chaunticleer, of course, is referring to the story of Adam and Eve in Genesis, a narrative of a man taking a woman's bad advice. But this example of bad female counsel will not provide any kind of "mirthe," nor will it "stint al this" strife between husband and wife—even if it exemplifies why he should refrain from listening to her about the (un)importance of dreams. To turn the subject to something else, while at the same time asserting his superiority, he'll have to talk fast. Thus, Chaunticleer mistranslates the Latin for Pertelote, turning his corrective of his wife into a compliment: "Womman is mannes joye and al his blis." The cock gets to have it both ways: he simultaneously insults her counsel and flatters her power over him, for an audience who understands the Latin she clearly does not.

Chaunticleer may not be wrong about the value of dreams, but he is distracted from his own knowledge by the attractiveness of his wife and the thoughts provoked by the allusion to Eve's seductiveness. In the process of arguing with Pertelote, he so is overcome by the memory of her "softe side" and those scarlet-tinged eyes that he "deffye[s] bothe swevene and dreem" (VII.3167, 3171), flying down from the beams in defiance of his dream's warning. Chaunticleer may be lording his superior masculine intellect over his wife's practical understanding, but his Latin knows more than he does. For in his clever quotation and mistranslation of Genesis, he unknowingly proffers a truth: woman is man's confusion *because* she is his joy and all his bliss. He has not confused her with his Latin translation so much as he has demonstrated his own confusion about its larger context and the male desire underwriting it. Repeating Adam's distraction from his knowledge, Chaunticleer rehearses the drama of the fall of man in the widow's garden.

Such is the greater significance of Chaunticleer's simple flight down from the beams. Setting up the bird's descent to the yard as an epic fall, the narrator prefigures the basic action of the fable and its hilariously pretentious terms:

> Real he was, he was namore aferd:
> He fethered Pertelote twenty time,
> And trad hire as ofte, er it was prime.
> He looketh as it were a grim leoun,
> And on his toos he rometh up and doun:
> Him deined nat to sette his foot to grounde.
> He chukketh whan he hath a corn yfounde,
> And to him rennen thanne his wives alle,
> Thus royal, as a prince is in his halle,
> Leve I this Chauntecleer in his pasture[.]   (VII.3176–85)

The concatenation of the narrator's description among the heroic claims of royalty and bravery ("he was namore aferd," "him deined nat to sette his foot to grounde") and his mundane chicken delight in finding a kernel of grain make up the very texture of this tale. It raises the ordinary far above its station, to the level of "the book of Launcelot de Lake, / That wommen holde in ful greet reverence" (VII.3212–13), only to let it plummet down to earth again. Nothing is outside the mockery of the mock-epic here: the behavior and aspirations of chickens, male confusion caused by sexual desire, and women's tastes in literature.

Earlier the distinction was made between plot and narration. The Nun's Priest's Tale takes that distinction to new heights, turning a fable with little plot into a narrative of extraordinary range and richness through its epic fabulation. The elaborate depiction of Chaunticleer and his wives has not simply been for laughs; it sets up the context for the entry into the garden where they dwell of the "colfox ful of sly iniquitee" (VII.3215). His actions are not provoked merely by the instincts of a hungry predator or as part of an effort to demonstrate the deceptive dangers of the world. The heroic register of the widow's chickens raises the fox's action to treason: nature's rivalries appear as epic betrayals and their conflict a matter of Fortune's machinations as well as of divine providence. These are the themes and propelling assumptions of a number of serious tales in the collection, principally the Knight's. We might well ask here whether the Nun's Priest's Tale mocks the chickens for their subjection to these forces or uses animals to mock humans for their own recourse to these ideas.

Once it finally gets going, the main action of the Nun's Priest's Tale remains the same as that of Marie's simpler fable. The fox coaxes the rooster into singing with his eyes shut, and the rooster escapes the fox's mouth by persuading him to boast of his success to those in chase. Both succumb to pride and a certain kind of flattery. And the two animals offer competing morals: "For he that winketh when he sholde see, / Al wilfully, God lat him never thee" (VII.3431–32) versus "God yive him meschaunce / That is so undiscreet of governaunce / That jangleth whan he sholde holde his pees" (VII.3433–35). Together they warn us to keep our eyes open and our mouths shut. But the tale is more than a race to this practical end. In its digressive learnedness, it has offered wisdom in excess of the practical maxims that "dremes been to drede" (VII.3063), that "mordre wol out" (VII.3052). It's also full of soothsaws about things like the cold counsel of women (VII.3256–57) and the bad luck of Fridays (VII.3341–52). But even directly following the two morals previously mentioned, the Nun's Priest offers an overarching moral, designed to generalize a level above both:

> Lo, swich it is for to be recchelees
> And necligent and truste on flaterye.   (VII.3436–37)

The structure of the story might make it seem as if things were building to this one conclusion, but it's a repetition of a wisdom cited earlier—"Redeth Ecclesiaste of flaterye. / Beth war, ye lordes, of hir trecherye" (VII.3329–30)—and thus we have moved around in a circle. Such repetition does not make the moral unimportant, but it does help the tale resist reduction to one, simple, concluding moral, turning our attention instead to more elaborate processes of moral making and interpretation.

In short order the Nun's Priest will urge *us* to simplify matters: "Taketh the moralitee, goode men. . . . Taketh the fruit, and lat the chaf be stille" (VII.3440–43). But a great deal of the morality and fruit is tied up in the very digressive, chaffy parts of the story that they are neither separable from nor reducible to. The Nun's Priest makes what seems like a simple gesture here, but his moral is a meta-moral on moral making, a decidedly self-conscious thing to do with this kind of story. And in fact, that self-consciousness has pervaded the Nun's Priest's Tale in the rhetorical, philosophical, and bookish ways previously discussed, making it a meta-narrative: a story about storytelling, particularly pertinent in a collection of competitively told stories.

These are the kind of narratively self-conscious moves that suggest the tale's quintessentially "Chaucerian" nature. So too are its references and quotations of a number of other Canterbury tales.[6] In putting such a highly self-referential, highly reflexive story into the mouth of a nearly invisible narrator, Chaucer re-creates the scene of his own narrative disappearing act, performed throughout *The Canterbury Tales* in the invention of its various pilgrim narrators as well as across his larger poetic career. It is Chaucer's signature move.[7] Chaucer appears as he disappears within the fictions he has himself worked to create. Quite a feat for a story about chickens.

---

[6] See my "Quoting Chaucer: Textual Authority, the Nun's Priest, and the Making of the *Canterbury Tales*," in *New Directions in Medieval Manuscript Study and Reading Practices: Essays in Honor of Derek Pearsall*, ed. Kathryn Kerby-Fulton and John Thompson (Notre Dame: U of Notre Dame Press, 2014), 363–83.

[7] That signature may lie more materially within the Nun's Priest's Tale in his protagonist's name as well. The Anglicized version of the French Chanticleer (literally, "clear song") includes and thus seems to encode Chaucer's name inside the cocky rooster's own: **Chaunticleer.**

THE SECOND NUN'S
PROLOGUE AND TALE

The tale told by the Prioress's "chapelaine" (I.164) is, like her superior's, one of the four rhyme royal performances, and the only example of the saint's life proper in *The Canterbury Tales*. It is also universally acknowledged as the paragon of Middle English hagiography: that is, the very best of the saint's lives composed in the language. But that admiration—remarkably high praise, given the genre's wide popularity and the numerous collections of saint's lives in the period—has not meant that the Second Nun's Tale is popular among readers or even frequently taught.

This tale is not closely connected with other stories in Chaucer's larger work, even those that share its pious aims, in part because the story was written before Chaucer began the storytelling collection: it never lost that independent character. The "Lyf of Seint Cecile" is mentioned in an earlier version of the Prologue to Chaucer's *Legend of Good Women* (as is the narrative that eventually became the Knight's Tale), written when he was experimenting with secularizing the saint's life into stories of (self-)martyred pagan women. The tale does not seem to have been much revised to fit *The Canterbury Tales*—or even the Second Nun herself. The narrator admonishes himself as an "unworthy sone of Eve" (VIII.62) in a prologue that in no way reminds us of the pilgrimage occasion or indicates a female speaker. These aspects of the Second Nun's Tale have both distanced the tale from its teller and estranged it from the Canterbury game and whatever lively entwinement its competition and frame might imply.

Though the genre is largely unfamiliar now, the saint's life was immensely popular in the Middle Ages; this type of story was closely related to the kind of virtuous romance narratives told by the Man of Law and the Clerk. Both of those tales made a kind of secular saint out of their heroines and their worldly tribulations. We might also include the Physician's Tale in this group for the way it emphasizes Virginia's virtue and the cruel fate she must endure. In fact, whereas the other tales invoke the contours of sanctity and piety in the suffering of their heroines, only the Physician's narrates a literal martyrdom in Virginia's submission to death. These similarities show how the stories of female piety in *The Canterbury Tales* rely heavily on the contours of hagiography, a genre, much like the Prioress's miracle of the Virgin, appropriate for a nun.

The sources of the Second Nun's Tale are various, because saint's lives were adapted to many uses and different kinds of books; but the life of St. Cecilia ultimately derives from the *Legenda Aurea* (*The Golden Legend*) by Jacques de Voragine, a large and rather popular collection of saints' lives. The Second Nun's Tale self-consciously plays on the poetical beauty of its rhyme royal form, which Chaucer reserves in *The Canterbury Tales* for stories of feminine virtue and piety. Here that lyrical meter fabricates another aestheticization of death and revels in the ecstatic violence directed against Cecilia, emphasizing a connection for which most saint's lives strive. The genre's conjunction of violence, eros, and religion, exalted by the form, tends to surprise modern readers. We don't have to wait until Cecilia resists the marital affections of her husband or suffers bodily abuse at the frustrated hands of her tormentors. The tale entwines the erotic and the religious from the very beginning in the way that it presents sin and its effects. The first lines of the Second Nun's Prologue, for instance, describe "the ministre and the norice unto vices," idleness, which is also the "porter at the gate . . . of delices" (VIII.1–3). Speaking in clearly moral and proverbial terms about the dangers of idleness, this figuration also alludes to the *Roman de la rose* and its signature personification of idleness, "Deduit," as the gatekeeper of the garden of Love. As I have been emphasizing throughout this handbook, the language, imagery, and thinking about the erotic and the religious are closely intertwined.

In adapting this earlier production into *The Canterbury Tales*, Chaucer gives his Nun a highly structured narrative that opens with a formal invocation to Mary and then offers an interpretation of the name of Cecilia, before the story proper begins. In some editions these two passages are separated from the tale itself by headings. The Marian address and its imagery are very much like the Prioress's opening hymn in praise of Christ's mother because both draw on the same prayer of St. Bernard from Dante's *Paradiso*, which addresses the particular power of the Virgin in its uniquely paradoxical terms.

> Thou maide and moder, doghter of thy sone;
> Thou welle of mercy, sinful soules cure,
> In whom that God for bountee chees to wone;
> Thou humble, and heigh over every creature,
> Thou nobledest so ferforth oure nature,
> That no desdain the Makere hadde of kinde,
> His sone in blood and flessh to clothe and winde.   (VIII.36–42)

The Virgin literally embodies the paradoxes of sanctity, which finds power in passivity and humility, and nobility (a social formation) in nature. The play on Cecilia's name prefigures some of the tale's attention to differing levels of signification and understanding, blindness and insight, embedded within her story. The exposition on her name seeks to locate the details and larger themes of her legend embedded there as well. Cecilia is inventively etymologized in these efforts in relation to a number of Latin terms—*coelo*, "heaven"; *lilia*, "lily"; *caecis*, "blind"—as well as the biblical name *Lia*, "Leah," rendering Cecilia "hevenes lilye" and "the way to blinde" (VIII.87, 92), for her good teaching and "lasting bisinesse" (VIII.98).

In some manuscripts, Latin headings separate these parts of the Prologue and Tale. But unlike the poetic disarray of, say, the Man of Law's prefatory material, where he changes from couplets to stanzas (while claiming to speak in prose), the Second Nun's performance is in one consistent metrical form. Also providing coherence is a pervasive emphasis on work and busyness, as remedies to the idleness through which sin operates. This part of the tale is also rather self-conscious of its *own* status as "faithful bisinesse" (VIII.24). The narrator strives to imitate Cecilia's "sondry werkes brighte of excellence" (VIII.112) as she narrates them.

Like other saint's lives, St. Cecilia's story focuses on her works and martyrdom, both of which, by definition, are imitations of Christ, particularly his sacrificial and triumphant death. Set in pagan Rome, before Christianity was accepted as its official religion, the tale narrates Cecilia's effect on her early Christian community, detailing how she marries a young man named Valerian and converts him on their wedding night to a chaste marriage. Sending him off to the reclusive Pope Urban hiding in the catacombs, Cecilia literally brings Valerian to see things as she does. When Valerian returns from his baptism by Urban, an angel arrives with "corones two" (VIII.221) of roses and lilies that are not fully sensible to others:

> Fro Paradis to you have I hem broght,
> Ne never mo ne shal they roten be,
> Ne lese hir swote savour, trusteth me;
> Ne never wight shal seen hem with his eye,
> But he be chast and hate vileinye.   (VIII.227–31)

Valerian can now see the angel Cecilia sees, because he has converted with an open heart. So far, so good in representing the crossed lines between literal and figurative, sensible and insensible worlds. The tale then crosses a line between genres, going in the opposite direction of what one expects. Because the young husband assented to Christ so quickly, the angel offers Valerian a rash boon of sorts, the kind of wish a romance's king grants to one who has pleased him. Immediately, Valerian initiates the conversion of his brother Tiburce, to "han grace / To knowe the trouthe" (VIII.237–38). The tale thus begins the series of conversions that show how Cecilia not only performs good works but also manifests the paradoxically pro-ductive power of virginity (contrary to the Wife of Bath's comments on the subject),[1] displaying everywhere "the fruit of thilke seed of chastitee" (VIII.193).

Despite her refusal of a married life and childbearing, Cecilia is shown to be capable, again and again, of producing more faithful followers of Christ. Her beauty and her teaching make her fruitful in ways that explode the traditional understanding of a woman's value, which is typically located in her sexual function. In her virgin state, Cecilia converts followers—particularly men—making for a surprising kind of increase and produc-tivity. When the Roman prefect, Almachius, sends in troops to detain these converts and force their obedience to paganism, Cecilia converts them too. At each turn, Cecilia is able to show them wonders that defy their earthly senses—the ability to smell flowers where none are visible and witness souls ascending to heaven in the presence of others who fail to see—prompting her converts to die happily for their faith. Almachius is eventually forced to detain Cecilia herself and to question her, but his language only winds up displaying what he doesn't know and cannot understand:

> Ther lakketh nothing to thine outter eyen
> That thou nart blind, for thing that we seen alle,
> That is a stoon—that men may wel espyen—,
> That ilke stoon a god thou wolt it calle.
> I rede thee, lat thyn hand upon it falle,
> And taste it wel, and stoon thou shalt it finde—
> Sin that thou seest nat with thine eyen blinde.   (VIII.498–504)

Cecilia's remonstrance to Almachius's order to "do sacrifice of Cristendom renaye" so as to escape death (VIII.459–60) displays the double valence of

---

[1] The Wife of Bath discusses virginity as "greet perfeccioun" but as sterile in her Pro-logue (III.62–146; quotation, 105).

the language of spirituality that characterizes the tale more broadly. It uses the literal and the figurative to show how the faithful attain a higher level of understanding that renders others, like Almachius, blind and dumb.

Finally, Almachius helps fulfill the hagiographical narrative by ordering Cecilia's death, which—in this genre's standard, miraculous way—he has trouble accomplishing. He tries to burn her in a bath of fire that does no harm. She spends three days preaching (and converting others) with her head nearly cut off before she literally gives up the ghost. Her possessions and her works provide for the founding of a church, which—as the Second Nun notes in her conclusion—is still extant "into this day" (VIII.552).

Once again, the plot does not drive the story in the ways we might expect. There is no comeuppance for Almachius, no conclusion to the political drama that attends Cecilia's disobedience. Instead, the saint's life revels in the performance of its miracles and the paradoxes of their significance, which are consistently sounded across the story in and through inversions of linguistic sense. Like Cecilia herself, the tale looks toward another realm of meaning, the spiritual, above and beyond this world. Playing a series of language games, the tale allegorically inverts matters, ultimately rewriting the very meaning of life and death. As Cecilia teaches, "Men mighte dreden wel and skilfully / This lif to lese . . . If this were living only, and noon oother" (VIII.320–22). Cecilia's focus, like the tale's as a whole, is on another realm. Thus she urges the heroic work on the men she has lately converted:

> "Now Cristes owene knightes, leve and deere,
> Caste al away the werkes of derknesse,
> And armeth you in armour of brightnesse.
>
> Ye han forsoothe ydoon a greet bataile,
> Youre cours is doon, youre faith han ye conserved:
> Gooth to the corone of lif that may nat faile—
> The rightful juge which that ye han served

> Shal yive it you as ye han it deserved."
> And whan this thing was said as I devise,
> Men ledde hem forth to doon the sacrifise.   (VIII.383–92)

Not only do Cecilia's words here position the converts as "knights" armed in the light of Christ, but her speech interprets their actions—their struggles to convert—as righteous battle. Chaucer subtly plays with the word "sacrifise," because Almachius's officers have detained Tiburce and Valerian in order to force them "to doon the sacrifise" to Jupiter that he commands. But an entirely different sacrifice is made when they accept death:

> But whan they weren to the place broght,
> To tellen shortly the conclusioun,
> They nolde encense ne sacrifice right noght,
> But on hir knees they setten hem adoun,
> With humble herte and sad devocioun,
> And losten bothe hir hevedes in the place:
> Hir soules wenten to the king of grace.   (VIII.393–99)

This passive behavior, setting themselves "on hir knees" in humility and "sad devocioun," *is* the heroic action that these knights perform and amounts to the sacrifice they are willing to make, inverting all the ways in which we tend to understand heroic action as well as the kind of sacrifice Almachius expects. Not only are these words shown to mean far more than they seem on their surface, but the spectacle of these knights' self-sacrifice converts Almachius's chief officer, Maximus, among others who watch "hir soules . . . to hevene glide" (VIII.402). By continually showing what is visible to those who display the faith, the tale reinterprets blindness and sight, pivoting on the importance of what only some can see (which may in fact be invisible) and what others, like Almachius, turn a blind eye to. Almachius's calculated spectacle of punishment in the public executions in this tale thus works against him as they become spectacles for conversion.

The tale itself works as a similar kind of display—hence its disruption of our typical expectations of story. But despite its redefinition of heroism and its rebuttal of the Wife's claims about the sterility of the virtue of chastity, the Second Nun's Tale does not feel to us as if it stages a contest with other Canterbury tales. We are likely reacting to the flatness of its narrator and its hermetic independence from the rest of the storytelling competition. Only a single line connects it to the more dramatically motivated intervention of the Canon's Yeoman: "Whan ended was the lif of Sainte Cecile" (VIII.554). Indeed, we hardly know whether the "lif" refers to the narrative or to the life of Cecile herself. For the Second Nun, there is not much difference between the two. Yet despite this independence, the tale's concern with language and the way it can be made to cooperate with the imperatives of genre appears typical of Chaucer's storytelling power in *The Canterbury Tales*.

THE CANON'S YEOMAN'S
PROLOGUE AND TALE

The sudden appearance of the Canon (a cleric attached to a cathedral, here probably Canterbury itself)[1] and the Yeoman, his servant, surprises everyone. Engrossed in the number of tale-telling figures before us, we've hardly given any thought to the possibility that new ones might materialize upon the way. The dramatic potential of the Canterbury frame is suddenly expanded when two latecomers catch up with the pilgrims just as they approach Boughton, a town near the Blean Forest and about five miles from their destination. Their arrival makes it impossible for us to perceive the General Prologue as a fixed introduction to the larger poem. Like all the other stories, which are responded to, reworked, and sometimes "quit," the General Prologue is something that can be exceeded, a possibility that adds spontaneity, liveliness, and vitality to Chaucer's collection at yet another level.

To this newest figure Chaucer assigns a tale of compulsive deception. Anyone who claims that the pilgrims are themselves unimportant and mere excuses to tell tales should be brought up short by the Canon's Yeoman. Chaucer had a handful of pilgrims left from the General Prologue who had not yet been assigned a story; he had no *need* to invent new ones.

---

[1] Regular canons (meaning those who follow the rule, in Latin *regula*) live communally, like monks, but they can also do parochial service, more like a parish priest. They straddle two different ways of clerical life, that of the cloistered contemplative and that of the active servitor.

That's not to say that the stories are simply psychological revelations of the pilgrims, an assertion that would be going too far in the opposite direction. But there is something dramatically alive in the fiction of the pilgrim tellers. The story of the false alchemist could not be assigned to just anyone, as Chaucer's late invention of the Canon's Yeoman makes clear to us. Its role is to be at least partially intrusive, and its truth is to be a different form of confession than those we have heard before.

Calling the Canon a "false alchemist" is something of a redundancy, as alchemy had a reputation for duplicity and deception by Chaucer's time. A prototype of chemistry, to which it is etymologically linked, alchemy is a science of material transformation. The word descends from the Arabic *al-kīmiyāʾ*, itself apparently related to the Greek *chēmeia* or *chumeia*, "the art of alloying metals," and perhaps to the Egyptian *keme*, or "black land" (as opposed to red desert sand). Alchemy is based on the idea that divinely made matter unites all of creation, and its etymology reveals the desire at its heart to fuse or unite with that originary form. Moving from east to west, from ancient to medieval worlds, alchemy eventually made its way to Mediterranean Europe via twelfth-century Toledo and the Latin translation of Arabic texts.

In a Christian culture that hoped to align rationalist principles and experimentation with faith, alchemy could ideally be part of the larger understanding of God's created universe, much like Nicholas's "astromye" in the Miller's Tale (I.3451). As such, alchemy was categorized as a kind of natural philosophy that explored the transformation and purification of matter, a practice that in theory could elevate base metals into higher, more valuable ones (notably gold and silver). The alchemists pursued the substance believed able to effect this transformation, the so-called philosopher's stone, which was also thought to produce an elixir that could offer immortality. By Chaucer's time, alchemy and its lore had moved from strictly philosophical and theological contexts to popular ones, where such practices and aims were subject to critical scrutiny and comic parody because charlatans had spread these ideas beyond intellectual circles.

Like the Wife of Bath and the Pardoner, with their long autobiographical prologues, the Canon's Yeoman uses his Prologue to situate his tale as a confessional revelation; and for him, too, that revelation emerges from the teller's profession (here, as an alchemist's servant) as well as from the drama of the frame story, which in this case appears a little suspect. The Yeoman and his master have made some effort to catch up with Chaucer's company, supposedly "for his [the Canon's] disport—he loveth daliaunce" (VIII.592). The initial impression they make is a wet and sweaty one, as if they had made a great effort in prodding their horses to overtake the pilgrims. In fact, the narrator's description of the Canon, whose "forheed dropped as a stillatorye" (VIII.580), is revelatory: such a mechanism for distillation predicts the Canon's secret craft.

The Yeoman offers the Canon to the company as a worthy companion, "a passing man" (VIII.614). Doing the introductions for his master, the Yeoman solicits the interest of the Host by boasting of the Canon's surpassing talents, expressed as the power to pave the streets with precious metals (VIII.623–26). The image draws on metaphor and literalism both, since the pursuit of precious metals is the Canon's particular skill. It sounds like something he has said before. But the praise also seems excessive and, to the Host, a little suspicious. The servant's description of this outstanding superior is belied by the shabbiness of his dress, "al bawdy and totore also. / Why is thy lord so sluttish[?]," the Host asks (VIII.635–36).[2] Harry Bailly presses the Yeoman on the contradiction between the Canon's looks and what's been said about him. The Host's questions about the appearance of these figures, the discoloration in their faces, and his general skepticism about what they say trigger a kind of defensive explanation from the Yeoman, in which he begins to complain about the hard work he does assisting his employer. Hearing his secrets leaking out from his servant's complaints, the Canon flees, giving the Yeoman opportunity to disclose even more.

---

[2] "Sluttish" here lacks its current sexual connotation; it simply means "slovenly" (*OED*, s.v. "sluttish" 1.a.).

The Yeoman tells a story of obsessive pursuits. As alchemists they "swinke sore and lerne to multiplye" (VIII.669), but that endeavor has not been successful, forcing them to "doon illusioun, / And borwe gold" with the promise of doubling it (VIII.673–74). The Host delights in the prospect of hearing the secrets of this work, and the Yeoman is equally happy to oblige, telling all he knows. But the tale is more than a revelation of trickery and a slander (that pretends otherwise) aimed at the rapacious Canon and his alchemical practice. It's also shows the Yeoman coming to terms with a philosophy and a "scientific" practice that obsesses him, as if confessing the truth about alchemy will purge him of the desire to pursue it. From the beginning that endeavor, like alchemy itself, seems designed for failure, linking language and the desire it tries to name and control.

The story is fascinating for its description of alchemical practices as well as of the hopeful quest for knowledge in the multiplication and transformation of elements promised by the practice. But that quest is also philosophically fraught. For one thing, such men pursue the very secrets of nature and creation that appear prohibited, delving into "Goddes privetee" (as the Prologue to the Miller's Tale would claim; I.3454), which might be better left alone. Their pursuit is full of psychological complexity, wrapped up in self-aggrandizement and unhealthy competitiveness with others. The cost of the science, which goes beyond the financial, is part of its attraction. The search for this secret knowledge—what the Yeoman calls "oure elvisshe craft" (VIII.751)—takes other tolls on its practitioners. Such men revel in seeming "wonder wise" while they exult in the failures of their fellow clerks: "For unto shrewes joye it is and ese / To have hir felawes in paine and disese" (VIII.751, 746–47).

From the beginning the Yeoman promises to reveal a secret and tell the truth of what he practices, the "sliding science" that possesses him (VIII.732). But that seems hard to do. In what is presented as part 1 of the tale, the Yeoman relates his frustration with the science he has studied for seven years (VIII.720–21) and the losses he has incurred, sharing some of the practice's special terms and concerns. He offers a mesmerizing list of elements and the specialized terms for transformation—"subliming, . . .

amalgaming and calcening" (VIII.770–71)—that have enraptured him. The Yeoman also admits to a certain amount of ignorance of the arts of alchemy while attesting to its lure:

> Ther is also ful many another thing
> That is unto oure craft apertening,
> Though I by ordre hem nat reherce can
> Bycause that I am a lewed man;
> Yet wol I telle hem as they come to minde—
> Though I ne can nat sette hem in hir kinde[.]   (VIII.784–89)

There follow lists of substances and equipment to be used in the "craft." And despite his recognition that "nat needeth it for to reherce hem alle" (VIII.796), the catalog goes on for pages, as if he is compulsively repeating what he has learned by association, one item or element leading to the next. His discourse falls into incantation:

> I wol you telle as me was taught also
> The foure spirits and the bodies sevene
> By ordre, as ofte I herde my lord hem nevene:
> The firste spirit quiksilver called is,
> The seconde orpiment, the thridde, ywis,
> Sal armoniak, and the ferthe brimstoon.
> The bodies sevene eek, lo, hem heere anon:
> Sol gold is, and Luna silver we threpe;
> Mars iren, Mercurye quiksilver we clepe:
> Saturnus leed, and Jupiter is tin,
> And Venus coper, by my fader kin!   (VIII.819–29)

Counterbalancing the Yeoman's revulsion for this "cursed craft" (VIII.830) is his excited recitation of this learning, "by my fader kin!" Instead of being a pure renunciation of the practice of alchemy, the Yeoman's tale winds up rehearsing its compulsive attractions in the very lists and explanations that he gets caught up repeating. The failure of each experiment provokes speculation on its cause ("Some saide it was long on the fir-making; / Some saide nay, it was on the blowing"; VIII.922–23). And like the shards of metal on the floor that they can sift from the debris of such failure, the explanations at which they grasp inspire them to try again:

> "Pardee," quod oon, "somwhat of oure metal
> Yet is ther here, though that we han nat al.
> And though this thing mishapped have as now,
> Another time it may be wel ynow.
> Us moste putte oure good in aventure."   (VIII.942–46)

Alchemy is presented as a science of "multiplicacioun," and we see that process of increase in the elements of alchemy—its ordered lists of planets, ingredients, objects, and operations—as well as the practitioners of the craft. This lore is a lure; the science is seductive, entrapping others to begin practicing the craft. In the Yeoman's tale the "foure spirits" (quicksilver, arsenic, armoniak [ammonium chloride], and brimstone; VIII.822–24) are met by, and even seem to produce, four alchemists, who argue about what went wrong with their last effort at transformation (VIII.922–31).

Unlike other models of corruption—for instance, the false indulgences sold by the Pardoner, which are underwritten by despair—alchemy is seductive and brings others under its power and into its secret fold, so that they become its practitioners and not just its targets. It entices and beguiles those who come into contact with it to pursue its work. The Yeoman's act of narration reproduces this dynamic, as he both disavows the Canon and his false art as the work of the devil *and* continues to pursue alchemical knowledge in enthralled detail.

Finally, given its disruptive function, it would seem somewhat hard to position the Canon's Yeoman's Tale in the pilgrims' ongoing debates and conversation. Neither the Canon nor his Yeoman were there to hear any of the previous stories, of course. (The tale is not even included in one of the earliest and most important manuscripts of *The Canterbury Tales*, the

Hengwrt MS, prompting some argument about its authenticity.) Emerging late in the game and close to what appears the end, it reminds us of what we've seen before: notably, the vexed relations of masters and servants often lurking at the edges of the main narrative. The Canon's Yeoman's Tale thus provokes us to rethink parts of the fabliaux and the Cook's fragmented tale, as well as the ideals of servitude presented in the Clerk's Tale and the Franklin's romance. We will see even more in the Manciple's Tale next.

THE MANCIPLE'S PROLOGUE
AND TALE

The Manciple offers a second tale indebted to the beast fable, this one descending from the Ovidian tradition and thus displaying a scene of transformation of the kind we associate with Ovid's *Metamorphoses*.[1] It offers an etiological narrative: that is, a story that explains the origin of something, in this case how the crow lost its beautiful voice and why its feathers turned from white to black. The story invites comparison to the Nun's Priest's as another tale ultimately concerned with tale-telling and participating in the self-reflexive economy of the Chaucerian collection. But this one is far less clever, mainly because its moral, "Keep wel thy tonge, and think upon the crowe" (IX.362), is awkward and has been confusing to many readers. It calls for self-conscious care about one's language, true, but it does so in no playful or seemingly knowing manner. Instead, the moral appears crudely tacked on to the tale's end. As part of a debate at the close of the collection about speech and its often dangerous power, it tenders a conservative lesson that falls flat after the celebratory exultation of the Nun's Priest Tale, and it ends the fictional collection reductively. While the Nun's Priest shows us a proliferation of meaning that can't be pinned down, the Manciple more simply tells us to avoid telling tales

---

[1] There is no one source of the Manciple's Tale, and the version of this story in Ovid is quite different from Chaucer's. See the discussion of it as memorial construction in Edward Wheatley's introduction to the sources of the Manciple's Tale in *Sources and Analogues of the Canterbury Tales*, ed. Robert M. Correale and Mary Hamel, vol. 2 (Cambridge: D. S. Brewer, 2005), 749–50.

"wheither they been false or trewe" (IX.360). How could someone saying this ever hope to win a storytelling contest? Perhaps he has other things on his mind.

The setup to the Manciple's story is a highly dramatic prologue that begins as an address to the Cook, who drunkenly lags behind the other pilgrims and provokes the Host's derision. At first he seems likely to be the next tale-teller, before the Manciple steps in and "excuse[s him] of [his] tale" (IX.29). Offering to speak in the Cook's stead, the Manciple keeps the game alive, but not without some open acknowledgment of the Cook's inebriated incapacity. There is a sense of familiarity among the London pilgrims here: the Host and innkeeper of the Tabard in Southwark; the Cook; Roger, who attends the five London guildsmen; and the Manciple, a steward who works for a group of lawyers, most likely at the Inns of Court. These figures inhabit the same urban locale and are associated with trades that deal in food and drink. Their familiarity slides easily into a kind of competitiveness. As men in more or less the same business, they know each other's economic secrets and shortcuts. The Host suggests as much when he warns the Manciple about reproving the Cook too baldly: "Another day he wol, paraventure, / Reclaime thee and bringe thee to the lure" (IX.71–72). But the Manciple just hands the Cook another drink and chalks up what he has said to play, praising Bacchus, the god of wine, "That so canst turnen ernest into game!" (IX.100).

The classical reference to Bacchus turns out to offer a foretaste of the Manciple's "classical" story, which opens with Phoebus Apollo at the time when he "dwelled here in this erthe adoun" as a "lusty bacheler" and superlative archer and musician (IX.105–15). Quite distinct from the Nun's Priest's Tale, the Manciple's is particularly interested in animal nature of various kinds and the human (especially masculine) desire to contain it. In a cage Phoebus keeps a snow-white crow, which counterfeits human speech and song. Similarly, he keeps his wife by watching suspiciously for any signs of infidelity and working hard to please her. From the very beginning, these two creatures are positioned as versions of each other, and in neither case is Phoebus's possessive gesture toward them a fruitful activity:

it is impossible "to destraine a thing which that Nature / Hath naturelly set in a creature" (IX.161–62). Both crow and wife are going to follow their natural inclinations, despite their treatment—or perhaps because of it. Making their alignment more clear, the Manciple's image for the futility of Phoebus's endeavor is, in fact, a caged bird:

> Take any brid and put it in a cage,
> And do al thyn entente and thy corage
> To fostre it tendrely with mete and drinke
> Of alle daintees that thou canst bithinke,
> And keepe it al so clenely as thou may,
> Although his cage of gold be never so gay,
> Yet hath this brid by twenty thousand fold
> Levere in a forest that is wilde and cold
> Goon ete wormes and swich wrecchednesse.
> For ever this brid wol doon his bisinesse
> T'escape out of his cage, if he may:
> His libertee this brid desireth ay.   (IX.163–74)

The example is followed by those of a cat and she-wolf, both of which reveal the compulsions of nature that no human comfort or care can overcome. The Manciple adduces them, he claims, as examples of "thise men / That been untrewe, and nothing by women" (IX.187–88), even though it's Phoebus's wife who reveals her "likerous appetit / On lower thing to parfournen hir delit" (IX.189–90). The Manciple tells us what he's not saying. A complex narration by disavowal motivates his story: in its own unusually inverted way, it denies what it has just claimed.

Witnessing Phoebus's wife's behavior from its cage, the crow uses his power of speech to alert his master of her deception, singing "Cokkou! cokkou! cokkou!" (IX.243). Imitating the cry of the cuckoo—a bird notorious for leaving its eggs in other birds' nests to be reared by them—the crow announces the cuckoldry he has witnessed, and then narrates what he saw in more detail. In his rage, Phoebus shoots his wife with an arrow and then breaks all his musical instruments. But once his ire is spent, he turns on the messenger, venting another kind of anger on the bird who told him what he does not want to believe and tried to prevent. In hindsight, he idealizes his wife and blames the crow for traitorous speech. Phoebus punishes the crow for his "false tale" by plucking out all his white feathers and "made him blak, and refte him al his song" (IX.293, 305). The tale thus not only explains how crows came to look and sound as they do, it exemplifies the importance of keeping silent, despite what one has seen or what one knows.

Like the Nun's Priest's Tale, the Manciple's story is about the language in which it is written and with which it is told. But there is no celebration of linguistic pyrotechnics here; instead, Chaucer offers a sharp turn away from the things language makes possible, afraid of the truth as well as the deceptions that it might convey. The swerve feels like a surprisingly reactionary gesture after the Nun's Priest's gleeful celebration, especially after the earlier fable's inventive allusions to so many of the other Canterbury tales—allusions that made for a narrative high point in the tale-telling game. By contrast, the Manciple is much more fearful and far more skeptical of what language can do. Throughout the story he has been subjecting his audience to its indirections, even as he plods forward with his etiological myth. (Perhaps this is why the Canon's Yeoman's Tale fits so well into this part of the collection too?) We saw that indirection when he turned from his examples of animals acting "naturally" as they resist the taming hands of humans to an indictment of men's desires, even though he was in the process of narrating the wife's infidelity with a man of lower degree. Similarly, he digresses on "knavissh speeche" when he calls the wife's lover her "lemman" (IX.205, 204). This word is appropriate for lovers of a lower class; such women might be called "ladies" when the aristocracy and their *fin amor*, or stylized courtly love, are spoken about. But the Manciple knows that the terms refer to the same thing: "God it woot, myn ownene deere brother, / Men layn that oon as lowe as lith that other" (IX.221–22). Citing Plato here on how "the word moot neede accorde with the dede" (IX.208), the Manciple offers a bit of the philosophy that the Nun's Priest exploited with such flair. Yet the Manciple's efforts have provoked confusion rather than laughter. His manipulations of his own speech are far less successful than the Nun's Priest's and have left his modern readers cold. Perhaps Chaucer is readying himself for the Parson's Tale, which, as we will see, rejects fiction altogether. That movement toward narrative renunciation has appealed to some audiences, especially as an alternative to seeing the Manciple's Tale as an imperfect fiction.

But what's so odd about this story of linguistic failure and mismatched intention is the contrast between a well-developed prologue and a stumbling tale that can't get out of its own way. The blame has been laid at the door of the Manciple as a failed narrator, but that answer has not been satisfying to most readers. It might be productive to revisit the Manciple as tale-teller, though perhaps examining not so much his failure as his success. If we return to the London drama of the Manciple's Prologue, we see the Host warning the Manciple that he may have overstepped the bounds of good sense by openly reproving the Cook "of his vice":

> Another day he wol, paraventure,
> Reclaime thee and bringe thee to the lure.
> I mene, he speke wol of smale thinges,
> As for to pinchen at thy rekeninges:
> That were nat honeste, if it cam to preef.   (IX.70–75)

As mentioned earlier, the Manciple invokes Bacchus to turn the rancor excited here in another direction. But this move also provides a way to read the following tale as a further line of defense against the future danger noted by the Host. For in the Manciple's story we can see a veiled threat to the Cook to abjure "tidinges, wheither they been false or trewe" (IX.360). Indeed, the conclusion of this story and its maternal advice might equally well refer to the situation of the Manciple himself. For the Manciple steals the Cook's place and talks when he should have held his tongue:

Thing that is said is said, and forth it gooth,
Though him repente, or be him leef or looth.
He is his thral to whom that he hath said
A tale of which he is now yvele apaid.
My sone, be war, and be no auctor newe
Of tidinges, wheither they been false or trewe.
Wherso thou come, amonges hye or lowe,
Keep wel thy tonge, and think upon the crowe.   (IX.355–62)

While this abrupt moral to the Manciple's Tale seems like a failure in storytelling, that very failure is also its success. For the Manciple has repeatedly staged failures in his story that help make his point. Even if the crow can see and report accurately to Phoebus, that truth can in no way save him from the blame and punishment that redound on him and define him evermore. By analogy, the Manciple issues a veiled threat to the Cook in the very language he claims is ineffective. And in that sense, drinking more wine and thinking on the crow have the same potential effect on the Cook. Language's failure to tell the truth in the Manciple's Tale only relays his message more emphatically, if covertly.

Reading the tale dramatically deepens the way we consider the thinking, particularly about tidings, language, and tales, at this lingering endpoint of fiction making in *The Canterbury Tales*. Its narrator complicates what only appears to be a ham-fisted attempt at moralization and skepticism about tale-telling and language. The Manciple's Tale does more than it says, paradoxically registering the power of language, tales, and speech in the very act of denying it.

THE PARSON'S PROLOGUE
AND TALE, AND CHAUCER'S
RETRACTION

The Parson tells the final tale in the Canterbury collection. Despite the seeming simplicity of this claim, its terms need some unpacking. That the tale is the last appears certain when the Host announces early in its Prologue, "Now lakketh us no tales mo than oon" (X.16). But this sense of an ending and of the completion of the Host's plan clashes with the design more fully elaborated in the General Prologue. Unlike the four-tale, two-way journey imagined for each pilgrim early in the poem, here the Host alludes to a simpler, one-way itinerary:

> Fulfild is my sentence and my decree;
> I trowe that we han herd of ech degree;
> Almost fulfild is al myn ordinaunce.
> I praye to God, so yive him right good chaunce
> That telleth this tale to us lustily. (X.17–21)

Some have enjoyed arguing that the Parson's Tale shows Chaucer nearing the end of his own life and modifying a grandiose design he could no longer achieve. But I find that argument unconvincing. The astronomical timetable offered in the Prologue's opening aligns it nicely with the similar opening of the Man of Law's Prologue, a beginning that appears to have been reshuffled into the work itself after the invention of the highly dramatic and interactive scheme of "quiting" in fragment I. It is entirely possible that the four-tale, two-way journey is itself a revision of an earlier design that was intended to conclude with the Parson's Tale just where it is.

Of course, no one—perhaps not even Chaucer—can know for certain just how Chaucer was altering his plans or what direction his revisions were taking. Evidence found in all the fragments, however, suggests that Chaucer was still undecided in places and moving things around. Moreover, the dramatic interactions of the tales in the first fragment seem so sophisticated, given their quotations from each other and structural repetitions, that it's difficult to see those stories as early and unrevised productions. They strike us forcefully as the product of Chaucer's mature writing.

But though we can read the Parson's Tale as a simpler ending to the collection that an expanded General Prologue plan may have been designed to replace, we cannot therefore conclude that the Parson's story is unrelated to or entirely separate from material in the General Prologue. In fact, much of what the Parson does is revise, by rehearsing, some of the General Prologue's terms, particularly the Host's "forward" or "behest" to the pilgrims. Like Harry Bailly, he gains the assent of his fellows before he begins his tale, which promises to be a refusal of tale-telling in the ordinary sense. "Thou getest fable noon ytold for me" (X.31), the Parson admonishes. "Why sholde I sowen draf out of my fest, / Whan I may sowen whete if that me lest?" (X.35–36). The Parson not only replaces the pleasures of fiction and fable with those of morality and "soothfastnesse" (X.33), he uses the Host's words against him, as if he doesn't really understand the meaning of the "end" he hopes the Parson to make. Harry Bailly had turned to the Parson—the last man standing, as it were—with the typical terms of play and derision he often used toward clerics:

> "Sire preest," quod he, "artou a vicary,
> Or arte a persoun? Say sooth, by thy fay.
> Be what thou be, ne breke thou nat oure play,

For every man save thou hath told his tale.
Unbokele and shew us what is in thy male!
For trewely, me thinketh by thy cheere
Thou sholdest knitte up wel a greet matere.
Tel us a fable anon, for cokkes bones!"   (X.22–29)

Harry repeats his own words from the conclusion to the Knight's Tale—
"This gooth aright: unbokeled is the male" (I.3115)—imagining the tale-
telling game as a purse whose strings have been opened.

The image is compelling, representing the Host's commercial outlook
generally. It is easy to envision him intent on getting his clientele's purse
strings undone in his place of business. The image thus suggests a way of
thinking about the assembly and their group relations. It also fore-
grounds the competitiveness structured into the work by pointing toward
its end, the purse or prize that will be awarded to the best story. Harry is
still thinking in these terms, perhaps unable to do otherwise. He imagines the Parson's contribution as a continuation to these plans: another
fable (from another cleric, like the Nun's Priest) from his own purse
("male") that will "knitte up wel a greet matere" that Harry's own opening plan set in motion. The terms for the entire contest are here reconfig-
ured as the Parson's means of concluding them. But the Parson resists,
using the Host's terms once more:

But trusteth wel, I am a southren man:
I can nat geeste rum-ram-ruf by lettre—
Ne, God woot, rym holde I but litel bettre.
And therfore, if you list, I wol nat glose;
I wol you telle a mery tale in prose,
To knitte up al this feeste and make an ende.
And Jesu, for his grace, wit me sende
To shewe you the way in this viage
Of thilke parfit glorious pilgrimage
That highte Jerusalem celestial.   (X.42–51)

What needs knitting up, according to the Parson, is the worldly nature of the "feeste" enjoyed by these pilgrims on their journey, which the Parson turns from a joyride to a matter of eternity: the pilgrimage to the heavenly Jerusalem. Happy to bring Harry Bailly's efforts to a close, the Parson seeks an entirely different end and asks for the assent of the others to do so:

> And if ye vouchesauf, anon I shal
> Biginne upon my tale, for which I praye
> Telle youre avis: I can no bettre saye.   (X.52–54)

Repeating, with a difference, the gestures of the Host at the start of the trip ("Holde up youre handes withouten more speeche"; I.783), the Parson asks for the same assent to his change of plan and his refusal of fiction in favor of what the pilgrims deem appropriate at this juncture: "To enden in som vertuous sentence" (X.63).

This gear-shifting appeal prefaces a treatise unlike anything else in *The Canterbury Tales* (despite some resemblance to the other prose contribution, Chaucer's Melibee). While it feels like a sermon from the wholesome parish priest who delivers it, the Parson's Tale is actually a penitential manual, derived from the Latin summae of Raymund of Pennaforte and William Peraldus, both Dominicans.[1] These are tracts meant to guide a reader (or priest) through the practice of confession. They organize their discourse around the three parts of penitence—contrition, confession, and satisfaction; and they focus on the seven deadly sins, anatomizing and categorizing their component parts. The tracts include information on the various species of each sin and the cardinal virtue that remedies it. Understanding sin was a way of understanding the self and carving out its interiority. Such manuals provided a model of the depths of human psychology and its compulsions. A number of inventive readers have explored

---

[1] Raymund's *Summa de casibus poenitentiae* and William's *Summa vitiorum* provided the Parson's material, together with other popular manuals, such as the Anglo-Norman *Somme le Roi* by Frère Laurent.

the Parson's Tale for the details about sin, pleasure, and desire that under-write its sterner injunctions.[2]

It is a rare undergraduate course that assigns the Parson's Tale in its entirety. Most make do with the Prologue, complemented by a taste of the tale's discourse, before proceeding directly to the Retraction. In that short statement appended to all manuscripts containing a complete copy of the Parson's Tale, "here taketh the makere of this book his leve."[3] The Retraction, as it has been conventionally called, has no explicit title, but it offers a title to Chaucer's storytelling collection in two places. It concludes with a colophon: "Here is ended the book of the Tales of Canterbury, com-piled by Geffrey Chaucer, of whos soule Jesu Crist have mercy. Amen."[4] And two sentences previously, a list of works that Chaucer claims to "revoke in my retraccions" includes "the tales of Caunterbury" (X.1086).

Other authors have written retractions. Augustine retracted some of his works, and Virgil famously wanted all copies of his unfinished epic, the *Aeneid*, burned upon his death. Such gestures can be read as elaborate forms of modesty, a literary repentance that may or may not be sincere. A key aspect of this passage is that in a time before the printing press stabi-lized the concept of authorship, Chaucer signs his name to all of his major works while retracting them: "the book of Troilus; the book also of Fame; the book of the five and twenty Ladies; the book of the Duchesse; the book of Saint Valentines day of the Parlement of Briddes; the tales of Caunterbury, thilke that sounen into sinne; the book of the Leoun; and many another book, if they were in my remembraunce, and many a song and many a lecherous lay" (X.1086–87). It's hard to balance the statements of repentance and rejection against the impetus toward permanency and stability in this gesture. As one critic has elegantly put it, we must see the Retraction as an ultimately ambivalent statement in the psychoanalytic

---

[2] Memorably, see Nicole Smith, "The Parson's Predilection for Pleasure," *Studies in the Age of Chaucer* 28 (2006): 117–40.

[3] This is the claim of the heading that separates the Retraction from the Parson's Tale.

[4] There is much variation in the layout of the tales manuscripts, making any generaliza-tion about headings, colophons (final statements), etc., nearly impossible.

sense, in that it registers how one feeling or intention competes with and contradicts the other.[5] It's not that Chaucer does not care one way or the other—the Retraction registers anything *but* that kind of ambivalence. Instead, it registers two competing responses simultaneously, making it hard for us to disentangle one from the other. As such, the Retraction has struck most as something more complicated and nuanced than the penance demanded by the Parson offers.

HERE TAKETH THE MAKERE OF THIS HANDBOOK HER LEVE.

This book is a highly unoriginal presentation of *The Canterbury Tales*. It depends on a long history of carefully reading the tale collection, comparing it to its sources, and thinking about its sophisticated deployments of language. The work of many decades of scholars has been recast as commonsense knowledge. I am aware of the many debts that I owe to those critics, and I want students to realize the tradition of laboring over Chaucer's *Canterbury Tales* that lies behind this handbook's efforts to make his work a bit easier to digest.

If I can be so bold, my efforts here—which align with those in my other scholarly forays into the *Tales*—have been to emphasize the productive value of the discontinuous in Chaucer's work. Instead of looking for cohesion, I've been at pains to present the fascinating way in which Chaucer's work seems intentionally to resist a coherent subordinating logic. Chaucer seems to me a poet enthralled by the power of the unexpected and the disruptive, as interested in what is missing and what goes unsaid as he is in what has been put forward. Such interests have generated a number of divergent readings of the tales as well as of the frame narrative structure, and this process shows little sign of abating. It's my hope that the reading and interpretive strategies presented here will inspire students to continue working at Chaucer in just this vein.

---

[5] See Patricia Clare Ingham, "Psychoanalytic Criticism," in *Chaucer: An Oxford Guide*, ed. Steve Ellis (Oxford: Oxford UP, 2005), 463–78.

SELECTED BIBLIOGRAPHY

Within each section, the arrangement is generally chronological rather than alphabetical.

Sources, Backgrounds, Biographies

Bryan, W. F., and Germaine Dempster, eds. *Sources and Analogues of Chaucer's Canterbury Tales*. Chicago: U of Chicago P, 1941.

Rickert, Edith, comp. *Chaucer's World*. Ed. Clair C. Olson and Martin M. Crow. New York: Columbia UP, 1948.

Crow, Martin M., and Clair C. Olson, eds. *Chaucer Life-Records*. Oxford: Clarendon P, 1966.

Benson, Larry D., and Theodore M. Andersson, comps. *The Literary Context of Chaucer's Fabliaux*. Indianapolis: Bobbs-Merrill, 1971.

Miller, Robert P., ed. *Chaucer: Sources and Backgrounds*. New York: Oxford UP, 1977.

De Weever, Jacqueline. *A Chaucer Name Dictionary: A Guide to Astrological, Literary, and Mythological Names in the Works of Geoffrey Chaucer*. 1987. New York: Garland, 1996.

Howard, Donald R. *Chaucer: His Life, His Work, His World*. New York: E. P. Dutton, 1987.

Blamires, Alcuin, with Karen Pratt and C. W. Marx, eds. *Woman Defamed and Woman Defended: An Anthology of Medieval Texts*. Oxford: Clarendon P; New York: Oxford UP, 1992.

Pearsall, Derek. *The Life of Geoffrey Chaucer: A Critical Biography*. Oxford: Blackwell, 1992.

Correale, Robert M., gen. ed., and Mary Hamel, assoc. gen. ed. *Sources and Analogues of the Canterbury Tales*. 2 vols. Cambridge: D. S. Brewer, 2002–05.

Andrew, Malcolm. *The Palgrave Literary Dictionary of Chaucer.* Basingstoke: Palgrave Macmillan, 2006.

Strohm, Paul. *Chaucer's Tale: 1386 and the Road to Canterbury.* New York: Viking, 2014.

Turner, Marion. *Chaucer: A European Life.* Princeton: Princeton UP, 2019.

General Critical Studies

Kittredge, George Lyman. *Chaucer and His Poetry.* Cambridge, MA: Harvard UP, 1915.

Muscatine, Charles. *Chaucer and the French Tradition: A Study in Style and Meaning.* Berkeley: U of California P, 1957.

Robertson, D. W., Jr. *A Preface to Chaucer: Studies in Medieval Perspectives.* Princeton: Princeton UP, 1962.

Burrow, J. A. *Ricardian Poetry: Chaucer, Gower, Langland and the 'Gawain' Poet.* New Haven: Yale UP, 1971.

David, Alfred. *The Strumpet Muse: Art and Morals in Chaucer's Poetry.* Bloomington: Indiana UP, 1976.

Howard, Donald R. *The Idea of the* Canterbury Tales. Berkeley: U of California P, 1976.

Owen, Charles A., Jr. *Pilgrimage and Storytelling in the* Canterbury Tales: *The Dialectic of "Ernest" and "Game."* Norman: U of Oklahoma P, 1977.

Olson, Glending. *Literature as Recreation in the Later Middle Ages.* Ithaca, NY: Cornell UP, 1982.

Kolve, V. A. *Chaucer and the Imagery of Narrative: The First Five Canterbury Tales.* Stanford: Stanford UP, 1984.

Lawton, David. *Chaucer's Narrators.* Chaucer Studies. Cambridge: D. S. Brewer, 1985.

Pearsall, Derek. *The Canterbury Tales.* 1985. London: Routledge, 1993.

Benson, C. David. *Chaucer's Drama of Style: Poetic Variety and Contrast in the* Canterbury Tales. Chapel Hill: U of North Carolina P, 1986.

Patterson, Lee. *Negotiating the Past: The Historical Understanding of Medieval Literature.* Madison: U of Wisconsin P, 1987.

Kendrick, Laura. *Chaucerian Play: Comedy and Control in the* Canterbury Tales. Berkeley: U of California P, 1988.

Dinshaw, Carolyn. *Chaucer's Sexual Poetics*. Madison: U of Wisconsin P, 1989.

Strohm, Paul. *Social Chaucer*. Cambridge, MA: Harvard UP, 1989.

Ganim, John M. *Chaucerian Theatricality*. Princeton: Princeton UP, 1990.

Georgianna, Linda. "The Protestant Chaucer." *Chaucer's Religious Tales*. Ed. C. David Benson and Elizabeth Robertson. Cambridge: D. S. Brewer, 1990. 55–69.

Keen, Maurice. *English Society in the Later Middle Ages, 1348–1500*. London: Allen Lane / Penguin P, 1990.

Knapp, Peggy. *Chaucer and the Social Contest*. New York: Routledge, 1990.

Leicester, H. Marshall, Jr. *The Disenchanted Self: Representing the Subject in the* Canterbury Tales. Berkeley: U of California P, 1990.

Patterson, Lee. *Chaucer and the Subject of History*. Madison: U of Wisconsin P, 1991.

Hansen, Elaine Tuttle. *Chaucer and the Fictions of Gender*. Berkeley: U of California P, 1992.

Lerer, Seth. *Chaucer and His Readers: Imagining the Author in Late-Medieval England*. Princeton: Princeton UP, 1993.

Crane, Susan. *Gender and Romance in Chaucer's* Canterbury Tales. Princeton: Princeton UP, 1994.

Cooper, Helen. *The Canterbury Tales*. Oxford Guides to Chaucer. 2nd ed. Oxford: Oxford UP, 1996.

Wallace, David. *Chaucerian Polity: Absolutist Lineages and Associational Forms in England and Italy*. Stanford: Stanford UP, 1997.

Mann, Jill. *Feminizing Chaucer*. New ed. Chaucer Studies. Rochester, NY: D. S. Brewer, 2002. Originally published as *Geoffrey Chaucer*. Feminist Readings. Atlantic Heights, NJ: Humanities P International, 1991.

Burger, Glenn. *Chaucer's Queer Nation*. Minneapolis: U of Minnesota P, 2003.

Miller, Mark. *Philosophical Chaucer: Love, Sex, and Agency in the* Canterbury Tales. Cambridge: Cambridge UP, 2004.

Mooney, Linne R. "Chaucer's Scribe." *Speculum* 81.1 (2006): 97–138.

Turner, Marion. *Chaucerian Conflict: Languages of Antagonism in Late Fourteenth-Century London*. Oxford: Clarendon P; New York: Oxford UP, 2007.

Clarke, K. P. *Chaucer and Italian Textuality*. Oxford: Oxford UP, 2011.

Scala, Elizabeth. *Desire in the* Canterbury Tales. Columbus: Ohio State UP, 2015.

The General Prologue

Bowden, Muriel. *A Commentary on the General Prologue to the* Canterbury Tales. New York: Macmillan, 1948.

Cunningham, J. V. "The Literary Form of the Prologue to the *Canterbury Tales*." *Modern Philology* 49.3 (1952): 172–81.

Donaldson, E. Talbot. "Chaucer the Pilgrim." *PMLA* 69.4 (1954): 928–36.

Hoffman, Arthur W. "Chaucer's Prologue to Pilgrimage: The Two Voices." *ELH* 21.1 (1954): 1–16.

Brooks, Harold F. *Chaucer's Pilgrims: The Artistic Order of the Portraits in the* Prologue. London: Methuen, 1962.

Mann, Jill. *Chaucer and Medieval Estates Satire: The Literature of Social Classes and the* General Prologue *to the* Canterbury Tales. Cambridge: Cambridge UP, 1973.

Sumption, Jonathan. *Pilgrimage: An Image of Mediaeval Religion*. Totowa, NJ: Rowman and Littlefield, 1975.

Leicester, H. Marshall, Jr. "The Art of Impersonation: A General Prologue to the *Canterbury Tales*." *PMLA* 95.2 (1980): 213–24.

Eberle, Patricia J. "Commercial Language and the Commercial Outlook in the *General Prologue*." *Chaucer Review* 18.2 (1983): 161–74.

Nolan, Barbara. "'A Poet Ther Was': Chaucer's Voices in the General Prologue to *The Canterbury Tales*." *PMLA* 101.2 (1986): 154–69.

Georgianna, Linda. "Love So Dearly Bought: The Terms of Redemption in *The Canterbury Tales*." *Studies in the Age of Chaucer* 12 (1990): 85–116.

Leicester, H. Marshall, Jr. "Structure as Deconstruction: 'Chaucer and Estates Satire' in the *General Prologue*, or Reading Chaucer as a Prologue to the History of Disenchantment." *Exemplaria* 2.1 (1990): 241–61.

Scala, Elizabeth. "Yeoman Services: The Knight, His Critics, and the Pleasures of Reading Historically." *Chaucer Review* 45 (2010): 194–211.

Rigby, Stephen, ed. *Historians on Chaucer: The 'General Prologue' to the* Canterbury Tales. Oxford: Oxford UP, 2014.

The Knight and His Tale

Muscatine, Charles. "Form, Texture, and Meaning in Chaucer's *Knight's Tale*." *PMLA* 65.5 (1950): 911–29.

Owen, Charles A., Jr. "Chaucer's *Canterbury Tales*: Aesthetic Design in the Stories of the First Day." *English Studies* 35 (1954): 49–56.

Hanning, Robert W. "'The Struggle between Noble Design and Chaos': The Literary Tradition of Chaucer's *Knight's Tale*." *Literary Review* 23 (1980): 519–41.

Minnis, A. J. *Chaucer and Pagan Antiquity*. Cambridge: D. S. Brewer, 1982.

Burrow, J. A. "Chaucer's *Knight's Tale* and the Three Ages of Man." *Essays on Medieval Literature*. Oxford: Clarendon P, 1984. 27–48.

Wetherbee, Winthrop. "Romance and Epic in Chaucer's *Knight's Tale*." *Exemplaria* 2.1 (1990): 303–28.

Fradenburg, Louise O. "Sacrificial Desire in Chaucer's *Knight's Tale*." *Journal of Medieval and Early Modern Studies* 27 (1997): 47–75.

Ingham, Patricia Clare. "Homosociality and Creative Masculinity in the *Knight's Tale*." *Masculinities in Chaucer: Approaches to Maleness in the* Canterbury Tales *and* Troilus and Criseyde. Ed. Peter G. Beidler. Cambridge: D. S. Brewer, 1998. 23–35.

Mann, Jill. "Chance and Destiny in *Troilus and Criseyde* and the *Knight's Tale*." In *The Cambridge Companion to Chaucer*. Ed. Piero Boitani and Jill Mann. 2nd ed. Cambridge: Cambridge UP, 2003. 93–111.

Fumo, Jamie C. "The Pestilential Gaze: From Epidemiology to Erotomania in *The Knight's Tale*." *Studies in the Age of Chaucer* 35 (2013): 85–136.

The Miller and His Tale

Donaldson, E. Talbot. "Idiom of Popular Poetry in the *Miller's Tale*." *English Institute Essays 1950*. Ed. Alan S. Downer. New York: Columbia UP, 1951. 116–40.

Harder, Kelsie B. "Chaucer's Use of the Mystery Plays in the *Miller's Tale*." *Modern Language Quarterly* 17.3 (1956): 193–98.

Olson, Paul A. "Poetic Justice in the *Miller's Tale*." *Modern Language Quarterly* 24.3 (1963): 227–36.

Rowland, Beryl B. "The Play of the *Miller's Tale*: A Game within a Game." *Chaucer Review* 5.2 (1970): 140–46.

Kolve, V. A. "The Miller's Tale: Nature, Youth, and Nowell's Flood." *Chaucer and the Imagery of Narrative: The First Five Canterbury Tales*. Stanford: Stanford UP, 1984. 158–216.

Prior, Sandra Pierson. "Parodying Typology and the Mystery Plays in the Miller's Tale." *Journal of Medieval and Renaissance Studies* 16.1 (1986): 57–73.

Patterson, Lee. "'No Man His Reson Herde': Peasant Consciousness, Chaucer's Miller, and the Structure of the *Canterbury Tales.*" *South Atlantic Quarterly* 86.4 (1987): 457–95.

Farrell, Thomas J. "Privacy and the Boundaries of Fabliau in the *Miller's Tale.*" *ELH* 56.4 (1989): 773–95.

Lochrie, Karma. "Women's 'Pryvetees' and Fabliau Politics in the *Miller's Tale.*" *Exemplaria* 6.2 (1994): 287–304.

Miller, Mark. "Naturalism and Its Discontents in the *Miller's Tale.*" *ELH* 67.1 (2000): 1–44.

Stanbury, Sarah. "Derrida's Cat and Nicholas's Study." *New Medieval Literatures* 12 (2010): 155–67.

The Reeve and His Tale

Tolkien, J. R. R. "Chaucer as a Philologist: *The Reeve's Tale.*" *Transactions of the Philological Society* 33.1 (1934): 1–70.

Copland, Murray. "*The Reeve's Tale*: Harlotrie or Sermonyng?" *Medium Ævum* 31.1 (1962): 14–32.

Delany, Sheila. "Clerks and Quiting in the *Reeve's Tale.*" *Mediaeval Studies* 29 (1967): 351–56.

Friedman, John Block. "A Reading of Chaucer's *Reeve's Tale.*" *Chaucer Review* 2.1 (1967): 8–19.

Brewer, Derek S. "The *Reeve's Tale* and the King's Hall, Cambridge." *Chaucer Review* 5.4 (1971): 311–17.

Plummer, John F. "'Hooly Chirches Blood': Simony and Patrimony in Chaucer's *Reeve's Tale.*" *Chaucer Review* 18.1 (1983): 49–60.

Harwood, Britton J. "Psychoanalytic Politics: Chaucer and Two Peasants." *ELH* 68.1 (2000): 1–27.

Cady, Diane. "The Gender of Money." *Genders* (2006). https://www.thefreelibrary .com/_/print/PrintArticle.aspx?id=179660978.

Crocker, Holly A. "Affective Politics in Chaucer's *Reeve's Tale*: 'Cherl' Masculinity after 1381." *Studies in the Age of Chaucer* 29 (2007): 225–58.

Epstein, Robert. "'Fer in the north; I kan nat telle where': Dialect, Regionalism, and Philologism." *Studies in the Age of Chaucer* 30 (2008): 95–124.

Sidhu, Nicole Nolan. "'To Late for to Crie': Female Desire, Fabliau Politics, and Classical Legend in Chaucer's *Reeve's Tale.*" *Exemplaria* 21.1 (2009): 3–23.

Taylor, Joseph. "Chaucer's Uncanny Regionalism: Rereading the North in *The Reeve's Tale.*" *Journal of English and Germanic Philology* 109.4 (2010): 468–89.

The Cook and His Tale

Stanley, E. G. "'Of this cokes tale maked Chaucer na moore.'" *Poetica* (Tokyo) 5 (1976): 36–59.

Scattergood, V. J. "Perkyn Revelour and the *Cook's Tale.*" *Chaucer Review* 19.1 (1984): 14–23.

Wallace, David. "Chaucer and the Absent City." *Chaucer's England: Literature in Historical Context.* Ed. Barbara A. Hanawalt. Minneapolis: U of Minnesota P, 1991. 59–90.

Strohm, Paul. "'Lad with revel to Newegate': Chaucerian Narrative and Historical Meta-Narrative." *Art and Context in Late Medieval English Narrative: Essays in Honor of Robert Worth Frank, Jr.* Ed. Robert R. Edwards. Cambridge: D. S. Brewer. 1994. 163–76.

Bertolet, Craig E. "'Wel Bet is Roten Appul out of Hoord': Chaucer's Cook, Commerce, and Civic Order." *Studies in Philology* 99.3 (2002): 229–46.

Fulton, Helen. "Cheapside in the Age of Chaucer." *Medieval Cultural Studies: Essays in Honour of Stephen Knight.* Ed. Ruth Evans, Helen Fulton, and David Matthews. Cardiff: U of Wales P, 2006. 138–51.

Pigg, Daniel F. "Imagining Urban Life and Its Discontents: Chaucer's Cook's Tale and Masculine Identity." *Urban Space in the Middle Ages and the Early Modern Age.* Ed. Albrecht Classen. Berlin: Walter de Gruyter, 2009. 395–408.

The Man of Law and His Tale

Schlauch, Margaret. *Chaucer's Constance and Accused Queens.* New York: New York UP, 1927.

Wood, Chauncey. "Astrology in the *Man of Law's Tale.*" *Chaucer and the Country of the Stars: Poetic Uses of Astrological Imagery.* Princeton: Princeton UP, 1970. 192–244.

Kolve, V. A. "*The Man of Law's Tale*: The Rudderless Ship and the Sea." *Chaucer and the Imagery of Narrative: The First Five Canterbury Tales*. Stanford: Stanford UP, 1984. 297–358.

Schibanoff, Susan. "Worlds Apart: Orientalism, Antifeminism, and Heresy in Chaucer's *Man of Law's Tale*." *Exemplaria* 8.1 (1996): 59–96.

Allen, Elizabeth. "Chaucer Answers Gower: Constance and the Trouble with Reading." *ELH* 64.3 (1997): 627–55.

Lynch, Kathryn L. "Storytelling, Exchange and Constancy: East and West in Chaucer's *Man of Law's Tale*." *Chaucer Review* 33.4 (1999): 409–22.

Lavezzo, Kathy. "Beyond Rome: Mapping Gender and Justice in *The Man of Law's Tale*." *Studies in the Age of Chaucer* 24 (2002): 149–80.

Nolan, Maura. "'Acquiteth yow now': Textual Contradiction and Legal Discourse in the Man of Law's Introduction." *The Letter of the Law: Legal Practice and Literary Production in Medieval England*. Ed. Emily Steiner and Candace Barrington. Ithaca, NY: Cornell UP, 2002. 136–53.

Heng, Geraldine. "Beauty and the East, a Modern Love Story: Women, Children, and Imagined Communities in *The Man of Law's Tale* and Its Others." *Empire of Magic: Medieval Romance and the Politics of Cultural Fantasy*. New York: Columbia UP, 2003. 181–237.

Barlow, Gania. "A Thrifty Tale: Narrative, Authority, and the Competing Values of the *Man of Law's Tale*." *Chaucer Review* 44.4 (2010): 397–420.

Nelson, Ingrid. "Premodern Media and Networks of Transmission in the *Man of Law's Tale*." *Exemplaria* 25.3 (2013): 211–30.

The Wife of Bath and Her Tale

Pratt, Robert A. "Jankyn's Book of Wikked Wyves: Medieval Antimatrimonial Propaganda in the Universities." *Annuale Mediaevale* 3 (1962): 5–27.

Carruthers, Mary. "The Wife of Bath and the Painting of Lions." *PMLA* 94.2 (1979): 209–22.

Robertson, D. W., Jr. "'And for My Land Thus Hastow Mordred Me?': Land Tenure, the Cloth Industry, and the Wife of Bath." *Chaucer Review* 14.4 (1980): 403–20.

Patterson, Lee. "'For the Wyves love of Bathe': Feminine Rhetoric and Poetic Resolution in the *Roman de la Rose* and the *Canterbury Tales*." *Speculum* 58.3 (1983): 656–95.

Fradenburg, Louise O. "The Wife of Bath's Passing Fancy." *Studies in the Age of Chaucer* 8 (1986): 31–58.

Knapp, Peggy A. "Alisoun Weaves a Text." *Philological Quarterly* 65.3 (1986): 387–401. Rpt. as "Alisoun Looms," in *Chaucer and the Social Contest*. New York: Routledge, 1990. 114–28.

Crane, Susan. "Alison's Incapacity and Poetic Instability in the Wife of Bath's Tale." *PMLA* 102.1 (1987): 20–28.

Hansen, Elaine Tuttle. "The Wife of Bath and the Mark of Adam." *Women's Studies* 15.4 (1988): 399–416. Rpt. in *Chaucer and the Fictions of Gender*. Berkeley: U of California P, 1992. 26–57.

Dinshaw, Carolyn. "'Glose/bele chose': The Wife of Bath and Her Glossators." *Chaucer's Sexual Poetics*. Madison: U of Wisconsin P, 1989. 113–31.

Ingham, Patricia Clare. "Pastoral Histories: Utopia, Conquest, and the *Wife of Bath's Tale*." *Texas Studies in Literature and Language* 44.1 (2002): 34–46.

Minnis, Alastair. *Fallible Authors: Chaucer's Pardoner and Wife of Bath*. Philadelphia: U of Pennsylvania P, 2008.

Scala, Elizabeth. "Desire in the *Canterbury Tales*: Sovereignty and Mastery between the Wife and Clerk." *Studies in the Age of Chaucer* 31 (2009): 81–108.

Tinkle, Theresa. "The Wife of Bath's Marginal Authority." *Studies in the Age of Chaucer* 32 (2010): 67–101.

Parsons, Ben. "Beaten for a Book: Domestic and Pedagogic Violence in *The Wife of Bath's Prologue*." *Studies in the Age of Chaucer* 37 (2015): 163–94.

The Friar and His Tale

Birney, Earle. "*After His Ymage*—The Central Ironies of the *Friar's Tale*." *Mediaeval Studies* 21.1 (1959): 17–35.

Richardson, Janette. "Hunter and Prey: Functional Imagery in Chaucer's *Friar's Tale*." *English Miscellany* 12 (1961): 9–20.

Szittya, Penn R. "The Green Yeoman as Loathly Lady: The Friar's Parody of the Wife of Bath's Tale." *PMLA* 90.3 (1975): 386–94.

Bloomfield, Morton W. "The *Friar's Tale* as a Liminal Tale." *Chaucer Review* 17.4 (1983): 286–91.

Hahn, Thomas, and Richard W. Kaeuper. "Text and Context: Chaucer's *Friar's Tale*." *Studies in the Age of Chaucer* 5 (1983): 67–101.

Ridley, Florence H. "The Friar and the Critics." *The Idea of Medieval Literature: New Essays on Chaucer and Medieval Culture in Honor of Donald R. Howard.* Ed. James M. Dean and Christian Zacher. Newark: U of Delaware P, 1992. 160–72.

Wallace, David. "Powers of the Countryside." *Chaucerian Polity: Absolutist Lineages and Associational Forms in England and Italy.* Stanford: Stanford UP, 1997. 125–55, esp. 136–44.

Kline, Daniel T. "'Myne by Right': Oath Making and Intent in *The Friar's Tale.*" *Philological Quarterly* 77.3 (1998): 271–93.

Somerset, Fiona. "'Mark him wel for he is on of þo': Training the 'Lewed' Gaze to Discern Hypocrisy." *ELH* 68.2 (2001): 315–34.

Bryant, Brantley L. "'By Extorcions I Lyve': Chaucer's *Friar's Tale* and Corrupt Officials." *Chaucer Review* 42.2 (2007): 180–95.

Weiskott, Eric. "Chaucer the Forester: The *Friar's Tale*, Forest History, and Officialdom." *Chaucer Review* 47.3 (2013): 323–36.

The Summoner and His Tale

Fleming, John V. "The Antifraternalism of the *Summoner's Tale.*" *Journal of English and Germanic Philology* 65.4 (1966): 688–700.

———. "The Summoner's Prologue: An Iconographic Adjustment." *Chaucer Review* 2.2 (1967): 95–107.

Levitan, Alan. "The Parody of Pentecost in Chaucer's *Summoner's Tale.*" *University of Toronto Quarterly* 40.3 (1971): 236–46.

Clark, Roy Peter. "Doubting Thomas in Chaucer's *Summoner's Tale.*" *Chaucer Review* 11.2 (1976): 164–78.

Hanning, Robert W. "Roasting a Friar, Mis-taking a Wife, and Other Acts of Textual Harassment in Chaucer's *Canterbury Tales.*" *Studies in the Age of Chaucer* 7 (1985): 3–21.

Mann, Jill. "Anger and 'Glosynge' in the *Canterbury Tales.*" *Proceedings of the British Academy* 76 (1990): 203–23.

Cox, Catherine S. "'Grope wel bihynde': The Subversive Erotics of Chaucer's Summoner." *Exemplaria* 7.1 (1995): 145–77.

Somerset, Fiona. "'As just as is a squyre': The Politics of 'Lewed Translacion' in Chaucer's *Summoner's Tale.*" *Studies in the Age of Chaucer* 21 (1999): 187–207.

Bowers, John M. "Queering the Summoner: Same-Sex Union in Chaucer's *Canterbury Tales.*" *Speaking Images: Essays in Honor of V. A. Kolve.* Ed. Robert F. Yeager and Charlotte C. Morse. Asheville, NC: Pegasus P, 2001. 301–24.

Travis, Peter W. "Thirteen Ways of Listening to a Fart: Noise in Chaucer's Summoner's Tale." *Exemplaria* 16.2 (2004): 323–48.

Olson, Glending. "Demonism, Geometric Nicknaming, and Natural Causation in Chaucer's Summoner's and Friar's Tales." *Viator* 42 (2011): 247–82.

Crane, Susan. "Cat, Capon, and Pig in *The Summoner's Tale.*" *Studies in the Age of Chaucer* 34 (2012): 319–24.

The Clerk and His Tale

Sledd, James. "The *Clerk's Tale*: The Monsters and the Critics." *Modern Philology* 51.2 (1953): 73–82.

McCall, John P. "The *Clerk's Tale* and the Theme of Obedience." *Modern Language Quarterly* 27.3 (1966): 260–69.

Frese, Dolores W. "Chaucer's *Clerk's Tale*: The Monsters and the Critics Reconsidered." *Chaucer Review* 8.2 (1973): 133–46.

Morse, Charlotte C. "The Exemplary Griselda." *Studies in the Age of Chaucer* 7 (1985): 51–86.

Ganim, John M. "Carnival Voices and the Envoy to the *Clerk's Tale.*" *Chaucer Review* 22.2 (1987): 112–27.

Georgianna, Linda. "The Protestant Chaucer." *Chaucer's Religious Tales.* Ed. C. David Benson and Elizabeth Robertson. Cambridge: D. S. Brewer, 1990. 55–69.

Morse, Charlotte C. "Critical Approaches to the 'Clerk's Tale.'" *Chaucer's Religious Tales.* Ed. C. David Benson and Elizabeth Robertson. Cambridge: D. S. Brewer, 1990. 71–83.

Wallace, David. "'Whan She Translated Was': A Chaucerian Critique of the Petrarchan Academy." *Literary Practice and Social Change in Britain, 1380–1530.* Ed. Lee Patterson. Berkeley: U of California P, 1990. 156–215.

Georgianna, Linda. "The Clerk's Tale and the Grammar of Assent." *Speculum* 70.4 (1995): 793–821.

Stanbury, Sarah. "Regimes of the Visual in Premodern England: Gaze, Body, and Chaucer's *Clerk's Tale.*" *New Literary History* 28.2 (1997): 261–89.

Denny-Brown, Andrea. "*Povre* Griselda and the All-Consuming *Archewyves.*" *Studies in the Age of Chaucer* 28 (2006): 77–115.

Sidhu, Nicole Nolan. "Weeping for the Virtuous Wife: Laymen, Affective Piety and Chaucer's 'Clerk's Tale.'" *Medieval Domesticity: Home, Housing and Household in Medieval England.* Ed. Maryanne Kowaleski and P. J. P. Goldberg. Cambridge: Cambridge UP, 2008. 177–208.

Scala, Elizabeth. "Desire in the *Canterbury Tales*: Sovereignty and Mastery between the Wife and Clerk." *Studies in the Age of Chaucer* 31 (2009): 81–108.

Schwebel, Leah. "Redressing Griselda: Restoration through Translation in the *Clerk's Tale.*" *Chaucer Review* 47.3 (2013): 274–299.

Normandin, Shawn. "'Non Intellegant': The Enigmas of the *Clerk's Tale.*" *Texas Studies in Literature and Language* 58.2 (2016): 189–223.

The Merchant and His Tale

Burrow, J. A. "Irony in the *Merchant's Tale.*" *Anglia* 75 (1957): 199–208.

Olson, Paul A. "Chaucer's Merchant and January's 'Hevene in Erthe Heere.'" *ELH* 28.3 (1961): 203–14.

Jordan, Robert M. "The Non-Dramatic Disunity of the *Merchant's Tale.*" *PMLA* 78.4 (1963): 293–99. Rpt. in *Chaucer and the Shape of Creation.* Cambridge, MA: Harvard UP, 1967. 132–51.

Donaldson, E. Talbot. "The Effect of the Merchant's Tale." *Speaking of Chaucer.* New York: W. W. Norton, 1970. 30–45.

Rose, Christine. "Women's 'Pryvete,' May, and the Privy: Fissures in the Narrative Voice in the *Merchant's Tale*, 1944–86." *Chaucer Yearbook* 4 (1997): 61–77.

Lucas, Angela M. "The Mirror in the Marketplace: Januarie through the Looking Glass." *Chaucer Review* 33.2 (1998): 123–45.

Crocker, Holly A. "Performative Passivity and Fantasies of Masculinity in the Merchant's Tale." *Chaucer Review* 38.2 (2003): 178–98.

McDonie, R. Jacob. "'Ye get namoore of me': Narrative, Textual, and Linguistic Desires in Chaucer's *Merchant's Tale.*" *Exemplaria* 24.4 (2012): 313–41.

The Squire and His Tale

Haller, Robert S. "Chaucer's *Squire's Tale* and the Uses of Rhetoric." *Modern Philology* 62.4 (1965): 285–95.

Goodman, Jennifer R. "Chaucer's *Squire's Tale* and the Rise of Chivalry." *Studies in the Age of Chaucer* 5 (1983): 127–36.

Miller, Robert P. "Chaucer's Rhetorical Rendition of Mind: *The Squire's Tale*." *Chaucer and the Craft of Fiction*. Ed. Leigh A. Arrathoon. Rochester, MI: Solaris P, 1986. 219–40.

Sharon-Zisser, Shirley. "The *Squire's Tale* and the Limits of Non-Mimetic Fiction." *Chaucer Review* 26.4 (1992): 377–94.

Lynch, Kathryn L. "East Meets West in Chaucer's Squire's and Franklin's Tales." *Speculum* 70.3 (1995): 530–51.

Lightsey, Scott. "Chaucer's Secular Marvels and the Medieval Economy of Wonder." *Studies in the Age of Chaucer* 23 (2001): 289–316.

Kordecki, Lesley. "Chaucer's *Squire's Tale*: Animal Discourse, Women, and Subjectivity." *Chaucer Review* 36.3 (2002): 277–97.

Ingham, Patricia Clare. "Little Nothings: *The Squire's Tale* and the Ambition of Gadgets." *Studies in the Age of Chaucer* 31 (2009): 53–80.

———. "Introduction: Newfangled Values." *The Medieval New: Ambivalence in an Age of Innovation*. Philadelphia: U of Pennsylvania P, 2015. 1–20.

The Franklin and His Tale

Gaylord, Alan T. "The Promises in *The Franklin's Tale*." *ELH* 31.4 (1964): 331–65.

David, Alfred. "Sentimental Comedy in the *Franklin's Tale*." *Annuale Mediaevale* 6 (1965): 19–27.

Riddy, Felicity. "Engendering Pity in the *Franklin's Tale*." *Feminist Readings in Middle English Literature: The Wife of Bath and All Her Sect*. Ed. Ruth Evans and Lesley Johnson. London: Routledge, 1994. 54–71.

Green, Richard Firth. "Rash Promises." *A Crisis of Truth: Literature and Law in Ricardian England*. Philadelphia: U of Pennsylvania P, 1999. 293–335.

Lightsey, Scott. "Chaucer's Secular Marvels and the Medieval Economy of Wonder." *Studies in the Age of Chaucer* 23 (2001): 289–316.

Ganze, Alison. "'My trouth for to holde—Allas, Allas!': Dorigen and Honor in the *Franklin's Tale*." *Chaucer Review* 42.3 (2008): 312–29.

Hume, Kathy. "'The name of soveraynetee': The Private and Public Faces of Marriage in *The Franklin's Tale*." *Studies in Philology* 105.3 (2008): 284–303.

Kao, Wan-Chuan. "Conduct Shameful and Unshameful in *The Franklin's Tale*." *Studies in the Age of Chaucer* 34 (2012): 99–139.

Narinsky, Anna. "'The Road Not Taken': Virtual Narratives in *The Franklin's Tale*." *Poetics Today* 34.1–2 (2013): 53–118.

Scala, Elizabeth. "'Ysworn . . . Withoute gilt': Lais of Illusion-Making Language in the *Canterbury Tales*." *Études Épistémè* 25 (2014). https://journals.openedition.org/episteme/230.

The Physician and His Tale

Middleton, Anne. "The *Physician's Tale* and Love's Martyrs: 'Ensamples Mo Than Ten' as a Method in the *Canterbury Tales*." *Chaucer Review* 8.1 (1973): 9–32.

Bloch, R. Howard. "Chaucer's Maiden's Head: 'The Physician's Tale' and the Poetics of Virginity." *Representations* 28 (1989): 113–34.

Lomperis, Linda. "Unruly Bodies and Ruling Practices: Chaucer's *Physician's Tale* as Socially Symbolic Act." *Feminist Approaches to the Body in Medieval Literature*. Ed. Linda Lomperis and Sarah Stanbury. Philadelphia: U of Pennsylvania P, 1993. 21–37.

Sanok, Catherine. "The Geography of Genre in the Physician's Tale and *Pearl*." *New Medieval Literatures* 5 (2002): 177–201.

Kline, Daniel T. "Jephthah's Daughter and Chaucer's Virginia: The Critique of Sacrifice in The Physician's Tale." *Journal of English and Germanic Philology* 107.1 (2008): 77–103.

The Pardoner and His Tale

Kellogg, Alfred L. "An Augustinian Interpretation of Chaucer's Pardoner." *Speculum* 26.3 (1951): 465–81.

Miller, Robert P. "Chaucer's Pardoner, the Scriptural Eunuch, and the Pardoner's Tale." *Speculum* 30.2 (1955): 180–99.

Steadman, John M. "Old Age and *Contemptus Mundi* in *The Pardoner's Tale*." *Medium Ævum* 33.2 (1964): 121–30.

Patterson, Lee W. "Chaucerian Confession: Penitential Literature and the Pardoner." *Medievalia et Humanistica* ns 7 (1976): 153–73.

Dinshaw, Carolyn. "Eunuch Hermeneutics." *ELH* 55.1 (1988): 27–51.

Leicester, H. Marshall, Jr. Chapters 1, 6, and 7 of *The Disenchanted Self: Representing the Subject in the* Canterbury Tales. Berkeley: U of California P, 1990.

Burger, Glenn. "Kissing the Pardoner." *PMLA* 107.5 (1992): 1143–56.

Kruger, Steven F. "Claiming the Pardoner: Toward a Gay Reading of Chaucer's *Pardoner's Tale*." *Exemplaria* 6.1 (1994): 115–39.

Dinshaw, Carolyn. "Chaucer's Queer Touches / A Queer Touches Chaucer." *Exemplaria* 7.1 (1995): 75–92.

Lynch, Kathryn L. "The Pardoner's Digestion: Eating Images in *The Canterbury Tales*." *Speaking Images: Essays in Honor of V. A. Kolve*. Ed. Robert F. Yeager and Charlotte C. Morse. Asheville, NC: Pegasus P, 2001. 393–409.

Minnis, Alastair. *Fallible Authors: Chaucer's Pardoner and Wife of Bath*. Philadelphia: U of Pennsylvania P, 2008.

The Shipman and His Tale

Richardson, Janette. "The Façade of Bawdry: Image Patterns in Chaucer's *Shipman's Tale*." *ELH* 32.3 (1965): 303–13.

Copland, Murray. "*The Shipman's Tale*: Chaucer and Boccaccio." *Medium Ævum* 35.1 (1966): 11–28.

Abraham, David H. "*Cosyn* and *Cosynage*: Pun and Structure in the *Shipman's Tale*." *Chaucer Review* 11.4 (1977): 319–27.

Scattergood, V. J. "The Originality of the *Shipman's Tale*." *Chaucer Review* 11.3 (1977): 210–31.

Schneider, Paul Stephen. "'Taillynge Ynough': The Function of Money in the *Shipman's Tale*." *Chaucer Review* 11.3 (1977): 201–09.

Nicholson, Peter. "The 'Shipman's Tale' and the Fabliaux." *ELH* 45.4 (1978): 583–96.

Stock, Lorraine Kochanske. "The Meaning of *Chevyssaunce*: Complicated Word Play in Chaucer's *Shipman's Tale*." *Studies in Short Fiction* 18.3 (1981): 245–49.

Adams, Robert. "The Concept of Debt in *The Shipman's Tale*." *Studies in the Age of Chaucer* 6 (1984): 85–102.

Hermann, John P. "Dismemberment, Dissemination, Discourse: Sign and Symbol in the *Shipman's Tale*." *Chaucer Review* 19.4 (1985): 302–37.

Finlayson, John. "Chaucer's *Shipman's Tale*, Boccaccio, and the 'Civilizing' of Fabliau." *Chaucer Review* 36.4 (2002): 336–51.

Dane, Joseph A. "The Wife of Bath's Shipman's Tale and the Invention of Chaucerian Fabliaux." *Modern Language Review* 99.2 (2004): 287–300.

Taylor, Karla. "Social Aesthetics and the Emergence of Civic Discourse from the *Shipman's Tale* to *Melibee*." *Chaucer Review* 39.3 (2005): 298–322.

Cady, Diane. "The Gender of Money." *Genders* (2006). https://www.thefreelibrary.com/_/print/PrintArticle.aspx?id=179660978.

Heffernan, Carol F. "Two 'English *Fabliaux*': Chaucer's *Merchant's Tale* and *Shipman's Tale* and Italian *Novelle*." *Neophilologus* 90.2 (2006): 333–49.

Epstein, Robert. "The Lack of Interest in the Shipman's Tale: Chaucer and the Social Theory of the Gift." *Modern Philology* 113.1 (2015): 27–48.

The Prioress and Her Tale

Lowes, John Livingston. "Simple and Coy: A Note on Fourteenth-Century Poetic Diction." *Anglia* 33 (1910): 440–51.

Gaylord, Alan T. "The Unconquered Tale of the Prioress." *Papers of the Michigan Academy of Science, Arts, and Letters* 47 (1962): 613–36.

Ridley, Florence H. *The Prioress and the Critics*. Berkeley: U of California P, 1965.

Frank, Robert Worth, Jr. "Miracles of the Virgin, Medieval Anti-Semitism, and the 'Prioress's Tale.'" *The Wisdom of Poetry: Essays in Early English Literature in Honor of Morton W. Bloomfield*. Ed. Larry D. Benson and Siegfried Wenzel. Kalamazoo: Medieval Institute Publications, Western Michigan U, 1982. 177–88.

Boyd, Beverly, ed. *The Prioress's Tale*. Vol. 2 of the Variorum Chaucer, *Canterbury Tales*, part 20. Norman: U of Oklahoma P, 1987.

Fradenburg, Louise O. "Criticism, Anti-Semitism and the *Prioress's Tale*." *Exemplaria* 1.1 (1989): 69–115.

Ferster, Judith. "'Your Praise is Performed by Men and Children': Language and Gender in the *Prioress's Prologue and Tale*." *Exemplaria* 2.1 (1990): 149–68.

Nolan, Barbara. "Chaucer's Tales of Transcendence: Rhyme Royal and Christian Prayer in the *Canterbury Tales*." *Chaucer's Religious Tales*. Ed. C. David Benson and Elizabeth Robertson. Cambridge: D. S. Brewer, 1990. 21–38.

Rex, Richard. *"The Sins of Madame Eglentyne" and Other Essays on Chaucer*. Newark: U of Delaware P; London: Associated U Presses, 1995.

Tomasch, Sylvia. "Postcolonial Chaucer and the Virtual Jew." *The Postcolonial Middle Ages*. Ed. Jeffrey Jerome Cohen. New York: St. Martin's P, 2000. 243–60.

Patterson, Lee. "'The Living Witnesses of Our Redemption': Martyrdom and Imitation in Chaucer's Prioress's Tale." *Journal of Medieval and Early Modern Studies* 31.3 (2001): 507–60.

Delany, Sheila, ed. *Chaucer and the Jews: Sources, Contexts, Meanings.* New York: Routledge, 2002.

Dahood, Roger. "The Punishment of the Jews, Hugh of Lincoln, and the Question of Satire in Chaucer's Prioress's Tale." *Viator* 36 (2005): 465–91.

Chaucer's Tale of Sir Thopas

Loomis, Laura Hibbard. "Chaucer and the Auchinleck MS: *Thopas* and *Guy of Warwick*." *Essays and Studies in Honor of Carleton Brown.* [No editor.] New York: New York UP. 1940. 111–28.

Burrow, J. A. "'Sir Thopas': An Agony in Three Fits." *Review of English Studies* 85 (1971): 54–58.

Gaylord, Alan T. "Chaucer's Dainty 'Dogerel': The 'Elvyssh' Prosody of *Sir Thopas*." *Studies in the Age of Chaucer* 1 (1979): 83–104.

———. "The 'Miracle' of *Sir Thopas*." *Studies in the Age of Chaucer* 6 (1984): 65–84.

Patterson, Lee. "'What Man Artow?': Authorial Self-Definition in *The Tale of Sir Thopas* and *The Tale of Melibee*." *Studies in the Age of Chaucer* 11 (1989): 117–75.

Lerer, Seth. "'Now Holde Youre Mouthe': The Romance of Orality in the *Thopas-Melibee* Section of the *Canterbury Tales*." *Oral Poetics in Middle English Poetry.* Ed. Mark C. Amodio. New York: Garland, 1994. 181–205.

Børch, Marianne. "Writing Remembering Orality: Geoffrey Chaucer's *Sir Thopas*." *European Journal of English Studies* 10.2 (2006): 131–48.

Purdie, Rhiannon. *Anglicizing Romance: Tail-Rhyme and Genre in Medieval English Literature.* Cambridge: D. S. Brewer, 2008.

Cannon, Christopher. "Chaucer and the Auchinleck Manuscript Revisited." *Chaucer Review* 46.1–2 (2011): 131–46.

Brantley, Jessica. "Reading the Forms of *Sir Thopas*." *Chaucer Review* 47.4 (2013): 416–38.

Chaucer's Tale of Melibee

Askins, William. *"The Tale of Melibee* and the Crisis at Westminster, November 1387." *Studies in the Age of Chaucer, Proceedings, No. 2* (1986): 103–12.

Kempton, Daniel. "Chaucer's *Melibee*: 'A lytel thyng in prose.'" *Genre* 21 (1988): 263–78.

Johnson, Lynn Staley. "Inverse Counsel: Contexts for the *Melibee*." *Studies in Philology* 87.2 (1990): 137–55.

Collette, Carolyn P. "Heeding the Counsel of Prudence: A Context for the *Melibee*." *Chaucer Review* 29.4 (1995): 416–33.

Burger, Glenn. "Mapping a History of Sexuality in *Melibee*." *Chaucer and Language: Essays in Honour of Douglas Wurtele*. Ed. Robert Myles and David Williams. Montreal: McGill-Queen's UP, 2001. 61–70, 198–203.

Walling, Amanda. "'In Hir Tellyng Difference': Gender, Authority, and Interpretation in the Tale of Melibee." *Chaucer Review* 40.2 (2005): 163–81.

DeMarco, Patricia. "Violence, Law, and Ciceronian Ethics in Chaucer's *Tale of Melibee*." *Studies in the Age of Chaucer* 30 (2008): 125–69.

Spencer, Alice. "Dialogue, Dialogics, and Love: Problems of Chaucer's Poetics in the *Melibee*." *The Canterbury Tales Revisited—21st Century Interpretations*. Ed. Kathleen A. Bishop. Newcastle: Cambridge Scholars, 2008. 228–55.

Taylor, Jamie. "Chaucer's *Tale of Melibee* and the Failure of Allegory." *Exemplaria* 21.1 (2009): 83–101.

Cannon, Christopher. "Proverbs and the Wisdom of Literature: *The Proverbs of Alfred* and Chaucer's *Tale of Melibee*." *Textual Practice* 24.3 (2010): 407–34.

The Monk and His Tale

Boitani, Piero. "The *Monk's Tale*: Dante and Boccaccio." *Medium Ævum* 45.1 (1976): 50–69.

Ramazani, Jahan. "Chaucer's Monk: The Poetics of Abbreviation, Aggression, and Tragedy." *Chaucer Review* 27.3 (1993): 260–76.

Kelly, Henry Ansgar. *Chaucerian Tragedy*. Cambridge: D. S. Brewer, 1997.

Wallace, David. "All That Fall: Chaucer's Monk and 'Every Myghty Man.'" *Chaucerian Polity: Absolutist Lineages and Associational Forms in England and Italy*. Stanford: Stanford UP, 1997. 299–336.

Neuse, Richard. "The Monk's *De casibus*: The Boccaccio Case Reopened." *The Decameron and the* Canterbury Tales: *Essays on an Old Question.* Ed. Leonard Michael Koff and Brenda Deen Schildgen. Madison, NJ: Fairleigh Dickinson UP, 2000. 247–77.

———. "They Had Their World as in Their Time: The Monk's 'Little Narratives.'" *Studies in the Age of Chaucer* 22 (2000): 415–23.

Fradenburg, L. O. Aranye. "The Ninety-six Tears of Chaucer's Monk." *Sacrifice Your Love: Psychoanalysis, Historicism, Chaucer.* Minneapolis: U of Minnesota P, 2002. 113–54.

Grady, Frank. "Seigneurial Poetics, or The Poacher, the Prikasour, the Hunt, and Its Oeuvre." *Answerable Style: The Idea of the Literary in Medieval England.* Ed. Frank Grady and Andrew Galloway. Columbus: Ohio State UP, 2012. 195–213.

The Nun's Priest and His Tale

Curry, Walter Clyde. "Chauntecleer and Pertelote on Dreams." *Englische Studien* 58 (1924): 24–60.

Young, Karl. "Chaucer and Geoffrey of Vinsauf." *Modern Philology* 41.3 (1944): 172–82.

Manning, Stephen. "The Nun's Priest's Morality and the Medieval Attitude toward Fables." *Journal of English and Germanic Philology* 59.3 (1960): 403–16.

Gaylord, Alan T. "*Sentence* and *Solaas* in Fragment VII of the *Canterbury Tales*: Harry Bailly as Horseback Editor." *PMLA* 82.2 (1967): 226–35.

Allen, Judson B. "The Ironic Fruyt: Chauntecleer as Figura." *Studies in Philology* 66.1 (1969): 25–35.

Pratt, Robert A. "Three Old French Sources of the Nonnes Preestes Tale." Parts 1 and 2. *Speculum* 47.3 (1972): 424–44; 47.4 (1972): 646–68.

Gallacher, Patrick. "Food, Laxatives, and Catharsis in Chaucer's Nun's Priest's Tale." *Speculum* 51.1 (1976): 49–68.

McAlpine, Monica E. "The Triumph of Fiction in the Nun's Priest's Tale." *Art and Context in Late Medieval English Narrative: Essays in Honor of Robert Worth Frank, Jr.* Ed. Robert R. Edwards. Cambridge: D. S. Brewer, 1994. 79–92.

Mann, Jill. "Beast Epic and Fable." *Medieval Latin: An Introduction and Bibliographical Guide.* Ed. F. A. C. Mantello and A. G. Rigg. Washington, DC: Catholic U of America P, 1996. 556–61.

Wheatley, Edward. "Commentary Displacing Text: *The Nun's Priest's Tale* and the Scholastic Fable Tradition." *Studies in the Age of Chaucer* 18 (1996): 119–41.

Finlayson, John. "Reading Chaucer's *Nun's Priest's Tale*: Mixed Genres and Multi-Layered Worlds of Illusion." *English Studies* 86.6 (2005): 493–510.

Mann, Jill. "The Nun's Priest's Tale as Reynardian Tale." *From Aesop to Reynard: Beast Literature in Medieval England*. New York: Oxford UP, 2009. 250–61.

Travis, Peter W. *Disseminal Chaucer: Rereading* The Nun's Priest's Tale. Notre Dame: U of Notre Dame P, 2010.

Scala, Elizabeth. "Quoting Chaucer: Textual Authority, the Nun's Priest, and the Making of the *Canterbury Tales*." *New Directions in Medieval Manuscript Study and Reading Practices: Essays in Honor of Derek Pearsall*. Ed. Kathryn Kerby-Fulton, John J. Thompson, and Sarah Baechle. Notre Dame: U of Notre Dame P, 2014. 363–83.

The Second Nun and Her Tale

Giffin, Mary. "'Hir hous the chirche of Seinte Cecilie highte.'" *Studies on Chaucer and His Audience*. Hull, QC: Éditions "L'Éclair," 1956. 29–48.

Reames, Sherry L. "The Cecilia Legend as Chaucer Inherited It and Retold It: The Disappearance of an Augustinian Ideal." *Speculum* 55.1 (1980): 38–57.

Hirsh, John C. "The *Second Nun's Tale*." *Chaucer's Religious Tales*. Ed. C. David Benson and Elizabeth Robertson. Cambridge: D. S. Brewer, 1990. 161–70.

Reames, Sherry L. "A Recent Discovery concerning the Sources of Chaucer's 'Second Nun's Tale.'" *Modern Philology* 87.4 (1990): 337–61.

Johnson, Lynn Staley. "Chaucer's Tale of the Second Nun and the Strategies of Dissent." *Studies in Philology* 89 (1992): 314–33.

Sanok, Catherine. "Performing Feminine Sanctity in Late Medieval England: Parish Guilds, Saints' Plays, and the *Second Nun's Tale*." *Journal of Medieval and Early Modern Studies* 32.2 (2002): 269–303.

Little, Katherine C. "Images, Texts, and Exegetics in Chaucer's *Second Nun's Tale*." *Journal of Medieval and Early Modern Studies* 36.1 (2006): 103–34.

Robertson, Elizabeth. "Apprehending the Divine and Choosing to Believe: Voluntarist Free Will in Chaucer's *Second Nun's Tale*." *Chaucer Review* 46 (2011): 111–30.

The Canon's Yeoman and His Tale

Grennen, Joseph E. "Saint Cecilia's 'Chemical Wedding': The Unity of the *Canterbury Tales*, Fragment VIII." *Journal of English and Germanic Philology* 65.3 (1966): 466–81.

Harwood, Britton T. "Chaucer and the Silence of History: Situating the Canon's Yeoman's Tale." *PMLA* 102.3 (1987): 338–50.

Scattergood, John. "Chaucer in the Suburbs." *Medieval Literature and Antiquities: Studies in Honour of Basil Cottle*. Ed. Myra Stokes and T. L. Burton. Cambridge: D. S. Brewer, 1987. 145–62.

Patterson, Lee. "Perpetual Motion: Alchemy and the Technology of the Self." *Studies in the Age of Chaucer* 15 (1993): 25–57.

———. "The Place of the Modern in the Late Middle Ages." *The Challenge of Periodization: Old Paradigms and New Perspectives*. Ed. Lawrence Besserman. New York: Garland, 1996. 51–66.

Knapp, Peggy A. "The Work of Alchemy." *Journal of Medieval and Early Modern Studies* 30.3 (2000): 575–99.

Epstein, Robert. "Dismal Science: Chaucer and Gower on Alchemy and Economy." *Studies in the Age of Chaucer* 36 (2014): 209–48.

The Manciple and His Tale

Shumaker, Wayne. "Chaucer's Manciple's Tale as Part of the Canterbury Group." *University of Toronto Quarterly* 22.2 (1953): 147–56.

Hazelton, Richard. "The *Manciple's Tale*: Parody and Critique." *Journal of English and Germanic Philology* 62.1 (1963): 1–31.

Scattergood, V. J. "The Manciple's Manner of Speaking." *Essays in Criticism* 24.2 (1974): 124–46.

Dean, James. "The Ending of the *Canterbury Tales*, 1952–1976." *Texas Studies in Language and Literature* 21.1 (1979): 17–33.

Fradenburg, Louise. "The Manciple's Servant Tongue: Politics and Poetry in *The Canterbury Tales*." *ELH* 52.1 (1985): 85–118.

Burrow, J. A. "Chaucer's Canterbury Pilgrimage." *Essays in Criticism* 36.2 (1986): 97–119.

Grudin, Michaela Paasche. "Chaucer's *Manciple's Tale* and the Poetics of Guile." *Chaucer Review* 25.4 (1991): 329–42.

Ginsberg, Warren. "Chaucer's Canterbury Poetics: Irony, Allegory, and the *Prologue* to *The Manciple's Tale*." *Studies in the Age of Chaucer* 18 (1996): 55–89.

Mann, Jill. "The Manciple's Tale." *From Aesop to Reynard: Beast Literature in Medieval England*. Oxford: Oxford UP, 2009. 206–19.

Fumo, Jamie C. "Domestic Apollo: Crises of Truth in the *Manciple's Tale*." *The Legacy of Apollo: Antiquity, Authority and Chaucerian Poetics*. Toronto: U of Toronto P, 2010. 202–28.

Bertolet, Craig E. "The Anxiety of Exclusion: Speech, Power, and Chaucer's Manciple." *Studies in the Age of Chaucer* 33 (2011): 183–218.

The Parson and His Tale

Allen, Judson Boyce. "The Old Way and the Parson's Way: An Ironic Reading of the *Parson's Tale*." *Journal of Medieval and Renaissance Studies* 3.2 (1973): 255–71.

Delasanta, Rodney. "Penance and Poetry in the *Canterbury Tales*." *PMLA* 93.2 (1978): 240–47.

Patterson, Lee. "The *Parson's Tale* and the Quitting of the *Canterbury Tales*." *Traditio* 34 (1978): 331–80.

Lawton, David. "Chaucer's Two Ways: The Pilgrimage Frame of *The Canterbury Tales*." *Studies in the Age of Chaucer* 9 (1987): 3–40.

Pitard, Derrick G. "Sowing Difficulty: *The Parson's Tale*, Vernacular Commentary, and the Nature of Chaucerian Dissent." *Studies in the Age of Chaucer* 26 (2004): 299–330.

Smith, Nicole D. "The Parson's Predilection for Pleasure." *Studies in the Age of Chaucer* 28 (2006): 117–40.

Winstead, Karen. "Chaucer's Parson's Tale and the Contours of Orthodoxy." *Chaucer Review* 43.3 (2009): 239–59.

Thomas, Arvind. "What's *Myrie* about the Prose of the *Parson's Tale*?" *Chaucer Review* 46.4 (2012): 419–38.

Chaucer's Retraction

Sayce, Olive. "Chaucer's 'Retractions': The Conclusion of the *Canterbury Tales* and Its Place in Literary Tradition." *Medium Ævum* 40.3 (1971): 230–48.

Dean, James. "Dismantling the Canterbury Book." *PMLA* 100.5 (1985): 746–62.

McGerr, Rosemarie Potz. "Retraction and Memory: Retrospective Structure in the *Canterbury Tales*." *Comparative Literature* 37.2 (1985): 97–113.

Travis, Peter W. "Deconstructing Chaucer's Retraction." *Exemplaria* 3.1 (1991): 135–58.

Vaughan, Míċeál F. "Creating Comfortable Boundaries: Scribes, Editors, and the Invention of the Parson's Tale." *Rewriting Chaucer: Culture, Authority, and the Idea of the Authentic Text, 1400–1602*. Ed. Thomas A. Prendergast and Barbara Kline. Columbus: Ohio State UP, 1999. 45–90.

Ingham, Patricia Clare. "Psychoanalytic Criticism." *Chaucer: An Oxford Guide*. Ed. Steve Ellis. Oxford: Oxford UP, 2005. 463–78.

Partridge, Stephen. "'The Makere of this Boke': Chaucer's *Retraction* and the Author as Scribe and Compiler." *Author, Reader, Book: Medieval Authorship in Theory and Practice*. Ed. Stephen Partridge and Erik Kwakskel. Toronto: U of Toronto P, 2012. 106–53.

INDEX

Note: The aim of this index is mainly to cover the tales themselves. Page numbers in **boldface** indicate principal discussions of individual tales.